WE'LL MEET AGAIN

Christie put her cap on at a dashing angle and turned to the mirror. A stranger looked back at her. She didn't look a bit like Christie Bellis of Hightree farm, she looked grown-up, self-confident, almost a woman of the world. What was more, the uniform suited her making her eyes look bluer than they really were, drawing attention to her small waist and slight hips. I like it, Christie thought almost unbelievingly. I really like it – I look good in it! Through the mirror her eyes met Meg's. They smiled.

'It's going to be all right, isn't it?' Christie said hopefully. 'We're going to be all right, aren't we? Funny what a difference seeing yourself in uniform makes. It makes us look ... oh, competent, I suppose. I don't feel quite such an outsider. And don't we get a lot of stuff?'

'If it has to last us till the war's over, we'll need lots,' Meg observed. She tugged at her belt. 'I wish this would go a bit tighter.'

'If they feed us the way they fed us earlier we'll all either eat it and get fat as pigs or leave it and fade away to nothing,' Christie said. 'Gosh, what a lot we've got to carry! We'd better start getting it together – is the paper carrier meant for our civvies?'

Civvies! The word had come easily to her tongue; already she was beginning to feel a part of it, a WAAF amongst WAAFs.

'Must be. Oh dear heaven, they're rounding us up again! Quick, we'd better hurry!'

About the author

Jenny Felix was too young to join the services in the last war but in the 1950s, with her future husband serving with the Royal Air Force abroad, she joined the Royal Observer Corps and worked for over two years in their underground ops room, plotting the aircraft on the big ops table as they moved across the sky outside.

Later, married with a young family and living far away from her Norfolk home, she undertook the cleaning of RAF billets in order to help out with family bills. 'As I cleaned latrines and cursed the great dirty marks made on polished floors by service boots, I never dreamed that one day I'd write a book about it all,' she says. 'But serving in the canteen, slapping bangers and mash onto extended plates, I picked up a lot of RAF slang without even noticing – now it has come in handy at last.'

Jenny has lived in several parts of Great Britain, and has used backgrounds with which she is familiar in the book, including Lincolnshire, home of the heavy bombers during WWII.

We'll Meet Again

Jenny Felix

CORONET BOOKS
Hodder and Stoughton

First published in 1994
by Hodder and Stoughton Ltd

10 9 8 7 6 5 4 3 2 1

A CIP catalogue record of this title
is available from the British Library.

ISBN 0 340 58371 1

Typeset by Keyboard Services, Luton

Printed and bound in Great Britain by
Cox & Wyman Ltd, Reading

Hodder and Stoughton Ltd
A division of Hodder Headline PLC
47 Bedford Square
London WC1B 3DP

Dedication

For my mother, Dorothy, who would have made a
lovely WAAF, but who chose to bring up two horrid
little children instead. Ta, Ma.

Acknowledgments

I am most grateful to all the people who helped me with this book, first and foremost in Lincoln, where the staff of the archives office and the central library found me a lot of very useful information and suggested other avenues I might find it worthwhile to explore. Also in Lincoln, Mrs Sheila Leggoe, who at the time was working at the SPCK bookshop in the city, spent a long time patiently explaining the differences between Lincoln in the nineteen-forties and Lincoln now and pointing me in the direction of other helpful sources.

In the same area, Anne and Richard Stamp not only invited my husband and myself to stay in their beautiful house whilst we did our research but introduced me to Alan Forman, late of the Royal Air Force and more recently of East Barkwith, who was stationed in Lincolnshire during the war and was thus able to fill in a great deal of background. Jean and Eifion Evans of Eastleigh told me a lot about their area and the RAF stations around Southampton and also put me in touch with Gilbert's Bookshop where Miss D. V. Surry helped me to find the information I needed on Winchester in the '40s – any errors are mine, the accurate stuff is hers!

In Nantwich I came across the inestimable Derek Hulland quite by chance and realised I'd found that goldmine, a local historian who really knows his stuff. I hope to make full use of the information he gave me in the future because there wasn't room for all of it in this book.

And last but not least, my heartfelt thanks go to Bert Mather, who not only checked the relevant parts of the MS, but also told me about his work in the control tower during the last war and his experiences in Aden.

And for giving me the flavour of married life in billets thanks go to LAC Hunter, A., and his wife Adelaide, who suffered under many a Mrs Denman and described such sufferings graphically!

1

There wasn't so much as a spare inch of space in the carriage and Christie's right foot in its stout school lace-up kept going to sleep. She wished, drearily, that she could follow suit but she was too cold and cramped. And what was more when she tried to wake her foot up, the small aircraftman squeezed between her and the window gave what she hoped was an apologetic grunt and tried to move over and a terrible miasma of unwashed feet, sweat and cheap hair oil rose from his vicinity, threatening to stifle her.

It was a bad start to adventure; in fact the whole business had turned from high drama to a sorry deceit as soon as Christie realised that her parents did not want her to join the forces. Her brothers, Frank and David, had gone into the Air Force and Navy respectively, but that simply meant she was needed more desperately than ever to work on the farm. Even a girl could be useful and Mummy had kept muttering that she was sure they could do something to get Christie officially on the strength, to make up for losing the boys and the younger farmhands. Bert and

Fred remained, but they were both in their seventies, set in their ways, dismissive of strange girls in strange uniforms coming to help out.

Christie sympathised with the old men, she even understood her mother's motives, but what her mother didn't realise was that Christie saw farmwork not as a job but as a familiar and boring chore. It was better than school perhaps, but what was the point of being seventeen and an adult if you couldn't have the dignity of choice? And Mummy just kept talking about the Land Army and pulling strings so that Christie could live at home, and all Christie wanted was to get away from the farm, to go abroad, to live dangerously, to meet on equal terms some of the glamorously uniformed men she saw striding the streets of Norwich when she was hurrying to and from school. I want to be a part of it, she told her best friend, Eleanor, when they discussed their futures. I want to do what the boys have done, not just put on breeches and a green woolly and go on being bossed about by my parents!

So she'd gone to stay with Eleanor for a few days just before Christmas and on one of them she had caught the train to Liverpool Street Station, in London. Her parents, in happy ignorance, continued with their lives whilst their only daughter set off alone to visit the wicked city.

Christie had never dreamed of going to London by herself, she had only rarely visited it with relatives, but she had no qualms about her ability to find her way. She knew which street she wanted and she guessed that the WAAF Recruiting Office would be identified by the number of Air Force uniforms going in and out.

Christie had hesitated for a moment on the pavement outside, wondering how she could possibly march in and announce that she had come to join up or sign on or whatever they called it; but then she saw that others were doing just that – girls no older than she, in lace-up shoes and navy coats – so she stuck her chin in the air and followed suit.

She went into the enormous building behind a blonde who looked, Christie thought, totally at home and in command of the situation, and took her cue from the other girl. She joined a short queue just behind the blonde and when she reached the head of it told a smiling clerk that she was seventeen – she produced her birth certificate – and wanted to join the WAAF. And after all her doubts, the whole business turned out to be totally straightforward. She was interviewed, underwent a brief medical examination, and was told to go home and await a telegram which would tell her whether or not she had been accepted.

On the train going home she had had some qualms. She had been deceitful, unkind. Her parents had loved and protected her, now she had gone behind their backs, done a mean thing. But her sense of guilt did not last. She had enjoyed the interview, liked the efficient friendliness of the staff at Bush House, even liked the other girls, several of whom had admitted to being here without parental knowledge. And when it was over and she was back on the chilly, crowded train, with a magazine and a rustling paper bag full of mint humbugs, she spent the journey imagining herself in various situations in which she scuttled the enemy, saved lives and won the war singlehanded. After all, she told herself defensively, getting out at Thorpe Station and crossing the road to catch her bus, if everyone tried to get out of it, where would we be then? Hitler would be laughing! As it was she and others like her might make just the difference to the war effort. It made her feel better, cheered her up.

The telegram came after a week of nail-biting uncertainty; she had been accepted, she should report to Bush House, in London, on a certain day, bringing with her a change of underwear and her washing kit.

After the telegram she had been forced to confess, of course, to hear Mummy's lamentations – 'Oh Christie, if you'd only *asked*, darling, we could have pulled strings, got you on the strength here . . .' – and to apologise for going behind their backs. But Daddy forgave her at once and hugged her and said she'd done the right thing and he was proud of her, couldn't wait to see his girl all in blue, getting some in.

That meant getting some service in, Christie knew. The boys had both joined up well before conscription started in May '39 and had been prodigal with such information when they came home on leave.

But because she hadn't felt she could explain to her mother that the Land Army simply wasn't what she wanted without also explaining why, she had withdrawn a little, perhaps she had even sulked. Consequently she'd found it impossible to ask for favours, such as a coat other than her navy burberry. It would have made her seem a child again, after her adult flouting of parental wishes. At any rate, on the day of departure she had donned her old school coat defiantly, stuck her darned green gloves on her hands, and hefted her leather satchel which contained the few possessions she had been told to take with her up onto her shoulder. If she had asked, no doubt her parents would have got her some decent clothes, but how could she ask, in the circumstances? She would soon be in uniform of a different sort and anyway she hadn't put on her black felt hat with its green and silver band, or her tie or blazer. No one would know it was her school uniform she was wearing – would they?

They drove her to the station, and there Mummy cried and hugged her and Christie had suddenly understood, for the first time in her life, that Mummy might have had dreams and aspirations of her own which did not include working on a farm for the rest of her life. She had been too young for the First World War but afterwards she had nursed for a while in the Norfolk & Norwich, perhaps she would have liked to volunteer to nurse again, but there was no chance of that whilst the farm needed her.

So they parted friends, after all. And Daddy, who had always loved her uncritically and called her his little ray of sunshine, had given her a hug and told her again how proud of her he was. Then he pressed a box of chocolates into her hand 'for the journey', and at the last minute he had walked away, straight-backed, towards the steamy buffet, and she had known he couldn't face waving her off because he would miss her so.

The train was crowded and late leaving, which was why at this present moment Christie was squeezed between the aircraftman and an extremely pretty Wren rating, praying for journey's end. The Wren was reading a romance and sucking peppermints; Christie had brought a book too, but it was in her satchel, out of reach, and the chocolates were no more than a memory. Doubts, which had been hovering, swooped, their black bat-wings beating round her head. Had she been a fool? She was so alone, she could have joined up with a friend, she could have asked around at school, seen if anyone else in the Lower Sixth had the same idea. With two of them this would have been fun; as it was . . .

She glanced across at the soldier sitting opposite her. His eyes were closed and his head was on one side. He was definitely asleep; probably sleeping was the sensible, adult way to pass a long, cold, boring journey.

Christie wriggled a little lower in her seat and let her chin fall forward on her chest. She would pretend to fall asleep, at least it was better than letting everyone see how out of place and miserable she was beginning to feel. But pretence soon became reality; now and then she jerked awake for a moment and knew where she was, felt all the uncertainty begin to seep back, but then dozed again.

The train jogged on, stopped, started, stood in a siding, started off again. Christie's head lay on the shoulder of the small, smelly aircraftman but he had long ceased to worry about such things. His own head, pillowed against the window, was jolted and jounced from time to time, but it did not disturb his slumber.

They all awoke when the train reached Liverpool Street. Outside the carriage, a few flakes of snow tapped the window glass and the wind froze the people waiting on the platform into blueness. Christie woke with a bad taste in her mouth and both her feet reduced to numbness, her right hand ice-cold and her left afire with pins and needles. She staggered off the train, amazed to find it was still daylight, then had to go back for her satchel. Still more asleep than awake, she dragged it carelessly off the rack and as it descended it caught her a glancing blow on the side of the head. Ruefully rubbing the spot, Christie fought an urge to sit down and cry. It was so cold, so unfriendly, so totally horrible – and now she must get on the underground or catch a bus and find her destination before it got dark. Once darkness fell she would be alone in the wilderness indeed.

Liverpool Street Station could not have been a pleasant spot even on a warm sunny day, Christie reflected, and on a late afternoon in mid-January it was gloomy and dirty. She wished she could have had a cup of hot tea in the buffet or could meet someone she knew, but both wishes were denied her; the buffet had closed early and although a great many people, most of them in uniform, milled around the concourse, she did not see a soul she knew.

7

Right! Pull yourself together, Christie Bellis, and get down to the tube, Christie ordered. No use hanging about feeling sorry for yourself; there's people worse off than you are, people who don't know where they're going. At least you've got a destination and enough money in your satchel to get you there.

It was warmer in the underground, and although the crowds were no friendlier, Christie felt less threatened. She consulted the coloured maps on the wall, caught the right train, emerged in the right place. She did not make the mistake of setting off into the grey streets however, but asked the newspaper vendor at the top of the underground steps, spelling out the address in case he did not understand her accent.

'Anuvver of yer?' he said however. 'See that gel wiv the brown ribbon in 'er 'air? Jest foller 'er – she's goin' to the depot an' all.'

Christie saw the girl; very tall and blonde and elegant she looked from the back. She thanked the news-vendor, then set off at a trot, overhauling the girl before they had gone far.

'Oh, excuse me,' she said breathlessly, touching the girl timidly on her camel-coated arm. 'The man selling newspapers said you and I are going to the same place . . . could we walk there together, do you think?'

The girl turned and smiled at her. She had a long, rather horsy face and a wide, mobile mouth. Her hair, which had looked sophisticated from the back, looked rather stringy and tired from the front, hanging round her face in wisps. But her smile was friendly; it was easy to see she was as glad to be approached by Christie as Christie was to approach her.

'That's the best idea I've heard this week, old love,' she declared in ringing, upper-class tones. 'I'm completely bowled over by the whole business, even wished I'd not been and gone and done it, but it'll be fun if there's two of us. I'm Adella Springthorpe . . . what's your monicker?'

'I'm Christie Bellis,' Christie said. 'Is it far to the depot?'

'Half a mile, according to the newspaper chappie,' Adella admitted. 'God, and my tootsies started killing me hours ago, on the old chuff-chuff from Tunbridge Wells. I never should have worn my mama's brogues; they must be at least two sizes too small.'

'Why did you?' Christie said curiously. 'After all, we'll be in uniform soon, I suppose.'

'No, not for ages if my spies have got it right,' Adella said. Christie, remembering various posters announcing that walls had ears, wished she would keep her voice down, but suspected that even at a whisper her new friend's tones would carry half a mile. 'They'll make sure they want us before they clothe us, old love.'

'Really? Could they kick us out, then?'

'Oh, sure. Or we could skedaddle, I suppose. But I intend to stick it; the uniform's fabulous if you've got blue eyes.' She turned and widened her eyes at Christie, revealing that her eyes were indeed blue and fringed with thick, fair lashes. 'See? I'll look *rather*

9

special, I flatter myself, driving someone most frightfully high-powered around in a car with a little flag on the front. And of course being a blonde's a bonus, don't you know.'

'Oh? Why?' Christie said rather breathlessly. Adella's long legs continued to stride out even when the girls were talking and staring into each other's eyes. 'Gentlemen prefer them, d'you mean?'

'Binky Carruthers, who's something frightfully high up, says he always goes for a blonde driver because they look so good in the uniform,' Adella said positively. 'Cool under fire, too, what?'

'Do you mean blondes look cool, or are cool?' Christie asked. 'We've none of us been under fire yet, have we?'

'Speak for yourself, old love! I've ridden to hounds, acted as beater to the guns on my uncle's grouse moor in Scotland, been tipped out of the laird's boat when he took me and my little brother salmon fishing. I stayed cool through all that, so why should I panic under fire? And there aren't many who can say that, I might add.'

'Very true,' Christie said politely, not sure whether to be amused or annoyed by this calm assumption of superiority. 'I've ridden most of my life, fallen in the broad when my brother David tipped our boat over, and tried to get out of the way when the boys shot at the rabbits bolting out of the last stand of corn . . . Do I qualify?'

'By Jove, yes! Pity you aren't a blonde, though your hair's a nice colour; what do you call it?'

'Hair,' Christie said, deciding to fight back a little. 'What do you call yours?'

If she expected her new friend to be annoyed by this remark however, she underestimated Adella, who brayed with laughter and caught her a friendly clip across the shoulder.

'Fool! The colour, I mean. It isn't red, nor brown. Do you rub it with a silk scarf to get that shine?'

'No, I just brush it,' Christie said, rather complimented that this assured, self-satisfied young woman had noticed her shiny chestnut hair. 'Ah, we've arrived!'

'Yes, this is it,' confirmed Adella – needlessly, since the stream of young women both in and out of uniform going through the gates spoke for itself. 'In we go, young Christie. Tummy in, tail down, as my old gym instructor used to say, and step out smartly, show 'em what we're made of!'

'Left, right; left, right,' Christie said, entering into the spirit of the thing. 'Lift those feet up, Aircraftwoman, and ha–alt!'

Giggling, the two of them stopped as they reached the end of the queue waiting to enter the building. Adella looked approvingly down at her companion.

'Well, well, you're made of the right stuff even if you aren't a blonde,' she said. 'Let's stick together, the two of us, if we get a chance. What do you say?'

'Sure,' Christie said recklessly. She still didn't know whether she liked Adella or not, but anything was better than being alone! 'Shunt along, Adella, the queue's moving at last.'

The depot, however, was just the start of it. In less than an hour the girls were on the move once again. Loaded on to a lorry, driven down to a station and herded aboard, ten to a carriage.

It was late evening when they reached their destination. Christie and Adella had become separated – first into different lorries, then into different railway carriages – and tired out and disorientated, Christie hadn't talked to anyone else as their train steamed slowly through the deepening dusk. By the time they reached their station she was cold and miserable as well as tired out. She looked round for Adella but could not see her so she allowed herself to be shepherded into yet another lorry, wondering, as her feet were trodden on and strange elbows dug into her sides, whether she could change her mind, go back home. She did not think she could stand much more. The lorry was an open one, chilling her already cold body even further, and somehow she found the darkness outside daunting in a way darkness at home never was. When an owl shrieked and a cow lowed plaintively she could not think of them as normal country sounds; they were coming from an alien environment where even the accent would be strange to her ears.

The lorry drew up. An officer ushered them down, bullied them into a line, led them through what seemed like total darkness, each girl clutching the one in front, into what proved to be a steamy, concrete-floored Nissen hut filled with wooden benches and long, scrubbed tables. The lighting fell harshly from unshaded bulbs, the windows were blacked out ... but there were tin mugs full of steaming cocoa and great vats of sausage and mash and plates piled with thick cheese sandwiches. The sight of food was welcome to young and hungry girls who had not eaten, in Christie's case, since breakfast.

Enthusiastically tucking in, Christie looked round her, but could see no sign of Adella. *I suppose they spotted that she was officer material and whisked her off somewhere special,* she thought wistfully. In their short acquaintance Adella had struck her as someone who would get what she wanted, rise naturally to the top. Christie finished her sausage and mash and wrapped her freezing hands round the hot cocoa mug, but as they warmed up her chilblains began to throb and itch so that she could have screamed with pain. She put the mug down and helped herself to a cheese sandwich, then turned to her neighbour, a short, fat cockney with greasy brown hair and flaky, patchy skin.

'What's next, I wonder?'

The girl shrugged.

'Dunno. Bed, I 'ope.'

'Bed?' jeered a bespectacled girl further up the table. 'It ain't six o'clock yet, you effin' idiot!'

The day had been interminable, almost unbearable. Yet, glancing at her wrist-watch, Christie saw that the bespectacled one was right; unbelievably, it was only twenty minutes to six.

The girl next to Christie began to argue that anyone

13

who expected anything from her after such a day had another think coming; someone else said cocoa was all very well but what she wanted was tea. Christie, putting her oar in, said that the cheese sandwiches were really nice and reached for another.

Gradually warming up, girls whose white faces and dark-ringed eyes advertised both their exhaustion and confusion, began at first to make the odd desultory remark, then to chatter. One or two names were exchanged; someone laughed, someone else announced that she could do with another cuppa.

'You won't git one 'ere, this is the Army, gal,' a peaky girl in a bright red coat called out.

'Garn, it's the Air Force,' someone else shouted. 'I'm almost sure I seen fellers in blue.'

Laughter; they were surrounded by Air Force uniforms, though the canteen staff wore calico aprons to protect their blues.

The atmosphere was growing warmer by the minute; Christie exchanged grins with several girls, the odd remark with one or two. Then an officer came in and began to round them up.

'Get into pairs,' she ordered them briskly. 'Your train was late, we'll have to get a move on! At the double, girls.'

She swept them into the dark again, and across to a big, echoing Nissen hut where she formed them into a queue for what she called an FFI.

'Free From Infection,' someone muttered knowingly; while the girl now ahead of Christie, a bottle blonde wearing a smart black suit and a perky little

14

astrakhan hat, said she'd a good mind to get out, she weren't having anyone pokin' round her, takin' liberties.

Christie, used to a certain amount of togetherness at school, was nevertheless a bit stunned to find herself told to strip naked. But she obeyed, as everyone else did, and stood clutching her clothes and feeling foolish as a couple of MOs toured amongst them, examining them for body vermin and other apparently unmentionable ailments. Christie looked straight ahead as she obeyed the murmured orders, knowing her face was scarlet, wishing she'd never come, hating the entire business ... but then the MO ran a quick hand through her hair and it was over. She was being told to get dressed and stand near the door, whilst from the pretty blonde in the black suit she heard arguing, sharp exclamations. The officer who had been examining the blonde was saying something about a haircut, a good wash in disinfectant ... my *God*, she's got nits, Christie thought, shrivelling inside for the other girl's embarrassment. Not that she seemed particularly embarrassed, dressing with angry care whilst using words which Christie had previously heard only on the lips of angry or injured farmhands.

'Everyone over here clear, then?'

A slim young woman in officer's uniform stood before them, addressing the growing group of girls near the door. Christie swallowed and nodded uncertainly.

'Yes, I think so. At least ...'

The officer laughed.

'Don't worry, you'd soon know if you weren't. Next hut for you, then. Follow me. And you, and you.'

Like a military pied piper she led the assortment of girls out into the sparkling frosty night and over to the next hut. Blinking in the doorway, Christie saw that this hut was equally large, equally cold, but this time crowded with equipment. Men in RAF uniforms stood behind long counters, doling out bedding. Other men handed out cutlery, which they referred to as 'eating irons'. Further along came uniforms, great piles of skirts, shirts, jackets, shoes. There must have been sufficient clothing to uniform the nation, Christie thought dazedly.

Having been issued with bedding and eating irons, the girls were directed to the uniform counter.

'Bust, waist, 'ips,' the fat sergeant behind the counter said in a bored monotone to each girl as she approached. 'Bust, waist, 'ips.'

'Thirty-four, twenty-two, thirty-six,' Christie whispered bashfully, hoping she had got it right, and received a pile of uniform, a positive heap of stuff. We're getting somewhere now, Christie told herself, clutching the clothing possessively. She followed the girl ahead of her into a large room where there were a few small mirrors and a great many wall-hooks, benches, and paper carrier bags. She saw, by watching, that you stripped to the skin and put on the pink brassiere, the ugly woollen vest, the long navy knickers, the suspender belt and grey lisle stockings and then of course the blues – blue shirt, blue skirt, blue jacket – and the thin black tie and the clumpy, clumsy black shoes which were very like the school ones which she had longed to shed in favour of 'something more feminine'.

She had struggled into the uniform and was trying to tie the tie without looking in the mirror when someone spoke.

'What'll you do with your hair?' a soft voice said behind her.

Christie looked round. A small, square girl stood at her elbow, twisting and untwisting a long mass of dark, springy hair.

'Have you tried your cap on?' the stranger said. 'Mine won't stay. It's my hair, it keeps sort of springing back.'

'I haven't tried, yet,' Christie admitted. 'But all the girls I've seen either have short hair or they've put it up, somehow. Tell you what, you do mine and I'll do yours. It'll be easier that way.'

'All right,' the dark-haired one said with alacrity. 'Only you'll have to bend down a bit – you're much taller than me.'

'Okay,' Christie agreed. 'I'll do yours first, shall I? By the way, what's your name?'

'Margaret Aldford. Only I'm called Meg, usually. What's yours?'

'Christie Bellis.' Christie wrestled with the other girl's wiry mop for a moment in silence, then turned to her new friend. 'Do you have any pins or anything, Meg? Only you've got very strong-minded hair, it doesn't want to be tucked up.'

'They gave us a sort of bootlace thing,' Meg said vaguely, gesturing to the mound of clothing on her bench. 'Was that meant to do the trick? That officer did say something about rolling it, but I don't think my hair means to come to heel that easily.'

Christie pounced on the 'bootlace thing' and found that it was indeed possible to subdue her new friend's riotous mop. She was firm with it, tying the bootlace in place, and in a few moments there was Meg in her uniform with her hair restrained and her cap on at last.

'You look awfully smart,' Christie said. 'If I sit on the bench, can you do mine?'

She knew that her own straight, chestnut-brown hair was slippery and difficult but Meg had it under orders in no time. Christie put her cap on at a dashing angle and turned to the mirror.

A stranger looked back at her. She didn't look a bit like Christie Bellis of Hightree farm, she looked grown-up, self-confident, almost a woman of the world. What was more, the uniform suited her just as Adella had said it would, making her eyes look bluer than they really were, drawing attention to her small waist and slight hips. And the stockings made her legs, which were thin, look slim and yet shapely, whilst the blue-grey shade did wonderful things for her fair skin. I like it, Christie thought almost unbelievingly. I really like it – I look good in it! Through the mirror her eyes met Meg's. They smiled.

'It's going to be all right, isn't it?' Christie said

18

hopefully. 'We're going to be all right, aren't we? Funny what a difference seeing yourself in the uniform makes. It makes us look . . . oh, competent, I suppose. I don't feel quite such an outsider. And don't we get a lot of stuff? Two of everything, and lots of knickers and stockings.'

'If they have to last us till the war's over, we'll need lots,' Meg observed. She tugged at her belt. 'I wish this would go a bit tighter.'

'If they feed us the way they fed us earlier we'll all either eat it and get fat as pigs or leave it and fade away to nothing,' Christie said. 'Gosh, what a lot we've got to carry! We'd better start getting it together – is the paper carrier meant for our civvies?'

Civvies! The word had come easily to her tongue; already she was beginning to feel a part of it, a WAAF amongst WAAFs.

'Must be. Oh dear heaven, they're rounding us up again! Quick, we'd better hurry!'

It was amazing how they settled. One moment outsiders, as Christie put it, the next a part of the whole. She and Meg were in the same billet, mostly by luck, and they stuck together during the day as well, finding they had a great deal in common. Both ex-pupils of Girls' High Schools, though one in Norwich and the other in Nantwich, both children of farming families; both determined, though for different reasons, to make a success of this, their first venture into the world outside school.

It was a different life, though. Their billet was in

one hut, the ablutions in another. Hightree was a rambling old farmhouse, the bedrooms icy in winter, but never before had Christie been forced to run in her pyjamas, with a greatcoat slung round her shoulders, across a strip of slippery, icy concrete in order to have a wash before she dressed.

Most of the girls in her hut – there were twenty-five of them – didn't bother. Most of them kept their underwear on beneath their striped pyjamas, dressed in the hut, then went to ablutions and had a sketchy wash in the cooling water which was all that was available. But in half-a-dozen of them the morning ritual was too strong to ignore. Collars turned up, feet slopping around inside unlaced shoes, numbed fingers clutching their washing materials, they would charge across the concrete to the accompaniment of ironic cheers from any Air Force personnel already about. Then they would have a strip-down wash in cold water, or a shower in tepid, depending on availability and courage. Meg and Christie always tried for the showers, but there were only two and if you weren't first in there simply wasn't time before breakfast.

Breakfast was pretty grim, too. Sticky, unappetising porridge followed by bread and margarine, with a concoction euphemistically labelled marmalade in a bowl in the middle of each long table.

'That stuff never saw a bloody orange,' Meg remarked after a week. 'If I wasn't so frigging starving . . .'

It was the first time that Christie had actually realised how thoroughly she and Meg were donning

protective coloration. Swearing, which was something they had been taught was an unpleasant habit
used only by the lower classes, was in such general use
that those who didn't pepper their every sentence
with obscenities were looked on as odd.

At first it had not seemed important, but then the
girl with the yellow hair – and nits – whose name
turned out to be Primrose Pluckman, told Christie
that she and her pal Meg were regarded as snobs by
most of the flight. Horrified, because they wanted
badly to fit in, Christie and Meg began to listen to the
other girls and to colour their conversation accordingly. Mummy would have a fit, Christie thought
apprehensively when Meg swore alliteratively at her
boots and she herself condemned her missing collar
stud in terms which would have raised a good few
eyebrows even in farming circles; but it didn't mean
anything, not really. We won't swear at home, nor
when we get our postings, she decided. It's just now,
whilst we're square-bashing, that we need it.

They grew wise in the ways of their new family.
They had been issued with shiny-peaked caps,
startling in their crisp and splendid smartness.
Admiring and envying the WAAFs who had been in
months already, they kicked and beat and trod on
their gleaming caps until they were crushed and
comfortable and elderly-looking. Then they turned
their attention to their buttons, cleaning them with
Silvo instead of Brasso until the yellow of new brass
was polished into gleaming, mature whiteness. After
that they attended to their stiff black shoes, gradually

increasing the shine to mirror consistency with constant wear and even more constant rubbing with spit and Cherry Blossom shoe polish.

Their initial training lasted for just over three weeks, then they were split up into two groups and assigned to general duties instead of the constant parade ground drill which had been their lot until then. After three weeks of being shouted at, it seemed to be accepted that they could wheel right and left, march, stop, start, dress, and eyes right, and do it well, what was more. They had learned to snap a salute to an officer at a moment's notice and to march on to the depot at the end of a day's tramp looking as fresh as when they had left it, though every muscle cried out for rest. Their uniforms were immaculate, their caps looked as though their owners had been around a bit and they carried themselves, Christie noticed, with an easy confidence which had certainly not been the case at first. So having made them into a unit the Air Force now brought them a further step along the road.

General duties they called it; Christie thought of it as a levelling out. Scrubbing floors and polishing linoleum, peeling potatoes and emptying garbage, might not make them into a fighting force, but it was as great a leveller as marching had been. Almost without knowing it, the ill-assorted, flung-together groups of girls from all walks of life were beginning to become a part of the whole – they were accepting the orders, carrying out the duties, laughing at themselves and each other, griping, belly-aching ... but getting on with it. Christie could see it happening now, and so could Meg.

And as time passed they also realised that the Air Force knew what it was doing. It might seem pointless, all the marching and cleaning and together-ness, the insistence on rules and regulations which were both antiquated and unfair, but it was not. It was turning them into WAAFs, and that after all, was the point of the exercise.

Once Christie had the time – and the energy – some small spark of fellow-feeling had persuaded her to conduct a search for Adella up in the admin offices, and she was amused to discover that the Hon. Adella Springthorpe had cut and run after her first official train journey with the WAAF.

'What was so awful about it?' Christie asked her informant rather plaintively. She could remember the cold, the weariness, but had put the uncertainty and fear of the unknown out of her mind. Now, she thought that curiosity, as well as patriotism, should have carried Adella at least as far as their destination.

'Too many people to a carriage and being met by open lorries,' the officer to whom Christie had addressed her query said. 'Used to better things, I imagine – she was twenty-eight, quite a lot older than most of your intake. So she upped and went . . . but she did write in.' She chuckled. 'Said it was disgusting, enough to put any decent girl off service life for ever!'

'Oh well, it takes all sorts,' Christie murmured

conventionally, but as she left the office she was aware of a treacherous feeling of relief. She and Meg were such friends, got on so well; and though she would have asked Adella to go into town with them this afternoon had Adella been somewhere on the depot, she doubted whether it would have added to anyone's enjoyment.

Because it appeared the Air Force now trusted them; having bullied them and screamed at them and put them on charges for the smallest and most trivial of offences, they were being offered an afternoon off – and not only off, but out. They were at liberty, for the first time in six weeks, to go off the depot, to visit the nearest town.

The exhilarating sense of freedom which this engendered had to be felt to be believed, Christie thought, as she and Meg polished buttons, brushed each other's tunics and pinned neatly out of the way every erring wisp of hair.

'I'm going to buy Mummy and Daddy a postcard and I'm going to eat the biggest, wickedest cake I can find,' Christie told Meg as they got ready for the treat. 'Oh, for a big flask of perfume! But talcum will do, if I can't find anything else.'

Their pay, too small for most purposes, seemed a fortune when saved up for six whole weeks.

'Shall we catch the bus?' Meg wondered aloud as she filed her nails with a borrowed emery board. 'Or shall we cadge a lift? Or walk?'

'We could bus,' Christie said. 'Unless there's a gharry going into town; if there is they'll take us.'

There was a lorry; they climbed aboard with others from their flight, all ridiculously excited, talking, laughing. They disembarked in the main street of the small town and split up, Christie and Megan finding a Woolworths and spending a luxurious hour combing the shelves for . . .

'Anything nice,' Christie said dreamily. 'Anything feminine and pretty or exotic, or . . .'

'Got any sweet coupons? There's Mars bars and liquorice allsorts but not much else,' Meg said, bringing the conversation down to earth. 'Let's try a chemist; we might get scented soap or talcum there.'

The street on to which they emerged was narrow, the buildings old. Service personnel seemed to have taken possession of it. The few civilians they saw seemed dull and lethargic; they dressed boringly, without so much as one brass button between them, and talked in low voices amongst themselves. Christie wondered what had happened in this dull little town before the forces came . . . Then they found a chemist whose shelves weren't entirely empty and bought rose-geranium soap and sweet violet talcum powder and gazed enviously at the perfume in tiny flasks marked up with huge prices.

'Can we have tea now?' Meg asked as they left the shop with their purchases tucked into their greatcoat pockets. It was another cold, grey day, the sort of day when a WAAF greatcoat could be truly appreciated. 'That place looks rather nice.'

'That place' was a tearoom with blackened oak beams, a roaring log fire and elderly waitresses in faded print overalls. There was a table vacant in the bow-fronted window and the two girls went in and sat down. The wind which had made them turn their coat-collars up and stick their hands in their pockets could now be ignored though the muffled-up passers-by made the girls feel even cosier in the firelit warmth.

'Where have all those girls come from?' Meg asked presently, after they'd asked the waitress to bring them buttered toast, tea and cakes, and were sitting back, waiting for their order to arrive. 'Well, they aren't from the depot, that's for sure.'

Glancing out, Christie knew what she meant. Outside, hurrying home, were girls from the local factories and shops – girls who were not WAAFs – and they seemed grey-skinned and slouching, with no pride in themselves, no spring in their steps.

'They're locals,' Christie said. 'Don't they look miserable, Meggie! It's as though you only have a sense of purpose when you're with our mob. But who wants to work in a factory or on the land, especially in February!'

'They're doing their bit, same as we are,' Meg said rather reproachfully; a neighbour's daughter had joined the Land Army and a cousin made tanks at Crewe Railway Works, to say nothing of a school friend who took the bus from Nantwich to Alsager each day in order to make munitions for the war effort.

'You can't believe that, not when you look at all those bent shoulders and miserable faces,' Christie scoffed. 'It's us that's going to win the war, us in blue

. . . 'ray, 'ray, 'ray for the WAAF and the RAF!'

The elderly waitress, coming over with their order, jumped and nearly spilt the tea. Meg glared at her friend.

'Don't make an exhibition of yourself, you'll have us turned out before we've had our tea! Gosh, don't those cakes look delicious!'

The waitress smiled and rested the tray on the edge of the table whilst she unloaded.

'Tea for two, cakes for two, and a plate of buttered toast,' she said cheerfully. 'Your first bit of time off, is it?'

'That's right,' Christie said. 'It's nice to see the real world again.'

'Oh aye . . . But you're a happy lot, you WAAFs. Well, enjoy your tea.'

Christie glanced at Meg as they ate the toast and sipped their tea. She had annoyed her friend, and she realised, suddenly, that for all her brave talk it was Meg who made life at the depot endurable, turned it from hard slog into something to be proud of, something to enjoy.

'Sorry, Meg, I shouldn't have yelled out like that. You can have first choice of the cakes to make up.'

Meg shook her head at her.

'You can't get round me that easy, Aircraftwoman. Anyway, you're right. It shouldn't scare me, being a part of it, but it does. I'm worried all the time in case we let anyone down.'

'It would be awful to let our flight down,' Christie agreed, relaxing again. 'Why, our little lot got top

27

marks for drill despite Evelyn's two left feet and
Primrose moaning about everything and thinking us
fools for going along with all the spit and polish.'

'That's because we're the best,' Meg said simply.
Her hand hovered over the plate of cakes, then
selected a mock-cream eclair. 'Besides, we're being
judged as a team, and we're a good team. What gets
me is the postings, though. The flight will be split up of
course, but I don't know what I'll do if you and me get
separated. The others are grand, but you and me
understand each other, you don't think I'm daft when
I worry about things. Still, in another five days we'll
know for sure.'

'Special duties! Both of us, what's more! I say, I was
dreading being turned into a full-time cleaner or a
cook or something. So you'd better get that snowy-
white kit-bag packed, Meg, and drop a line to your
people.'

The two girls were walking back to their billet
through a snowstorm, but even the weather couldn't
damp their high spirits. No one knew precisely what
special duties would consist of, but it was clear from
the small numbers going on the course and the fact
that most of them had done well at school that it was a
superior sort of thing to do. Meg and Christie had
both passed their School Certificate and had been
studying for their Higher when they decided to join up
instead.

'What did the old battle-axe say to you? She said I
was officer material,' Meg said. She straightened her

shoulders and smiled into the blizzard. Christie could see that Meg had been immensely heartened by the officer's words, as she herself had.

The Squadron Officer i/c WAAFs had interviewed everyone at the end of their training for a few minutes. She had made a deep impression on Christie, and judging from Meg's expression now, Christie thought her friend had felt the same. Miss Fortescue was a hard-working, sincere woman who lived for the Air Force and wanted 'her girls' to do well in their service careers.

'Yes, she said I was officer material, too. She's not a bad old thing, is she? You could tell she meant every word.'

Christie's reply was muffled by the collar of her greatcoat, turned up to shield her face from the driving flakes, and she had to raise her voice a little to be heard above the squeak of their leather-soled shoes on fast-settling snow.

'Yes, she was all right.' Meg slowed her pace as they neared their billet. 'She made me feel much better about things: much braver, somehow. She said perhaps I should get my hair cut, said it was neater and would save me time in the mornings.'

Christie laughed.

'She must say that to everyone; you going to do it? Cut your hair, I mean.'

'Nope. Well, not yet, anyway.'

'Nor me,' Christie agreed. She liked her hair long, in peacetime she had worn it in a pageboy, the ends turned under. Daddy liked the satiny shine of it and the way it moved when she did, he said; but it wasn't easy rolling it each morning. Short hair would definitely be more efficient.

'I suppose she said it because most officers seem to have short hair,' Meg said. 'But I don't think I want to be an officer. For one thing I couldn't tell other people what to do, and for another, officers will spend the war training people like us to do interesting work. Personally, I'd rather do the interesting work.'

'Me too. I wouldn't mind being an officer one day, though. Have to wait and see what these "special duties" amount to.'

The girls reached their hut and pushed open the door, hurrying inside and hastily closing the door again on the cold and the snow. Other girls were sitting on their beds, doing their hair, shedding coats and kicking off their shoes. There was a small stove glowing away in the centre of the room; it made little impression on the chill though body heat made it a good deal warmer than outside.

'What'll we do now?' Christie said, hanging her snow-damp coat up on its hook and sitting down on her narrow bed. 'How about cadging a lift in a gharry if someone's driving into town? We could see a flick, then have fish and chips for supper. We ought to celebrate being on special duties and we aren't on duty again until tomorrow. And the day after we're off to the new posting, so we might as well say cheerio to the town.'

Meg looked doubtful. She had taken her coat off too and hung it up, now she sat down on her bed, kicked off her shoes and began to massage her toes.

'We–ell, I've not written to my people for ages, I really ought to let them know I'm moving on. Besides, my coat's damp already, I don't want to sit in the picture-house in soaking wet clothes and get pneumonia just at the start of special duties. Why don't we go over to the cookhouse, get some grub, write our letters, and then have an early night for a change?'

Christie sighed and nodded.

'I suppose we should, only it seems so dull not to celebrate in some way. We might go over to the NAAFI after we've eaten and have a sing-along, I suppose, though that isn't exactly exciting. I wonder what life will be like on a real RAF station? I wonder what it'll be like doing the special duty training, come to that?'

'You spend too much time wondering,' Meg said comfortably. 'You should wait and see, like I do. I'm going to wear my gas cape to go across to the cookhouse, though, not a damp coat.'

'I'm going to wear my towel,' Christie said. 'Wrapped round me. Oh, but if I do I shan't have anything to dry on tomorrow morning. Perhaps I'll wear my gas cape, too.'

It was a constant battle keeping clothing and equipment dry and mould-free in the chilly, echoing Nissen huts.

Primrose Pluckman, who was *not* destined for special duties, turned from contemplating her reflection in the small square of mirror above her bed. She had put her hair in curl papers and was carefully

31

applying pencil to her eyebrows but she stopped for a moment to speak.

'You're nutty, you two are,' she said frankly. 'Worryin' about gettin' wet when you never goes anywhere worth goin'. Me an' Ethel and the rest's goin' to the pub later. Why don't you come dahn there? You'd enjoy it, 'ave a bit of a knees-up.'

'Yes, why not?' Christie said with an alacrity she was far from feeling. The village pub was small, the locals not always welcoming. But she realised it would be a gesture of togetherness which, in her heart, she wanted right now, when they were so soon to be separated. 'What d'you say, Meg?'

'Are we walking? We'll get drenched,' Meg said doubtfully.

Primrose giggled.

'Walkin'? Us gels? 'Course we ain't walkin', we're goin' in the fellers' waggon. They'll stop by the NAAFI to pick us up an' drop us off at closin' time. A date then, is it?'

'It's a date,' Meg agreed. 'Now let's get some grub!'

2

Meg and Christie travelled down to their training centre by rail, amazed to discover that, in the soft south, the first signs of spring could already be seen in woods and meadows.

'Snowdrops, drifts of them,' Christie exclaimed rapturously as the train chugged through ancient woodland. 'And there are crocuses in the gardens, and daffodils in bud. We'll be quite near the coast at this place, perhaps we'll be able to get down to the beach.'

'If we don't get kicked out because we aren't good enough,' Meg mumbled. 'Have a sandwich.'

The staff at the depot had handed out packed lunches to those moving on – two corned beef sandwiches, a small bar of chocolate and a currant bun – so now the girls got their packages out and opened them. The other occupants of the carriage, seeing what they were doing, produced food of their own. A sailor, delving into his kit-bag, began to eat a huge Cornish pasty and a woman with three children handed her offspring miniature meat pies and small jellies in little paper cups. Two ATS girls, giggling over a letter and making eyes at the sailor every now and then, had a big flask of hot soup and lovely crusty rolls.

I expect everyone else is coming from home, so they've got food made by the family, Christie thought, eyeing her dry and curling sandwiches with distaste. Still, food is food, might as well eat as go hungry.

She sank her teeth into the first sandwich and it wasn't too bad, though margarine on the bread or some pickle would have helped; and she would have given a small fortune for a hot drink, the chocolate only made her thirstier.

She said as much to Meg and the sailor leaned forward, brushing crumbs of pasty from his trouser-legs.

'The train stops at a small station in ten minutes; there's a feller on the platform sells coffee in paper cups. Want me to get you a couple?'

'Oh, that would be marvellous,' Christie said gratefully. 'How much are they?'

'Dunno; prices keep goin' up. But you can pay me when I get back aboard,' the young man said cheerfully. 'Where are you headin' for, then? Not Southampton?'

'No, Christie said, smiling back at him. We're getting off the train there, but we're actually going...'

'Careless talk costs lives,' Meg said reprovingly. 'But thanks for offering to get us the coffee; we're dying for a drink. What time are we due in?'

The young man shrugged, smiling at Meg this time to show he wasn't offended.

'Four forty, so it'll probably be sevenish. I've never worked out why trains can't run on time just because there's a war on.'

'Nor us,' Meg agreed. 'Still, sevenish wouldn't be too bad. So long as they save us some grub in the cookhouse.'

'They're bound to, surely?' Christie said, dismayed by the implication that they might be allowed to go hungry after their extended journey. Meg shrugged.

'I dunno. Remember arriving at the depot?'

'Yes, of course I do; we had sausage and mash.'

'True. But remember Jennifer Stalker, whose train was even later than ours? Just dry bread and a tiny bit of cheese.'

'Oh, blow,' Christie said. 'We'll wish we'd not eaten both the sandwiches by bedtime.'

'Still, we're bound to get a hot drink,' Meg said. 'Aren't we?'

She was addressing Christie, but her question went right to the heart of every member of the forces present. Faces mirrored Christie's own sudden doubt. Meg sighed and slid further down in her seat.

'I'm going to sleep,' she said. 'Wake me at the coffee-station.'

Special duties, for both girls, turned out to be working in the operations room, as plotters. On this particular station they were training only ops room staff and very intensively at that. In four weeks, they were told on the first morning by an upright, silver-haired Wing Commander, they would get their postings and start the job in earnest; until then, they were not to talk about what they were doing, would not leave the station, and must do their very best.

'If you can't cope we'll know, but if the work brings you out in a rash somewhere where we can't see it or gives you nightmares tell someone. The lives of a great many young men will depend on you!'

It was a good, lively lecture and started them off on the right foot from the very beginning. The Wingco who talked to them was a fatherly, understanding sort of man. As well as telling them how they would train he also told them they were privileged, top of their intake, or they wouldn't be here; and that having the mental ability to do more intelligent work brought with it responsibilities and pains which the less able might never suffer.

'Your superiors at the depot believe each one of you is capable of setting a good example and leading your peers; in other words, that you're officer material,' the Wingco explained. 'Try to live up to their expectations and you'll go far.'

Furtive grins were exchanged; they had already, after only a few hours in each other's company, realised that all of them had been pinpointed as officer material. They might scoff – well, they *did* scoff – but secretly, Christie thought, they were all as thrilled as she and Meg were. Even if they chose not to lead their fellow WAAFs, at least the Powers that Be thought they had the ability.

On that first day the new intake were handed over to a pretty, efficient-looking WAAF officer in her mid-thirties, who led them across the airfield, down a flight of concrete steps to a thick, baize-covered door, and into the artificial lighting of the operations room. As they entered, Meg gave Christie's arm a quick squeeze. This, the gesture said, is what we've been waiting for: important war work!

The room was a bit like a circular theatre, with a big table painted with a gridded map taking the place of the stage. Where the audience would have been, rising in tiers, were men in Air Force uniform, some wearing headphones and some not, either watching the table intently or using the equipment before them.

Around the table men and a few WAAFS stood, holding sticks like billiard-cue rests which they used to move to and fro across the grid objects which looked like toy galleons. The men and women wore head-sets and were clearly obeying instructions received through these sets. There were one or two other WAAFs and RAF, standing back behind the plotters, now and again coming forward and handing them something or speaking a quiet word in an ear.

The officer responsible for their training drew the small group of girls aside.

'This is where air movements are plotted,' she whispered. 'Presently I'll link each of you up with a plotter and you can hear what's happening. Each of the pieces represents a plane, the enemy's have swastikas, ours are the arrows with their numbers and of course our colours. The sticks the girls use are called rakes, the pieces slot into the tip of the rake and can be easily moved from square to square. The controllers make sure everyone knows what's going on and keep in touch with the observers – they are the people who tell the plotters where each plane is. In an hour or two, perhaps you'll begin to understand a little of what's going on; in a day or two, you'll be able to take over at quiet periods. This is a very intensive course though, you won't be here for more than six weeks, so make the most of it.'

The next few hours were interesting, exciting, frightening . . .

'You name it, I felt it,' Christie told Meg that evening as they sat in the cookhouse eating bully beef stew. 'I know we're supposed to be bright, but goodness, it's all so complicated! All those numbers and little ship-things just for a start, then all the voices, and you have to listen out for the one who's talking to you, you have to find the aircraft, move it into the right square . . . I don't believe I'll ever be able to do it properly, without someone holding my hand. Imagine getting something wrong – you could muck up the whole board!'

'Yup. But we're being trained so we don't muck up,' Meg said through a mouthful of potato. 'Christie, this is the most worthwhile thing I've ever had a chance to do and I don't intend to balls it up.'

Christie looked sideways at her friend. She and

Meg knew each other pretty well, or so she had thought, but now she wondered if they really knew each other at all. Meg was not a girl who talked about her worries and uncertainties much, but somehow Christie had always felt that she led and her friend followed. Now she stared thoughtfully at Meg across the table. Pink-cheeked, frizzy-headed, eating solidly, yet this Meg wasn't quite the girl she thought she knew. Until today Meg had been uncertain of a number of things, unsure of her own abilities in this strange new world that they had been hurled into. But the new Meg had determination in every inch of her small, puggy face and her eyes shone with purpose and self-assurance.

Yet I, who have felt the stronger of the two of us, the one who handed out reassurance and platitudes, am really worried in case I make a mess of plotting and risk lives, Christie realised. Meg is absolutely right, we're being given this chance to do something really worthwhile, to become a force to be reckoned with, it's up to each one of us to accept the challenge and take the training more seriously than we've ever taken anything before.

'You're right, Meg,' she said humbly. 'And it *is* important work, since apart from anything else, the Wingco said every WAAF plotter releases a man for a more active role. I won't balls it up either. We'll be the best plotters Fighter Command has ever known!'

'The best *bloody* plotters,' Meg corrected without the hint of a smile. 'This is the WAAF, aircraft-woman, not sodding civvy street!'

* * *

After the course, Meg and Christie passed out as fully fledged plotters and were posted, together again, to an airfield nearby. It was a pleasant spot, within reach of several large towns, Southampton being one of them, and they soon settled down, taking their work in their stride though the skies over their part of the grid were getting busier day by day.

They arrived at the new airfield in April. By July they were no longer 'new girls' but a tried and trusted part of the team which was made up almost entirely of WAAFs, as the men were posted to other positions and other airfields.

It was becoming clear that Hitler's planned invasion could not take place without air superiority, which meant crushing the RAF once and for all, so a night seldom passed without the drone of the heavy bombers going over to bomb the big cities and the roar as their own aircraft were scrambled to intercept. Christie tried to keep pace with the progress of the war as a whole, but most of the time she was just too tired. France and Belgium fell, the troops were evacuated from the Dunkirk beaches, radar became a new and important tool in the effort to keep the sky-invaders at bay. But in the ops room they were too busy to discuss the larger international battle; in their billet, tired out and sometimes depressed, it became more important to find out where Maureen had got her new lipstick or why Sheila had stopped going out with Mark.

They had not yet had any leave because of the

pressure of work, but home had grown hazy; their parents, though still much-loved, seemed less real than the girl beside you at the table, the man's voice speaking in your ear.

Meg and Christie had just come off the one a.m. to five a.m. night watch and were walking to the cookhouse in the quiet grey dawn. It had been a busy night, with constant movement over their part of the grid; when their reliefs arrived the girls simply took off their headsets and left, almost too tired to talk.

Halfway across to the cookhouse, however, Christie remembered something.

'Meg, tomorrow's our big day! We aren't on again for two days and we're going to meet those chaps. I'd not given it a thought for hours . . . oh bliss! Come on, Meg, the sooner we eat the sooner we can sleep.'

Catching Meg's hand she began to run and found herself waking up as she did so, taking great breaths of the sweet, grass-scented air, enjoying the feeling of well-being as the blood began to circulate briskly once more. The two of them burst into the cookhouse and got in the queue. The girl in front of them turned round.

'Hello, gels! Oh Gawd, not that so-called stew *again*! I swear Cooky arranges for that bloody stew and suet duff every time I'm on the last flippin' night watch. What's more, if I ate it my bum would spread out sideways and I wouldn't be able to get into the bloody cook'ouse. Last time I ate some I spent the next two weeks on the bloody bog, gettin' rid of it. If there was any meat in it it wouldn't be so bad, but all I

41

ever get is bloody turnip and that awful Oxo gravy.'

Ellen Rafferty shared a billet with Meg, Christie and a couple of dozen others. She was a friendly soul who talked like a stand-up comic, making them laugh with her criticisms of life on the station, whether about the food, the bedding or the officers to whom they had to pay respect. A plump woman of indeterminate age, Ellen might have been thirty or fifty, with badly bleached hair, a great sense of humour and no fear of authority whatsoever. She also happened to be extremely good at her job, which was why people put up with her, Christie supposed. Now, she was complaining about the food whilst standing with her plate held out so that the girl in charge of the stew could fill it.

'There's cabbage, Raffs,' Christie said, peering through the steam. 'You could have cabbage and spuds. And if you asked one of the girls she might let you have just custard instead of the duff.'

'Hmm. Look at you, gel, just skin and bone, yet you eat the god-awful muck; don't let on you leave it 'cause I've seen you, puttin' it away.'

The girl doling out the stew dipped her ladle into the heaving mass and deposited a large helping on Ellen's plate.

'Come on, Raffs, give us a break,' she urged. 'It's what they give us to cook, not what we do with it.'

'Ah well, you would say that, wouldn' cha? Still an' all, mebbe it smells better than it did last week.' Ellen heaved an exaggerated sigh. 'Oh well, I'll give it a go. Come on, gels, grab a seat.'

The three of them sat down at a table, Christie looking at her stew with almost as much suspicion as Ellen. The one a.m. to five a.m. night watch was cordially hated by one and all, and Christie wasn't hungry, particularly for stew. Few people can do justice to a meal like that at five-thirty in the morning, and as for sleeping with that in your stomach . . .

Opposite her, Meg chewed her way stolidly through her plateful. The poor girl looked exhausted, Christie thought, and no wonder. It had been a hell of a shift, with heavy raids in their area so that they had been plotting non-stop for more than their regulation four hours. And it took it out of you; you might start fresh and eager, but the tension, the emotion, got to you in the end. And two hours into their shift there had been a tragedy over their own station – two fighter planes flown by men they saw strolling around the station when they were off-duty, had collided in mid-air when coming in to land. Both men died in the crash and when she heard, the duty officer had gone so white they thought she was going to faint; later someone realised that the officer had recently got engaged to one of the dead pilots.

So stew wasn't what they'd had in mind when they came in for their meal. Still, it was here, and if she didn't eat anything and went to bed hungry Christie knew from experience that she probably wouldn't sleep, either. But a few mouthfuls would be quite enough, plus a cup of the incredibly stewed cook-house tea and a very small helping of suet duff.

Ellen ate with a good appetite, considering her

43

earlier remarks. She worked shifts on the exchange, putting calls through to the outside world and dealing with incoming ones. She had been a telephone operator in civvy street and dealt with her job here with the same efficiency and despatch; callers who waited and complained were rare when Ellen was on duty. She was a motherly soul though and presently, having eaten all her own stew and polished the plate with a thick wedge of bread, she turned to Christie.

'You look like death, the pair of you,' she announced . 'Get to bed, go on. No plans for today, eh?'

'Just to sleep,' Christie said. 'It's the end of our week, though; we're not on tomorrow, so we might get off the airfield for a bit.'

She and Meg exchanged small grins. Highly illegally, Christie had been conversing with an officer who was putting in some time on an observer post one quiet morning and he had suggested that it might be fun to meet. 'Me and my pal, you and yours,' he had said. 'How about a night on the town? How about meeting at Waterloo Station under the clock at eight on Friday evening? '

Blind dates were all the rage, but this would be a first for Meg and for Christie too. The officer was a fighter pilot, as was his friend; the girls had agreed to go chiefly because they were always hard up and were beginning to find that a plotter's life, with the strange shifts and the constant fear of missing a move on the table, was so highly charged and tense that they desperately needed time to relax and forget about the war. And leave, even a precious forty-eight, was not yet on the cards for them.

'So now we'll have a good day's sleep, then tomorrow we'll spend our time beautifying ourselves, and in the evening we'll go on the razz,' Christie said as the two of them made their way to their billet. They had left Ellen in the cookhouse, entertaining an air-crew who had just come in for a quick meal. 'Do you realise, Meg, that this will be my first date since I left school? I went out with boys in school, of course, but that didn't mean much.'

Meg giggled. 'I should hope not! Schoolboys aren't exactly big romantics. Want a drink or anything before we turn in?'

'No thanks. I'm going to sleep for eight precious hours and then I'll have a shower and we'll catch a bus into town and try to find ourselves tea and toast or perhaps a light lunch.' The two of them almost lurched into their billet, to find all the other beds empty, their usual occupants having decided to go out whilst they could, whilst the girls who were doing day shifts were either working or entertaining themselves elsewhere.

God, I am *so* tired! I don't know how the others do it, gadding off round the station, I'm just about out on my feet. Don't let's bother to change, Meggie, let's hit the hay.'

It felt like only seconds later when Christie was woken by someone roughly shaking her and shouting in her ear.

'Wake up, woman! Aircraftwoman, wake up, are you deaf? Oh hell, didn't you hear the warning? Do wake up!'

'Whassamatter? Go 'way, I'm asleep,' Christie droned. She tried to curl up, to get her head under the covers, but small, cruel hands wrenched the blankets down, exposing her to the light.

'Look, there's an emergency call out, chuck, it's a daylight raid, a bad one! They sent me to check the huts – your oppo gorrup in her sleep I think, but you didn't stir. They want you over in ops, they need plotters desperately and there's a good few of you either already in the shelters or off on the town, so just wake yourself up!'

Christie opened bleary eyes, focusing with some difficulty first on her wrist-watch – it was just noon – and then on the face above her. It was a face she didn't know, a small, fair face, crowned with blonde curls. Christie frowned at it, then sat up slowly, still only half awake.

'Whatever is it? I've only just come off watch, you can't . . .

'Emergency. You've gorra report straight to the ops room.' The girl sighed and then unceremoniously pulled Christie out of bed, shaking her slightly as she did so. 'I've gorra go, there's other huts . . . You won't go back to sleep?'

'I'm awake,' Christie said with a groan. 'Where's Meg, though?'

'In the ops room. I were sent in here to fetch anyone still sleeping and your oppo woke first shake. But not you, friend, you was still snoring. Look, do get a move on! Your pals won't have waited, they'll have left, but you can use a bike, you'll get there almost as quick as them.'

She left. Christie got out of bed, thankful that she was not in pyjamas but in her underwear, and only needed to slip on stockings, shoes, and uniform to be properly dressed once more. Respectable, though both crumpled and dazed, she was at the door of the hut and about to leave when she heard the noise.

Aircraft.

That should have been nothing new, but after weeks and weeks of listening to them leaving and returning she knew the sound of those fighters attached to the station well enough to realise that she was hearing strange engines. And wasn't that gunfire? The little blonde had said something about a raid . . .

Christie opened the door cautiously and poked her head out. A plane was coming down towards her, spurts of flame spitting from its guns, flanked by others like it. She could see the black crosses where roundels should have been – it was the Luftwaffe, they must have managed to break through the British defences!

The noise was awful. As she ran, bending double, for the bicycle which she could see propped against a nearby hut, she heard bombs fall and was abruptly knocked off her feet by the blast. She skidded along the concrete on hands and knees and ended up with her nose inches from the bike's front wheel. She looked round wildly, then up: the belly of one of the attacking planes zoomed overhead, looking close enough to touch. She could see the wheels, the bomb hatch, everything, but wasted no time in staring. Instead, as soon as the planes had passed over, she grabbed the bike and vaulted into the saddle.

It was a man's model but she heaved her skirt up round her thighs and pedalled as fast as she could along the concrete path, heading towards the ops room. It occurred to her suddenly, as she rode, that there was no one about, not a soul. Still dazed by deep sleep interrupted and none too sure she was not dreaming, Christie pedalled on. An aircraft loomed into view, low, the tail fin half blown away. One of ours. No one came running and the pilot must have pulled back on the stick because the nose suddenly lifted and she was airborne once more, climbing steadily to where, high above, a covey of other planes, spitting smoke, seemed to be engaging in a dog-fight right above the main runway.

This really is serious, Christie told herself, bending to her work and sending the bicycle shooting forward. Better get into the ops room fast, it's underground, which will be safer, and they'll need me by the look of things.

She reached the well-hidden concrete steps, dumped the bike and fell down into the corridor. She could have traversed it in her sleep and since the lights seemed to have gone out she very nearly did, then opened the door leading into the ops room and saw it smoky, dim, strangely unlike its usual self.

Someone at the table turned; it was Meg, a grin splitting her pale face.

'My God, it's Bellis – I tried to wake you but it was like trying to wake Rip Van Winkle! I left some little blonde screaming at you like a guards officer, she must have done the trick. You all right to start work? They've hit the electricity supply, but the Group Captain got the emergency ones going; you can just about see if you peer. Here, take this head-set.'

The emergency lighting, Christie saw, was half-a-dozen hurricane lamps. Some hung from the light fittings, others stood on any surface where they could shed a glow on the proceedings, and by this unlikely illumination the plotters worked, although as Christie reached out a hand for the babbling head-set she could see that there was almost as much confusion on the table as there was outside on the airfield.

She waited a moment to orientate herself, then repeated the call-sign and grid number which was coming to her over the ether and moved the wooden arrow representing that particular aircraft into its new position. A duty controller called across to one of the WAAFs servicing the table and she slipped out of her seat and brought more wooden arrows down to the frantic plotters. Christie heard a deep roar through her headphones and even as she wondered what it was, heard an observer remarking dispassionately, 'Two down that time, one Beaufighter, two Ju 88s. Did you get that, control? Take them off the table.'

Christie's stick stole two blacks and a colour and pulled them out of play. You have to think of it like that, she told herself, not for the first time. You mustn't let reality get to you or you couldn't do the job properly; and the men on the ground who master-minded the battle raging in the air needed to be able to see what was happening up there.

Beside her, Meg pushed another piece towards her part of the grid, then another. The voices switched from Meg's frequency to Christie's as the observers on the ground, in air traffic control towers, on ships, gun-sites, balloon batteries, observatories, radioed in the new positions of the dots in the sky.

At some point Christie looked at her wrist-watch and it was four o'clock; she glanced round the table, seeing the fierce concentration, the hooded eyes, the way the rakes reached out, patted, pulled, pushed, were drawn back again, all without the plotters' expressions changing. Above her the faces in control were dimmer than usual, the men leaning forward to see better, moving markers on their own, smaller, maps, glancing up occasionally at the huge map of the southern half of Britain above them on the wall; plotters were working on that, too, shifting the tiny aircraft slowly across the map, mimicking their flight.

An hour to shift change – but who would come? Someone said a shelter had been hit. WAAFs had been down there, the men were digging . . .

A hand touched hers. Startled, Christie looked up to see Patty, her relief, ready to take over. As it happened, things were quiet in her sector so she slid the head-set off and Patty jammed it on to her sleek dark hair while Christie stepped out of the way, realising as she did so that she ached in every limb. Meg had already been relieved and stood back too, massaging her upper arms. She was short, so the effort it took to reach the end of her grid was correspondingly greater than for Christie; and the greater effort meant Meg got muscle pains in the arms and sometimes cramp in the calves as she strained to retrieve or reposition from the centre of the table.

'All right?'

Meg smiled and nodded, still rubbing her arms.

'Oh, sure. Let's see if we can get a cuppa, shall we?'

They went outside. It was strange to go from dimness into full sunlight, to hear birdsong, to smell crushed grass. Downstairs in the ops room it was always night, being below ground and windowless, and with that dreadful air battle raging Christie had somehow come to think that it was night outside, too. And it was not only grass she could smell but gasoline, and that horrible smell of brick dust and soot and damp plaster which seems to hang round bombed buildings.

One of the huts was leaning sideways, like a drunk on the verge of falling flat on his face; nearby there was a huge crater with rubble in the bottom. Something else was different too, though Christie could not quite make out what it was. Then Meg grabbed her arm.

'The cookhouse isn't there! Nor's our hut!'

'Our hut? Oh, my God! Who . . . what . . . ?'

'It was empty,' Meg said firmly. She frowned, her voice suddenly less certain. 'Wasn't it?'

'Don't know, can't remember. Oh Meg, all those girls!'

Uselessly, pointlessly, they began to run towards the ruins of their hut.

3

It was chaos, of course, but organised chaos. People got themselves sorted out, beds were arranged, bedding drawn from the stores. The death-toll was seven WAAFs, all killed when the shelter was bombed, and four men who died when a German plane had strafed the runway they were repairing.

In the makeshift cookhouse, with tepid food brought in from heaven knew where, Christie and Meg scarcely talked at all and the others were as quiet. Christie couldn't get over her narrow escape: if that little blonde had decided to leave her to have her sleep out, if she'd not taken the bicycle and gone over to the ops room despite the raid, if she'd decided to get into the shelter until the worst was over – the different options were all too possible and could all have ended fatally.

Even her ability to sleep through anything could no longer raise a laugh. The other girls looked at her soberly, knowing that each of them, in one way or another, was lucky to be alive. Their mess had been taken over, so when they finished their meal they had nowhere to go but to their billets and presently, still quiet and pale, they did just that.

Meg and Christie were re-billeted in the hut nearest to the smoking ruins of their erstwhile home. Most of the dispossessed would be billeted in the nearest village; but because of the need to have plotters actually on the airfield, those who worked in the ops room were rehoused on the station, even though it meant a certain amount of overcrowding.

The evening after the bombing raid Christie and Meg made their way to their new premises, with as much borrowed equipment as they had been able to scrounge in their arms and bedding draped about them.

They found the occupants of the hut moving their beds closer to make room for the newcomers. Two bedsteads were waiting and gaps had been made so that there was just about room to squeeze them in. A few remarks were exchanged as Meg and Christie laid the three 'biscuits', which together made up the Air Force mattress, on the flat wooden stations and then began to arrange their bedding on top, but by and large the girls were quiet. They had all known the seven WAAFs who had been killed in the air-raid shelter and their corporal had been dating one of the dead aircraftmen. Their welcome was subdued, therefore, and presently, without exchanging more than a few words, Meg and Christie undressed and got into bed, sliding between the strange, chilly blankets in their borrowed pyjamas.

Christie, glancing round her at the dimly lit room, suddenly realised that she did not even have a toothbrush – or a bar of soap to call her own. She had nothing. Her photograph of Fly, the border collie who her father often said was his right-hand woman on the farm, had gone up in smoke along with her cherished silk stockings, the dark brown ribbons she used to roll up her hair, and the pin-up picture, cut from a magazine, of Clark Gable and Vivien Leigh. Her little purse with a few shillings in it, her Basildon Bond with matching envelopes, even her autograph book had gone. She felt suddenly stateless, bereft.

'Hope there isn't another raid tonight,' someone said apprehensively. It was what they were all thinking, but a chorus of comfort greeted the remark. Lightning never struck in the same place twice, Jerry would be too busy licking his wounds to think of a return bout so soon, and why don't we get what sleep we can, gels, because tomorrer's goin' to be one 'ell of a day?

They agreed and settled down. Christie lay there watching with some interest and not a little amusement as the girl in the next bed pinned her long, lank red hair into tiny snail-like roundels against her scalp. On the far side of the red-head a small girl with fair curls smeared her face with cleansing cream, wiped it off on the sheet and then snuggled down, heaving the blankets up over her ears. The two seemed to be friends, they had whispered a few words as they got ready for bed, much as Meg and Christie had done. Talk like that – light, perhaps inconsequential – had all the comfort of familiarity.

Christie did not think she could possibly go to sleep

but somehow the strains and stresses of the day acted as the very best sort of soporific and she scarcely had time to notice the unfamiliar feel of the newly issued bolster beneath her cheek before she was dreaming.

Next morning Christie woke to find the early morning light stealing across the room, falling on the humped figures of twenty-six sleeping girls. Outside birds shouted a joyous chorus and began their day-long search for food. If the end of the world came, if we all blew each other up, I suppose the birds would still shout when the light arrived to prove that they'd survived the night, she thought. Sometimes I feel just like that – that I ought to sing and pray to show God that I've noticed I'm alive, that the new day which has just dawned, dawned for me, too.

But that was a bad thought, because it immediately made her think of those others, for whom this dawn had never happened. Four young men, seven young women, who yesterday had snuggled down beneath their blankets when reveille shrilled, or jumped out of bed, or cursed the noise and tried to muffle it with a bolster, each according to his or her nature. Today those eleven souls heard nothing, knew nothing, were as the dust.

And it might have been me . . . oh, shut up, Christie Bellis! Stop feeling so bloody sorry for yourself and get out of your pit, stack your biscuits – which meant make your bed – and go and take a look at the dew on the grass. And thank your stars you're still around to get wet feet – wonder what happened to the girl who woke me up: she could have been killed, might have been, come to think of it. If she went straight to the shelter . . .

But depressing thoughts like that could not possibly help. What I should be doing, Christie told herself, getting out of bed, is finding out who that girl is and whether she's still all right. After all, she saved my life whichever way you look at it. At the time Christie had been so dazed and disorientated that she had scarcely registered anything save that the girl was fair. In fact it had been all she could do to stumble out of the hut and along to the ops room. If it hadn't been for Blondie she would have stayed in her bed. Even the bicycle had played its part – if it hadn't been there it would have been easier and quicker just to nip to the shelter . . .

Christie began to fold her blankets and stack her mattress and then sat down on the black iron bedstead to consider. How could she find out about the blonde? There must have been something else besides her hair colour which had stuck in her mind . . . but if there was it escaped her now. Oh, yes, an odd sort of accent . . . But since she didn't recognise it that wouldn't be much help. But later, when everyone was up and about, she would do her best to discover the blonde's name and whereabouts, so that she could thank her properly.

In the meantime she might as well get a shower; she was certain of being first, for once. Christie picked up her borrowed soap and a newly issued towel as well as the hanky which would have to do service as a flannel and made her way to the ablutions at the end of the hut. The hot water situation here was not as bad as at training camp, but even so the earlier you got up the better your chance of a warm shower. She selected a cubicle, stripped off her borrowed pyjamas and stepped into the shower. As she was luxuriating in the patter of hot water on head and shoulders she remembered the blind date which she had totally forgotten the previous day; a little spurt of interest, a genuine curiosity, brought her mind back out of the blank of sadness and loss which threatened to ruin the new day.

What were their names, those two RAF blokes? Phil and Bob or something like that. Something ordinary, unremarkable. And she and Meg were meeting them under the clock on Waterloo Station. She stayed in the shower until the water began to cool, wondering what the fellows would be like; then rubbed herself dry, put on her newly issued underwear and went back to the main part of the hut.

She sat down on her bed and glanced around her. Everyone slumbered still, Meg snoring quietly, like a very small, distant motor-bike. The red-haired girl slept neatly, on her side, hand beneath cheek. By craning her neck Christie could even make out the girl with the fair curls, flushed with sleep, mouth open, breathing stertorously but not snoring, or not now, at any rate.

With her mouth open like that, the fair girl reminded her of someone. Christie frowned, trying to bring the resemblance to mind – school friend, film star? – then shrugged and gave up. It was like watching a kettle boil; if you just left it it happened, if you watched it... She would remember in the fullness of time. Now she intended to go out on to the airfield and why not? After the horrors of the previous day no one was likely to get up before they needed to do so and a glance at her watch showed that even if the Tannoy system was still working, it would not be reveille for another hour.

The blackout blinds were always drawn back by the duty corporal after lights out to let some fresh air into the hut and also in order that the daylight might waken them, so now Christie looked out of the small, square window nearest her. The sun wasn't up but the sky was blue and a lark lifted from the long grass near the trees which sheltered the entrance to the ops room, its liquid, bubbling notes rising with the tiny singer as it soared skywards.

Christie glanced a trifle wistfully at Meg, sleeping still, then shrugged and let herself quietly out of the hut. Meg was worn out, and besides, she needed to be by herself for a bit. The morning was clear and fresh as spring-water, the dew thick on the grass. She crossed the concrete, eyeing the sleeping huts, then heard the first planes returning. She knew the engine notes well enough to be sure that this was just last night's fighters coming back home and waited, looking across, hoping that everyone would land safely, that they would not need to add more losses to those suffered on the previous day.

Out on the airfield itself there was a hum of activity

now, as men and machines moved purposefully about. She knew the ops room would be busy, counting them back, that the tower would be fully manned. Soon the aircrews would be coming in for a meal, only to find the cookhouse in ruins, but they would go to the WAAF mess instead and doubtless there would be food waiting for them.

She decided to walk for half an hour, going round the perimeter of the field, and was half-way back, her mind gentled by the peaceful morning, the birdsong and sunshine, when she heard the distant hum of approaching aircraft. Another batch coming in... Spitfires, she rather thought. She slowed, gazing up into the blue, listening hard. Yes, Spitfires, she recognised the throb of the engines, the note which was peculiarly theirs.

An officer came out of a nearby hut, trim in her uniform, heading for the Tannoy, probably. She saw Christie and Christie's right hand immediately flew to the salute.

'Morning, ma'am.'

'Morning. You all right, Aircraftwoman? You're about early.'

'I'm fine thanks, ma'am. Since I was awake, I thought I'd take a stroll before everyone else got up.' She recognised the officer as a girl whose boyfriend flew Spitfires. She was probably checking to make sure he was all right. 'They're coming in now, ma'am, I heard the first one land five minutes ago.'

The officer smiled and suddenly she was just the girl Christie thought her, a girl with anxious eyes.

'Yes, I thought I heard them. I'll just stroll over to the ops room, I believe, see how things went.'

She disappeared, not at a stroll. Christie stood for a moment looking after her and then, with a sigh, returned to her billet just as the Tannoy shrilled out its morning message.

In the hut, people were already on their feet, some heading for the ablutions whilst others still struggled to wake. Meg yawned and sat up, glanced at Christie's empty bed, frowned, looked around – and saw Christie grinning down at her. In the next bed the red-head swung her feet on to the lino and yelped, then stood up, swaying a little, and knuckled her eyes.

'Morning, Meg,' Christie said. 'I'm just making up for oversleeping yesterday. You going for a wash? You won't get a shower, because I was in early and I've already run off most of the hot water.'

Meg moaned theatrically and from the bed on the further side of the red-head a voice said sepulchrally, 'Oversleepin'? That's the understatement of the year, gal!'

It was the fair girl with cherub curls, and all in a moment Christie knew her. She pointed and stared, eyes positively popping.

'It's you! You're the girl who came into our hut and woke me up yesterday – if you hadn't I'd have been dead as mutton. You saved my life, girl!'

'Oh aye? ' said the blonde, patently uninterested. 'I did wonder whether you run for the shelter or the ops room. You must've wondered what to do for the best, with them Jerries shriekin' over'ead like bloody vultures, and all hell breakin' loose around us. Just goes to show, there is some point in obeyin' orders. I weren't too sure, before,' she added thoughtfully.

'I went to ops, but I was still half-asleep when I got there,' Christie admitted. 'What's your name? What do you do?'

'I'm Sue Collins. I'm a driver,' the blonde said. She got out of bed and pushed her feet into her unlaced shoes, then began to shuffle off towards the ablutions, a pink floral sponge-bag swinging from one hand 'Who are you, then?'

'Christie Bellis. I'm a plotter. Thanks, Sue. If it hadn't been for you . . .'

'You said it once,' Sue said over her shoulder, still shuffling. 'Get a move on, Shanna, or you'll be late for breakfast.'

'Did she really save your life?' the red-head said. She had a clear, bell-like voice with a pretty Scottish accent and she was somehow managing to dress under cover of her pyjamas – or had she not removed her clothing the previous night? Some people never undressed completely, and often it was the girls who made up heaviest and spent all their money on clothes and other adornments who apparently considered washing an overrated pastime. 'She's a good wee girl, is Sue!'

'I'll second that,' Meg said. 'I'm going to get a wash, even if it is in cold water.'

Whilst Meg and Sue washed, Christie made Meg's bed and she and Shanna chatted.

'I'm from Glasgow and Edinburgh mostly,' Shanna

said when Christie asked her which part of Scotland she came from. 'I've lived in both.'

'But Sue isn't Scottish,' Christie observed, folding the blankets from Meg's bed into a neat pile. 'Did you know each other before you joined up?'

'No, but we were the only ones from our intake to come down here,' Shanna said, scrambling her covers off the bed and folding them into an approximation of the neat squares she should have produced. 'Sue's from Liverpool, do you no' recognise the accent?'

'I thought it was north-country somewhere,' Christie said. 'I'm from Norfolk myself, and Meg's from Cheshire. We've been together right from the start.'

'That's good,' Shanna observed sagely. 'If you've got a pal you can laugh when things go wrong. It's no' so easy on your own.'

'You're right. And of course it's easier for Meg and me because we both work in the ops room. Not that we're always on the same shift, mind you, though we can usually work it.'

'Aye; but a driver's always on her own, and I'm no' sticking in admin for ever,' Shanna said. She abandoned her own bed and started on Sue's. 'Here, lass, if you'll gi' me a hand we can go to breakfast as soon as the others are back.'

Christie gave her a hand willingly and presently Sue and Meg returned, with damp hair and shining faces, and the four of them made their way to the makeshift cookhouse. Wonders had been performed, Christie saw. A long counter had been erected, a number of catering saucepans and containers had been brought in, and WAAF cooks stirred pans or tended kettles over paraffin stoves.

'Necessity's the mother of invention,' Sue said when Christie pointed out that someone was going to have to lend them plates and 'irons', since theirs had been flattened by the Luftwaffe. 'Hold out your cap, chuck, and they'll fill it with porridge for you.'

Everyone laughed, including the duty cook, but she found some extra plates from somewhere and told the girls that they would get reissued with eating things just as soon as possible.

'Until then, you can use our spares,' she said.

With porridge, mugs of tea and fried potatoes, the girls took themselves off to sit round a card table and eat. Sue was first to break the silence.

'You're plotters then, you two?'

'Yes, that's right,' Meg said. 'What do you and Sheila do?'

'It's Shanna, no' Sheila,' the red-haired girl said. 'Shanna Douglas. I'm a clerk in admin. Sue is Sue Collins, she's a driver. Wish I could drive.'

'They'll teach you, I told you,' Sue said.

Shanna turned to Meg. 'Where are you from? How long've you been in?'

'We've been in six months. I'm Meg Aldford, I'm from Nantwich in Cheshire. I know Sue's from Liverpool, she told me earlier, and I can tell you're from Scotland. Whereabouts?'

'Glasgow, mostly. We've been in six months, too; this is our first posting.'

Same as us,' Christie said. 'Do you reckon we'll stay here for a bit?'

'Yes, whilst the big air-push goes on,' Sue put in. 'Especially plotters; they need you real bad, I heard my officer talking about it. Shanna thought she might get trained for plotting. They shove you into anything at first, I think, but you can retrain.'

'What's it like in the offices?' Meg asked curiously. 'We only go in when we're paid.'

'It's no' bad,' Shanna said cautiously. 'A wee bit boring, mebbe. But at least it was warm in the winter, when Sue froze in that draughty car, waiting for her officer.'

'I'm going for a mechanic's training, I've already put in for it,' Sue said. 'What'll we do today, though? We're off out, Shanna and me.'

'Help! we're off too, to London to meet a couple of chaps, a blind date,' Chris said, remembering. 'Oh, and me with only laddered stockings! Still, we can explain.'

'I'll lend you some new ones,' Shanna said, eyeing Christie's slim legs. 'We're about the same size, wouldnae you say? And Sue's sure to have some for . . . Meg, was it?'

'That's right. But in fact, though I'm wearing my one and only pair, they're all right so far,' Meg said. 'Still, if you've got a pair you could lend I'd be grateful. You can have my new issue, when we get them.'

'It's all right; Sue's friendly with the sergeant on equipment, she only has to smile at him to get new issue,' Shanna said. 'More tea, anyone?'

* * *

It was fun, getting ready for a date.

'It takes me back,' Christie said dreamily, as she and Meg combed their hair, powdered their noses and brushed imaginary flecks from their tunics in the ladies' toilet on Waterloo Station. 'Apart from the fact that it's summer, and I've not just been to my dancing lessons, it's just like when I saw Derek for the first time.'

'Oh? Was he a blind date?' Meg said, leaning nearer to the mirror and examining her forehead anxiously. 'Oh lor', is that a spot? And there's nothing you can do about a spot. Help, it's two spots! Oh my God, I only have to think about a date and spots come rushing to the surface, determined to let everyone know what a rotten skin I've got.'

'At least you've got black eyelashes, not pale ones,' Christie said, scrubbing away with a nearly bald brush at a tiny, worn cake of mascara. 'If I don't see some mascara for sale soon the world will just have to get used to me with light lashes. As for Derek, he was at the grammar school and I never did get to go out with him, I just used to follow him round after my dancing lessons. You see, I did Greek dancing with . . .'

'You, Greek dancing?' Meg gave a squawk of laughter. 'Did you wear a little white tunic and one of those laurel wreath things on your head?'

'Don't be daft! Anyway, I don't know why I brought the subject up, except that it's rather nice to be meeting a bloke; rather special. Oh, say, they'll out-rank us, so do we salute?'

66

'Yes, since we're in uniform,' Meg said, but doubtfully. 'Actually, it's easier because we don't know them – I mean we'll automatically salute everything we see in RAF blue. I always look away from army and navy, just in case they're really men from the electricity company.'

Christie, who had saluted an elderly scout leader and a bus conductor when she first joined, giggled.

'Yes, I know, me too. Still, if we salute them once and then haul them in somewhere where we can take off our caps. That'll be all right, I suppose.'

'Oh, sure to be. I know it isn't allowed, officially, but there's a lot of it about. After all, Millie Trotter's a warrant officer, which is a lot further down the scale than Dougie Trotter – he's a Flying Officer – but they only salute when they spy each other for the first time.'

Christie tucked up a stray strand of red-brown hair, then perched her cap on the back of her head so her hair showed to best advantage. She looked at herself critically in the mirror. 'That looks rather good, don't you think? I say, imagine your father and mother saluting. Honestly, isn't it *bizarre*?'

'My mum's small and round and my dad's tall and gangly; it's odd enough just seeing them dance together,' Meg said. 'As for letting my imagination go any further ... well, I simply can't. What about yours?'

'Same, except that my parents are both tallish, I suppose, and Mummy's very slim whereas Dad's like most farmers, broad, sort of, and pretty strong. Look, we'd better go and lurk or they'll think we've stood them up and I never would, I think it's a rotten trick.'

'Ye-es..., but suppose we can see them, and they're a couple of real stinkers?' Meg said uneasily. 'Suppose they're old and fat and bald? Or suppose they're really young and spotty and weedy?'

'We go through with it,' Christie said firmly. 'Oh God, Meg, I must have been mad to say we would! That's the trouble when you live and work mainly with women, you're so keen to get a bloke that you dive straight for any man who offers. Anyway, we can meet them and be awfully polite and say our leave got stopped. Look, tell you what, if you say "As my friend Sally always says", I'll know you want to quit, and if I say it, you'll know I do, and then we'll back each other up and make an excuse. How about that?'

'I know what you've just thought,' Meg said, hefting her shoulder bag. 'You've just thought that I might get a handsome one and you might get an ugly sister. Oh, all right, all right, it's a deal. What was the word again?'

'Sally. As Sally always says. Shall we go?'

Side by side, they emerged from the ladies' toilet and began to saunter across the station in the general direction of the clock. The hands pointed at eight, the station was crowded, yet no one actually seemed to be standing directly under the clock. Meg, clutching Christie's arm, said as much in a low, breathy mutter.

'Well, there are those two ATS, and there's a couple of WAAFs as well, only no men,' Christie agreed. 'Oh no, the WAAFs have wandered off. Oh my Gawd, look at the size of *that*!'

A huge RAF officer, his cap decorated with gold braid, sauntered up to the clock, peered up at its face, checked his wrist-watch, shook his head, then glanced round hopefully.

'It can't be him, he's sixty if he's a day and an Air Chief Marshal at least,' Meg said. 'How soon can we go? I feel such a fool hovering about here, staring at people. If a bobby was to come along he'd probably think we were spies or prostitutes and arrest us.'

'Spies or prostitutes? In uniform? Margaret Aldford, you are a rotten, lily-livered coward, and if you won't go and stand under that clock then I will,' Christie said with a shaky attempt at bravado. How could she have been such a fool in the first place? She just knew that somewhere on this station the two ugliest, nastiest men in the world were lurking, waiting to pounce. And an evening in London was a rare event, it would be awful to have to run back to the airfield, where Sue and Shanna would be awaiting their return, and admit they hadn't gone through with it.

The four girls had spent most of the day together, and though Sue was a bit sharp and Shanna seemed to think of nothing but dating and boys, they had enjoyed each other's company. Shanna and Sue had had quite a number of blind dates already and had taken it for granted that, if the boys were unattractive, Christie and Meg might just walk away from them, but Christie thought that this was downright rude.

But if Meg and I walk quietly away right now,

Christie caught herself thinking, we might easily meet someone nice in a pub or at the flicks, and we'd never have to admit that the blind dates weren't quite . . .

But it would not do. My principles are firm, Christie told her shaking knees. I shall keep my side of the bargain – to meet and go out with two strange young men – and even if we have a dull evening, or if we feel stupid, it's only one evening, for God's sake! It can't exactly ruin our lives.

'Right, I'm with you,' Meg said. She linked her arm with Christie's. 'Quick march. Oh God, salute . . .'

They unlinked arms just in time. A WAAF officer with a steely eye had opened her mouth to reprimand them but the brilliance of the heel-clicking salutes they threw at her disarmed her – or at least shut her mouth as she reciprocated, coming to attention and then, rather pink-cheeked, hurrying away.

'Bet she'll keep her eyes to herself in future,' Christie said smugly. 'Bet she felt even more of a fool than I did. I'm sure half Waterloo Station is staring at us.'

They stopped under the clock. People continued to mill around. An Air Force officer approached, then veered off, greeting a golden-haired woman in an exotic fur coat who flung her arms round his neck, knocking his cap askew. Her perfume, heady and musky, nearly made Christie's eyes water as the couple swayed amorously near them, quite literally wrapped up in one another.

'Toby, *darling*!' the golden-haired one squeaked. 'Oh, *darling Tobeee*!'

'Well, that one isn't ours,' Meg said rather gloomily. He was, Christie observed, very good-looking. 'And if he was, I doubt he'd welcome me wrapping myself round him like that. What were their names again?'

'I can't remem . . .' began Christie when two more Air Force uniforms began to converge. Meg dug her in the ribs.

'Salute, you fool!'

The men were undoubtedly heading in their direction; they would have to be saluted, unless Christie had the gall to discover her shoelace needed tying or something of that nature. She thought about it, then she and Meg clicked to attention. The officers saluted back, a little shamefaced, then glanced round with that air of almost-casualness which was, Christie thought, the biggest clue of all to their reason for being under the clock. They were waiting for someone . . . someone they did not know well enough to recognise.

One of the young men was tall, tanned, fidgety. He looked at them, then quickly away. He had high cheekbones and Christie was almost sure a blush stained them. Quite young, she estimated, probably no more than twenty-one. Rather nice.

The other was chunkier, with a square chin and a nose which looked as though it might have been broken at some time. He looked across at them, half grinned, then looked away. Then he looked back and began to come across towards them.

'I say, I'm most awfully sorry, but my friend and I

71

are meeting . . . You wouldn't be Christine, by any chance?'

'No, but I'm Christie, and this is my friend Meg,' Christie said. Relief was flooding over her in waves, positively deluging her in fact. They were all right! Better than all right, they were really decent-looking blokes. Oh hell, what were their names again?

'That's wonderful,' the square one was saying. 'I'm Andy and this great beanpole is my friend Patrick – Pat to you. Look, let's get away from here. Have you eaten? We thought perhaps you'd like a couple of drinks and a meal somewhere, and then we could go to one of the big hotels and dance. We're on standby tomorrow night so we've got to be back at the field by dawn which means catching a train tonight; would you rather do something different, though?'

Christie had marked Pat down as hers, yet found herself with Andy, and was soon glad of it. He was just so nice, the nicest man she had ever met. He made her laugh a lot, teasing her about her dread of saluting, saying her hair was so nearly red that he would never dare to cross her. She was glad that Meg and tall Patrick were getting on well too, but couldn't get over her own luck. A blind date, they could have been stinkers, and not only were they good-looking, they were nice, too!

The boys took them to a small Italian restaurant where the food and wine were good and reasonably priced. At first they were all rather shy, but the spaghetti soon changed that. Christie had never eaten it in public before, Meg had just never eaten it; the boys showed them how, teased them, called the waitress over and said the ladies would like soap and a flannel before they chose their dessert . . . Meg was helpless with laughter, Christie clutched her side and vowed vengeance.

And the ice, having been broken, could not re-form. They were suddenly good friends, swapping stories of service life, telling Andy and Pat about their homes, their families. Andy had been to Italy and talked of the wine-growing areas, the big cities, the friendliness of the peasants up in the mountains. Pat talked about his twin sister, who was a WAAF on a station in Yorkshire, and Christie found it easy and natural to tell stories of the things she, Frank and Dave had got up to as kids. Even Meg, an only child, reminisced about her parents and her country childhood.

After the meal, relaxed and at ease with one another, they walked slowly down to Fine's Hotel, where the men said the dancing was good. Meg and Pat walked ahead, Christie and Andy dawdled behind. By then they had agreed to catch the same train home since Meg and Christie would get off two stops before Pat and Andy. Once they reached the hotel the girls hurried to the cloakroom to repair their make-up and compare notes.

'Pat flies a Hurricane, thinks it's the best aeroplane going,' Meg said, cleaning her teeth with the edge of her hanky and patting her powder puff briskly across her shiny nose. 'He's younger than I thought, only twenty-one, he went in before the war started so he's got more experience than some of the boys. He comes from a little village in Derbyshire, I'd never heard of it, he was at university when war broke out . . . What about yours?'

'Andy flies a Hurricane too, he's from a village on the Wirral, near you. He's older than yours – twenty-three – and he went straight into the RAF when he was eighteen because he wanted to learn to fly. I'm going to listen for his call-sign when I'm on his part of the grid,' Christie said. 'I say, aren't they *nice* – and after all our worries, too!'

'It was lucky, ' Meg agreed, straightening up and eyeing herself critically in the glass. 'Wish we weren't in uniform . . . I can't imagine doing a really romantic tango in this skirt!'

'Nor me, but we'd better go and join the fellows or they'll find someone else,' Christie said. 'Meg – does anything bother you about them?'

'Bother me? No. Why should it?'

'I don't know, exactly. It isn't *them*, they're grand, it's something else which keeps niggling away at the back of my mind.'

Meg shrugged and began to speak and then they were out of the cloakroom and in the ballroom itself. After weeks of concrete huts and the ops room it looked incredibly glamorous, like a Hollywood film set. The circular wooden floor gleamed gold with polishing, the romantically dim lighting made all the women look beautiful, all the men handsome. Patrick and Andy stood up as Meg and Christie crossed the floor towards them. They had taken a table with four chairs round it right on the edge of the dance-floor and had put their caps on the table, but now they laid them on their chairs and smiled expectantly at the girls.

'Shall we? Better tip your chairs forward and put your caps on the table; it's going to get pretty crowded in here presently.'

That was Patrick, holding out a hand to Meg. She put her own small hand confidingly in his and he swung her into the dance. Christie and Andy watched for a minute. Considering how small and square Meg was she danced surprisingly well, moving with a sureness and grace which Christie knew she would be unable to match. She said as much and Andy grinned down at her.

'Good, because I've got two left feet and I'm tone deaf,' he said. 'Shall we?'

Christie put her cap on the table by Meg's and glided into his arms. He danced well enough for her, she decided after a moment. It was the first time she had danced with someone who was virtually a stranger and apart from an initial shyness at having his arm round her, guiding her firmly, they got on well. Their steps seemed to fit, they were a good height for each other, and very soon they were chattering away and not thinking too much about their steps, as they waltzed, fox-trotted and quickstepped around the floor.

By the time they paused for a drink they felt they had known each other for years. Andy had put both arms round Christie during a dreamy slow waltz and instructed her in the art of dancing with both arms up round his neck so that their bodies were lightly touching. Christie knew her mother would say she was being common, that her father would raise his gingery eyebrows and look worried, but she did not care. She was a woman, a WAAF who had risked her life by being on the airfield when it was bombed and strafed by enemy fire. Surely she was entitled to cuddle a man on a dance-floor if she so desired?

'We'll go to the bar; it's in the basement,' Andy said as they came off the dance-floor. 'There's Pat – your friend's with him, they're heading for the bar, too. Whoever gets there first can order the drinks.'

It was whilst they were squashed into a corner of the bar, with other people's elbows in their faces and their drinks held tight against their chests, that the certain something about Patrick and Andrew which had eluded Christie all evening suddenly clarified itself in her head. She nudged her companion.

'Andy ... why did you tell me over the head-set that your name was Bill? When you came up to us I *knew* there was something wrong – well, not wrong, different – only you seemed to know us at once. It was the names.'

Andy looked sheepishly across at Patrick, who had gone brick-red. Then he grinned down at Christie.

'Caught! Well, sweetheart, to tell you the truth we're here under false pretences. You see a squadron can be given a forty-eight and then they suddenly need you, so Bill and Bob found themselves a bit tied up and rather than let you arrive at Waterloo and think you'd been stood up ... It wasn't as if anyone could actually get in touch with you ... I say, are you *very* cross? We meant it for the best, honest injun!'

'Did Bill and Bob ask you to meet us?' Meg asked suspiciously. 'Or did you just offer? Do they know what's happened? Isn't it odd that we neither of us realised the names were different, though!'

'They didn't exactly ask, but we know them pretty well; they would have been distressed to think you'd wasted an evening in London because they couldn't make it,' Patrick volunteered. 'We meant to explain, honest, but you didn't query the names and I suppose we just let things slide. Was it so bad of us?'

'No, I think it was kind,' Meg said, whilst Christie was still thinking it over. 'I've never been stood up but it must be horrible, I'm really grateful you saved us that.'

'Yes, it would damage one's self-respect, I think,' Christie said thoughtfully. 'It wouldn't have crossed our minds that the chaps had been unable to make it, we'd always have believed that they'd turned up, taken a look at us, decided we weren't pretty enough, and moved on.'

'Oh, Christie, as if anyone could think such a thing,' Andy said. His free hand was on her waist; now he slid his arm round her and pulled her close. 'You're the prettiest thing I've had the good fortune to meet since I joined up. I hope we'll meet again, the four of us.'

'Rather,' Patrick said. 'I'm glad that's off my conscience, I felt bad about it and I'm sure old Andy felt the same. Drink up and I'll get another round.'

77

'Sure. And then we'll have a couple more dances and make for the station,' Andy said regretfully. 'We dare not miss the last train, and expect you're in the same boat. Look, the crowd round the bar's about twelve deep, why don't we have another hop and then go out and walk along the Albert Embankment; there's a fellow down there with a little cafe who sells mugs of coffee and cheese rolls and at this time of night there won't be much of a queue. I could do with a bite to set me up for the rail journey; what does everyone else think?'

It seemed a good idea to all of them. They danced, cuddling, then the girls returned to the ladies' cloakroom to tidy themselves up, which meant combing their hair and repositioning their caps, straightening ties and rubbing a handkerchief over shoes which were dusted with French polish from the dance-floor. Then, with the boys' arms round their waists, they set off through the summer night in the direction of the Embankment.

'No moon,' Andy said with satisfaction as they threaded their way through the dark streets, Meg and Patrick ahead of them. 'That means there's a good chance we won't have a raid. Have you been in the underground?'

'Not lately. But some of the other girls have; they say it's awful, seeing all those pale, weary people sleeping on the platforms and all over the stairs.'

'It is,' Andy said soberly. 'It makes it easier to go up when you think of our people living like moles because of Jerry.'

78

'Yes, I suppose it must. Andy . . . do you ever feel scared?'

'Not much; only every time I fly,' Andy said ruefully. 'We're only human, Chris. Tell you something, though.'

'What?'

'Well, in future when I'm down on the deck again and I know I'm safe then I won't just be thanking my lucky stars, I'll be thanking a little girl with a rake in her hand who has been leaning over that table in the ops room, plotting me back, whose hard work has enabled the bods in command to see the situation up in the air as clear as though they were up there too. You're all heroines – well, I knew that already – but getting to know my own little plotter will help me far more than you'd believe.'

'Oh, Andy, what a lovely thing to say,' Christie said, much moved. 'That makes it so much easier to keep up with the work and not panic when the kites pile up in my bit of the grid and things threaten to go wrong.'

They were walking along beside the river now, the water gleaming like pewter under the dark and cloud-filled sky. The leaves rustled above their heads as a breeze touched them, somewhere a bird chirped and a cat, stalking along ahead of them, looked thoughtfully up into the branches above. Andy pulled Christie gently to a halt and took her in his arms.

'Shall we have a kiss?' he whispered. 'Before we catch up with the others and get our grub? Just a little kiss, between friends?'

79

Christie was new to kissing; she held up her face and his mouth closed with warmth and gentleness over hers. His arms caught her to him, his body seemed to fuse with hers, his hands, strong capable hands, moved soothingly up and down her back even as his mouth moved on hers, awaking in her emotions which had never stirred her before.

A shout from ahead made them break the embrace; they drew apart comfortably, leisurely, though Christie's heart was bumping hard, her breathing ragged. So that was what kissing a man was like, compared with kissing a boy! She liked it, though she was not so sure about the extraordinary feelings which had rampaged, roughshod, through her whole body as their mouths met. What a good thing we're on the Embankment with people about, she thought. Otherwise I might have ... well, I might have forgotten myself!

'Come on you two, stop snogging and let's get something to eat,' Patrick called. 'The train leaves in forty minutes.'

'Or should,' Meg pointed out as Christie and Andy, clumsily clutching one another, galloped breathlessly up and skidded to a halt beside them. 'Knowing what the trains are like, though ...'

'If we're on the platform we've done our best,' Christie said righteously. 'Is that the place? I hope so, because something smells awfully good.'

Ahead of them the tiny, shack-like cafe bulked against the gleaming river. It was blacked out but the door, opening outward, showed a soft glow of light.

Inside, the cafe was lit by hurricane lamps which showed tables and chairs of white-painted deal, whitewashed walls and checked tablecloths. The short counter was manned by a cheerful old man in a stained white coat; his rosy face puckered, now, against the heat from the small paraffin stove he was tending. There were servicemen and women sitting at one or two of the tables but the place, though it had clearly been busy earlier, was beginning to wind down. Patrick went straight to the counter.

'Hey, Jim; anything left for us?'

The old man looked up, then grinned at them.

'Coffee an' a cheese roll? he suggested in a broad cockney twang. 'Or baked beans on toast, or scrambled egg?'

'No time,' Patrick said briefly. 'Coffee and rolls then, Jim, four times.'

The four of them huddled round a table warming their hands on the thick white mugs, for though it was high summer the night was nippy now. Christie and Meg ate the food eagerly, then drank the coffee. It was hot and bitter but nevertheless welcome. Andy glanced at his watch and then got to his feet.

'Okay, people,' he said briskly. 'Better get moving. Can you run, girls?'

They could and did. They scooted desperately up the road, following Patrick, who clearly knew the way very well indeed, and found themselves back at Waterloo with five minutes to spare.

The train was late and crowded. There was no chance of a seat but they positioned themselves in the corridor and sat on the floor, legs pulled up, leaning against one another. They did not sleep but occasionally Christie must have snoozed, because twice she jerked awake, her heart bumping, wondering where she was and what she was doing on the floor.

Just before they reached their station, Christie thought of something.

'Andy, you know you said you'd phone or write next time you've got some time off, so's we can go out again?'

Andy rumpled her hair, then slid a hand round the back of her neck. 'It's been such a short time, yet I feel I've known you for years. You want to do it again, don't you?'

'Oh, yes ... but look, what about Bill and Bob? What will they say if they find out it's us you're dating? I mean stepping into the breach so we didn't think we'd been stood up is one thing, going on seeing us is another.'

Andy heaved a sigh. Then he sat up properly and turned her face so that he could look into her eyes.

'Sweet Christie, I didn't want to tell you this, but you've forced my hand. It didn't occur to either of us that we'd want to see more of you, you see, and now that it has we'll have to tell you a bit more.'

'You didn't tell them you were going to meet us, did you?' Christie said wisely. 'That's it, isn't it?'

'Yes, that's it. Only ... they won't mind, baby. They won't mind at all. They bought it the day Jerry got through our defences and bombed your airfield.'

There was a moment when Christie just stared,

then she felt her eyes fill with tears. Was he trying to tell her the boy was dead, the one with the light, amused voice, who had dated her over the head-set? And the friend he had spoken of? No, that couldn't be what he meant, death happened all the time, but not to friends, not to people you knew or almost knew. She had always known when she scooped a plane off the table ... but she'd pushed the knowledge back, refused to believe. It was only a game, after all.

The train slowed, slowed, rattled over points, slowed some more. People began to push towards the doors at either end of the corridor and Andy gave her a quick, hard hug.

'Poor Chris! But you never actually met them.'

'No, of course not. It's just a bit of a shock,' Christie muttered. She got to her feet, automatically straightening her tie, casting a quick look down at herself to make sure she was presentable. 'You'll – you'll be in touch?'

'Sure will. Take care of yourself, sweetheart.'

He stood up, fighting through the good-natured crowd with her, jumping down onto the platform and then turning to catch her as she jumped in her turn. He held her for a moment, then kissed her mouth lightly. His nice, plain face understood her shock, sympathised. He squeezed her shoulders, then got back into the train behind Patrick and slammed the door shut.

'Be good ... we'll be in touch!'

The girls stood on the platform and waved until the train began to move and then they had to run to catch the lorry which would take them back to their hut and their duties.

'Have a good time?' someone asked when they were all squeezed inside and the lorry was lurching forward. Christie looked across the dim interior and saw that it was Shanna, her careful pin-curls limp now, untidy, damp-looking. She had her skirt hooked up over her knee and a man's hand rested possessively half-way up her thigh. The man was an AC1, low-browed, aggressive-looking. Shanna pushed him off and raised her brows at the girls. 'Meet them, did you, Christie?'

'Yes, we met them. We had a good time, too. And you?'

'No' so bad,' Shanna said demurely. 'Wullie, will you stop that?'

Willie, if that was the AC1's name, ignored her, continuing to fondle her leg with one hand whilst the other gripped her thin shoulder. When she tried to push him away again he bent his head and nuzzled her neck. Christie averted her eyes and concentrated on Meg, sitting beside her and telling the girl nearest her about their evening.

'We went dancing,' Meg was saying. 'The blokes were lovely, honest, ever so kind. They paid for everything, never even suggested we might go Dutch. But they were aircrew of course – pilots. Yes, we had to salute them; but only once; after that . . .

The talk became general. And presently the lorry disgorged them on to the concrete apron in front of the makeshift cookhouse and they took their separate

ways to their billets. Christie and Meg hung back to
wait for Shanna but she had disappeared so they
bundled into the hut and found Sue, face shining with
cream, sitting up in bed reading.

'Shanna with you?' she said as they entered. 'That
girl's goin' to be in trouble one of these days, she's
always late.'

'She was on the gharry, ' Meg said, beginning to
undress. Lights out was strictly adhered to and their
corporal would be doing her rounds in ten minutes.
'She disappeared though. We tried to wait for her but
she'd just vanished.'

Sue sighed and nodded. 'Oh aye; with a feller, was
she?'

'Yes, an AC plonk.'

'Well, she'll be sayin' goodnight to him. Behind the
hut I daresay. She'll come in when she's finished.'

'He was almost eating her in the gharry,' Christie
commented, taking off her borrowed stockings with
sheathed nails and great care. 'I didn't notice him
going out, but perhaps he was on a different lorry.'

'Or perhaps she didn't know him then,' Sue said.
'Likes the lads, does our Shanna.'

It was not said censoriously, but Christie shook her
head.

'Oh no, it was someone she knew well, all right,'
Christie insisted. She lowered her voice, leaning
nearer Sue. 'He had his hand up her skirt, and she
wasn't at all put out.'

'She wouldn't be; Shanna needs fellers, she's . . . oh
well, you'll find out for yourselves soon enough.'

'Find out what?' Meg said, picking up her sponge-bag. 'Coming for a wash, Christie?'

'Never mind; you trot off,' Sue said absently, returning to her book. 'Ah, talk of the devil . . .'

Shanna slid in through the door, kicking off her shoes, wrenching off her jacket and tie as she came. Christie and Meg went to pass her and Christie saw, on the white stalk of her neck, a great black and purple bruise. She nudged Meg and jerked her head at the mark as Shanna pulled her shirt off over her head, then put her pyjama jacket on without removing her bra.

'He must have tried to strangle her,' she hissed as they walked over to the ablutions. 'Poor kid!'

'I dunno,' Meg said. 'She's a funny one, that Shanna.'

She sounded disapproving, Christie thought, surprised. She had expected Meg to be full of pity for one so cruelly marked.

'You mean she's funny not to screech out when someone grabs her neck?' Christie asked, filling a bowl with tepid water and beginning to splash. 'But maybe she did, maybe we just didn't hear.'

Meg hissed her breath in through her teeth as though exasperated.

'Christie, how old are you? That bruise must be what they call a love bite.'

'A love bite? Never heard of it. It was a bruise, he must have . . . what do you mean, a love bite?'

Meg groaned.

'Oh God, girl, men get a bit of skin in their mouths

and sort of suck it into a bruise. That's a love bite.'

Christie's eyes flew open and got filled with soap. She squeaked and lurched back to the bowl, splashing water up into her face until the pain eased.

'What a barbaric, horrible . . . I didn't know that! Are you kidding me, Meg Aldford? Well, I'm shocked. How do you know, has anyone . . . ?'

'No, they haven't,' Meg said hastily. 'And I agree with you that it's barbaric, but I do know it happens. That's why they make jokes about girls who wear scarves and high collars.'

'Oh,' Christie said feebly, having thought it over. 'Meg, is Shanna . . . well, did Sue mean . . .'

'Get washing or we won't be back for lights out,' Meg recommended briskly, brushing her wiry hair until it crackled. 'We'll find out in due course, like Sue said. Do come on, Chris!'

It was not until she was in her bed once more, with Shanna already apparently sleeping on one side of her and Meg snuffling away on the other that Christie had time to consider anything other than Shanna's white neck with its ugly purple bruise. And then she remembered again what Andy had told her, and wondered why she hadn't passed the information on to Meg. But why should she? It would only hurt her friend, as it had hurt her. Meg might need to know one day, but not yet, not just yet.

They were dead. Bill and Bob were dead, that was why they had not waited under the clock. Another time it could be Andy and Pat who didn't turn up, couldn't turn up. Her mind cringed away from the reality of the thought; she couldn't bear it, she just couldn't bear that Andy might die, crashing out of the sky in flames, drowning in the sea, being smashed into nothingness by tracer or cannon.

She tried to turn her thoughts back to Shanna and her boyfriend, the mysteries of love-making which could include a vampire-like bite on the neck, but her mind refused to be sidetracked. Instead it kept going back to those two boys, Bob and Bill, and to Andy and Pat. She knew she should stop thinking about it, that she could do nothing but harm to herself by dwelling on what had happened; but it continued to haunt her until she cried herself to sleep.

4

Shanna was scrubbing the canteen floor. She wasn't doing it with a very good grace, or with very much energy, because this was punishment fatigues and you didn't do your best when some nasty bitch of a sergeant had taken a dislike to you and put you on jankers out of sheer, green-eyed jealousy. So she scrubbed as slowly as she dared, remembering that if she did it too badly the cookhouse corporal, a fat and vindictive man with a broken nose and cauliflower ear, would get his own back, possibly by refusing her a cup of char presently, when everyone else got one, or even by slapping spud peelings on to her plate when the workers were fed later with their mince, potatoes and cabbage. The vegetable refuse was always cooked up for the hens which bickered and squabbled outside the cookhouse corporal's billet in the village; it would not be the first time that cooky had humiliated an enemy by serving them hen-food.

So Shanna scrubbed on, hating the floor, which was filthy and covered in spilt food, and Sergeant Shaw, who was responsible for her presence here, and Flight

Officer Sussman, who had decided on a day of floor scrubbing as a reasonable punishment for whatever sin she had committed.

Once or twice she raised her head from her work and glanced wistfully towards the doors, open to let in hungry aircrews and the long, soft gold rays of the September sun. If only Sergeant bloody Shaw hadn't walked behind the hedge and stumbled, not only into the ditch, but also into Shanna and Aircraftman Rab McIntyre, she with her skirt up round her neck, he with his trousers round his ankles! Sergeant Shaw had screamed and then let fly with a stream of obscenities which the startled Shanna had seldom heard used all together like that. Then the sergeant, red in the face and with her eyes glittering like mad marbles, had hit Rab McIntyre across his bare bum with her respirator case and clawed at Shanna's legs and Shanna, furious and humiliated and aware that she was already in deep trouble, had thrown caution to the winds and told Sergeant Shaw exactly what she thought of her.

It was lucky, actually, that Sergeant Shaw really was the dried up, bitter old spinster Shanna had called her. Because when it came to the rub, when she had marched her captive in figurative chains before the Flight Officer, Sergeant Shaw did not have words to explain the depths of Shanna's evil.

'Insubordination to a non-commissioned officer,' she brayed, meaning, Shanna imagined, that she herself had been sworn at by the wicked aircraftwoman so ignominiously hauled into the office.

'Unbecoming conduct – dreadful language, ma'am – muckin' arahnd wi' a feller, ma'am, shamelessly!'

'Ye didnae say nothin' aboot attackin' ma feller,' Shanna muttered under her breath, just loud enough to reach Sergeant Shaw's ears. 'Batterin' the wee mon's bum the way ye did. Och, we all know what you'd rather ha' been doin'.'

She always spoke broad Scots when annoyed, which was fortunate, since Sergeant Shaw, an East-ender, rolled a furious but totally uncomprehending eye at her and continued with her complaints.

'Uniform all any'ow, didn't show respect for me rank...'

Shanna bit her lip to stifle a grin and saw Flight Officer Sussman doing exactly the same. The thought of anyone complaining that a WAAF had not shown respect for rank whilst on the job was something only Sergeant Shaw could have contemplated.

'Called me names, ma'am, used language like wot you wouldn't believe,' Sergeant Shaw ended righteously, conveniently forgetting her own stream of obscenities. 'Bad for discipline, ma'am.'

Flight Officer Sussman had sighed and agreed, the enormous warrant officer who had marched Shanna into the office marched her out again, and Shanna was incarcerated in the cookhouse until twenty-one hundred hours. So far she had scrubbed the floor, emptied garbage, scrubbed the floor again, peeled twenty million potatoes, scrubbed the floor again – and the worst of it, she thought rebelliously, her scrub-brush worn almost down to the wood already and it wasn't even teatime, was that the floor went on getting filthy. Air- and ground-crews brought mud in, dropped food on the floor, ground out their cigarette butts underfoot, and behind the counter the cooks stirred carelessly, served carelessly, nipped out for a quick fag and brought mud in . . . it was endless, soul-destroying.

What was worse, Shanna and Christie had planned a night out tonight. Sue and Meg were both working but there was a good film on in Winchester, so Shanna and Christie had agreed to go together. It might not sound much – a seat in the stalls followed by a fish and chip supper afterwards – but Shanna would have enjoyed it. You never knew who you might meet when you were with a pretty, lively girl like Christie, and though Shanna wouldn't have dreamed of spoiling the evening by chasing a feller, that didn't mean she might not meet someone and make a quick, private arrangement for tomorrow night.

Now that Shanna came to think about it, it was odd how very well the four of them got on. At first she'd almost resented Meg and Christie, thinking perhaps that they would try and get between her and Sue. But it hadn't worked like that, not a bit. Meg and Christie were a pair, they went out in a foursome with their boyfriends, they worked together whenever they could, sat with their heads together in the evenings, ate together in the cookhouse, giggled together.

But because of Sue saving Christie's life, Shanna

supposed, the other girls had started to bag seats for them at mealtimes, or on the gharry going to and from Southampton or Portsmouth. Now the four of them sat and talked endlessly, or queued for new kit or flicked stockings from bed to bed when the officer's back was turned at kit inspection. They helped each other out in a hundred ways; made telephone calls for each other, wrote down messages, ran errands. Lending and borrowing became a matter of course, and Shanna, who had tended to clutch her possessions to her own bosom and to steal when her supplies ran out, found that her friends' acceptance of her needs, even their expectations of Shanna's generosity, was something to be cherished and lived up to.

Soon she saw that this togetherness, which she had once despised, meant that they kept each other out of trouble and shared the bad luck with the good, so that having three friends was even better than having one. When Sue was working or unavailable, Shanna only had to ask and either Christie, or Meg, or both if they were free, would welcome her to their ranks.

It would have worked like that today, had she not been on floor scrubbing. Sue's officer had been told to attend a meeting up in Lincolnshire and Sue was driving him, so that was her out of the running; and Meg was on the eight to midnight shift, but Christie had been free this evening and only too happy to go into town. Christie, whose father owned a big farm and whose brothers were officers, would have gone happily out for the evening with Shanna, who had never met her own father, could barely remember her mother. At first, Shanna thought wisely, scrubbing patiently away, her brush making big soapy circles in the filth, Meg and Christie had been a bit shy of her, a bit uncertain. They had been a couple of innocent schoolkids, with no experience of life to fall back on. She remembered the way they had looked at her when she picked up a feller; the silence which fell, sometimes, when she came in a bit mauled after a session behind the hut.

But that had been in the early days. Now they scolded her for being what Christie called promiscuous, and warned her of the evils lying in wait for girls who went with too many fellers; but they hated it when anyone called her the station bicycle and protected her as best they could.

They didn't understand, that went without saying. How could they, coming as they did from loving homes? Even Sue, who seemed to have innumerable brothers and sisters, all brought up in a small house off the Vauxhall Road in the great city of Liverpool, didn't totally understand. Sue's mam and dad loved all their kids and wanted the best for them. Sue got lots of letters, badly written but written with love, from her parents down to five-year-old Sammy. Family meant everything to Sue.

Sue had been the one who found her, though. She had been wandering the London streets the night Leonard from Glasgow had finished with her, so Sue had a pretty fair idea what Shanna's life had been like before the WAAF.

'You ain't a bad kid, considerin' you're a bloody

furriner.' The cook's voice, almost pleasant as he looked down on Shanna's handiwork, broke across her thoughts. 'I dunno when I seen that floor so clean, so 'elp me. Leave orf for a minute an' 'ave a mug o' char.'

'Oh, thanks,' Shanna said, scrambling to her feet. 'I'd best wash my hands first, though.'

She went across to the sink, rinsed her hands and dried them on a rough khaki towel, then gratefully took the proferred mug.

'Rest your arse for a mo,' the corporal said. 'No 'arm; Sergeant Shawski the Russian commandant's gorn orf to 'ave a fag.'

Shanna sat down and sipped her tea. She wondered whether Christie would go into town without her but doubted it. Anyway, she would ask her presently, when Christie came in for her supper, and if her friend was staying on the airfield then they could go along to the NAAFI together for a bit.

'Finished? Good gal. Best give Monica an 'and wiv the peelins. I want 'em in the bin wiv a number free on the side. Right?'

'Sure, corp,' Shanna said, glad to find herself popular, and just for carrying out punishment fatigues, too. 'We'll get that done in no time.'

Monica, a sturdy, big-faced girl with flushed cheeks and tangled hair, began to tip the first cauldron of peelings into the number three bin. Shanna heaved the next cauldron off the heat and staggered over to the bin with it. She took her time pouring the heaving contents out, not wanting to spoil her clean floor with splashes, then went back for the next. When the bin was full she went over to the cook.

'Done it, Corp. What next?'

The corporal was sweating as he tried to get the meal dished up. The waiting airmen and WAAFs had formed a long queue, plates held out in supplication as they moved along the line with one WAAF cook slapping on the mashed potato, another supplying cabbage, another doling out a skinny little chop whilst the corporal presided over the gravy and kept an eagle eye on helpings. He did not take his eyes from his staff for a moment but spoke to Shanna out of the corner of his mouth.

'Spuds runnin' low, gal. Drain another pan an' mash 'em.'

'Right, Corp. Won't take me a tick.'

It didn't, either. But the queue hadn't got any shorter and very soon Shanna was draining cabbage too, pressing it into the big tin collander for a moment and then heaving it out into the metal serving dishes. And when she thought they must all have been fed they were queueing again, for jam tart and custard now, and the floor was dirty once more, someone had dropped a tart jammy side down . . . It didn't need the corporal to tell Shanna what needed doing this time, in fact she nearly missed Christie as she began to scrub her way across the floor yet again.

'Shanna!'

Shanna looked up and grinned.

'Oh, Chris . . . this is going to last until nine o'clock. I'm awfu' sorry, I'm afraid the flicks is out.'

Christie sighed.

'I knew old Shawski would choose something horrible for you. Oh well – I'll be in the NAAFI at nine, then. See you there.'

It gave Shanna ever such a warm glow, to think that Christie wouldn't even consider going to the flicks without her. That was friendship if you like, real friendship.

'Thanks, Christie,' she said. 'In the NAAFI at nine; I shan't be late.'

Left alone to her scrubbing, her mind returned to that night in London when she'd first met Sue. God, she'd been at a low ebb, walking along by the river aching in every limb, crying, no money, no possessions, her face bruised, a cheekbone split, a tooth knocked loose. She'd stood at the side of a busy road and actually contemplated walking under a bus, because what else was there for her? She didn't have the money to go back to Glasgow, and anyway, what was the point? No one wanted her there either. Gus, the man she'd worked for in Glasgow, would break her neck if he ever set eyes on her again because she'd run out on him, lured by Leonard's pretended admiration, his avowed intent to marry her, keep her all to himself.

All he'd wanted was her earnings, of course. Just like Gus. The lovely flat he'd promised her had turned out to be a seedy room with a creaking, over-worked double bed in the middle and a cupboard where . . . She snatched her mind away from all that and returned it to the edge of the Charing Cross Road, to the girl with the yellow curls and the heart-shaped, happy face, swinging along with a little overnight bag in one hand and glancing at her in passing, suddenly stopping, turning to stare ... then retracing her steps.

'Hello, chuck – you all right? You've cut your cheek ... hey, what's the marrer? Tell Sue.'

As simple as that; Shanna remembered her own ugly, cracked sobs, the way the tears had simply pelted down her cheeks because of this one act of kindness. Then the feel of the little blonde's arm round her shoulders, steering her into the warmth and brightness of a nearby coffee bar. The girl had sat her down and ordered coffee and buns ... and listened whilst Shanna, in a mutter, had told her story. Leonard's liking her, bringing her down to London in a hired car, putting her in the room and bringing a friend back ... only the man hadn't been a friend, she'd been frightened, they'd beaten her until she let them ... let them ...

'But you gorraway,' Sue said practically, applying more hot coffee, like a poultice on a wound. 'You're safe wi' me, chuck.'

'But I have no clo'es, no money,' Shanna had sobbed. 'Nor anyone to want me, not down here in England. And with no money I canna get home.' Pride stopped her from admitting that no one wanted her up in Scotland, either. 'I might just as well be dead; I wish I were dead.'

'Don't talk rubbish; you're young and pretty, you've got plenty of good times ahead,' Sue said bracingly. 'As for money, I haven't got much meself, but money isn't everything. Tell you what, queen, why don't you come wi' me, earn yourself a few bob? I'm joinin' up today. Joinin' the WAAF. They'll feed us, clothe us, and pay us! What could be better than that, eh?'

'They wouldnae take me,' Shanna had snuffled. 'I dinnae have a trade.'

'So what? What did you do in Glasgow?'

'Clerical work,' Shanna mumbled. 'Shopwork, sometimes. I've nice, neat handwriting, see, an' . . .'

'Fine. Same as me. Are you on, then?'

And Shanna had looked into the bright little face so near her own, felt the warmth, not just of the coffee but of Sue Collins herself, and had nodded, at first hesitantly, then purposefully.

'Aye, I'm on! If you say they'll take me I guess they will.'

Sue stood up and smiled as Shanna followed suit.

'Atta girl! We'll be on our way before dusk. A pal of mine joined up last week. Wonder what they'll give us for our tea?'

That had been months ago, but Shanna knew she'd struck gold and had clung to Sue like a burr ever since. And even when Sue shouted at her, said that she herself had been scared to join up alone, that Shanna had been as useful to Sue as vice versa, Shanna only smiled and loved her the more.

'Hey, you . . . little miss jankers! Come on, there's a plate o' food goin' beggin'. Get outside o' that.'

Shanna grinned at the corporal. He could be a bad-tempered blighter but it was true what the kitchen staff said – that cooky looked after his own. And plainly, anyone who scrubbed his floor properly became a member of his flock. Shanna, who wanted to belong more than she wanted almost anything else, decided that punishment fatigues weren't so bad. Over the corporal's shoulder she could see the clock; less than another hour to do and she'd be free to join Christie in the NAAFI, free to try to wash the smell of cabbage and greasy gravy out of her hair. The Flight Officer, who wasn't a bad sort really, had said she'd not put the offence in the book which meant it wouldn't go down on Shanna's record. FO Sussman, Shanna concluded, must have felt a bit sorry for anyone caught in a compromising position by old hairy-legs Shawski.

'Thanks, corp,' she said cheerfully, now. 'Mind if I just finish off? Only the bit in the corner to do and then I can give a hand wi' the garbage cans.'

The corporal nodded. He looked rather pleased than otherwise to find Shanna's previously well-hidden love of work suddenly showing.

'You do that; I'll see you git a bit o' meat wi' your veggies,' he said. 'Git yourself over 'ere, Monica; scoff's up!'

Sue, who had driven as fast as safety allowed ever since leaving Hampshire, enjoyed the long drive even though for most of it Wing Commander Bingham was too busy with a mass of papers to talk. He told her to pull over at noon and they went into a pub for a snack but they did not hang about, the Wingco drinking a beer and Sue a glass of lemonade in record time, then taking their ham sandwiches to eat in the car.

'Sorry to do you out of a proper meal, Susie,' James Bingham said remorsefully as he leaned back and began to put his papers back into his official briefcase. 'The truth is this meeting's damned important – something to do with a new weapon, I believe. I said we could be there by three and I don't want to be any later.'

It was first names when they were alone in the car. Sue turned her head to smile at her boss. He was a likeable, handsome man probably in his mid-fifties and they had always got on well, both appreciating the other's businesslike approach and calm efficiency.

'Do me good; it's easy to put on weight, sitting behind the wheel all day. I quite often skip the midday meal back at the station.'

'Well, you shouldn't,' James said, but absently. He turned his head to look out at the passing scene. 'I hope Dilly doesn't do anything so daft as miss a meal – not that it seems likely, she loves her food. Not far now, then you can get some cookhouse grub and have a rest. In fact you'll be free until after lunch tomorrow. We'll leave around two o'clock, I expect.'

Sue, concentrating on the grey ribbon of road unwinding ahead of her, nodded. Dilly was her boss's only child. She was twenty-three, three years older than Sue herself, and an officer in the WRNS stationed at Portsmouth, or Pompey as James called it. Sue had never met Dilly but liked the sound of her and it was clear that James adored both his lively, intelligent daughter and his capable, affectionate wife, who ran the WVS in her area with the same sort of efficiency which her husband brought to his work with the Air Force.

A signpost and a right-hand turn loomed up. Sue knew the signpost would be painted out to baffle invaders and looked for the barn with the tiles repaired in two different colours. Her instructions were explicit, easy to follow, though James always pretended that it was Sue's interpretation of them which got him across the country, always on time, always smiling on arrival. For her part, Sue, scared of being held up by military convoys, insisted that they start out early. Some men would not have allowed her to put her oar in quite so often, she knew that, but James valued her and let her have her say. As a result, their spot-on navigation was legendary.

'Right here? Yes, I remember a right turn ... are you sure, Susie my dear? Ah, you're not looking at the signpost ... oh well, you've never been wrong yet.'

James Bingham, who had leaned forward anxiously as the car slowed, relaxed once more and Sue, hearing the rustle as he produced yet more papers, allowed her thoughts to turn back to the station they had left earlier in the day, and to her friend.

Shanna. What a blessing it had been, spotting her that day! Sue, the confident and efficient Sue, had been feeling very lost, very lonely. Back home in Liverpool she had done clerical work at Tate & Lyle's until it became clear that war was going to come, and then she'd got a boyfriend to teach her to drive. She passed her test at the first attempt and then war came so she got another job, this time driving a large delivery van, and stayed with it until her younger sister, Lizzie, had joined the ATS and had been posted to the wilds of Scotland. Sue had been very envious and more than a little annoyed. Pipped at the post by a mere seventeen-year-old, and she about to be nineteen in a couple of months! She had fully intended to join one or other of the services, but somehow, with the driving job being so interesting and her mam so dependent, she'd put it off and put it off. But no more; the kids 'll manage fine without me, Sue decided. And it's about time Mam realised she can't lean on me for the rest of her life, she's got to be independent. It can be her contribution to the war effort.

Ada Collins's husband, Donald, had worked the ferries for years and joined the Merchant Navy as soon as war was declared. Her eldest son was in the engine room of a destroyer and her brother Solly was afloat too, so she had had hysterics when she heard Lizzie had joined the ATS. Ada, however, had always worked hard, she was a school cook as well as the mother of eight assorted young Collinses, and when she'd finished weeping and wailing and declaring that her heart was broke and all she was fit for was the grave, she sighed, mopped her eyes and told Sue that, as the eldest, she would simply have to stay home and give a hand there. Home was an underfurnished, painfully clean little house just off Vauxhall Road.

Accordingly Sue, not above a little deceit if it made life easier, didn't say anything about the WAAF or her own intentions. She just said she'd been offered a better job driving a delivery van in London, and since it would mean living down south she intended to accept the job, find herself accommodation, and visit home as often as possible.

Oddly enough, this news did not bring on the fainting fits or the screaming habdabs. Ada Collins took a deep breath, let it out in a long, gusty sigh – and then asked how much money Sue would be sending home each week. When Sue said rather tartly it would be as much as she could afford, her mother hugged her convulsively and said that Sue was a good girl, none better.

'You'll do well, queen,' she said, with tears brimming her eyes and chasing each other down her round, rosy cheeks. 'I won't hold you back, but don't you go forgettin' us now, 'cos we do love you.'

The younger kids cried and clung to her, the older ones – privy to her secret since they promised not to tell Mam until it was too late to stop her – cast envious glances at her, and Mam did all Sue's ironing and promised to send her clothes on when she'd found herself digs. Mam then curled her hair, made up her face and donned her best coat, wept a little weep when she saw Sue packing a weekend case, and came to the station and waved her first-born off without further fuss. So Sue caught a London-bound train from Lime Street, talked to a WAAF in the same carriage who was going back to her airfield down south, and got instructions from her on how to join the WAAF. The ATS was all very well, but she thought the WAAF uniform much more attractive, especially on a blonde.

She left Euston after the rail journey with a brand-new *Geographia* of London grasped in one hand and her weekend case in the other, feeling more uncertain than she had ever felt in her life before. Leaving home was something she had often contemplated wistfully, but now that it was actually happening she found she wasn't as independent as she had always supposed. London seemed big and lonely, and she was trying to nerve herself up either to book into a guest-house or to go straight to the depot and join up, when she saw the thin, forlorn red-head swaying on the kerb, and immediately all the natural protectiveness which had been the trademark of Sue's dealings with her younger brothers and sisters surged to the fore.

'Hello chuck – you all right?'

Shanna had thought herself rescued, befriended. So she had been, but only Sue could know how much stronger and more positive she felt herself, once she had someone else to look after. Even when she began to suspect that Shanna was going to be trouble, she stuck by her. Once they were through their basic training indeed, she tried to change Shanna's more disreputable ways, but she didn't worry much over her inability to do so. Shanna's life had been hard beyond Sue's understanding, but she did see that her new friend most desperately yearned to be needed.

Shanna didn't like herself much, didn't see herself as worthy of any deep or genuine emotion such as real love. But when a feller groped her in the cinema or threw her down on the grass behind the hut she felt, not insulted or outraged, but accepted, wanted. Needed, even.

Sue had worried about this for a long time. She knew such an attitude was dangerous, but she didn't know how to stop Shanna feeling like that. Whilst she was on the spot it wasn't too bad, she could see that Shanna didn't get too low, but when the two girls were apart she was uneasy ... or had been. She didn't worry now, though. Trying to analyse the sudden easing of responsibility made her realise that being friendly with Meg and Christie had made all the difference.

Right now, for instance. A few months ago she would have been worrying over what Shanna would do with Sue so far away. Now, she knew Shanna would be all right. She wouldn't run away or choose the wrong feller on too dark a night and end up with her throat slashed from ear to ear. She would have Meg and Christie, unobtrusively keeping an eye on her, taking her round with them until she, Sue, returned.

'Well, Susie, looks like we've arrived. Got our passes?'

'All present and correct, sir,' Sue said, leaning over and taking the passes out of the dashboard dive. 'I say, lots of activity!'

The airfield positively hummed with people, some

standing around in small groups, others walking more or less purposefully. And all over the place the large, slow-moving figures of the Air Force Police.

'That's it. Secret weapons always mean doubled security and a huge audience.' The car slowed, they were challenged and Sue rolled down the window and showed their passes. The sergeant who had stopped them peered at the paperwork, let his eyes dwell lovingly on Sue's neat figure for an instant and then saluted with a heel-jarring crash, his arm flying up like a train signal as he stepped back.

'Orfficers' mess to the ri', cook'ouse a bit further on, visitors' billets be'ind the mess,' he said in a bored monotone. 'Everywhere's signposted today, you shouldn't 'ave no trouble findin' your way. You can park the vehicle beside your billet.'

Sue thanked him, engaged first gear and began to drive forward once again.

'I'll take you to the officers' mess, sir, since you'll have an hour to kill – we're early.'

'Thanks, my dear,' James said. 'Don't forget, you're to have a decent meal presently, and an early night. You've been assigned a guest-room so you won't be kept awake by snoring WAAFs.'

'This is a big place,' Sue said presently, as they drove across the airfield towards the officers' mess, half hidden by a convenient group of trees. 'I wonder if they show films on the station?'

'Quite possible. I suppose watching a picture is more relaxing than talking to total strangers, which is what I'll probably end up doing. Did the gate sergeant tell you where you could park the car?'

'Yes sir, he said right next to my billet.' Sue slowed the car and drew it to a halt right outside the officers' mess. 'See you tomorrow, sir.'

Meg's evening started quietly, but an hour into her shift things suddenly hotted up; it was a moonlit night and raiders began coming in over the Channel, intent on reaching London and other major cities. Meg's arms were soon aching as she leaned across the board but adrenalin kept her going, excitement, distress, triumph attacking her in turn as the British planes began to close on their Hun counterparts. Presently however the enemy moved away from their table.

'All right? Shift change in less than an hour, girls. You can knit if you want for a bit.'

The officer who had spoken grinned encouragingly at them and sat back in his chair and Meg began to massage her arms, a trick which she had found useful at mid-shift. Her calf muscles ached too, from standing on tiptoe; not for the first time Meg wondered how she had come to be picked as a plotter, short as she was. But no one had ever complained about her skills, so perhaps it hadn't made any real difference and besides, she loved the work.

'Meg, if you haven't got any knitting you might hold my wool.'

Jane Griffiths, sitting next to Meg, held out a great, untidy mass of wrinkled wool. She had obviously been unpicking a jersey and still hadn't got round to balling it up. Meg sighed and held out her hands.

'Oh, give it here, I might as well have a go – only get it out of sight fast if there's a report.'

She glanced up at the big board of southern England as she began to try to get the rough skein round her wrists in the approved fashion, then snatched her eyes away. She was still sensitive about Patrick, though she had not told anyone else yet, not even Christie.

They had met for the fourth time a week ago, on a Sunday. It had been one of those golden and glorious September afternoons which don't happen often, when the weather seems to be trying to revert to high summer yet the blue of the sky is misty, the gentle breeze has the scent of bonfires and roasting chestnuts on its breath.

Patrick said he wanted to walk, so they went to the New Forest and set off, at first all four of them together. But then Andy and Christie loitered and Patrick strode out; and before Meg had really realised what was happening she and Patrick were alone in the sun-dappled forest with the subdued September birdsong the only sound apart from their footsteps on the soft leaf-mould underfoot.

'Should we wait for the others?' Meg asked, but Patrick shook his head.

'It's all right, I arranged with Andy to go back to the car for our picnic, that's why we didn't bring the food with us. I – I wanted to talk to you, Meg.'

'Go on then,' Meg said at once. 'Is something wrong?'

'No, not . . . yes! Meg, I'm fond of you, you know I

109

am. I like you better than any girl I've met since I joined up, but I think we ought to stop seeing one another.'

Meg's heart gave a sickening dive. She stared ahead of her, digging her hands into the waistband of her skirt, trying to look casual, uncaring. She dared not risk a glance at Patrick, so tall and golden and gorgeous . . . but then she'd never expected anything of the relationship, not really. She was short and squat, dark and uninteresting, it had been too good to be true . . . and he did like her, he'd just said so.

'Meg? I wouldn't hurt you for the world . . .'

There was something in the way he said it which gave her a clue. She turned her head, looked up at him. There was a flush on his cheekbones and a look of great discomfort in his narrowed blue eyes.

'You're married, aren't you?' she said, almost relieved, because if he was married then she could scarcely expect to retain his affection – would not want to do so. To be dropped by a fellow for no reason would have been agony, but if he really was married . . . 'What's her name?'

He went redder, hesitated, then stopped walking and turned towards her. When she would only look at his tunic buttons, which happened to be where her eyes fell naturally, he took her chin in one hand and lifted it so that their eyes met.

'What sort of a cad d'you think me? But I am engaged. She – she's a nice girl, but . . .'

'But you were forced into the engagement at gunpoint,' Meg said. She had meant to sound gay, laughing, but it came out bitter, somehow. 'It doesn't matter, Pat. Thanks for telling me, though I can't help wishing you'd said something at the start.'

'It does matter! And at the start it didn't seem . . . I never should have behaved the way I did, but Gillian's a long way off and I was lonely . . . I never meant it to go beyond the first time but we had such fun . . .'

'And now you're calling a halt, having had such fun,' Meg said, trying to sound practical. 'You're doing the right thing, now at least no one will get hurt. Tell me, is Andy . . . ?'

'No, he's not married or engaged. He's fancy-free so far as I know,' Patrick said moodily. 'And it isn't true to say no one's been hurt because I've felt awful, as though I were being torn in two. Meg, I'm really fond of you. Andy said I'd simply got to spill the beans but . . . I'll miss you badly. If it hadn't been for Andy I'd not have said a word because in a way, I – I need you.'

'Yes. Well.' Meg looked down at the leaf-mould underfoot because she could feel tears beginning to build behind her eyes. She could guess how much having someone to cuddle had meant to him, caught up in all the terrors of flying fighter planes. She could even understand the evasions now; he had never lied to her, he had simply made sure she never asked the wrong questions. If I'm hurt, then it's my own fault because he never pretended it was anything but friendship, she told herself, moving out of Patrick's reach and continuing to study her feet. He made a little noise, similar to the noise a puppy makes when you won't open the door for him, and she looked up at last and tried out a watery smile.

'We've not hurt anyone, anyway,' she observed. 'It's only been a few kisses and a lot of laughs, I've not taken anything from your Gillian.'

'Well, not deliberately. Meg . . . now that you know will it make a great deal of difference? We can still meet, can't we, as friends? I can't bear the thought of managing on my own again, being without you.'

'Patrick, your opening remark was that you thought we ought to stop seeing each other, and you were absolutely right,' Meg pointed out. The dreadful sinking sensation had lifted; he's nice but not that important, she realised, amazed at herself. She was in complete control what was more, the pain of rejection at least eased by two things: the realisation that he didn't want to end the friendship and oddly enough, the fact that Andy had made him tell, that left to himself he would have continued to deceive her. 'Look, I'll miss you very much, but I do see it's for the best.'

'I could tell Gillian about you; I'm willing to do that,' Patrick said eagerly, thereby sinking his last chance of continuing the relationship, Meg thought crossly. So she was the kind of girl that a fiancée couldn't possibly object to, was she? Good old Meg Aldford, everyone's friend, no one's lover, certainly not an object of desire. Anger, a cleansing emotion, began to replace the last vestiges of loss in Meg's mind. How dare this tall, golden young man value her so little!

'Thanks, Pat, but it would be too difficult to act naturally,' Meg said, letting him down lightly, she felt. She glanced round her, at the sunshine, the leaves fluttering in the summery breeze. She felt lighter, almost as though a burden had dropped from her shoulders – yet she had so enjoyed talking about her boyfriend, anticipating their next meeting! I'm shallow, she told herself, but she knew it wasn't true. She hadn't known him well enough to love him; she had a lot for which she should be thankful.

To change the subject, and also because she found that despite not loving Patrick she still rather liked him, she said, 'Do you have a photo of your fiancée? I'd love to see it.'

Patrick mumbled something, then took out his wallet. Meg could see that he was rather disappointed that she had not taken his defection harder, made more of a fuss. But he extracted a photograph and held it out to her with a fairly good grace.

'There. She's twenty, older than you.'

Meg took the picture. The girl was blonde, slim, beautiful. Poised and posed, she sat at an angle to the camera but with her face turned towards it. Her hair shone and there was a sweet, provocative smile on her face. She wore a light-coloured evening gown which left her shoulders and the tops of her breasts bare, showing off her white and flawless skin. Even Christie and Sue would acknowledge that Gillian was stunning and again this helped Meg to understand Patrick's behaviour. There was no shame in losing out to a girl like that, she told herself stoutly; no shame at all.

'She's very beautiful, Pat. You should be proud. Is she in one of the services?'

He took the picture back. Oddly enough now his face was closed, guarded, as though by showing the picture he had given himself away to Meg and regretted it.

'Yes. She's in the WRNS. She's up in Scotland at present, something to do with submarine trials, I believe.'

'I expect she looks marvellous in the uniform,' Meg said wistfully. Everyone envied the Wrens their black silk stockings but Meg, remembering how long she spent trying to pick white lints off her blue serge, thought that navy must show every mark and be horribly difficult to keep clean and tidy. 'Is she an officer?'

'I don't know. She's only joined recently. Look, we ought to turn back now, the others will wonder where we've got to.'

They turned back and presently came upon Andy and Christie, wandering along hand in hand, flushed and happy.

'I'm not going to say anything yet,' Meg whispered as they overhauled the other couple. 'Let's not spoil everyone's day, Pat.'

So the picnic, and the drive home, had gone far better than they might have done. Patrick volunteered to drive, which meant that the other two sat and cuddled in the back seat, and Meg talked and laughed and wondered what Christie would say when she told her that she wasn't going out with Patrick any more. Chris would be upset because she enjoyed the foursomes, but she'd understand.

And I'll meet someone else some day, Meg comforted herself, but next time I'll know what questions to ask before I start cuddling up. I'll never be caught like that again, never. After all, I was lucky he came clean on our fourth meeting, otherwise goodness knows how heavily I might have got involved. Once bitten twice shy, though. Next time . . .

'Right, everyone . . . aircraft approaching, get ready!'

Fortunately Jane Griffiths was just rolling up the last of the wool. Meg snatched up her rake as a male voice sounded in her earphones. For the rest of her hour she manoeuvred the pieces briskly across the grid, then as the aircraft began to land and the raiders moved out to sea she sat back once more, automatically rubbing her arms, and let her thoughts stray back to Patrick and their non-existent relationship.

Even if she had never been in love with him she would miss him, that went without saying, and she dreaded the moment when she would have to tell Christie what had happened between them. But on the other hand she had always known in her heart that he was not the sort of fellow to go with a girl like her. Suppose he had wanted to accompany her home one day? It did happen, other people had talked of taking boyfriends back to meet Mum and Dad. Because she had been with Christie whenever they met she had let Patrick believe they shared a similar background.

Thinking it over now though, Meg realised that in a way she had done just what Patrick had done. She had made sure that no one asked the wrong questions about her home circumstances.

Everyone, even Christie, took it for granted that since Meg had been a pupil at Nantwich High School, her parents were at least comfortably off. In fact Meg had won a scholarship to her school and since her father was a farm labourer they had neither money nor property. The Aldfords lived in a flat over the small newsagent and tobacconist shop which Mrs Aldford ran with comfortable efficiency. Meg's father cycled three miles to work each day on a farm; he was a valued farm labourer but that was all.

Meg loved her parents and her home, never thought it unfair that she – and they – had lacked material things. Her father was easy-going and kind, his wedding photograph showed that he had been extremely good-looking too, and her mother, Sarah, was intelligent, with a capacity for absorbing knowledge which had stood both mother and daughter in good stead when they were at school. Sarah had been a very clever girl but she had fallen in love with Ben and that had been the end of her interest in education. The young couple had moved into the flat, she had taken on the shop, and so far as Meg knew had never looked back, far less regretted her circumstances. Sarah Aldford never complained or grumbled, but had been unable to hide her joy when Meg had got the scholarship.

'Don't you go wastin' it, girl,' she advised. 'I'm not

sorry for what I did, your dad's worth it all, but I wouldn't want you to do the same.'

Meg took her mother's advice. Long ago, in self-defence, she had shed her flat Cheshire accent and learned not to talk about her background. School-friends knew, of course, but they accepted her. Nantwich was a friendly little town and no one had ever thought the worse of Meg because her mother kept a shop and her father worked on a farm.

It should have been far easier in the WAAF; for a start the polyglot mix meant that others, too, came from working-class backgrounds. Sue, for instance, would go far, though she came on her own admission from a Liverpool slum. Indeed, had Meg been frank from the start she would have been accepted by everyone for what she was. But she'd said her father farmed and ever since then regretted it.

Because Christie's father really was a farmer, she and her brothers rode and fished and mixed with county people, took the good life for granted. So Meg, who otherwise could have come clean, found herself letting people believe an untruth, just like Patrick had.

Perhaps it's a lesson to me, Meg thought now, taking off her head-set and handing it to Martha, waiting beside her. Perhaps, if I'd been honest, I never would have got Patrick in the first place so I wouldn't be losing him now.

But that was silly, because she'd enjoyed her outings with Patrick, would look back on them with pleasure, and you can't lose what you've never had.

The truth is, Meg told herself, I enjoyed Patrick's company and was proud to have caught myself a pilot officer, but that was about all. But I'll feel I'm letting Chris down, because the foursomes were fun and convenient for us both. Only it's daft to think that because Chris will understand; she always does.

'Coming, Meg?'

That was Jane Griffiths, tugging impatiently at Meg's sleeve. Meg nodded, cast one last valedictory look at the almost empty board, and headed for the outside world, the cookhouse and her bed. Tomorrow, she told herself, I'll tell Christie what happened between Patrick and me. She's a very understanding person, she'll help me over it. Why, if all goes well I might even tell her the truth about Dad and Mum.

But she knew she wouldn't; not yet.

5

Christie was walking over to the mess to telephone
Andy, keeping her torch in her pocket as she could
see quite well in the faint starlight. The moon was
new, just a nail-paring of a moon spreading almost no
radiance, and anyway small cloudlets kept hiding its
face; but the stars were twinkling away, guiding
Christie to her destination, though she knew the
airfield so well by now that she could probably have
found the WAAF mess blindfold.

Christie's coat collar was turned up, her breath
fanned into mist around her face and her feet
crunched across grass thickly furred with frost. It
was hell in the billets now; even with every garment
they possessed spread in a tottering heap on top of
their bedding the girls were always cold. Christie
thought wistfully of home, the big fire in the kitchen,
and the goosefeather eiderdown on her bed. Still, she
would be back there in just over a week and in the
meantime walking briskly would help to keep her
warm.

The WAAF mess was in darkness of course, the
blackout complete, but there was always something

which guided you to a building full of people; a smell of cooking, perhaps, or a faint, residual warmth. Christie swerved off the grass and on to the concrete, pulling her hands in their blue woolly gloves out of her pockets in order to turn the door handle. As always when she was about to call Andy's airfield, she began to feel that horrible sinking sensation in the pit of her stomach – suppose he wasn't available to answer the call? Suppose there was the little silence she'd been told about by other girls, followed by a kind but impersonal voice saying: 'Sorry, he doesn't seem to be back yet.' What would she do? If something happened to him, how could she bear it?

But the door-knob was beneath her hand, she was pushing the door open, slipping in, shutting it behind her. Don't meet troubles half-way, she scolded herself, heading for the telephone. Damn, there was someone using it . . . never mind, her hands and feet were freezing, she could have a warm by the fire whilst she waited.

Shanna and Meg were playing cards by the fire; they waved to her. Christie always felt awkward when she telephoned Andy with Meg there. Meg had been so proud of Patrick, so happy in his company, all her protestations that they had only been friends didn't always ring true. She wouldn't meet Pat again, for a start, which must mean, surely, that she had been emotionally involved and didn't want to become involved again?

Sue said it was nonsense though, that Meg had more sense than to fret for a man she'd only met four times, and Sue was probably the most sensible of them all regarding emotional entanglements. She didn't exactly steer clear of men, but she didn't get involved. You couldn't imagine Sue shedding tears over some feller – she'd shrug and move on, the way she thought all girls should do.

Christie crossed the room and went to stand beside the card players, partly because they were nearer the fire than anyone else so she could have a good warm whilst talking.

'Chris – want to join in? If so, do tell Shanna not to cheat!'

'It's no' cheatin' to win three times runnin',' Shanna said smugly 'Your face is too open, Meggie. I can read you like a book!'

'She peeps,' Meg insisted. She grinned up at Chris, her puggy little face flushed with the heat from the fire. 'Otherwise she's psychic and that I'm not prepared to believe.'

'I'm no' cheatin',' Shanna insisted. 'Come on, hand over that tanner, you tight-fisted sassenach!'

'Oh, all right,' Meg muttered. 'Does that mean you've finished bleeding me white for the evening? If so, chuck over my knitting. I want to finish my jumper in time for Christmas.'

The jumper was a lacy, frothy affair, low-necked, sleeveless, which Meg had been knitting in her spare time for several months. In fact, one reason why it was lacy and frothy was because Meg was using any spare scrap of pink wool which crossed her path, and when the pinks were noticeably different she just knitted in some love-knots or a fringe and pressed on regardless. And so far, Christie thought, passing the jumper and needles to its creator, it was paying off. The garment looked high fashion rather than desperate, and that was all to the good since Meg intended to wear it at the mess Christmas party in ten days' time.

'Thanks, Chris. Did you come over for a game of cards? Because if so, you can take on Shark-Shanna here. I refuse to be beaten any more tonight ... besides, she's taken my only spare tanner.'

'No, I'm not playing cards, I'm making a phone call. Or I would be, only Corporal Sutton's using the ... Help, she's off. See you in a moment!'

Christie waved a hand and scuttled across the room and out into the corridor. Corporal Sutton looked glum; Christie paused for a moment.

'Everything all right, Corp?'

The Corporal came from Norwich and had been at the same school as Christie, though six years earlier, so despite their difference in age and rank she and Christie were on good terms. They knew each other's families vaguely, and occasionally gossiped wistfully about school, the city or mutual acquaintances.

'Oh ... Bellis, it's you. I was speaking to Mummy, apparently Cousin Cathy was killed in the raids on Sheffield yesterday. She was staying with her boy-friend's family. It is so sad, such a waste.'

'I'm sorry,' Christie murmured. 'Everyone thought the bombing would ease off now winter's here, but it doesn't seem to happen like that.'

'No. Still, at least our immediate families are both

in the country; if you're ringing home give your parents my regards.'

'I will,' Christie said. She never told anyone when she was ringing Andy, just in case. 'I'm going home in just over a week – are you?'

Corporal Sutton shook her head.

'No, I'm having New Year. Well, hope you get through all right. The lines are busy – but when aren't they, in wartime?'

She left, pushing the door open and letting it swing noisily shut behind her.

Christie put her hand on the receiver and started to pick it up, then hastily clattered it back on to its rest. She closed her eyes, stood on one leg and said a short, fervent prayer. It was just stupid superstition, of course, but so far she'd always followed the exact routine before asking for the number she required, and so far Andy had either answered the phone himself or come straight away when he'd been paged. She opened her eyes and glanced at her wrist-watch. Yes, the time was about right – you couldn't promise to ring at any exact time because of other people making calls and the lines being perpetually busy, so she and Andy had agreed that they would try to ring between seven and eight. Please God, Christie prayed, let Andy be there, let him be waiting!

Closing her eyes again, she lifted the receiver off its rest and waited. Presently the operator's cool, impersonal voice said, 'Number, please?' and she recited the number which was as much a part of her as her own service number.

'Put four pennies in the box, please.'

Christie complied. The coins clinked down, there was a series of clicks, some heavy breathing, and then a young masculine voice shouted into the telephone.

'Hello?'

Not Andy. Impossible not to feel that awful plummeting of the heart, though there was no need for it, not yet.

'Could I speak to Flying Officer Todd, please?'

'Yes, sure, he's right here; who shall I say . . .'

But he got no further. There was a brief scuffle, a breathless exclamation, and then Andy's voice sounded warmly in her ear.

'Chris darling, is that you?'

Christie's heart, which had been beating fast and unevenly, slowed and steadied. Happiness enfolded her like a warm pink cloak.

'Yes, it's me; what would you have done if it was your mother?'

Andy laughed.

'I always know when it's you. The chaps tease me by trying to get you talking. Everything all right?'

'Everything's fine, now. I – I do worry, though I know it's stupid and pointless.'

'Damned pointless. But I'm glad you do it. I'll tell you all about it when we meet but . . . Look, I'm off for twenty-four hours, any chance of a quick get-together?'

His voice sounded strained; he had flown a great many ops and the weariness was beginning to show.

'Yes, definitely. Where? When?'

'Well, what are your shifts tomorrow?'

'I'm on earlies; five a.m. until ten a.m.' Christie said. 'Then I'm free until ten a.m. the following day. I suppose you don't know about Christmas, do you? I'm off from Friday 20th for a week. I'm going home. Could you come with me? I'd love my parents to meet you.'

'And I'd love to meet your parents, but the blighters haven't said a word about leave yet,' Andy said. 'If there's the slightest chance I'll bag that week, or a part of it . . . actually, I'll have a word with Bucky, my squadron leader; get him to put in a good word. About tomorrow, though. It's too cold to take a picnic anywhere, but we could go into Winchester, grab ourselves some food and see a flick.'

'Right,' Christie said at once. Life was too short and precious to waste it carping about where and when, you just grabbed every opportunity which came up. 'Meet you by the clock tower?'

'Lovely. At two o'clock? That will give you an hour or so to rest after your shift.'

'I don't need any rest after the five to ten shift, it's an early start, that's all. Say noon at the clock tower, then we can have lunch together.'

'Right.'

Christie was beginning to say something else when the operator's voice overrode hers. 'Your time is up, caller. I've other calls waiting.'

'Sorry,' Christie said quickly. 'Cheerio then, darling; see you at noon tomorrow.'

125

* * *

'I like Andy; give him my love,' Meg said when Christie told her she was going into Winchester by bus. 'If you're going round the shops do see if you can find some elastic. And four little pink buttons.'

'I don't know that we're going shopping, but if we do I'll keep my eyes open,' Christie promised. 'What's the elastic for?'

'For my pompoms. I'm going to string them on a piece of elastic so that they can hang across the pram. My cousin Cecilia's got herself in the club, so I thought I'd make a toy for the baby when it comes.'

'How could I forget, when you grab every milk-bottle top which comes within a mile of us?' Christie said. 'What'll you do if we can't find some elastic though? It's pretty scarce, like everything else.'

'I'll fillet a pair of old knickers,' Meg said. 'Thank God that sergeant in the stores still thinks the sun shines out of Sue. Actually, I could do with another pair of stockings . . . it's odd you know, my legs aren't long but I'm always laddering mine. Yours keep whole for ages.'

The two girls had come off the early shift and were in their billet, Christie changing into clean stockings whilst Meg brushed her hair until it stood out round her head like a furze bush.

'If you've got some really holey stockings, let Elsie have them when the new ones come; she's making her mother two cushions for Christmas and stuffing them with cut-up stockings,' Christie said. 'They lost most of their furniture when they were bombed out. At least it makes Christmas presents less of a problem; they're grateful for anything, Elsie says.'

'Okay, I'll do that. Sure you don't want to come into town with me, Meggie? Andy would be only too pleased to take us both to lunch.'

Meg snorted derisively and threw her hair-brush down on the bed, then began to subdue her hair with the aid of a length of ribbon and a good many hairpins.

'I'm sure he would! Go along with you, Shanna's off after lunch. We're going to rehearse our act for the Christmas revue, and then two of the chaps said they'd give us a game of table tennis.' Meg snorted. 'I do hate that expression – give you a game. I expect we'll beat them hollow, but they'll go on pretending they let us win because we're women.'

'Which chaps are these?' Christie said suspiciously. She had been told long ago that Patrick and her friend had parted, but she'd not heard of socialising amongst the revue cast before. 'I shouldn't have thought Shanna's taste in chaps and yours were exactly similar.'

'You can play table tennis with a fellow without wanting to climb into bed with him,' Meg said. 'They're all right, we get on okay. So you toddle off and have fun with Andy, and give him my love, as I said.'

'Right. Be secretive and keep me in the dark,' Christie muttered. 'Is one of the chaps Frank Myers?'

'M.Y.O.B.,' Meg chanted, then grinned at Christie's scowl. 'Oh well, one of them is Frank and the other

. . . but if you want to know any more, you'll have to come to the revue when it happens.'

'If it happens,' Christie said, setting her cap carefully on her smoothly shining hair. 'I bet you go and do it whilst I'm on leave – that would be bloody typical, that would.'

'We're doing it three times, so you'll probably catch one of the performances,' Meg said. She pulled a hideous face, crossing her eyes and putting her tongue out as far as it would go. 'So you'll see me swanning round the stage in my smallest swimsuit, being a Great Star,' she added, drawing her tongue in again and uncrossing her eyes. 'Do get a move on, Chris, or you'll miss your bus and what would poor Andy do then?'

'Wait, I hope,' Christie said, but she bolted for the door nevertheless. 'Bye, Meg; see you later!'

Christie enjoyed the journey into town. The bus was crowded, with everyone in holiday mood, talking about Christmas, trying not to mention the war. The conductress rattled out her tickets, clinked change, shouted raucous jokes to a couple of servicemen sitting on the front seats.

They were on time, too, which was a bonus. Andy, standing at the bus stop, must have arrived early and decided to wait here rather than by the clock tower. An extra five minutes, Christie thought gleefully, getting to her feet. Half the passengers were getting off here, so she joined the slowly shuffling queue and peered at Andy through the window as she did so, rather enjoying the opportunity to take in his familiar, much-loved appearance whilst he was oblivious of her presence.

He was in uniform, of course. His cap was on the back of his head and she saw that he looked tired, with dark smudges under his eyes and his dark, wavy hair a little longer than he usually wore it. But haircuts took time, and time was so precious!

He saw her as she reached the step and his eyes lit up. They were lovely eyes, a surprisingly reddish brown when contrasted with his hair which was almost black, and when he smiled his eyes seemed to sparkle. They sparkled now as he sketched a salute, then stepped forward to take her in his arms. They clung unashamedly, Christie feeling the tension in him even as her own tension began to drain away. He was here; for ten whole hours they could be together and even after that she wouldn't have to worry for a bit because he wasn't flying until tomorrow and if the weather stayed bad, he might not be flying then.

Andy heaved a sigh and held her back from him, then kissed the tip of her nose, her cheeks, her mouth. Then he put an arm round her waist and began to lead her away from the bus stop.

'Sweetheart, it's wonderful to see you, absolutely wonderful. What shall we do?'

'Oh, I don't mind. Just wander, shall we? It's a nice day even though it's so cold.'

'Tell you what, I'll take you into the Copper Kettle and we'll have a cup of coffee to warm us up. How's that?'

Anything was fine, anything which meant they were together, away from the war for a bit.

'That sounds lovely. I *am* rather chilly.'

They found a quiet table in a dark corner and ordered coffee and a teacake apiece, then they just stared at each other. Hungrily, passionately, both of them trying to have something to keep, something for tomorrow. Christie saw new lines on his face, a darkness in his eyes, as well as the signs of fatigue which a quiet day might help to smooth away.

'Andy? What's happened?'

She knew it was something bad. He looked down at the cloth, then up at her again, his eyes full of pain.

'Patrick.'

She was stunned, yet just because he didn't see Meg any more that didn't mean he was not important to Andy. He and Pat were close still, Andy talked about his friend a lot, though Christie had not set eyes on him since he and Meg parted.

'Patrick? Hurt?'

'Mm hmm. He bought it, sweetie. I saw it.'

She wanted to take him in her arms, kiss away the pain, but it wasn't possible. Pain like that didn't just disappear. She reached across the table and took his hands, squeezing them gently, trying not to cry because she had no right, she'd never been that close to Patrick.

'Are you sure? Couldn't he have . . . oh God, Andy, what happened?'

'We'd been escorting bombers to Düsseldorf;

Patrick's kite was hit, I don't know what got him, it might have been flak, but I'd bet on a JU88 myself. His kite broke up ... he didn't have a chance, he plummeted past me ... I can't tell you how bloody *helpless* I felt, how sick to my stomach! He didn't have time to pull his parachute cord, I doubt he was even conscious ... I got myself back on an even keel somehow ... but coming back I threw up all over myself. Twice.'

The waitress brought the coffee and teacakes. No one spoke as she placed them carefully on the table. Christie just held his hands and watched as the slow, painful tears came to his eyes and trickled slowly down his lean cheeks. Andy bent his head; she could hear his breathing change as he fought for control – and won.

Presently he looked up, took his hands away from her and wiped his eyes unashamedly with the heels of both hands. It was a boyish gesture, but there was nothing boyish about the look in his eyes. He sighed and picked up his teacake but made no attempt to eat it.

'So you see, I knew he was a goner. I watched him down as far as I could ... no 'chute.'

'Poor old Pat,' Christie said softly after a moment. 'And how agonising it must have been for you, seeing it all but being powerless to help. Do you want to leave here now? If you can't face it ...'

'No, it's all right.' Andy bit into the teacake. 'Life goes on – Pat would be the first to say that. But it really makes you think. So many of us, the ones who

131

flew together from the beginning, who've messed together, have gone for a burton. You can't help wondering when it'll be your turn.'

'It won't – it can't . . . don't talk like that,' Christie said wildly, leaning across the table again and taking his free hand. 'Please, Andy darling, don't talk like that. There's a future for us, the war will finish and we'll be together, I'm sure of it.'

He shrugged, finished his teacake, picked up his coffee cup.

'Perhaps. Perhaps. But I've got such an empty feeling inside, Chris my old darling. Such an aching, empty sort of feeling.'

Christie abandoned her own coffee and stood up.

'Right. Come on, I can't stay here; let's walk.'

Out in the cold, sunny street again she glanced indecisively around her. Where to go? She knew, suddenly, that she wanted to be alone with Andy, that for her at any rate, there was only one way to comfort him properly. She told him she was taking him to an hotel and he nodded, letting himself be led through the town until they reached the Old Bear, a pub with a few rooms for letting over the main bar.

Christie pushed him into a chair and went over to the woman behind the desk. Filled with aching pity, she felt no shame at her enquiry.

'Do you have a room, please? Just for a few hours. My husband's so tired, he needs to rest.'

The woman glanced quickly down at Christie's bare left hand, then across at Andy, slumped in the chair, his eyes fixed vacantly ahead. She opened her mouth, closed it again, and pulled a large, leather-bound book towards her, opening it and running a finger down the page.

'Number 6, second floor,' she said. 'That'll be ten and six, my dear.'

Christie only had five shillings. She looked appealingly at the woman.

'We don't need a room for the night ... just for a few hours. I – I've only got five bob on me, and I don't want to trouble my husband for money.'

The woman behind the desk shrugged. She was elderly, in her fifties, with thickly curling grey hair and tired blue eyes.

'Five bob will do,' she said. 'You can be out by six?'

'Yes. Thanks very much.'

Christie handed over the money, then went back to Andy.

'Get up, darling. I've got us a room for a few hours. We'll lie on the bed and talk and ... here, have the key. It's on the second floor.'

Andy sat where he was, frowning down at the key she had thrust into his hand. Then he stood up.

'I don't know why, but I'm absolutely exhausted. Are you coming up as well?'

'Yes, for a bit. I'll leave when you go to sleep if you like,' Christie said as they mounted the stairs. 'I thought you'd prefer a room to trying to sleep in the cinema.'

'Thanks,' Andy mumbled. They reached the first landing and Christie ushered him up the narrow, uncarpeted stairs to the second floor. There they found a tiny room with a sloping ceiling and a large double bed. There was just about room for the washstand with a mirror standing on it and a rickety chair. But it was fresh and clean, the window half-open to let in the iced wine of the winter sunshine, the bed-sheets crisp and white.

'Take your shoes off,' Christie ordered Andy as he slumped down on the bed. 'Better take your uniform off too – I'll turn my back.'

Andy, undressing, looked up at her suddenly and grinned. It was a pale grin, but she could see that he was coming out of the horror that had engulfed him when he told her of Patrick's death.

'Never, in my wildest dreams, did I imagine that you would try to seduce me like this, Christie Bellis! Ordering me into bed . . . and what will you do whilst I snore away?'

'Never you mind. I'm taking my skirt off though . . . and my jacket. Just imagine the fuss if I went back to the station all rumpled, without a proper explanation.'

She intended to lie on top of the covers, to comfort him with her nearness. She slid her skirt and jacket off, then undid her tie and kicked off her shoes. Andy, already down to underwear, turned and looked at her, his eyes widening, the expression on his face changing subtly from humorous amusement to smouldering desire.

'Christie . . . oh my God, let me hold you!'

He crossed the narrow space between them in a stride and she was in his arms, clutched convulsively close to his broad chest. Christie clutched back, suddenly aware that Andy was not the only person in the room with appetites which, until now, had seemed under at least a semblance of control.

No longer. They collapsed on to the bed, Christie shivering with excitement and suspense whilst Andy undid her suspenders, stripped her stockings off one by one, gently wriggled her out of her dreadful RAF blackouts, and even managed to extract her from her issue suspender belt, doing it all so neatly, so expertly, that the awful suspicion crossed Christie's mind that he must undress WAAFs often. She struggled into a sitting position and tried to pull the covers over her but he took her hands and opened them up and kissed the palms, then kissed up her arms to her shoulders, her neck . . . her lips. And suddenly nothing mattered but Andy, what he had done was done lovingly, with care and gentleness . . . all she wanted was to please him, to help him to forget the loss of his friend, and if undressing her helped in this then he might undress her with her blessing.

'Andy? I didn't mean . . . you must think me dreadful . . .'

He pushed her gently back onto the pillows and stroked her cheek. He said, 'Hush,' and pushed the damp hair away from her neck, spreading it out on the pillow with great care, his hands trembling. She could feel her face hot with shyness and awakened desire but she met his eyes, did not look away. Having arranged her hair to his satisfaction Andy knelt beside her, looking down at her, letting his gaze sweep the length of her body. Christie was sure she could feel his eyes drawing a rose-pink blush across her flesh and so strong was the impression that she looked down at herself, curious suddenly over her own nakedness which could bring such an awed look to the face of a man she knew to be strong, self-reliant.

Milk-white and tender, her naked body lay on the blue bed-cover, with the soft dark blur of her pubic hair and the brighter, deeper pink of her nipples the only splashes of colour. I look like a painting, Christie thought, ever so much nicer than I look with clothes on. I wonder why nudity is somehow wrong? I look like Eve must have looked, in the Garden of Eden, like a woman was meant to look, yet if anyone else saw me like this they'd think *how shocking, what a shameless hussy*!

She transferred her gaze to Andy's face, still with that look of awe imprinted on it. As she watched, his hand stole out and touched her breast, then cupped it firmly. Immediately, the nipple hardened, peaked, standing to attention like a small soldier on parade.

The thought brought an involuntary bubble of laughter rising to her lips. She glanced up at Andy, about to share the joke, and the laughter died unborn. Andy was crying. He released her breast to scrub at the tears which were running down his face just as they'd done in the cafe, over their cups of coffee.

'Andy? What is it?'

'You're so beautiful, so bloody beautiful! I want you . . . well, you can see that, but it wouldn't be fair, it isn't on.'

136

He sat back on his heels, still in his underpants and socks. His underpants looked uncomfortably tight and Christie realised that this must be what Shanna referred to, rather oddly, as a hard-on, the physical manifestation of his wanting her. She took his hand which had balled itself into a fist and uncurled the fingers, then kissed his palm, only moving her mouth from his flesh to question his last remark.

'What isn't on? I don't understand. Andy, darling, I love you and I want you to be happy. Let's get under the covers, though. I'm getting most awfully cold.'

'It's not on to take advantage of you, when . . . when I know I can't offer you anything, not even a future,' Andy said. 'I didn't intend . . . I'm not the sort that carries a rubber johnny wherever I go on the off-chance, I can't let you take the risk . . .'

Christie rolled over and got off the bed. She pulled the covers back and dived inside, then shivered exaggeratedly, hugging herself with her arms crossed over her breasts.

'Stop pontificating and help me to get warm, even if you don't want to do anything else. Then we'll go happily off to sleep for a few hours and we'll both feel better.'

He sighed, then rolled into bed with her. He kept his back to her so Christie curled round him and put her arms around his waist and then, as they grew warm and comfortable, she slotted her hands into the elastic of his underpants and pressed her chilly fingers on to his warm, well-muscled stomach, kneading the firm flesh.

He gave what might have been a groan and turned like a whiplash in her arms. Strong hands caressed her back, her waist, slid down to her buttocks, pulling her urgently close. Then he began to kiss her. Christie's arms went round his neck and she strained against him, feeling the whole length of his aroused body against hers, enjoying the sensations which arrowed through her; love, desire – even fear, spiced as it was with a wild anticipation of what was to come.

His hands and his mouth seemed to know just what her body wanted, needed. Yet when something he was doing drove her to cry out, to move with him, he drew back suddenly, took her by the shoulders, stopped the frantic, shuddering movements of her pelvis against his.

'Chris . . . is it all right? Can I . . . ?'

'Oh Andy, Andy . . . don't stop, don't stop!'

Unexpectedly, he chuckled.

'Dearest Chris! I love you, love you, love you!'

He bent his head and kissed her, long and passionately. Then he flipped her on to her back and began to stroke the insides of her thighs, to kiss her neck, her breasts. When he had gentled and coaxed and brought her to a point where he could have done anything with her, when she was on fire for him, he took her at last.

Christie clung to his strong shoulders and clenched her teeth and screwed her eyes up until she saw scarlet and black patterns inside her lids and felt the sudden, tearing pain and accepted it gladly because it was only through pain that she could give Andy the forgetfulness he needed. And then the pain was gone, forgotten, and ecstasy replaced it as, together, they began the slow, sensuous climb to the heights.

Christie woke. She was warm, cosy, comfortable. The room in which she lay was grey with fading light . . . where the hell was she? She moved, and felt an arm looped round her waist and in the same moment, realised that she was naked, as was the owner of the arm.

She opened her eyes properly this time and saw Andy's wrist-watch, still on his wrist, lying on the pillow only inches from her eyes. She read the face and it was five o'clock. Remembrance came flooding back; Patrick's death, Andy's deep unhappiness . . . their love-making. Remembered pleasure brought heat rushing to her cheeks; so *that* was what it was all about – gosh, she understood a lot of things now which had been a closed book to her before. Why Shanna was prepared to do all the things she did . . . if *that* was the carrot dangling on the end of the stick no wonder she went to such lengths! Christie picked up the hand lying on her waist and transferred it to her breast; it automatically tightened on her and Christie's breathing speeded up. All over her body little pulses and nerves began to sit up and take notice; watch out, she's going to start all that business again – are you ready? Her stomach, normally a staid and respectable member of the body politic, gave an extraordinary surge of anticipation which sent startling sensations arrowing all over her body, strong enough to make Christie give a little mew of protest. Andy was asleep, he needed his rest, he'd had a bad time . . .

His face nuzzled against her neck, his hands pulled her round to face him.

'Christie? Oh my God, what's the time? Should we get dressed, get out of here?'

'We've got another hour,' Christie murmured. 'It's five o'clock, we've got the room until six. But I suppose we might as well go now, since we're both awake.'

The mouth which was kissing along her collar-bone smiled; she could feel it, knew he was smiling.

'An hour? Oh, in that case, I can think of something far nicer to do than getting dressed. Pretty, pretty little Chris, we can make love again!'

'I don't think we should,' Christie murmured unconvincingly. 'What about getting ourselves a meal? We missed lunch, you know.'

'So we did. Which would you rather . . . *this*, or beans on toast?'

Christie sighed and squiggled closer.

'Guess,' she said.

At six they left the room and went wandering out into the icy darkness. They held hands, didn't talk much. They found a tiny restaurant in a side street where they paid the regulation five shillings apiece and had an adequate meal but probably neither of them could have said what they had eaten. They held hands under the table and smiled into each other's eyes and were very polite about the food when the elderly waiter asked them if they'd enjoyed their meal.

'I suppose I'd better catch the transport at ten-thirty,' Christie said presently, as they wandered up to the King George Hotel and went into the bar for a last drink. It was warm in here, and dimly lit. Sitting at a quiet corner table they could hold hands, talk, plan their next meeting. 'I think the last bus has probably gone and I used all my money on the room.'

Andy chuckled. He was looking relaxed, easy, his cap on the back of his head, his reddy-brown eyes sparkling, the curly smile much in evidence. What a wonderful thing love-making is, if it gives a bloke back his hope for the future, Christie found herself thinking. If everyone did it once a day, the world would be a happier place. Why, Hitler might not have bothered to declare war if only he'd had someone to make love with on a regular basis!

But it didn't work like that, of course, or Shanna would be the jolliest girl in the whole world, and the happiest. You didn't have to be a psychologist or whatever to know that Shanna was very unhappy a lot of the time. Indeed, one or two of the girls in her billet had said that they felt deeply depressed after having it off as they termed it, with some lucky feller.

You've got to be in love with the feller, Christie decided at last, sipping the small sweet sherry which Andy had bought her to keep the cold out. Not that she needed anything to warm her, not with happiness and contentment filling her to bursting point.

'Christie? Sweetheart, we took a helluva risk this

afternoon, d'you realise that? What if . . .' Andy lowered his voice even further. 'What if you find you're . . . you know?'

'Pregnant, d'you mean? Well, I leave the WAAF and we get married,' Christie said. 'Or don't you want to? We'll do what you want, of course.'

She said it, but it was lip-service only. She knew Andy wanted to marry her because that would mean being together for always and that was what they both wanted most in the world, she knew it without being told.

'I'd marry you tomorrow,' Andy said at once. 'Sooner, if I could. But . . . things happen to blokes like me. Look . . . look at Pat.'

The shadow of it was back in his face, his eyes. Just for a moment he looked like the haunted, exhausted man who had met her off the bus. Then she put her hand on his and the look fled.

'No, don't look at Pat or any of the others. You're all different people, you fliers, and you're going to come through it, my dearest love. How many more ops have you got before you go armchair flying?'

'Before I'm desk-bound, I suppose you mean. Dunno. Eight? Ten? Something like that.'

It was an affectation to pretend that you weren't counting, didn't care. She smiled at him tenderly, loving him more with every moment that passed. She was strong, confident – strong enough for both of them.

'Well there you are then. Take great care, love me very much, and we'll be all right. Honest.'

'And ... and if there's a baby? If something happens and I can't marry you? Oh Chris, I never should have done it, I shouldn't have let you persuade me.'

He grinned at her, but there was unease behind the grin, she could sense it, almost see it.

'If there's a baby ...' she paused, thinking about it. A baby! The last thing she wanted ... or was it? It would be Andy's baby ... that was a good thought, something to cling to. 'If there's a baby it'll be a part of you, so that's all right,' she ended.

Around them the pub buzzed with conversation, laughter, shouts. In their corner they held hands, smiled into each other's eyes.

'You're a great girl, Chris. I don't deserve you, but I'm so bloody glad we chanced it, found each other.'

'I'm glad too,' Christie said. 'And don't forget, you're going to speak to whatsizname about leave over Christmas.'

'Squadron Leader Buckingham, you mean. I won't forget. I'll have a word tomorrow and ring you between seven and eight. Unless you can get off again?'

Christie pulled a face.

'Not tomorrow. I'm on ten till two and then midnight to five a.m. I hate it when the shifts double up like that but it doesn't happen often. I'll be in the mess between seven and eight, then. Oh, Andy, I do hope you can swing it; I'd so love to take you home with me!'

'I'll do my best. And now let's make tracks; we've

got about ten minutes to reach the square and get aboard our transports.'

Shanna and Meg were walking across the concrete towards the mess when the gharry from town drew up. Meg tugged at Shanna's arm.

'I bet Christie's aboard since she must have missed the last bus. Come on, let's go over.'

Shanna was agreeable; she liked Christie and anyway she wanted to see who else was on the gharry. There was a bloke who she quite fancied . . . she'd not seen him this evening, he might well have gone into Winchester. If he was alone then she might have a word, if he was with a WAAF then at least she need no longer waste a thought on him.

Shanna's bloke was nowhere to be seen but Christie was aboard. She climbed down and smiled a greeting, then linked arms with them, Shanna on her right, Meg on her left.

'Hello, girls, nice of you to wait for me. How did the rehearsal go?'

'Grand, thanks. And we won at table tennis, didn't we, Shan, so we're feeling quite pleased with ourselves. How's Andy?'

'Wonderful,' Christie said. She squeezed their arms. 'He's going to try to get leave so he can come home with me at Christmas. Oh, I can't tell you how much I want to show him everything – the farm, my parents, the dogs . . . everything!'

'Well, good luck,' Meg said. 'What did you do? See a flick?'

There was a short silence, then Christie hurried into speech.

'No, we didn't go to the cinema; Andy wasn't in the mood. We walked, had – had a meal, went into a pub . . .'

'You walked?' Meg said incredulously. 'You walked from ten in the morning until ten at night? Tell us another!'

'Oh well, as I said, we ate, and walked, and talked, we had a couple of drinks . . . good gracious, I can't remember exactly what we did.'

'Well, did you go shopping?' Meg said, whilst Shanna stared from one face to the other. 'Did you buy my elastic?'

'We looked everywhere for some, but we couldn't find any, not even a tiny bit,' Christie gabbled. 'Nor the buttons . . . I'm awfully sorry, Meg, but as I said we did try and it took quite a while, too.'

'Oh well, never mind. There's a lorry going into Southampton at the weekend, perhaps I could try there. I know the bombing has been awful, but there must be some shops still standing.'

'Right. Look, I'm going to see if I can get a shower before we go to bed. See you presently.'

Christie unlinked her arms from theirs and hurried off and Shanna tucked her hand into Meg's elbow.

'Well, what about that?' she said. 'She couldnae fool a babe in arms, that one.'

'Why should she want to?' Meg said, as they strolled into their billet. 'She's ever so straight-forward, is Christie.'

145

Shanna chuckled.

'Spent twelve hours walking and talking? My foot,' she said derisively. 'Carryin' on in corners, that's what they were doing. You mark my words, she'll be after that Andy now like a cat after a mouse.'

Meg shook Shanna's hand off her arm and turned to give her a long, chilly look.

'Don't judge others by yourself, Shan,' she said coldly. 'Christie's not like that, she's just crazy for Andy, that's all.'

'Oh aye? Mebbe, mebbe,' Shanna said. 'It's none of my business, anyroad. Sorry I spoke, I'm sure.'

'You should be,' Meg said, not mincing words. 'Wash your mouth out, Aircraftwoman! Are you coming to the ablutions?'

'I dinnae think I'll bother,' Shanna said, beginning to remove her clothing. 'I'll wash tomorrow.'

'Or the next day,' Meg said, but her voice was teasing, comfortable once more. Shanna thought herself forgiven and was glad of it, but she was still sure she was right. That Christie had been having it, whatever anyone said.

Meg heard Christie singing gaily in the shower and called out to her, then began her own wash. Presently Christie emerged from the cubicle, pink and damp-haired, with her eyes shining and a gloss on her which Meg hadn't seen for some time.

'You look pleased with yourself,' she observed. 'What's up?'

'I am pleased; Andy and I do feel ... well, I

think we'll probably get married when the war's over.'

Meg beamed.

'Congratulations; what brought this on?'

She was watching Christie's face and saw the flush suddenly drain away, leaving her friend pale, her eyes shadowed.

'Oh . . . oh Meg . . . I wish . . . oh, I'm such a selfish, horrible person, I never thought, I . . .'

Meg looked down at her feet in the sturdy black shoes, then at her hands, gripping her flannel as though she was trying to wring its neck.

'It's Patrick, isn't it? He's dead, isn't he?'

'His plane broke up in the air,' Christie said helplessly. 'Oh Meg, poor Pat, and poor Andy. They were so close.'

'Poor bloody Gillian,' Meg said softly. 'Such a pretty girl . . . I'm really sorry about Pat but I'm glad you told me. I'd rather know.'

'I'd forgotten,' Christie said humbly. 'Andy was so upset you see, it put it out of my head. Who was Gillian, anyway?'

'Pat's fiancée. I thought I told you about her.'

'I don't think you told me her name. Oh Meg, I'm so sorry.'

Meg began to run water into a basin.

'Damn, it's nearly cold,' she said absently. 'I suppose you ran off most of the water for your shower. It's all right, I said. He was a nice bloke, though. I shan't forget him.'

'Nor me,' Christie said remorsefully. 'I was upset

when the two of you broke it off, but now... perhaps it was for the best.'

'Probably,' Meg said calmly. She soaped her hands, face, and neck, then rinsed herself briskly in the almost cold water. She groped blindly for the towel and felt Christie press it into her grasp. Rubbing hard, she dried herself off then bundled her washing things back into her sponge-bag and set off for the billet. 'Come on, race you back to bed!'

They reached the billet with Christie a whisker ahead and burst, laughing, into the room. Sue was already in bed, Shanna just a hump under the bedclothes. Meg and Christie put their clothes on their lockers, hung their greatcoats on the hooks beside their beds and got into bed. Within two minutes they had got out again, dragged their greatcoats off the hooks and spread them over their blankets.

'My nose always freezes outside the covers, but if I put it under I nearly asphyxiate,' Christie remarked. She sat up in bed in her blue and white striped pyjamas and reached for her clothes. 'If I wrap my cardigan round my head and sort of cuddle my nose into it . . .'

Shanna emerged from her covers like a tortoise poking its head out of its shell. She fixed round, accusing eyes on Christie.

'Chris, what's that mark on your neck?'

Meg watched as her friend's pale complexion slowly deepened from rose through to beetroot. She glanced curiously at the v of Christie's pyjamas. There was a mark . . . you could only just see it, but there was something . . .

'Shut up, Shanna! I must have caught myself on something in the shower.'

'On a feller, I reckon,' Shanna mumbled under her breath. 'Och well, at least I'm no' the only one.'

Sue snorted. Christie dived under the covers again. Meg arranged her greatcoat primly to give maximum coverage and then lay down again herself. She thought of Patrick, the golden boy, lying dead. She thought of Gillian the beautiful, mourning him. She thought of Christie being loved by Andy, and of Shanna restlessly searching for a reason for living.

And what about Meg? Plain, practical Meg was doing very nicely without any bloody man to muck her life up.

She thought about the rehearsal, about the two young men they'd played table tennis with, laughed with, had a drink with. Presently, calmly, she slept.

She dreamed of Patrick, dying with him a hundred times. And wept in her sleep.

6

'Well, what's the verdict? Any leave at all?'

Christie, Meg, Shanna and Sue were clustered round the notice-board on which Christmas leave had just been posted. Christie and Meg already knew they were having Christmas week because they hadn't had a proper leave before; but now Shanna and Sue turned to them, Sue smiling rather guiltily, Shanna determinedly.

'Five days for us both, only it's mucked up our plans, rather,' Sue said. 'I'm from six a.m. on Saturday 21st and Shanna's from six a.m. on December 30th, which takes in the New Year. A bit of a bloody nuisance since we meant to go home together. There's always room for another one in my house but no chance of that with those dates. I'm real sorry, Shan, love. Still, Mam and the kids 'll be glad to see me – I can just about make Liverpool if I leave last thing the day before.'

'By train?' Christie said doubtfully. 'I didn't know there was a train that ran that late. And it'll mean going through London, won't it?'

'No, not by train; I'm not that mad,' Sue said,

pushing her cap forward onto her nose and raising her chin like a guards officer to peer at Christie under the peak. 'I'll hitch-hike. Someone will give me a lift.'

'What about you, Shanna?' Meg asked. She and Christie had already plotted their own journey, with much delighted anticipation. Andy had not managed to get the same leave as Christie, he only had three days, but he would join her in Norfolk on Christmas Eve if everything went according to plan. Since his mother was dead and his father lived in London with his second wife, he was delighted to be sharing Christmas with the Bellises.

Shanna smiled.

'I'll be fine, just fine. I'll mebbe go up to Town, see a show or something. Even if I only lie in bed for five days it'll be a nice change.'

'I don't think Meg was talking about your leave; it's being alone here over Christmas,' Christie said gently.

Shanna shrugged.

'They say Christmas is good on the station – to make up for being here, I suppose. And Sue will be back on Boxing Day and you two on the 27th, so I'll only be on my tod five days.'

'I suppose it's not so long,' Sue admitted. 'But it's right over the holiday . . . I wonder, if I went to see the FO . . .'

'It doesnae matter,' Shanna insisted. 'It'll no' be too bad – what's five days, after all?'

'Yeah, you're right, and anyway it's time we got to work,' Sue said suddenly. 'I've got an officer

152

champing at the bit, waiting for me to take him somewhere. See you later, girls.'

'I want to go into the village, see if I can get those buttons,' Meg said as Shanna and Sue hurried off to their respective jobs. 'Or we might cadge a lift into Portsmouth; you did say you couldn't find any buttons in Winchester, didn't you?'

'I forgot the buttons; it was the elastic we couldn't find,' Christie said, tongue in cheek. What a liar she was becoming! When Andy had told her he couldn't get the full week off she had actually contemplated ringing her mother up and pretending that some of her own leave had been cancelled – it was only the fact that she and Audrey Robbins, who lived in Bury St Edmunds, had agreed to journey together most of the way that made her put the thought aside. Audrey was new to the station, having recently retrained as a plotter, and had confessed to Christie that she had been dreading the long and lonely journey home. Besides, quite apart from keeping an eye on little Audrey she knew that since Andy would either be flying or on standby she wouldn't be able to see much of him during that time anyway. And the rail journey was such a beast of a trek, she would probably spend her extra days travelling.

Of course this applied to Andy too; he had an eighth share in the small car which he occasionally used, but he didn't have either the juice or the money to drive to Norfolk and back, even if he had felt justified in taking the car away for such a prolonged period.

Still, there was hitch-hiking. Perhaps he could do that and arrive a bit sooner. Christie, with her rail pass and a whole week at her disposal, knew she would go by train. Sue might hitch-hike, Shanna wouldn't think twice about doing it, but even the thought of such a thing made Christie nervous. Anyway, Andy had said it was risky and life was fraught enough without taking chances which hadn't been forced upon you.

'Are you telling me that I might get the buttons in Winchester?' Meg said suspiciously. 'When are we on?'

'This evening. Five till ten.'

'I thought so. Is there a bus from the village into a town? The transport won't be going until late afternoon . . . Christie, do stop gazing into space and grinning; are you coming shopping with me or not?'

'I'm coming, I'm coming,' Christie said hastily. 'We might find some scented soap – my mother loves scented soap, particularly rose-geranium.'

'Pigs might fly,' Meg said caustically. 'Scented soap indeed – you'll be suggesting perfume next!'

'Sometimes I feel as if I've spent most of this last year in trains, going from one place to another, like some sort of modern Flying Dutchman,' Christie said, helping Audrey to gather her kit-bag and paper carriers together as the train approached Stowmarket. 'But at least we'll sleep in our own beds tonight. Have a lovely week, Audrey.'

On the first stage of their journey Meg and another girl, Ruby, had been with them but now it was just she and Audrey and a carriage full of strangers, though most were in uniform of one sort or another. Two soldiers, a naval rating and a leading aircraftman, an ATS private and a smart-looking girl clad in the distinctive land-army gear meant that most if not all of the services were represented.

'Thanks, Chris; I hope you have a super time, too,' Audrey said. 'Look, I'm going to have to hang about a bit at the station until my connection comes; would it be a good idea if I were to ring your parents, tell them you'll be arriving in Norwich Thorpe in an hour or so? I'm going to ring my own parents, so it's no trouble.'

'Oh Audrey, would you? I'd be most awfully grateful. It would save me hanging about, though I s'pose I could go in the buffet, if it's open. Let me give you some money . . .'

'It's all right, honestly, you'd do the same for me,' Audrey said as the train slowed. 'Could you possibly give me a hand with my kit-bag? I've never really got the knack.'

Christie heaved the kit-bag, already hung about with various extras, onto Audrey's shoulder and picked up the carrier bags which contained, she knew, the family's presents. She looked around the carriage, but everyone else seemed comfortably ensconced, no one else seemed about to get off, so she let down the window with a rattle – it wasn't a corridor train – and leaned out, trying to see the station through the windy darkness. It couldn't be far, she could hear voices . . . ah, but they probably came from other passengers on the train, also leaning out. Better wait until the train came to a complete halt.

'Oy, moi woman, pull you that winder up, can't you? Tha's fair cuttin' me in two and I weren't exactly 'ot to start with!'

The uninhibitedly broad Norfolk dialect warmed Christie's heart and she turned and grinned at the grubby little soldier who had spoken. He grinned back, revealing a mouth full of broken and blackened teeth.

'Sorry,' Christie said, pulling up the window again. 'I'm always scared of missing a station – the next one is Stowmarket, isn't it?'

'Oh ah, tha's Stowmarket next all right,' the soldier agreed. 'But not for another mile or more – I keeps an eye open for Talbot's duck-pond and when that come up then I start gettin' moi traps togither. I've got to know this jarney blindfold so I won't let you miss it, don't you frit.'

'It's not her, it's me, ' Audrey said. 'Oh, I do hope the train does stop, I'd never dare to pull the communication cord, but I can't bear to think of missing my connection – we've spent the whole of our first day's leave travelling as it is and we're still a way from home.'

'You aren't alone,' the soldier said, and there were nods from several other servicemen and women in the compartment. 'They give me three days ... three days, I ask you, what can I do in three blummen' days?'

'Not a lot, when you have to spend one day getting there and one getting back,' Christie agreed. 'But we've been in since January and this is our first proper leave, so we're really looking forward to it.'

'Yes, but I *still* don't want to spend it all on Stowmarket platform because I've missed the connection for Bury,' Audrey put in. She looked hopefully round the carriage, shyness suspended by need. 'I suppose there isn't anyone else here going to Bury St Edmunds?'

Heads were shaken.

'No, I'm for Norwich . . . I'm goin' through to Great Yarmouth . . . I'm gettin' out at Diss . . .'

'Never mind, moi woman,' the soldier said cheerfully. 'I'm out at Stow, I'll see you on to your train . . . here, siddown, I'll tell you when.'

Christie, nose pressed to the glass, still missed the famous duck-pond but the soldier heaved his kit-bag off the rack over his head, slung it on one shoulder, and took Audrey's carriers in one calloused hand.

'Right; don't git down till I tell you,' he ordered as the train slowed to a crawl. 'Ah . . . here come the platform . . . any minute now!'

He crashed the window down, jumped out, steadied himself and then held out a hand to Audrey.

'Out wi' you! Well, where's a porter or someone in a fancy cap what'll tell us where to go next?'

'Cheerio, Chris . . . don't forget, we're going to catch the same train back,' Audrey gasped, turning to slam the door shut again. 'You'll be aboard first . . . oh, I'll ring you!'

'Bye, Audrey, love to your parents. Happy Christmas!' Christie shrieked, leaning out of the window as

JENNY FELIX

her friend's laden figure trudged away from her. 'Have a great time. See you in a week!'

She waited until Audrey and the soldier disappeared, then drew back inside the train again and pulled up the window. She smiled round at her fellow passengers through the faint haze of cigarette smoke.

'Well, only another hour or so and we'll be in the city,' she declared. 'I hope there won't be a raid tonight.'

'Not likely,' the leading aircraftman said judiciously, staring out of the window at the clouds racing across the dark sky. 'We might get some snow. But it's too wild for a raid I'd guess.'

'Can't be sure, though,' someone else reminded them. 'All you need is one blighter wanting to win medals . . . one bomb . . .'

'Or a clear sky,' someone else put in. 'It ain't clear here, but that don't mean to say it ain't clear over Norwich.'

'They're certainly doing their damnedest to flatten the whole country,' the ATS said bitterly. 'My mum's living with my grandfather; Southampton got wiped out, near as dammit, three weeks ago. I got compassionate leave, but now I'm rejoining my regiment in time for Christmas.'

'Southampton? I'm stationed near there,' Christie said, but all this information earned her was a reproving frown.

'Walls have ears,' the ATS girl reminded her. 'Mind, I guessed it when you said you'd not had leave. Work with a rake, do you?'

158

Christie, abashed, nodded, realising that most of the compartment would have no idea what she and the other girl were talking about. The ATS girl, however, smiled knowingly.

'Same as my sister Pansy. She was saying last time I spoke to her . . .'

'Not Pansy Wilberforce? Good Lord, isn't it a small world? Pansy said she'd a sister in the ATS. You must be Violet.'

The ATS girl grinned and nodded vigorously.

'That's it – Vi Wilberforce, that's me. And you?'

'Christie Bellis,' Christie said, holding out a hand. They shook vigorously. 'We were so sorry for Pansy when the news came – but it could have been a lot worse – none of your family were hurt, were they?'

'How are you, Christie? Pansy's mentioned you. Nah, it were only the house what was hit, Mum an' the kids was all in the public shelter in the vaults under the town walls . . . bit of luck, because it was the first time they'd gone there.'

'Well, let's hope there's not a raid tonight, not anywhere,' Christie said fervently. She had been told by Southampton people about the horrendous raids on the last night in November and the first in December, in which almost four hundred people had been killed. 'Where was your dad during the raid, or is he in the services, too?'

'ARP,' Violet said laconically. 'Busy night for him, but he'd seen the family off to the shelter before he left for work; one comfort. But me aunt was dug out of the ruins – she had a flat above a sweet shop – and she's still in hospital.'

'It's a terrible war,' Christie said. 'Sometimes I think we're having it easier in the services than people in civvy street.'

'Could be,' Violet said. 'I hope the transport's at Thorpe Station to meet me, but I'll get some shut-eye now, just in case I spend the rest of the night hanging about on the platform.'

The nearer they got to Norwich the more excited Christie felt, so falling asleep was out of the question. But she must have snoozed for presently she became aware that the train, which had slowed, was picking up speed, and then she felt a lurch and heard a crash and woke, startled.

'What was that?'

'Buffers,' the ATS private explained kindly. 'Reckon the driver wasn't braking quite hard enough and ran into 'em . . . just enough to wake us all up the hard way!'

'Wake us . . . have we arrived then? Is this Norwich Thorpe?'

'It's your home town, not mine,' Violet said, but she let down the window and put her head out. 'Aye, we're at journey's end. Come to think of it, where else could we hit the buffers but at the terminus?'

There was some good-natured laughter at this and people began to get their gear down from the racks and someone flung the window up and wrenched the door open.

'Cheers, Chris; have a good leave,' Violet said,

heaving her kit-bag up onto her shoulder. 'Happy Christmas, one and all!'

'Bye; I'll tell Pansy we met when I get back to the station,' Christie called as the other girl in her khaki uniform climbed down onto the platform. 'Happy Christmas, Vi!'

The platform was long and dark, the lighting in the station foyer dim. But Christie saw her brother Frank at once, looking taller and handsomer than ever in his best blues. She yelled his name, her voice shrill with excitement, and despite the noise and bustle – for though it was getting on for midnight the station was crowded with travellers and those meeting them – he heard her immediately. He pushed through the crowd towards her, his smile much in evidence, took her kit-bag and gave her a hard brotherly hug and a smacking kiss on one travel-stained cheek.

'Hi, Christie . . . did you salute? I'm your superior officer, you know! Good God, girl, is that your cap? What did you do with it – sit on it? The bloody train's late, of course, but a friend of yours telephoned. Dad's got a gilt farrowing so I said I'd come and meet you . . . Mum's doing a marathon bake, Christmas cakes for the boys I gather . . . is it terribly trite to say you've grown, changed . . . I don't know, you look different, anyway. Come on, little sister, let's get weaving.'

He hustled her out of the station and across to the car. Christie remembered his little sports model which she could hear approaching the house two miles away, but this was not Frank's car. She raised an eyebrow.

'Dad's,' Frank said. 'He sold the Armstrong Siddeley and bought this Ford truck – the Armstrong drank juice, you know. Besides, this is much more practical.'

'Why d'you call him Dad and not Daddy though?' Christie asked as she climbed into the passenger seat. 'It sounds odd.'

'Yeah, but Daddy and Mummy sound like an old Shirley Temple film,' Frank said, climbing behind the wheel and slamming his door shut. 'Dave and I talked about it; we decided Dad came more naturally to us than Father, which was the alternative. Mind, do you?'

'No,' Christie decided after some thought. 'In fact I never say Daddy in the mess, just to him, I suppose. Will they mind if I use it as well?'

'Don't suppose they'll notice,' Frank said, starting the engine and putting the truck into first gear. 'You've got a week?'

'Leave, d'you mean? That's it, one measly week. And . . . Frank . . .'

They drove out of the station concourse and turned right on to Thorpe Road. Christie strained her eyes through the darkness but could make out very little. She was home. Of course the village was her real home, but ever since she started at the High School she'd grown to know and love the city and to regard it as her special place.

'Yes old girl?'

'I – I've asked a friend home for a few days. He's coming the day after tomorrow, all being well. His name's Andy Todd.'

'Oh? Who's gone and got herself a feller, then?'

She couldn't tell from his voice whether he was pleased or upset; he sounded amused, but that was Frank all over. He never revealed his true feelings. Though he probably didn't care much about her feller one way or the other; brothers didn't, they had their own lives to lead.

'I have. Andy's . . . oh, Andy's special. You'll like him – not that I care, I mean he's too important to me to worry even if you and Dave hate him. Only you won't, because . . . are you still seeing Paula?'

Christie hadn't liked Paula, a beautiful, poised young woman from a wealthy family, who despised other members of her own sex. At least she had despised Christie and Christie's friends, and had been heard to make slighting remarks about Christie's older cousins Janet and Helen, who were very pretty and never made slighting remarks about anyone.

'Paula? Good lord, what a memory you've got, I'd almost forgotten Paula. No, she's what you might call a part of my past, I suppose.'

'Good. I don't like girls with cutaway nostrils,' Christie said lazily, leaning back in her seat.

They had just passed the end of Harvey Lane. Her favourite cousin lived on the corner there, in a big house set amongst tall beech trees with a marvellous garden and a lily pond which had been the scene of several childhood scrapes years ago. She and Bea had spent happy holidays up to their knees in mud and newts . . . Bea was a year older than Christie, though, and had got herself involved in something very senior and hush-hush in the Army. She'd gone abroad in '39 and though the two girls had exchanged letters for a bit, somehow the correspondence had lapsed.

'Did Paula have cutaway nostrils? How ghastly . . . well, Celia's got a pert little nose, with not a cutaway nostril in sight,' Frank said dreamily. 'What are cutaway nostrils, anyway?'

'Who is Celia? ' Christie countered sharply. She was half asleep . . . ah, there was the River Green, looking as romantic as ever . . . and had no desire to describe Paula's hated nostrils to anyone.

'Who is Celia, wha-a-at is she-he, that all her swains comme-hend her,' Frank sang, bumping the heel of his hand on the horn at the end of each stanza and probably waking half Thorpe St Andrew as they swept through. 'She's my latest floozie, dear Christie.'

'Oh? Celia who?'

'You don't know her. She wasn't at school with you, she doesn't ride to hounds or belong to the Pony Club. But she's the best thing that's happened to me this side of Christmas . . . or that side, either.'

'Good,' Christie said contentedly. 'Tell me about her.'

'She's small, she's got light brown hair, big blue eyes, a most delectable figure . . . you'll like her, she's great fun – but even if you didn't it wouldn't matter, because I'm going to marry her. In the spring, if I live . . . if all goes well, I mean.'

Christie had been leaning back in her seat, letting Thorpe St Andrew slide by like a lovely, remembered dream. The riverside pubs, the railway arch over the road which wasn't a railway arch at all, really, but a road which ran from one side to the other, linking the big hospital, then the flat fields stretching away to the horizon as they left the city behind. But Frank's words brought the war roaring back, an ogre which could swallow all their gentle contentment, their small personal happiness.

'If I live that long,' Frank had been going to say. She'd heard it so often on the lips of Andy and his friends, young men who took their lives in their hands day after day, to try to win this bloody dreadful war so that girls like Celia – and herself – could lead normal lives with a husband who didn't kill for a living, with children who didn't have to spend half their lives in shelters or dugouts.

But she couldn't let Frank know she'd noticed his slip of the tongue; she didn't know why to do so would be wrong, she just knew it deep inside her. So she answered as though she'd not realised the significance of the words.

'Oh, Frank, a spring wedding! We might get married when Andy's tour's finished, then we could get leave together, a sort of wartime honeymoon. How many ops have you done, Frank? You're higher up than he is . . . he's just a pilot officer, you're a flight lieutenant, aren't you?'

'That's what those silly old rings mean, duckie – those symbols we work so hard to acquire. You shouldn't have to be told that, Christie, not working amongst us chaps like you do.'

'Of course I know what your rings mean ... but I haven't seen you in the light yet, stupid. Anyway, I do write to you from time to time and I like to address the letters properly, so your rank is important. Which reminds me, you hardly ever reply to my lovely, newsy epistles.'

'When you last wrote I was probably a pilot officer myself, it's been such ages,' Frank said drily. 'Still, I get your news; Mum passes it on. To tell you the truth, writing letters isn't my long suit.'

Christie giggled.

'I know; you'd rather do something physical, whether it's driving a tractor or an aeroplane. Considering you like to be considered almost illiterate, isn't it strange that you did so awfully well at school!'

'A fluke, my school cert was,' Frank said. 'God, how this truck rattles! Want to be a bridesmaid?'

'Not terribly; if she's small, and you said she was, then I'll probably tower over her and look all feet and hands,' Christie said. She was beginning to feel terribly tired and fought to keep her eyes open and her mind active. 'Want to be *my* bridesmaid, Frankie? Because I might easily get married first you know.'

'You won't. Mum and Dad will say wait, and you'll have to, because you aren't twenty-one for a couple more years. Whereas I, as a man of twenty-six, cannot be told what to do.'

'They can't stop me, but if they try we'll simply live

together,' Christie said calmly. 'Don't tease, Frank; this is the most important thing that's ever likely to happen to me and I have to take it seriously. I'm in love. You'll understand when you meet him.'

Frank glanced sideways at her; she saw the movement of his head, the momentary flash of eyes and teeth, then he was facing front once more, eyes fixed on the unwinding ribbon of road ahead.

'But Christie, my poppet, you're only a kid, you could be making a terrible mistake! It's only because we're all so fond of you that we advise a bit of caution, you know. Let's all meet him ... remember that in wartime things aren't as safe and settled as they are in the peace; if the two of you rush into a hasty marriage ...'

'It's just the same with you,' Christie reminded him. The truck ate up the miles, rain now and again spattering the windscreen. She could see the hedges on either side of the road being tossed by the gusting wind, the long, winter-whitened grass on the verges flattening beneath the downpour. 'How old is this Celia of yours?'

'Umm ... well, she's twenty, but ...'

'Then unless you want to put off your wedding for at least a year, dear brother, don't you go putting any spokes in *my* wheel,' Christie advised him grimly. 'I need Andy and want him; if you don't understand then it's your loss. How do *you* feel about Celia?'

There was a pregnant silence. Stealing a sideways glance at her brother's handsome profile, Christie saw his brows draw down over his eyes; he was actually thinking, taking her seriously, not just dismissing it as a kid sister's fantasy.

'Well, Frank?'

'I – I feel the same. Celia and I just want to be together. All right, if it comes to the crunch I'll tell Mum and Dad that you're old enough to be trusted with a very responsible job so you're old enough to choose the right man. And I look forward to meeting Andy.'

'I look forward to meeting Celia,' Christie responded at once. 'Especially if she hasn't got cutaway nostrils.'

Frank snorted, then they reached the King's Head crossroads and he wound down his window and indicated he was turning left.

'I tell you she's just about perfect and what's more important, she's a darling. Even if she was ugly I'd still love her, she's got that certain something . . . so don't let's talk nostrils. Besides, we're nearly home.'

The village street looked just the same. There was the post office, the Swan public house, the general shop. To the right the doctor's, where Christie had sat shivering whilst Dr McIllvray advised her mother to see a surgeon about her daughter's enlarged tonsils. To the left the library, where Christie and Eleanor had so often met, each with an armful of books, to spend an exciting Saturday morning choosing new ones. Ahead of them the village school where a million memories, good and bad, lay in wait.

The Ford van went past the row of thatched cottages and swerved right beside the school. At the

T-junction, the truck turned right again, fields and shaggy hedges all that showed up in the car's dim lights. A mile further on and a left turn this time, into a narrower, shaggier road.

They reached the farm. Frank turned left off the road into the curving driveway and stopped outside the kitchen door with a scatter of gravel. The blackout was complete, but in the faint and patchy starlight Christie sat still for a moment, staring at the dear, familiar bulk of the house, the walnut tree outside her bedroom window, the horse-trough by the long white gate which led to the orchard. Still here! Unbattered, unblistered – untouched, apparently, by the worst war Britain had ever known. She gave a deep sigh and Frank got out and opened her door, then leaned over and picked up her kit-bag from the back seat.

'Come along, Christie . . . good to be home, isn't it?'

Someone inside must have heard their voices. The back door opened a crack and for a moment they glimpsed firelight, the reflections in a row of gleaming pans, before a woman's figure emerged, shutting the door carefully behind her.

'Christie, darling! Oh it's so good to see you, chicken . . . not that I can . . . what a horribly dark night!' Warm arms enclosed her in a tight hug, then her mother linked arms and drew her towards the door, chattering as she went. 'Come along, it's freezing cold out here but we've got a lovely log fire blazing indoors, though I turned the lamp down so I wouldn't show a light for Jerry to home in on us by.

169

There's a shepherd's pie in the oven and a milk jelly on the marble slab in the pantry – I remember how you used to adore the dullest food when you were little. Daddy's out with his pigs, but he'll be in presently ... oh Christie, we've missed you dreadfully, though your letters are lovely, much better than Frank's and David's.'

'Thanks, Mum.' Frank drawled from behind them. He slung his sister's kit-bag down in a corner and walked into the centre of the room, reaching up to trim the lamp back into brilliance. 'There, that's better. Now we can see one another and you can say, *Christie, darling, how you've grown!'*

Becky Bellis laughed and gave her tall son a poke in the back.

'No cheek, or you'll forfeit a share of that shepherd's pie!' She turned to examine her daughter in the light from the gently hissing lamp. 'You haven't grown, but you've changed; I suppose you've grown up. And you've not cut your hair; the thing which worried Daddy most was that you might come home with all your pretty hair cut off.'

Christie laughed and began taking off her cap and greatcoat, hanging them carefully on the old deer-antlered coat-stand behind the door.

'No, I shan't do that; Andy likes my hair long, too. I think a lot of fellers see long hair as being more feminine.'

'Andy?'

Her mother's voice was sharp, almost apprehensive. Christie nodded. 'Yes, Andy. We've been going around together for several months. I told you I'd invited a friend back for Christmas, Mum, I said he'd got a few days leave. Well, that's Andy.'

'Oh! He's a boy, then?'

Frank guffawed and Christie giggled nervously.

'Of course Andy's a boy, Mum! What on earth made you think . . . ?'

'Oh dear, and now you'll think I'm stupid, but I'm not, it's David's young woman, dear,' Becky Bellis said, causing Christie even more confusion. 'Her name is Andrea, but David sometimes calls her Andy. So naturally, when we got your letter, we thought . . .'

It was possible, Christie supposed reluctantly, that someone who didn't know might assume him to be a girl, a fellow WAAF, presumably. So perhaps Mum's mistake was understandable. Christie hadn't said much about Andy in her letters, not wanting to start parental wonderings, and besides, she knew that once they met him they'd love him as she did, she just hadn't bargained on them believing him to be a girl!

Frank came to the rescue.

'Fellow, girl, what does it matter? Any friend of my kid sister's is a friend of mine. Though I'd have preferred a blonde with a big bust,' he added, winking at Christie. 'When's this paragon arriving?'

'Christmas Eve; and he's not a paragon, he's a Hurricane pilot,' Christie muttered. She felt that in some way the wind had been taken out of her sails, her credibility questioned. It was almost as if her mother was saying that a girl like Christie wouldn't have a

171

boyfriend, would naturally be bringing home a fellow WAAF and not a handsome young pilot officer with a string of successful ops to his credit.

'Well, that's very nice, dear,' her mother said soothingly. I've just heard on the wireless that nearly 12,000 evacuees from Gibraltar have arrived safely in Britain – isn't that good news? At least we've done something right.' She patted Christie's arm, then dived over to the Aga and opened the oven door. A delicious smell of cooking wafted across the kitchen. Christie had to stop herself from closing her eyes and sniffing ecstatically, nose in air, like one of the Bisto kids.

Mrs Bellis withdrew a golden-topped, savoury pie and stood it down beside the Aga. Then she stooped lower for two old-fashioned blue and white vegetable tureens, one filled with potatoes, the other with a mixture of carrots, swedes and finely chopped winter cabbage. She carried each dish, one at a time, over to the table, put them down on the scrubbed wooden surface with a thump and turned to her eldest.

'Frank, if we leave it any longer the food will be overcooked and I couldn't countenance that, not with a war on. Do go and give Daddy a call, tell him I'm serving up in ten minutes. Tell him if his wretched gilt hasn't farrowed by then I'll take over to give him a break.'

'I'll go,' Christie said quickly.' I'd like to, honest.'

She grabbed her greatcoat, struggled back into it and headed for the back door.

Outside it was pitch-black at first to eyes recently

accustomed to the lamp's bright glow, but the habit of years carried her across the paved yard and into the piggery. It was a good-sized brick building, the three farrowing pens on the right of the door. Christie could see her father as soon as she entered, squatting beside the mountain which would be the farrowing gilt. He turned at the sound of the door and grinned, his face lighting up with genuine delight.

'Chris, old girl! Oh lor, Mummy will have words . . . I meant to be sitting in the kitchen all clean and neat by the time you got back, but Minerva's only just finished . . . sixteen littl'uns, quite a war record I should think, with everything so hard to get, including pig-meal. Though our pigs eat pretty well, we get all the swill from the village school and so on.'

As he talked he was standing up, a hand on his back, unconsciously rubbing the ache there. Christie leaned over the low wooden wall of the stye and kissed him on the point of his five o'clock-shadowed jaw. He was wearing his mucking-out mac, huge rubber boots, an ancient cap which kept his bald patch warm. He grinned shyly and kissed her cheek, being careful not to touch her though his hands looked pretty clean for someone who had just helped a large sow to deliver sixteen pink sugar-pigs.

'Darling Daddy, I don't care where you are, it's just so good to see you again. But Mum says come in so we can eat together . . . are the piglets all right? Can they be left?'

The new-born young were all huddled up together under a lamp which shone redly down upon them.

'Yes, they'll be fine, now. I'll put them to the teats later, after supper. Frank will give me a hand. What do you think of the proud mum, eh? Her first litter and no trouble, it was like shelling peas. She's tired out now, mind you.'

Christie looked at the enormous pig, reflecting that the animal did look tired with her huge, cabbage-like ears flopping forward and almost hiding her tiny, pale blue eyes fringed with bristly white lashes.

'She's grand, a real winner,' she said sincerely. 'Shall I open the gate for you to come through?'

'No, you're clean,' Dan Bellis said. 'Might as well stay that way. Now, what's your news? My goodness, you look so lovely in that uniform, I could eat you up!' He swung the door of the pen shut, then caught Christie's shoulders with his fingertips and turned her to face him, surveying her with pride, his eyes shining. 'It doesn't suit everyone of course, but you look grand, sweetheart! Happy, are you?'

'Yes, awfully. Daddy, I've got a friend coming to stay; a boyfriend. Andy Todd.'

Her father squeezed her hand, then snatched his own away, tutting with exasperation at himself.

'Sorry, I keep forgetting I'm a bit piggy; I want to give you a great big hug . . . Mummy said something about a guest. Nice, is he?'

No frowns or awkward questions, no pretending that he'd assumed the friend would be a girl. She snatched his hand back and planted a kiss on the back of it, then put her arm round his waist and gave him a squeeze.

174

'Oh Daddy, I do love you! Yes, Andy's terrific, you'll approve. And now let's go and eat that shepherd's pie before it goes cold.'

I wonder if all leaves go as fast as this one's going? Christie asked herself, as she stood on the platform, watching Andy's train drawing into the station. Beside her, Frank's Celia waited, and beyond her, Frank himself. Celia was a small delicate-looking girl with soft, golden-brown bobbed hair and a gentle, rural accent. She wasn't in the least like Frank's usual type of girl which was one point in her favour, and after spending a couple of hours in her company Christie had been absolutely astonished to discover that Celia was a WAAF despatch rider, and rode a powerful motor-bike all over the place, carrying various papers and messages.

'I'm stronger than I look,' Celia murmured when Christie let her surprise show in an unguarded moment. 'Mind, I don't fancy getting muscle-bound when I have to contend with ice and snow. I've said I'll re-muster as a lorry driver if that happens. I can drive most of the waggons on the station.'

'What does Frank think – about you riding a motor-bike, I mean, and driving a lorry?' Christie asked with genuine curiosity. Frank's previous girl-friends had not only been tall, handsome and generally horrible, they had also been snobbishly sure of themselves and their place in society. They might have ridden motor-bikes for a lark but would certainly not have done so in inclement weather or as a means of earning a living. And heavy lorries would have been totally beyond the pale.

Celia laughed. She had a v-shaped, elfin grin and a bubbling gurgle of laughter which was extremely infectious; Christie smiled too.

'When we met I was coming round a corner a bit sharpish,' Celia said. 'And I skidded on a pile of leaves. I flew off and Frankie fielded me . . . he didn't seem to mind my motor-bike then!'

Celia had arrived at three in the afternoon and since Andy wasn't reaching the station until five the two girls had a couple of hours to get to know one another. Frank, having met the train and kissed Celia very thoroughly, introduced her to Christie and told the two of them that he was off to the city hall to talk about pig licences but would meet them again at the station when Andy's train was due.

'Have a look at the shops,' he suggested.' Buy yourselves some tea. Chris, I entrust you with this quid, don't go mad and don't forget I want my change. Have fun, darlings.'

Two hours in a country city with only a quid and no coupons to spend might not sound exciting to some people, but to a couple of girls normally bound by service rules, with almost no money and less spare time, it was a rare and delectable freedom and they made the most of it.

It was a freezing cold day with a brisk wind blowing but they enjoyed spending Frank's quid, having tea at Lyon's Corner House on Gentleman's Walk, touring the market for bargains and finally catching a bus from the centre back to the station, talking all the while and finding themselves more and more in accord.

Frank arrived at the station very soon after they did and because Andy's train was – predictably – late, treated them to another cup of tea in the buffet and a railway bun as well. It was nice in the buffet, warm and steamy, with passengers in holiday mood, laughing and joking, women laden with holly and mistletoe and last-minute presents and men carrying bottles with exaggerated care.

Frank examined their shopping and produced a small piece of mistletoe which he pinned on to Celia's cap – she was still in uniform, though Christie, having been home a couple of days already, was comfortable in her old school burberry with a scarlet scarf of her mother's round her neck and gum-boots on her feet.

'There you are, sweetheart; no defence,' he said, and as Celia, cuddled into the crook of his arm, smiled up at him, Christie suddenly recognised something in their expressions and knew they were lovers.

Like me and Andy, she thought, awestruck. Is it that obvious, then? Does a simple act like losing one's virginity show with such startling clarity on every face? If so, suppose Mum and Dad just look at Andy and me and know at once ... suppose Frank's the same ... how will I face them?

But then the train drew up and Andy got down, looking anxiously up and down the platform, seeing her, dropping his kit-bag, clutching only the bottle, with holly round its neck, which he'd probably clutched all the way from the airfield, and scooped her up into his arms.

Ah God, she loved him! He had his cap on the side of his head, a lock of dark hair dangled across his brow . . . Then his mouth came down on hers and she forgot everything else but Andy, forgot fears that they might not like him, that they might realise he was her lover . . . all that mattered was that he was here, his arms enfolding her.

At last Andy let her go with a little sigh and she introduced him to Frank and Celia; they smiled and shook hands, commiserated with him on the length and fearfulness of his train journey, took his kit-bag, told him that Mrs Bellis had cooked a goose, hoped he liked roast goose . . .

Andy put his arm round Christie as they walked to the truck. They sat in the back and cuddled, content with nearness for now. Later, they would want more but after a week apart, just to be close was enough.

Christie leaned her head against Andy's shoulder and decided that she was happier than she had any right to be. She had him now for two whole days, two days when he wouldn't be flying and she wouldn't be afraid. She heard her own voice, telling him about her journey home, how the evening after she'd arrived they'd been disturbed by the steady thrum of enemy aircraft overhead, making their way to some unfortunate inland target . . . how they had heard later that Liverpool had been attacked . . . she'd thanked her stars that Sue wasn't due to arrive there until the following day.

Andy listened, and nodded, and every now and then turned his head and nuzzled into her neck, reducing her to a jelly because desire was beginning to rear its head. For two whole days and three nights they were going to be under the same roof ... but she and Celia were sharing her room and Andy would be in the tiny spare room behind hers, right next door to the cloakroom where, tomorrow morning, she would empty her hot-water bottle into the wash-basin so that she could have a slightly-less-than-freezing wash – baths in wartime were a once-a-week affair.

The truck rattled along the familiar roads; it was a clear night, bright and moonlit. As they turned left into the village Christie began to tell Andy who lived where, which building was what. She saw that Celia had drawn very close to Frank and presently, when they turned down beside the school, the truck began to slow. At the T-junction Frank turned right, then slowed more and more, until they were hardly moving. Then he turned round and addressed them.

'I'll stop for five minutes if you like. Just so we can have a cuddle.'

Andy said, 'Good idea,' and turned Christie neatly in his arms, then unbuttoned her coat and slid his hands – chilly-fingered – up under her blue angora jumper. Christie gave a little shiver, whether of excitement or cold she could not quite determine, and put her arms up round his neck. For a blissful moment they kissed and cuddled, finally ending up with Christie more or less prone on the back seat and Andy more or less on top of her. When Christie opened an eye and squinted at the front seat, there was no one visible, but she could hear heavy breathing and little mutters. Since she was making the same noises herself she simply sighed, closed her eyes again and thrilled to Andy's touch as his hands conquered obstacles and found her warm, willing flesh.

'Time to move on,' Frank said presently. His voice was calm, but Christie could hear the reluctance in it. 'Tidy yourselves up, ladies; if there is smudged lipstick or untidy buttoning, put it right. Mothers do not approve of smudged lipstick or untidy buttoning, not on their little ewe-lambs, anyway.'

'What about their little ram-lambs?' Christie asked indignantly, pulling her angora jumper into respectability and pushing her tousled hair into what order she could manage with neither light nor a mirror to guide her. 'I imagine that mothers can get very annoyed indeed if little ram-lambs appear unbuttoned.'

From the front seat, Celia's delightful gurgle of mirth rang out.

'You tell 'em, Christie-love,' she said. 'Anyway, Andy, at least there's two of us. If Mrs Bellis accuses us of leading her kiddies astray, we'll stand up for each other.'

'True,' Andy said. He took out his handkerchief and scrubbed what was left of Christie's lipstick off his mouth. 'Good lord, you girls, why do you have to wear that lipstick stuff? It doesn't suit us blokes one bit!'

This rather feeble joke seemed the epitome of humour to Christie and Celia; they laughed helplessly as Frank started the truck and began to drive it through the moonlit countryside once more.

'Sober up, ladies,' Frank said as he turned into the farm drive. 'There's nothing more annoying than a joke you can't share. We want to make a good impression, don't we?'

'Let's give them some carols,' Andy suggested as they crunched across the frost-crisp grass towards the back door. 'God rest ye merry . . .'

Singing lustily, they formed a small half-circle outside the back door and presently were dragged inside to drink hot cocoa and eat mincepies and be introduced, fussed over, welcomed.

'Wasn't it a grand evening?' Christie said, tumbling into bed as Celia, neat and sweet in pink pyjamas, came in from her visit to the cloakroom. 'They liked Andy, didn't they? And they loved you, Celia.'

'We got on pretty well,' Celia admitted, climbing into bed. 'Your parents are nice, Chris. But it's all very well them being kind to Frank's floozie – what about when Frankie tells 'em we want to get married?'

'They'll be happy for you,' Christie said. She sat up in bed, hugging her knees and looking dreamily out across the moon-bright fields. 'I hope they'll be happy for me and Andy, too, when we tell them the same.'

'Ah . . . I thought you looked a bit dewy-eyed,' Celia said. 'What does Andy do in civvy street? Is he a farmer?'

'Goodness, no. He joined up as soon as he was old enough because he thought there was a war coming.

He's only twenty-three, you know.'

'I didn't realise; he seems older,' Celia observed. She was sitting up too, now, and staring out through the square bay window, as Christie was. 'So many of 'em seem older, now.'

'I know. But what does it matter what Andy did in civvy street? I mean the war's now... God knows when it will end.'

'Oh ah. But ... I'm not a country girl, see? I'm scared of all these yur fields an' cows an' that. If Frankie and me get wed, how'll I manage?'

'Don't worry, Frank will see you right,' Christie said, having thought it over for a moment or two. 'I don't know that he'll even want to farm when the war's over. People change.'

'That's true.' Celia lay down, pulling the cover up round her shoulders. 'No point in meeting troubles half-way, any road. It's now that matters, right now. And tomorrow's Christmas Day. Can you remember Christmas Day last year, the year before? I'd rather have what Frank and I have got now than anything else, anything at all.'

And Christie, lying on her back and watching the moon get caught in the black branches of the walnut tree whilst Andy's dear, anxious face floated in her mind's eye, could only agree with her.

7

Christmas without them will be fine, if I'm sensible, Shanna had been saying to herself, over and over, ever since she'd seen Sue off on the first leg of her trip home. Everyone will be in a good mood, there will be mistletoe, kisses, presents . . . it'll be good fun, it'll be something to remember. And anyway, on Boxing Day Sue will be coming back, with her presents and her chatter . . . I'm no' *dependent* on Sue, I just love her, feel safer when I'm with her. I'll be just fine without her.

Even so, waking on Christmas morning was strange. The voice from the tannoy reminding them that it was 'seven o'clock, ladies and gentlemen, time to rise and shine,' was full of unnatural bonhomie for a start; and driven by some obscure feeling that it would please Sue, Shanna bounded straight out of bed and rushed into the showers, using all the tiny amount of hot water available and bringing down upon her head a good few nasty remarks from those who habitually washed each day.

'Shanna, did you have to have your once-yearly on Christmas Day? I particularly wanted to be spotless for this afternoon. When I come off duty there's a Christmas tea-party at the vicarage . . .'

'Shanna, you selfish cow, this bloody water's freezing, why did you run it for so long, don't you ever think of anyone but yourself? Ah God, I'm all soapy but I can't stand it any longer, my tits are *blue* – just wait till you want a favour doing!'

Apologies, mumbles that she hadn't realised, hadn't thought . . . didn't get her far, either. She had spoiled their morning showers – and it was no use pointing out that she did not, as a rule, use her fair share of the hot water; that was her choice, not their wish.

'If you washed more often you'd know how hard it is to make the hot water stretch,' grumbler number one said plaintively. 'It isn't even as if you're coming to the party – you aren't, are you?'

There was enough anxiety in the last words to put Shanna's back up as far as it could go.

'A party at the *vicarage*?' Shanna said incredulously, as though the other girl had suggested playing strip poker on the altar. 'I'm no' that desperate for amusement.'

'Your idea of amusement ain't the same as others',' grumbler number two said acidly. 'You're a mucky blighter, Shanna – they don't call you the station bike for nothing . . . oh God, I'll be sticky all bleedin' day now!'

So it was good to escape from the ablutions, get into her uniform and head for the cookhouse. The staff, usually cheerful, were a bit glum but the place had been decorated with holly and there was a good deal of talk about the turkey – or at least the chicken – they had been promised for their dinner. Breakfast, however, consisted of the usual horrible dried eggs though accompanied by half a sausage which was ninety per cent breadcrumbs.

'They won't come over today, at any rate, which is one blessing,' the girl at the next desk said to Shanna, rattling away on her ancient typewriter until it sounded like machine-gun fire. 'What a lousy day, eh? Not even nice crisp snow, just clouds and drizzle.'

'They bombed Manchester the night Sue got home,' Shanna said nervously. 'It's quite near Liverpool, isn't it?'

'Nah . . . about fifty, sixty mile off,' someone said. 'She'll be okay, Shanna.'

Shanna nodded as though she'd known it all along and only asked to test them, then got up to answer the telephone.

'Admin . . . yes, sir, I'll tell her.'

She put the phone down and turned to the WAAF sitting on her right.

'Lucy, the boss wants a word.'

Dinner was rather good, despite everyone's inner reservations. They had been promised that the officers would serve them and sure enough several officers did turn up; but though in peacetime other ranks would have enjoyed the situation to the full, would have chucked food around, embarrassed the officers and had a marvellous time, no one had the heart to so much as lob a portion of swede at an officorial head; and shortages being what they were, anyone chucking food would probably have to avoid cooky with a swinging meat axe, to say nothing of greedier colleagues, who always complained about the size of portions.

Shanna wasn't a girl who cared much about food so long as she got enough to keep body and soul together; but she tucked into her turkey, sprouts and roasties with quite an appetite and pulled a cracker with a red-haired airman, then stuck her paper hat on at a jaunty angle and tried not to count the hours to bedtime.

It was half-shifts in the office today, so she was free after the meal finished. There were various parties planned – to be fair to her fellows, she had been invited to most of them, the exception being the one held at the vicarage – but after the unaccustomed pudding and the glass of sherry which had preceded the meal and the beer which had accompanied it, Shanna felt more like a lie-down on her bed then a knees-up in the sergeants' mess. However, after half an hour of lying on her bed and miserably contemplating the arched ceiling above and the length of time before Sue would come whistling home she swung her feet to the floor, got her greatcoat off its hook, slapped her cap on her strangely clean and shiny hair – she had washed that as well in the shower – and set off for a walk round the camp.

Others had the same idea. Ahead of her a group of WAAFs sauntered. Presently they were joined by a group of aircraftmen. Shanna decided to go in a different direction; away from the airfield, into the nearby sodden countryside, because it was still drizzling with rain.

Sue will be back tomorrow; and I needn't take my leave, no one is forced to take leave, she reminded herself. I've no home to go back to, no family waiting. No money . . . unless I go up to London and – and see if I can find some fun?

But the WAAF had done its work well; no sooner did she think of cruising the streets of London than a wave of nausea swept over her. She was a WAAF with a pride in herself, her work. She most certainly would not go up to London alone . . . besides, Sue wouldn't approve.

She was thinking of turning back, of going along to the sergeants' mess after all when she noticed someone trudging along the road ahead of her. An aircraftman, his forage cap stuck on the side of his head – how did they do it? – and something dark on his shoulder. And then she heard his voice. He seemed to be talking to someone but he was alone, the lane here wound onwards between two wide grassy verges. She would have seen anyone else around . . . there was no one!

Curiosity kept her at his heels; he was rattling on, now and then he laughed . . . then her blood ran cold. She was not listening to one voice but two; two quite similar voices, but one deeper, a trifle hoarser! She looked round wildly – nothing but the encroaching dusk, the occasional gust of wind and the light, drizzly rain blowing into her face. And what was more, no one, save for the stumpy figure ahead.

And then, even as she was about to turn and run for it, the dark object on the airman's shoulder moved, turned. It was a bird – the bloke had a bloody parrot or something, she wasn't going mad after all. Relief made her start to laugh and when the man stopped short and turned to stare behind him she continued to laugh as she hurried to catch him up.

'Gosh, I'm awfu' sorry, you must think I'm mad, but I didnae see your bird. I thought you were talkin' to yoursel' – then I heard another voice . . . it gave me a right turn.'

She had caught him up, he started to smile at her and they both stopped short in their tracks.

He was about Shanna's height but a good deal more thick-set. He had soft, soot-coloured hair, tufty and ill-cut. His grey eyes surveyed her through thick, short lashes. Even in the dusk she could see the blue shadowing on his jaw, the uniform which was neither crisp nor particularly clean. So why . . . why did she feel like this? Warm, wanting to touch him? And God, the bird on his shoulder was a big green parrot with an enormous beak . . . She meant to take a step back but found she'd stepped forward instead, saw that her hand was creeping towards him as though to touch him. Hastily, very embarrassed, she turned the gesture into a half-wave, then dropped her hand to her side.

'Hey-up! You give me quite a scare, gal. I fought I was alone, din't know you was follerin' me.'

He was a cockney, she knew it as soon as he opened his mouth. She disliked Londoners, they reminded her of that dreadful time, the time before Sue. But this voice seemed to hold no threat, it was as if she knew him, his voice, his face, even the way he walked, talked . . . God, she really must be going mad, whatever was she thinking of? Just because it was Christmas Day and she was lonely . . .

'I wasn't exactly following you. Does the bird talk? I thought . . .'

'What, talk, old Jacko? You want to try to stop 'im, that's all. All parrots is the same, once they start jabberin' you can't stop 'em. And learn?' He grinned and his face lit up, almost glowed, with pride in the bird. 'Why, there ain't nothin' you couldn't teach 'im. 'E's a clever feller is Jacko, ain't you, old chap?'

'Clever feller,' the bird said, its voice sounding very like its owner's. 'Clever feller, clever feller, ain't you, old chap?'

Shanna, startled, laughed. The bird stared at her, head on one side, then laughed too.

'Ha-ha-ha! Clever feller, clever feller!'

''E's took a fancy to you,' the airman said. 'Jacko don't try to copy many voices. Did you 'ear 'im, takin' you off?'

'I don't laugh like that, do I?' Shanna said, half offended, half amused. 'Eh, but he really is a clever feller. What else can he say?'

'Oh, no end,' the airman said. 'Tell the lady to 'ave a nice Christmas, Jacko. Tell 'er . . .'

''Appy Christmas, 'appy Christmas,' the bird

shouted, cocking its head again. 'Gi's a beer, Dolly!'

'Who's Dolly? I do think you're clever, Jacko,' Shanna said. She put a hand out, then stopped. 'Does he bite?'

'Nah . . . not 'is friends any road. Give 'is 'ead a rub; 'e likes that.'

Shanna daringly smoothed the bird's head with two fingers. He did seem to like it, making a sort of purring clatter beneath his breath and sinking his head to encourage further petting.

'There, you see? You're the lady's pal, ain't you, Jack?' He turned from contemplating the bird to stick out a hand. 'I'm Colin Blacker; Col to my friends. And you're . . . ?'

'Shanna Douglas. Nice to meet you, Col.'

As their hands met, his large palm closing warmly round her smaller one, Shanna felt a stab of excitement dart through her, sizzling up from their joined hands to arrow deep into her stomach. This was absolute madness – she was getting more pleasure from this young man's touch than she did when submitting to the most intimate caresses by other men! She took her hand away and held it against her hot cheek.

'Where were you going, you and Jacko?'

'Dahn the pub, but it's closed, would you believe? On a bloomin' Christmas Day, when there ain't much for a feller to do. So we come on a walk, didn't we, Jacko? And 'ad a piece of luck.'

'What piece of luck?' Shanna asked. She expected him to say he'd been invited out in the village, or had found half-a-crown, but instead he looked straight at her and spoke seriously.

'We met you, Shanna. And Jacko likes you. 'Ow about comin' over to the NAAFI wiv me, later? There's a dance – I wasn't goin', but if you'll come along as well . . .'

'Well, thanks, since it's Christmas I'd like to have a dance,' Shanna said. 'Will Jacko come too?'

Col laughed.

'You can't always rely on 'is good manners, that's the trouble,' he said. 'One day 'e'll be good as gold, the next 'e'll fart in the CO's face or swear at an officer. But 'e's ever so good in my billet at night. Just kips down, quiet as a child, till the light wakes 'im. So I leave 'im in his cage on my bed, most evenings.'

'What's he like in summer?' Shanna asked as the two of them turned back towards the station, walking side by side, the bird on Col's shoulder nearest to Shanna. 'I mean does he wake at dawn then, and start chuntering on? That could make you pretty unpopular I should imagine.'

Col shrugged.

'I dunno. I don't think 'e's very old, probably last summer 'e was just an egg. I bought 'im in early September, dahn in Pompey. The pet-shop had been bombed, they was gettin' rid of the stock, cheap. I wanted a monkey – nice little chap, but I didn't 'ave enough tin, an' whiles I were 'angin' round, this cheeky bugger started givin' me lip. So I couldn't resist, could I? Bought 'im for a ten bob . . . best ten bob I ever spent.'

'It's odd I've no' seen you before, nor the bird,' Shanna remarked as they reached the gates. 'Have you been here long, Col?'

'Nah, only a couple o' days. I'm ground-crew – flight mech on Spitfires – an' when our flight moves, we move too. They sent me 'ere while we wait for a postin', dunno where to yet but I wouldn't be surprised if it were North Africa. A lot go there.'

'I see.' Shanna, who had known this young man about ten minutes, felt her heart lurch boot-wards. 'You won't be here long, then?'

'Can't tell. It could be several weeks, an' then they only do tours over there ... so many months and you're back in Blighty. Where do the WAAFs 'ang out 'ere, then? I disremember seein' you when we 'ad our dinners.'

'I'm in that hut.' Shanna pointed. 'We could meet in the NAAFI, though. You don't want to hang about waiting for me; no sense in it.'

'You sure? Right ... what time, then?'

Shanna thought. She found she wanted a bit of time to tidy herself up, clean her shoes and so on. For the first time, she was glad that none of the others were back. Just for this one evening, she could be the belle of the ball ... well, not the belle of the ball, but at least a girl with a feller who wanted her company.

'Suppose we say eight o'clock? At the bar?'

'Fine. See you then, Shanna. I'll look forward to it. Me an' Jacko kip dahn over there.' He pointed. 'So we'll make tracks now.'

He turned, the bird pressed against his head, and

walked towards his hut. Shanna watched him through the increasing dusk until he had disappeared from sight, then went into her own hut with a light heart and a dancing step.

He really liked her – and she liked him, she liked him very much. He hadn't been here long, he didn't know how stupid she'd been with other fellers, he'd accept her as a decent girl, a girl like Sue, or Meg, or Christie. Of course she'd thought other men had liked her, when it had all been a ploy, but she didn't just think it with Col, she knew, inside, that they were somehow the same. Two of a kind.

We clicked, she thought ecstatically as she polished her shoes and borrowed someone's hair-brush to add a last-minute burnish. Or was it love at first sight? Think of all the men I've known, been with, and I've never had this warm, safe sort of feeling with anyone before, never known with this inner certainty that this was special.

Doubts set in when she was carefully applying a thin layer of lipstick, dabbing powder on the tip of her nose, brushing flecks of dust off her shoulder and lapels. She had imagined it – he must have heard she was easy, plotted to get to know her . . .

But that was just plain silly. He had only been here a couple of days. Oh to hell with it, Shanna, stop imagining all sorts of rubbish and just enjoy being with the feller, she told herself, admiring her shining hair. A pity she hadn't had time to curl it up, but perhaps he would prefer it long and straight, like a curtain of flame.

Curtain of flame? Where the hell had she heard that? It's just bloody *hair*, you fool, not anything special, she reminded herself. But she was fascinated by the shine on it, the colours which came from being thoroughly washed and then allowed to dry naturally, without being tortured into curlers, and then simply brushed until it crackled.

And as though happiness was infectious others, also getting ready for the NAAFI dance, were nice to her, friendly, flattering.

'Your hair looks a treat,' Ellen from three beds down said. 'It's ever such a pretty colour – you didn't oughter stick it in curlers, not on a dance night.'

'You've got good legs, Shanna. Them stockings don't do anyone no favours, but you've got the slimmest ankles in this hut, I reckon. I'll lend you some silk stockings if you like.'

The silk stockings were wonderfully smooth; she ran her hands up and down her legs, loving the feel of them.

'Thanks, Dawn, I'll take real good care of them,' Shanna said, and wondered again why everyone was being so nice, until it occurred to her that perhaps it was easier to be nice to someone who was happy and relaxed than to someone who was edgy, bad-tempered, anxious.

'You goin' to the dance with a bloke, Shan, or d'you want to come with us?'

That was the girl who had sworn at her for using all the hot water. Shanna tried out a smile and found it returned.

'I'm meeting one of the mechanics in there,' she said. 'But I'd like to come over with you, if that's all right.'

'Sure it is. Come on, then, if you're ready.'

They went across to the NAAFI in a big, straggly group, everyone excited, sure of having a good time. Men always outnumbered women by about five to one, so most of the girls would find themselves eagerly sought as partners; but a dance was good fun anyway, the band knew just how to please the dancers, the refreshments were being provided free and included mincepies and lots of fizzy lemonade as well as beer.

In the NAAFI, stripped for action with chairs and tables pushed against the walls and the band already tuning up, Shanna took a very small glass of lemonade and glanced towards the door just as it opened to let Colin Blacker in. Her heart gave a delighted skip and she knew her face broke into a broad smile. He was with several other chaps; a purist might have noted that they were mostly taller than he, mostly better-looking, certainly smarter; but Shanna was not a purist and anyway, she was looking at Col with the prejudiced eye of love.

How delightful were his sooty hair, his lean jaw, his twinkling eyes! When he saw her and came across the room even the way he moved seemed to Shanna to be superior to the way others strode across the floor.

The band struck up a waltz. Shanna, who got by on the dance-floor because she followed her partner closely, melted into Col's arms. Together, they seemed to dance well, or perhaps it was just that they

195

danced the same; certainly there was no standing on toes, no gasps of stifled pain. Shanna found she did not have to concentrate. She simply relaxed and let her body do what Col's body did, and behold, they were dancing.

Usually, men danced with Shanna meaningfully, making sure she wouldn't object, when they took her outside, to being pushed against the wall whilst they snorted and heaved at her clothing and tried to get inside her knickers. Col treated her like a lady. He fetched her drinks, kissed her gently as they danced, stroked down her back as though unable to believe his luck. Later, when they went out for a breath of air, he strolled beside her, an arm loosely around her shoulders, and made her laugh with stories about Jacko, and asked her to tell him about herself.

'There's no' much to tell,' Shanna confessed. 'My mother ran away from my dad when I was small, then my father dumped me wi' a stepmother who couldnae stand me . . . I got away from home as soon as I could. I worked in a shop, then in an office in Glasgow, but as soon as I could I came down south . . . and joined the WAAF. What about you, Col?'

'Oh, my mum was only a kid an' she didn't want me at all,' Col said airily. 'Dumped me on an orphanage, she did. They was awright, in their way, but I got out soon's I could. Worked in a garage, got real useful . . . then the boss sent me to night school to learn about other sorts of engines and I saw an advert for mechanics in the Air Force so I put my name down. Been with 'em ever since. I was a boy-entrant. Is it rude to ask you 'ow old you are? I'm twenty-two.'

'I'm twenty,' Shanna said quickly. It wasn't true, but it was what he wanted to hear and it was her first lie tonight. *I won't lie to him again*, she told herself defensively as the words left her lips. *What does age matter, anyway? It's people who are important, not their ages.*

'There you are, I knew we was made for each other! Want another dance?'

They returned to the NAAFI and danced until the band packed up. Then Col walked her back to the hut, gave her a shy kiss on the side of her mouth and asked if he might meet her again.

'We could go to the flicks, or take a bus into the country, see 'ow old Jacko behaves in the New Forest, wiv all them trees,' he suggested. 'We was in Norfolk, before. Jacko's never seen a forest – nor me.'

'Oh, *yes*,' Shanna whispered ardently. 'I'd like that, Col. Either the flicks or the forest . . . it would be fun.'

They parted with another of Col's gentle kisses, then Shanna went into the hut and was about to tear off her clothes and hop between the sheets when she hesitated. She wanted to be a nice girl, like Sue, Christie and Meg, she wanted to be a nice girl for Col So she really ought to wash . . . they always washed, and brushed out their hair and cleaned their teeth. They hung their clothes up, too. And dug dirt from under their nails with an orange stick and put skin-stuff on their face . . . well, Sue did and Sue was beautiful.

She hesitated, her fingers on her tie. She could wash in the morning, do it really properly, and clean her teeth and everything. But right now she was tired, and wanted her bed, longed to pull the covers up round her ears and start thinking seriously about Col.

But when you start a new life you do it properly. Sighing, rebellious, she nevertheless undressed, hung up her clothes, went along to the ablutions with her greatcoat over her shoulders and had a cold but thorough wash, cleaned her teeth, brushed her hair . . .

And climbed at last into bed, so tired that she scarcely thought at all before plunging gratefully into sleep.

Because Sue had hitch-hiked most of the way, there had been no chance of letting her mother know what time she would be arriving. This of course meant she could not be met, but that did not worry Sue. The Collins family would all be waiting for her; she knew the sort of boisterous welcome she would have and had been dreaming about it for most of the journey.

The journey had not been too bad, either, despite her fears. She, had hitched a lift as far as Crewe, what she thought of as a 'straight' hitch since the Air Force corporal in the heavy lorry was going there to collect an engine, he told her. Then she was picked up by a delivery van driven by an old man who smoked a very pungent pipe and grumbled all the way from Crewe to Chester. And on the outskirts of Chester, after she had walked half a mile, she got another lift, this time from an army lorry taking spare parts to a depot in Birkenhead.

And now here she was, stepping out of Lime Street underground station, sniffing at the cold, familiar salty smell and smiling into the wind as it roared straight across St George's plateau from the Mersey, almost tearing the hair from her head. It was late and the blackout meant that city darkness was deep and complete; a few blue-lit vehicles made their way slowly along the streets and a special policeman grinned at her as she hurried along, one hand on the wall, her kit-bag over her shoulder, making for the nearest tram stop.

'All right, Miss? Where're you headin'?'

'Vauxhall Road,' Sue said briefly. 'Any chance of a tram or a bus? I'd walk, but it's cold as well as dark.'

The man sucked in his breath.

'Which end o' Vauxy, queen?'

'About half-way; up by Tate's.'

'That's a good walk in the dark; if you get a move on there'll be a tram standin' at the stop on the Old Haymarket. Leaves in a few minutes. Here, I'll walk wi' you, see you right, being as 'ow it's almost Christmas.'

Sue thanked him and they walked companionably through the dark streets and up to the tram depot on Old Haymarket. Sue, looking round her, began to get her night eyes and was pleased and relieved to see that no major changes had taken place. Home was still home, thank God.

'That's the one,' Sue's new friend said as they reached the terminus, indicating a tram at the head of the line. 'Get you 'ome 'fore you know it. Goodnight, Airwoman.'

He saluted and grinned and Sue smiled her thanks and got aboard the tram, glad to get out of the cold, though it wasn't that much warmer in the dismal, blue-lit vehicle. There were only half-a-dozen passengers, huddled up on the slatted seats beneath the blacked-out windows, whilst the Mersey wind whined in through the open doorway.

Sue handed the driver her fare, then took a seat near the door, despite the draught. She saw little likelihood of recognising her stop unless she really concentrated on the passing streets.

But she was in luck. The tram was about to pull away when there was a shout and a gaggle of girls in their early teens piled on board, giggling and pushing each other. Sue glanced casually at them, then stiffened. At the back of the queue were her twin sisters, Deirdre and Emily, known in the family as Dee and Eee. They did not notice Sue, obviously seeing her merely as a uniformed adult, and would have jostled further down the tram without giving her a second glance had Sue not grabbed Dee as she drew level with her.

'What's all this? Don't you know your own flesh and blood no more, our Dee?'

Dee stopped, squealed, then threw herself into Sue's arms.

'Oh Sue, we've missed you! Eee, look who's here!

Our Mam'll be made up when we take you in, she said you'd never get 'ome tonight!'

After mutual huggings the twins sat down, one on either side of her, and plied her with questions; did she like forces life, had she got many boyfriends, what was the food like, had she brought them sweets? Sue, laughing, said they would have to wait for her stories until they got home since she hated repeating herself, and asked the girls rather censoriously where they had been at this time of night?

'To the flicks; King's Cinema, on London Road,' Dee said promptly. She was the taller twin, a round-faced, yellow-haired girl who bossed her shy sister. 'It were a Christmas treat from Uncle Syd, he sent us the money, didn't he, our Eee? It were a wizard fillum – it had that feller in, the one we like ... oh what's 'is name, our Eee ...'

'The fillum were *Gone with the Wind*,' Eee chipped in. She was like a shadow of Dee, Sue reflected, but much the cleverer of the two. 'I know, it were Clark Gable.'

'That's it, Clark Gable ... ooh, I love 'im,' Dee declared with relish. 'Eh, come on girls, our stop next!'

The three of them piled off the tram, scuffled around for a moment getting their bearings and then set off, arm in arm.

'How did you know it was our stop?' Sue asked curiously as they walked, three abreast along Vauxhall Road. 'I couldn't see a thing.'

'You just gets to know,' Dee said vaguely. 'We can see in the dark now, can't we, Eee?'

'Aye,' Eee said laconically. 'Shall we give Mam a surprise? Shall you wait outside an' then go in and say *boo*?'

'Yes, if you like . . .' Sue was beginning, when she heard the familiar wail of a siren. Sue felt her stomach first drop into her boots and then begin the slow, uncomfortable churning which always heralded a raid. 'Oh dear, sounds like trouble. We'd better hurry.'

They turned into their street on the words and began to run.

'It'll probably not be much,' Dee said breathlessly as they charged down the back entry. 'We 'ad it bad three weeks ago, reckon they won't do much now. Best get into the 'ouse, though, in case.'

It was a horrendous night; usually the family made for the shelter at the end of the road but by the time they decided it was going to be a bad one it was too late. The sky was lit up with flares and bombs were dropping thick and fast. Mrs Collins pulled the heavy old kitchen table across the room and wedged it against the cupboard under the stairs and they all crawled inside. Blankets were produced, and pillows, and everyone settled down to trying to forget the whine and crash of the bombing and the dreadful rumbling roar of dwellings being razed to the ground.

It was impossible, of course. Fear dried Sue's mouth, made it difficult to speak naturally; but the twins told her they didn't think it was as bad as the raid three weeks ago and they'd survived that, hadn't they, and Mam was calm, crawling out and making a pot of tea and some sandwiches during what she optimistically called a lull. And Sue found comfort in being surrounded by her family. She took five-year-old Sammy on her knee and told him stories and cuddled him to sleep whilst Mam dealt with Annie, who was seven, and handed out tea at intervals.

'I didn't notice any signs of bomb damage as I walked up to the tram terminus,' she said to her mother at one point. Mrs Collins snorted, then winced as a bomb whistled down nearby, the impact shaking the house and waking the sleeping Sammy, who began to cry drearily.

'You'll notice tomorrer,' Mrs Collins said grimly. 'The last lot were bad, now there's this lot, too.'

'I guess I will notice,' Sue said, trying to keep her voice steady and rocking Sammy soothingly. 'Wharra welcome 'ome, Mam! '

Morning came and with it, the spirits of the Collins family revived in a manner marvellous to behold. Sue was very impressed, especially with her mother's calm acceptance of the terrible damage, the shops and offices which had been reduced to rubble, the homes ruined, even the lives lost.

'They didn't have our number on last night,' she said to Sue as the two of them went shopping up and down the Scottie, hoping to find something interesting for their Christmas meal. 'Another night we'll make for the shelter in good time, though they might give us a break now, hammer some other poor buggers.'

Sue widened her eyes at her mother. Mam, swearing? Mrs Collins noticed her daughter's surprise and grinned guiltily.

'I know, it isn't like me . . . we're all goin' to have to be different, now, queen. Do you like herrings? Mr Evans said he'd keep me a few.'

Next night the bombing seemed, to Sue, to be even more severe. The noise was terrifying, the crashes closer, but at least, at Mam's insistence, they were no longer cramped up under the big table. As soon as the first siren wailed they had scooped the kids out of bed, wrapped them in blankets and hurried them along to the shelter at the end of the road.

'It's a good, deep one,' Mrs Collins panted, clutching a very large basket with a flask, cups and sandwiches in it. She was wrapped in her best coat and had her handbag with all her most precious possessions tucked into its capacious folds. 'Keep a hold on Tibby, Sue love. She hates the shelter and she hates the bombs; dunno which is worse. Twins, give Annie a hand with the Madeira cake, we don't want her droppin' it half-way down the road.'

They were warmly greeted in the shelter by neighbours already in residence whilst the damp brick stairs behind them echoed to other footsteps. Most of the road was abandoning ship tonight for the safety of a foot of concrete all round.

'Move over, sonny, give the gals a bit o' space,' an elderly man advised his young son. 'I reckon the 'ole of Worship Street's 'ere tonight, 'cep for old Mrs Bishopp.'

'She's too old to move,' Mrs Collins explained in a quiet voice to Sue as the children began to get themselves organised. 'She is eighty.'

'Let's 'ave a song,' someone called as the first shriek and whine of what sounded like a landmine descending came to their ears. 'Come on . . . let's 'ave a song!'

They sang. They played round games. They even tried to sleep a little, whenever the noise would let them. But Sue sat with Sammy in her arms and rested her chin on his curly head and prayed.

Morning found them pale and worn out; but as they struggled up the steps into the first faint, grey daylight Sue was aware, suddenly, of a sort of desperate optimism and hope. The air was cold and clean in sharp contrast to the air in the little concrete box overfilled with humanity in which they had spent the last ten hours.

'Well, it's good to be out of that,' Mrs Collins remarked as they emerged. The pavements were furred with frost and their footsteps rang on the icy pavement. 'Oh, my God!'

They had turned into what was left of their road. Last night, as Sue had descended the steps, with the family cat, protesting loudly, clutched beneath her arm, she had looked back at the narrow street, the neat houses. They were ordinary houses, the homes

205

of ordinary people, and there were an awful lot of them, hundreds probably.

Now they weren't there. Not the first dozen or so anyway, though here and there a wall stood, a door, or an entire window, even the glass unshattered, whilst the house smoked in ruins around.

'Where's number twenty-eight?' Mrs Collins said, her voice hoarse, strained. 'Where's me little 'ome?'

Behind her, a voice said, 'Christ! Don't I even 'ave a doorstep?'

The woman who had spoken sat down suddenly on the splintered pavement. She was smiling, but tears ran down her face.

Sammy, swathed in blankets, recognised something was wrong and began to cry. His nose was running. Sue bent down and picked him up, which meant putting the cat down, and tried to comfort him.

'It's all right, Sammy, we're all here, don't cry, we're all safe, a house is only a house, after all. It's not important.'

The twins were in full flight after the cat, shrieking as they ran. Sue guessed it was a reaction to finding themselves suddenly homeless and watched, with a lump in her throat, as Dee and Eee belted up the pavement.

'Tibby, come back, Tibby, it's dangerous, come back!'

'Dee, Eee, come back yourselves,' Mrs Collins shouted, suddenly galvanised. 'Don't you go near them ruins . . . they could fall on you, squash you flat . . . girls!'

Dee grabbed the cat, was scratched, held on. She trotted back to them, triumphant, bloodstained, grinning.

'It's all right, Mam,' she said. 'We're all safe, even if the old 'ouse isn't. Will we go to Granny Sutton's, over in Midgy?'

'I dunno,' Mrs Collins said. Her voice was flat suddenly, lifeless. 'Granny Sutton's very old . . . Dear God, where'll we go?' she turned to Sue. 'We've got nothin', chuck, only the clothes we stand up in. What'll we do?'

Sue looked around her; at the neighbours who had laughed and sung all night in the shelter now wandering aimlessly up the shattered pavements, staring, blank-faced, at what had once been their homes.

'Mam, we've got our lives,' she said bracingly. 'We'll go to Aunt Florrie, in Formby. She'll take us in until they find us somewhere else to live. As you say, Midghall Street may easily have been hit, but Formby's a way out; they ought to be safe.'

'Oh Sue, love, I don't know if she'll manage all of us. Even wi' you older ones away there's our Annie, our Sammy and the twins and me . . . that's five, an' when your da comes 'ome . . .'

'She'll find us somewhere,' Sue said comfortingly. 'Leave it to me, Mam.'

'Oh but they'll want you back as soon as Christmas is over. We'll never settle nothing wi' the holiday an' all.'

'I'll get compassionate leave, I won't budge till

you're settled,' Sue assured her. 'Chin up, Mam! We won't let that old bugger Hitler gerrus down!'

'Meggie! Did you have a good Christmas? Did you go anywhere exciting, meet anyone new? It's odd how the days fly when you're on leave, it seems no time at all since I last stood in a queue for a meal.'

Meg was standing, eating irons in hand, waiting for her breakfast, but she turned at the sound of her friend's voice and smiled broadly. She had found herself glad to be back, much though she had enjoyed her leave, and seeing Christie, pink-cheeked from fresh air and hurrying, set the seal on her contentment. Now Christie joined her, pushing her loose hair behind her ears; she must have come pretty well straight from the station, Meg supposed, noting the train smut on her friend's forehead and the crease-marks on her skirt. No doubt she had just cantered into their billet, slung her kit-bag onto the bed, and rushed over here for something to eat.

'Hiya, Chris! Everything was wonderful, thanks – how did your Christmas go?'

Chris heaved a great sigh and closed her eyes for a second.

'It was bliss, absolute bliss. Andy loved everyone and everyone loved him, my brother Frank's got the nicest girlfriend, her name's Celia, we got on like a house on fire . . . But why didn't you ring me? You did say you would, I kept hoping . . .'

'Sorry, but I did try several times and your line was always engaged. And there's always a queue at the public call-box now, with everyone wanting to get in touch with someone else.'

'Oh well, fair enough. And the line was awfully busy, you're right there. Cousins, brothers, even Mummy and – I mean Mum and Dad – seemed to get an awful lot of calls. So what did you do?'

Meg considered. Looking back, it hadn't been a particularly exciting leave, but it had been just what she needed. The flat above the shop had been warm and homely after life in billets; and her bedroom overlooking the river with its steep, willow-laced banks and the old, old stone of the Welsh bridge just visible if you squinted sideways, was a haven of peace. Familiarity can also bring contentment. Her father, cycling three miles to the farm at Burland where he worked at the crack of dawn each morning; her mother, getting up with Dad to see to the newspapers, serving breakfast in relays as she had always done, then opening the shop dead on eight o'clock so that tradesmen hurrying along Welsh Row into Nantwich or catching the red bus to Crewe, the nearest big town, to open their own shops might pop in for a copy of the *Chronicle* and – if they were lucky – ten Woodbines or an ounce of shag.

Meg, lying in her bed beneath the sloping ceiling which, if she lay on her right side, was only six inches above her nose, woke when Dad clattered downstairs, then snoozed until she felt inclined to move. Then it was breakfast – real eggs every morning, from Dad's hens on the allotment, real bacon from the farm's autumn pig – then chatting to Mum, helping to serve in the shop, great excitement when someone from school, smart in service uniform, came sauntering in and found her there.

She'd wandered round the town, at first alone, then with Lenny Bowdler, the estate agent's bright, restless son, now a rear gunner in a Wellington bomber. The Bowdlers' estate agency was only a few doors up from the Aldford's, though five years ago they had moved from the flat over the shop to a beautiful Georgian house in Dysart Buildings, near the parish church. But Meg and Lenny were old friends; Meg remembered him from infant school when he had knocked over her bricks and then let her play with his sand-tray, and they had roamed the streets together as kids, been screamed at by their mums when they played on the banks of the river Weaver or roller-skated down Beam Street, imperilling not only their own lives but the lives of anyone on the pavement.

As they grew older they had grown apart a little, until the school holidays when Meg was fifteen and Lenny seventeen. They had spent blissful weeks, clad in old dungarees, taking his newly acquired second-hand motor-bike to pieces and putting it together again in the small cobbled yard behind his father's premises. Meg remembered how annoyed he got because she was better at it then he, seemed to have an in-built understanding of the way engines worked.

'It's bloody unfeminine,' he had grumbled. And then he'd bought a new exhaust for his bike, a great roaring curly thing, and she had put it on for him whilst he watched and dabbed oil on the tip of her nose and laughed at her.

He'd not taken her to the flicks though, or kissed her in the back row. It had hurt her, but he'd called her a kid, said she was too young for 'that sort of thing', so she hadn't bothered unduly about it.

Now together again, more by luck than design, Meg told herself, they strolled beside the river talking of their schooldays, popped into the Crown Hotel on High Street for a five-shilling dinner and honoured the Boot & Shoe, the Wilbraham Arms and several other local pubs with their custom in the evenings.

'You're so good with engines, Meg. I just wish you worked with my ground-crew,' Lenny told her as they sat on the bank below the Welsh bridge, watching the swans gliding up-river. 'We could do with someone who seems to know by instinct how an engine feels . . . but there you are, I suppose we need plotters, too.'

'Clerks (special duties),' Meg reminded him, smirking. It amused her that everyone thought plotting a glamorous job and found it hard to believe that their job-description could possibly be anything as mundane as clerk (sd). 'Well, they say there will be postings in the New Year – perhaps I'll go for flight mechanic training then.'

'You should; you're the only girl I know who looks pretty with oil on her nose and her hair tied up in an old duster.'

She swung at him, he dodged, caught her hand . . . kissed the palm, cuddled her, sighed against her hair.

'I never thought I'd regret leaving all this behind,'

he said, with a gesture which took in the town, the bridge, the fast-running, brownish water of the river. 'You know what they say about rear gunners, Meggie?'

'No? What?'

'Oh well; we don't live to a ripe old age, as a rule. Did I tell you about my mate Tommy Elcott?'

'No, I don't think so. What about him?'

He stared at the swans for a long moment, then he told her. In a dry, unemotional voice which did not fool Meg for one moment.

'He was a rear gunner, like me. We were over Germany – the Ruhr, it was. His kite got a direct hit, it broke in two, I saw it happen, but there was nothing I could do about it . . . I saw Tommy, too.

'Meg, he was in the rear gunner position, in half a plane. He was grinning, still firing . . . he had no idea the front half of the plane wasn't there.'

'That's terrible,' Meg said at last. 'That's so terrible, Len.'

'Yes. So . . . perhaps this place wasn't so bad after all.'

But they both knew life must go on, and the following evening Lenny took her dancing at the country club. Next day he acquired fishing rods and he and Meg sat on the cold river-bank and cast for trout until it grew dark, when they got a green Crosville bus into Chester and visited the Christmas fair on the Roodee, the flat water meadow by the race-track. Lenny's dad was a bit of a wide-boy, Lenny always had money, but they'd spent all Mr Bowdler handed out that day, having a go on everything from the roundabouts and swingboats to the hoopla and shooting stalls. Lenny had given her all his winnings – a kewpi doll with a simpering smile on its celluloid face, a tiny goldfish in a jam jar, two sticks of unbelievably pink rock. They missed the last bus and had to hitchhike home – a lorry-driver picked them up and Meg had fallen asleep against Lenny's shoulder as the lorry roared homewards.

When her leave ended – Lenny had another day's leave still to go – he had humped her kit-bag to the station and insisted on climbing into the carriage with her.

'You made my leave for me, chick,' he had said, with both arms round her and the carriage door closed despite Meg's fears that he would find himself carried off to Euston. But she clung to him, responding warmly when his mouth slowly, lingeringly, covered hers. He drew back when the porter came along, slamming carriage doors, bawling a warning that the train was about to depart, and swung lightly down on to the platform. She hung out of the window to hear his parting words: 'Let's do it again, next time we're home – you will write, Meggie?'

But it was the sort of thing air-crew said, Meg knew it, and they said it because life was so short, so fraught, if you were a rear gunner in a Wellington bomber. There was no point in a plain girl like Margaret Aldford pining for the fascinating Lenny Bowdler. Best put the whole episode behind her and get on with her life.

'Come on, Meg ... don't dream! What happened on your leave?'

Christie's voice jerked Meg back to the present. Lenny Bowdler's lively, triangular face crowned with mouse-brown curls faded, along with the willow-girt river, the winding streets of the old town, the shop with its newspapers, sweets, tobacco. Mum and Dad faded too, becoming a part of her past again, almost dreamlike, almost unreal.

'What happened? Well, not a lot. I slept late, ate a lot, went out a few times ...'

Never lie to your best friend, Meg thought desperately, trying, on the spur of the moment, to remember just what she had told Christie, just what Christie would expect to hear. Why had she let Christie assume that she came from a well-to-do farming family? Why hadn't she said straight out, *My dad's a farm labourer and my mum keeps a newsagent's shop*?

'Yes? Who did you go out with?'

'Oh, a bloke called Lenny; a neighbour's son, we've known one another for years. It was just friendship, though. He's a rear gunner in a Wellington, so we had the service in common.'

'Just that? Nice, is he?'

'Very nice. But we may not see each other again, not until after the war, anyway. What did you do, Chris?'

'All sorts. This and that. Have you seen Sue yet? Shanna?'

'Ah, you don't know, of course. Sue's got special

leave. Her home has been bombed, she's staying to see if she can sort things out.'

'Oh, poor Sue! Yes, now you mention it I remember seeing in the papers that the Jerries had raided Liverpool before Christmas. We heard planes going over, wave after wave of 'em. Oh, Meg, how dreadful for Sue. Was anyone in her family hurt, do you know?'

'No, I don't think so. Just shocked ... and with nowhere to live, of course. But Sue's so sensible; she got on the telephone at once and spoke to the CO and explained what had happened. And of course he told her to stay on until she had sorted things out.'

Whilst they talked the girls had had their plates filled with one of cooky's ubiquitous stews. They took their food to an empty table and sat down, then Christie looked around.

'Where's Shanna? It must have hit her very hard. She's awfully dependent on Sue.'

'She's got a half-day. And she's bearing up pretty well. She's gone off on a bike today, believe it or not, to visit the New Forest.' Meg took a mouthful of stew, then gestured with her fork to the doorway, through which they could see snowflakes lazily drifting. 'Trust Shanna to pick a day like this – she'll be frozen by the time she gets back.'

'Oh, well. Who's she gone with?'

'Some bloke,' Meg said indifferently. 'You know Shanna.'

Christie smiled.

'I know what you mean, but perhaps we're all a bit like Shanna in wartime. We all want some closeness.'

Meg pulled a face.

'We aren't all promiscuous, but ... yes, I suppose you're right. I think I understand Shanna and the way she behaves better because of being with Lennie, this leave. I say, it's jam roly for pudding; my mouth yearns for it but my hips aren't so keen. What about you?'

'I ate too much all over Christmas, I really shouldn't ... but what the hell? I won't be seeing Andy for a whole fortnight, I'll lose weight tomorrow,' Christie said recklessly. 'Is there custard?'

That night, Shanna lay in her bed and listened to the thrum-thrum of heavy bombers flying overhead and guessed it was the Luftwaffe, off to attack inland once more. She tossed and turned restlessly for a bit, unable to drop off, which was unlike her. Usually Shanna was fast asleep within seconds of her head touching the pillow. But not tonight; her mind was too active for sleep and nothing she did brought the longed-for slumber.

Whilst the aircraft roared overhead she even tried counting planes, hoping that would be more successful than counting sheep, but there were too many, the formations too close. And then, of course, the reverberating, hateful sound made her think of Sue, up there in Liverpool sorting her mother out, minding the kids, organising everything.

She missed Sue but it wasn't Sue who was mainly on

her mind. It was Col. She had known him rather less than three days, they had spent as much time as they could together, but their intimacy, so far, had only stretched to some kissing and cuddling.

How, then, was it possible that he had become so very important to her? Men had never mattered – she had been secretly rather proud of the fact. She needed men but she didn't like them or think about them or, indeed, expect them to like or think about her. Yet here, out of the blue, like a wonderful gift, was Col Blacker. And he mattered. He was waiting for a posting abroad, he had told her so from the first, he might be gone within days. Yet she, who had let more men than she cared to remember have their way with her, could not offer herself to him – would not.

He respected her; she thought he loved her, knew she loved him. Such a rare, wonderful thing was not to be treated lightly, not even if he was going away. He touched her with a deference and delicacy which was foreign to her – but she loved it. In return, she behaved as he expected her to behave, with affectionate circumspection, and wished with all her heart that she was as virginal as he believed her to be, so that her giving, when it came, could be honest, total.

She knew they would be lovers. Her mind and body cried out for him. She wanted to give, to please, to become a part of him, subservient to his every wish, eager only for his gratification, his happiness.

Before, her love-making had scarcely justified the name because it had been such a totally selfish emotion. She had lain under anonymous young men, or leaned against hut walls with her skirt up round her shoulders and her knickers round her ankles, intent on two things; the great, whooshing rush of pleasure which intercourse gave her and the warmth and power which came from being desired.

And now? Now, when she would have done anything to please him? Now she had to wait for him to make the first move, and the waiting was driving her mad, sending her mind round in circles, forbidding sleep.

He had said he didn't know when he'd be posted, that the call might come at any time in the next few weeks. But Shanna, her mind sharpened by the fear of losing him, was sure that it would be sooner than later. She thanked God – in whom she did not believe – for making him ground-crew and not air-crew because she could not have borne the worry every time he took to the sky. Shanna did not have a particularly vivid imagination but she understood at last how others felt; how Christie must feel, with two brothers at risk as well as her lover. Christie had arrived at the station young and rosy, with a good deal of quiet self-confidence and the natural, delightful charm of one who usually gets her own way. No more. She was slimmer, paler ... she jumped at sudden sounds, wept when the News coming over the wireless was bad, couldn't open a letter without losing her colour.

I don't want to be like that, do I? Shanna asked herself uneasily, and knew that she had no choice. When you love, when you give hostages to fortune, then fear enters your life, sapping your confidence, nibbling away at it until you, too, jump at sudden sounds, weep over trifles, dare not open a letter for fear of what it might say.

But hand in hand with love and fear goes hope, Shanna suddenly realised. Hope of better things, better times. Hope that one day, you and your lover will be together, free from fear, free to love unreservedly. So though suddenly she and Christie were sisters under the skin, though the experiences through which they were going were painful ones, they had a goal. Peace. The end of all this carnage. Children, even.

Children? But I've never wanted to have kids, it hurts, Shanna thought, so surprised that she sat upright in bed, staring blankly at the window opposite her, at the dark sky and the stars. Why should I suddenly see kids as desirable in any way?

But of course, the answer was that they would be Col's kids. A baby, warm and soft, tugging at her breast, Col's arm round her shoulders, his eyes shining with pride as they met hers. Col would like a child, so she would like one, too.

Very slowly, she lay down again. What made her think she could have a child, anyway? God knew she'd been with enough fellers and she'd never quickened yet, had looked askance at girls panicking because a period was late, desperately gulping gin and taking hot baths. Yet deep within her, a quiet certainty was growing. She could have children – one day, she would have children.

The thought, for some reason, calmed her, as though her mind had come full circle and satisfied the itch of need within her for the time being at any rate.

Presently, she slept.

Christie was on duty and heard the planes going over, saw the British fighters begin to appear on the board. She was on the first day of her period and stomach cramps kept attacking her but she swallowed a couple of aspirin with a cup of lukewarm tea and carried on. As soon as she sat down at the table these days she put herself onto what she secretly thought of as automatic pilot and now despite the pain in her stomach she did just that and began her work, listening to the voices coming in over the ether. Someone said a hundred bombers had droned past ... it didn't matter, numbers were irrelevant, what mattered was getting it right, moving the pieces when you were told, and telling yourself that Hurricane V for Victor, with Andy at the controls, was all right, fine ... had probably landed safely already.

It was a sticky shift, though. Midnight to five a.m. often was. Observers reported a Hurricane spiralling down into the sea. Christie waited for the number but it didn't come. They rarely managed such firm identification at night and with the worst of the air battles behind them, most of Andy's flying was done after seven in the evening.

But she wouldn't consider ... She heard another voice in her ear ... an ack-ack battery on the coast had hit a German plane, it, too, had come down in the sea. There were crooked crosses on the board; she picked one at random and took it out of play, for one ghastly moment putting herself in the place of that poor devil, hearing the terrible howling of an engine out of control as it dived, the rush of air, of flames, feeling the tremendous, breath-stopping blow as he emerged from the cockpit into the madness of the night, struggling to find the ripcord of his 'chute ... then the sea roaring up to meet him, the desperate prayers for the 'chute to open before it was too late, before the sea claimed another victim ...

'Christie? Can you hand over yet?'

Audrey, Christie's relief, took the head-set gently from her nerveless fingers and slid into the seat which Christie hastily vacated. She adjusted it and turned sympathetic eyes up to meet the other girl's gaze.

'Bad night, Chris?'

'Yes, pretty nasty,' Christie said briefly. 'It should quieten down soon though; it usually does.'

'Good. You get some rest,' Audrey advised. 'You look washed out.'

'I feel it.' Christie touched the other girl's shoulder briefly. 'Thanks, Aud; see you tomorrow. I'm going to bed when I've eaten.'

'Good idea.'

Audrey turned to the board and Christie made her way out of the operations room and across to the cookhouse. She felt terribly sick and knew she must replace her sanitary towel soon or she'd mark her uniform. But sometimes food helped. She took a plate of vegetable soup and some bread and marg but

221

couldn't face a meal, not feeling as she did. What was more, she knew very well she wouldn't sleep . . . not until she'd heard from Andy, at any rate. She'd ring his station at seven a.m. even if he'd gone to bed someone would know he was back.

Or not. But she didn't allow herself to consider that. Instead, she had a few spoonsful of soup and half the bread and marg, then got wearily to her feet and went across to her billet. Dawn was a long way off but familiarity got her across to her own bed. She found an issue sanitary towel and clean knickers, put her greatcoat on over her uniform, picked up her towel and soap and set off for the ablutions. So it was early . . . at least having a good wash would freshen her up and give her something to do. When she and Meg were on together they went into the mess and played cards or talked, but tonight she was the only one from her billet on duty. If she was quick she could have a proper shower, that would wake her up with a vengeance, make her feel more like herself.

The water wasn't hot, but it wasn't freezing cold, either. She showered, dried, cleaned her teeth, dressed again. She felt stiff and creaky, and her back ached as though she'd been up and about for weeks instead of just a few hours. Then she walked through the icy darkness towards the mess. She would doze in a chair, or read a book, or just sit and pray . . . but it was pointless undressing in the billet when she only had an hour until she could ring Andy.

The hour passed slowly. At seven on the dot she made her way to the telephone, feeling alive for the first time since the previous evening, when she and Andy had spoken briefly. The number was engaged for the first ten or fifteen minutes, but at least she was doing something, though the girl on the exchange must have got pretty fed up with her. But what did she matter, when Andy was at stake?

At last she got through. Yes, Pilot Officer Todd and V for Victor were both down safely; Pilot Officer Todd had grabbed some breakfast and gone straight to bed . . . was there a message?

'No . . . just tell him Chris rang,' Christie said. Great waves of relief were washing over her, making her positively euphoric. She could go back to her billet now – she'd sleep like a baby, knowing him safe.

In the hut, everyone else was waking up. Christie undressed, grinning at Shanna, who had somehow managed to get to the ablutions first and looked sparklingly clean and almost pretty. Something's different about Shanna since Christmas, Christie thought, lining up her shoes in front of her locker. She's happier looking – perhaps it's because she's realised she can manage very well without either Meg and me or Sue.

She pulled her pyjamas on and looked lovingly at her pillow, at the coarse grey blankets and her greatcoat which she would presently spread over herself. Meg's bed was stacked – she was on the five to ten shift and had probably relieved someone just before Christie herself was relieved. How awful I am, I never even looked for her, Christie remembered, stricken. But I felt so sick, and my stomach ached so much . . . the trouble is, I'm so preoccupied with Andy that nothing else seems real, somehow.

She climbed into bed, expecting immediate sleep, but her head was whirling, and the pain in her back defied description. I'll break in half if this goes on, she thought crossly. Who'd be a woman? It seemed so unfair that she should have to cope with this as well as everything else.

Lying there hurting, she kept her eyes tight shut, trying to ignore the whirling feeling in her head, hearing the girls chatter off to breakfast whilst she lay deliberately still, courting sleep.

It would not come. Instead, her limbs kept cramping up so that a leg would kick involuntarily, startling her out of whatever doze she had dropped into, or she would suddenly realise that her eyes had opened of their own accord and she was staring blankly at the roof above her head. And the pain went on, intensified, became a part of her.

After two hours of this she was like a violin string, stretched so tight that if someone had touched her she would have twanged. She thought about more aspirin, then remembered she had taken the last two earlier. She would have to get over to the NAAFI for more. She plainly wasn't going to get to sleep anyway, so she stumbled out of bed, dressed, and lurched towards the door. Half-way there the hut began to waltz crazily about her, the roof and the floor changed places, and a bed appeared to career towards her hitting her violently and painfully on the front of both calves.

She cried out as darkness swam up to meet her.

The MO was a middle-aged, fair-haired man with a sensible bedside manner and more sympathy and understanding than Christie felt she had any right to expect. He didn't tell her she had been silly to go on duty when she was suffering from bad period pains, nor did he try to say that all she was suffering from was a natural feminine affliction. In fact he took her collapse seriously, which was just what she needed.

'It's nervous exhaustion,' he said when he'd examined her. 'The bad period pains were just an aggravation of an existing condition. You passed out because you were simply too tired to go on, neither your body nor your mind could take any more. It happens to men as well as women, believe me. Now tell me again what you did when you came off duty?'

'Took a shower, read a book, rang my boyfriend,' Christie said weakly. 'It's all right, he was down safe. I thought I'd sleep after that, but I was so muddled, and my back was really bad, so I thought I'd go over to the NAAFI for some aspirin ... the rest you know, as they say.'

The doctor smiled.

'And your boyfriend is an operational pilot?'

Christie nodded. To her horror she felt the tears begin to form in her eyes and trickle down her cheeks.

'Yes; he flies a Hurricane,' she whispered. 'My brother Frank is a flight lieutenant, too. He flies Beauforts. They're bigger than Hurricanes; he has a crew with him.'

The doctor patted her hand.

'It's all right, there's no shame in tears, now and then. Any other brothers or sisters?'

'No sisters, but another brother. David; he's in the navy.'

'At sea?'

'Yes. On a destroyer.'

'Well, there you are, then. And you're a plotter, so you must wonder, every time . . .'

She turned her head away and spoke loudly, drowning him out.

'No! I don't wonder, I don't let myself. It's just a game . . . you have to think of it like that – just a game.'

He said nothing and after a moment she turned her head and looked up at him. His fair, kind face reflected the pain, the misery, which she had told herself she must not feel. But when he saw her watching him he smiled and patted her hand.

'Right. Well, you must stay in bed for the rest of the day and I'll write you down for three days off . . . not leave I'm afraid, but you won't be on ops for three days. And then I suggest you re-muster. They're posting WAAFs away from here now, the need for you in the ops room isn't so urgent . . . My dear, I know you won't believe me, but you'd be better doing almost anything else, situated as you are.'

'But I must be near him, we must take what we can, while we can.'

'Going to get married?'

'Yes. He hasn't asked me, I think he feels it's unfair

whilst everything's so – so uncertain. But we will marry.'

'Grand. So stay very quiet and calm for a few days and then pick up where you left off . . . except you've had your warning. Don't push yourself too hard another time. Tell someone how you feel, go sick, come to me or one of my colleagues. If there's a repeat of this it may not be so easy to bring you back.'

He made as if to get up and Christie's hand grabbed his sleeve.

'Don't go. I want to ask you something.'

He sat down on the bed again, smiling gently.

'Ask away.'

'Is it always like this? Loving someone, I mean? Does it always have to go hand in hand with such terrible worry and fear?'

He was silent for a moment, looking down at her, then he spoke.

'Only in wartime, my dear,' he said quietly. 'Only in wartime. And to balance that, you'll never feel things quite so vividly again, not love, not pain, not loss.'

'Good,' Christie muttered. 'Thanks, Doc. I think I can sleep, now.'

8

There was a letter board in the WAAF mess right next to the bulletin board and every morning it was surrounded by girls eager to see if they had any mail. Usually Shanna never bothered; why should she, when she knew very well that no one would ever write? But now that Sue was away she hurried with the others, because Sue had sent her two postcards already, both saying cheerfully that she would be back at the station by the time Shanna's leave finished and explaining just what she was trying to do.

But of course Sue didn't know that Shanna had delayed her leave because she wanted to be with Col. They had been surprised, in admin, when she'd explained that her boyfriend was due to be posted abroad and had asked if she might delay her time off to coincide with his embarkation leave, when it came. But the CO said he supposed it would be all right, and let Shanna continue at her desk, sorting out wages and using the clattering little calculating machine which was the Air Force's idea of modern technology.

So on New Year's Day, when Shanna would have

been enjoying a well-deserved rest had she let her leave stand, she hurried into the mess with Christie and Meg to see if Sue had written and found an official notice, with her name on it, stuck on the bulletin board.

She nearly didn't read it because it looked sinister, as though it might be a dental appointment or the news of a failed job interview. In fact she turned away, only Meg said, 'Oh, hell!' and pointed to her own name, just above Shanna's. 'It's a list of postings; God, half the hut's on it . . . anyone got a pencil? We'd better jot the details down.'

Shanna couldn't believe it. A long while ago she'd tentatively told one of the officers that she'd like to be a driver, then she'd forgotten it. How she wished the officer had; but there it was, in black and white: ACW Douglas, S., to report to RAF Weeton in Lancashire for MT training. And the date was less than a week away.

'They cannae do it,' Shanna muttered, staring round-eyed at Meg. 'Wha' does yours say, Meggie?'

'Retraining, same as yours . . . some godforsaken airfield way up north. Lord, someone's made a muck-up here; I'll see if I can have a word with the Wingco,' Meg said. 'Better get over to the cookhouse now, though, Shanna, or we'll miss our brekker.'

Shanna followed Meg, kicking dispiritedly at the snow as she went. Today was going to be a good day, too. She and Col – and Jacko in his light bamboo cage – were going off on the transport into Winchester after work, despite the snow which lay thickly on the ground, to see a flick and have a fish and chip supper afterwards. It was a simple enough treat, but one to which Shanna had been looking forward ever since Col had suggested it. Now the posting had ruined her pleasure in the day; all she would be able to think about was how to get out of it.

In the cookhouse, Shanna and Meg joined Christie, already eating a plateful of porridge. Christie had a letter from home, she was reading it propped up in front of her as she spooned porridge into her mouth. Now and then she chuckled; she looked better than she'd done after that funny turn which had ended in her being sent to the sick bay, but she still wasn't right; even Shanna could see that.

Meg, having finished her porridge, sat back and stared disconsolately at Christie.

'Chris, when you went to get your post, did you look at the bulletin board?'

'Briefly. Nothing on it for me, though. Why?' Christie finished perusing her letter and glanced across at her friend.

'Because Shanna and I have got postings; Shanna's off to Weeton on an MT course, I'm off to Northumberland.'

'You've been posted, Meg?' Christie frowned. 'Shanna too?'

'Aye. I dinnae ken what I've done,' Shanna said, taking refuge in broad Scots as she always did when she was upset. 'They cannae just post me as if I were a bluidy letter, can they?'

'They can,' Meg pointed out. She stared broodingly

at the table top. 'Someone said they wanted WAAFs on the bomber stations now . . . I suppose it's all to do with that. I'm not sure it's such a bad thing anyway, except for leaving you lot. I wouldn't mind learning something different, but . . . I'll see the Wing Officer. If it's definite there are things like rail warrants . . . you'd best do the same before you go off on leave, Shanna.'

'But that's just ma point – my leave's been deferred . . . If I'm up at this Weeton place what'll happen . . . what'll I do . . . oh, Meg, I willnae go!'

'See the Wing Officer,' Christie said. 'My God, if you two are posted and Sue has to stay away for long, I'm going to end up on my own here!'

She sounded so horrified that Shanna had to laugh, though in truth she felt exactly the same. If she meekly accepted the posting and went to Weeton she, too, would be alone, with the added disadvantage of being in a strange place. I'll run away, she thought wildly, I'll go to Col, explain I can't leave . . . he'll think of something. I could be a land-girl, they must need land-girls round here, there's an awful lot of countryside . . . then I could be near Col until he goes.

'I don't see the point of the WAAF training you as a plotter and then calmly announcing that they'd rather you learned a new trade,' Christie was muttering. 'Did you say there was a *list* of postings? I wonder who else had one?' She glanced round the table, eyebrows raised.

'Anyone else got a posting?' Meg asked.

'Yes, I have.'

'And me.'

'Me, too.'

'Bloody hell, it's half our hut,' Meg gasped. 'I wonder whether everyone's heading north? If so, at least we may be able to meet up now and then. What's the betting you have a posting in the next couple of days, Chris old bean?'

'I wouldn't be surprised if you were right,' Christie said gloomily. 'The MO said they were going to start shifting us around. Oh well, I'll have to put a good face on it, I suppose. Unless Andy decides we can get married, in which case I'll be off out of it.'

Shanna stood up.

'I'm away to see the Wing Officer,' she said, her voice trembling a little. 'Coming, Meg?'

Shanna walked out across the snow, heading for the NAAFI, where she had arranged to meet Col and Jacko. The Wing Officer had been awfully nice and had explained things rather well; but she had said, firmly, that it was either take the retraining or leave the WAAF. Shanna, who would have said that she found service life bearable but far too formal and hide-bound, suddenly knew that she had been happier this past year than at any other time in her life. In civvy street just getting by had been one long struggle. She had worked hard simply to keep body and soul together, to clothe herself and to have a roof of some sort over her head.

In the WAAF, though she had grumbled as much as

the next girl, her worries about food, clothing and somewhere to live had disappeared. She realised, now that there was a possibility that it might be taken from her, that she needed the WAAF as much as she needed Sue. No, she would have to put up with the posting, the enforced separation from both her friends and Col, because the alternative was too awful to contemplate.

Nevertheless, she would see what Col said. He was sensible, far more so than she. He would advise her sensibly, she was sure of it. And despite the posting, they could still have their evening out.

She reached the NAAFI and went in. Outside it was dusk and here the blackout blinds were down, the curtains drawn across – and Col was waiting for her, two mugs of tea on the table in front of him. Jacko was perched on the back of the second chair and Col was feeding him a digestive biscuit dunked in the tea, a treat which Jacko was noisily enjoying. Col looked up as the door opened and waved.

'Come and sink this tea; we'll catch the transport if you like, Shanna. But I rather want to talk to you.'

Shanna sat down opposite him and drew the mug of tea towards her. Jacko bounced down from chair-back to seat and screeched a greeting.

''Appy Noo Year, 'Appy Noo Year! Get that bloody bird out o' this place, go on, get 'im out!'

'Shut up, you old fool,' Shanna said, leaning across the table to ruffle the bird's soft green neck plumage. 'Let Shanna drink her tea.' She took a long, satisfying drink, then turned to Col. 'Can't we talk now?'

'Oh sure, yes. Look, no messin' about. We're leavin' for an unknown destination in a week. So my embarkation leave starts right now.'

Shanna's eyes widened.

'Well, if that isn't...' she fumbled in her coat pocket. 'Read this.'

Col read the instructions she had copied off the board then looked up at her and smiled.

'Ain't that downright weird? You're off too, on the self-same bloody day! I'll write ... you must give me your address.'

'I'll only be at Weeton a few weeks or something though,' Shanna pointed out. 'But if you write here the RAF will pass it on. So we're both off, then.'

Col's eyes brightened.

'You've got leave, too? A week, like me?'

He had misunderstood her; he thought she meant that she, too, had embarkation leave. Shanna opened her mouth, shut it again, picked up her mug and sipped whilst she gathered her thoughts, then spoke decisively.

'That's right, I've got a week from this moment, just like you,' she said. 'What'll you do?'

He grinned at her.

'What'll *we* do, you mean. Game to come away wi' me? It's freezin' cold and pretty dam' miserable wi' the snow dahn, but I've saved quite a bit ... There's a little cottage where the woman lets a couple o' rooms, it's not twenty miles from 'ere ... would you like that? Or we could try a small 'otel, only it ain't everyone what'll put up wi' Jacko.'

'The cottage,' Shanna said at once. 'And now that's settled, shall we catch the transport into town? Are you packed? But we can do that when we get back from the flicks.'

Col stood up, smiling delightedly.

'You're a great girl, Shanna,' he said. 'You've not even asked me wherrer it's one bedroom or two!' His face softened. 'You trust me ... you're right, you can.'

'I know,' Shanna said, standing up as well. 'Let's get a move on; I'll be as quick as I can ... say five minutes?'

'Say fifteen; that's when the transport leaves. Matthew's lookin' after Jacko for me for this evening; Jacko can ruin a good picture and 'e's a glutton for fish an' chips.'

Shanna laughed with him, then made for the door.

'I'll just run over to the offices and make my final arrangements. See you in quarter of an hour.'

'What d'you mean, *she's on leave*? She should have been back ages ago. Don't say she's gone AWOL.'

Christie had been sitting on her bed mending a hole in her stocking when Sue came bursting into the hut. It was lovely to see Sue, so reassuringly normal and fit-looking, her cheeks and nose pink from the cold, her curls furred with snowflakes. And to do Sue justice, she flung her kit-bag onto her unmade-up bed, gave Christie a quick hug, shouted a greeting to the other girls present, and asked immediately for Shanna.

'She changed her leave,' Christie explained, getting up to light the Primus stove so that she could make Sue a cup of tea. 'She deferred it. She didn't go until this morning, early. She'll kick herself when she finds you've come back sooner than she expected. Is everything okay at home, Sue? Did you manage to get everyone settled before you left?'

Sue heaved her greatcoat off and hung it up, then took off her cap and shook her snowy curls vigorously.

'Gawd, what weather! Yes, I got Mam and the kids in with me Aunt Florrie, out at Formby. They're sleepin' on tables, under 'em, all sorts, but they'll be safe enough there until they can be rehoused. Did you have a good leave, Chris? Meg's on duty, I suppose.'

'Super thanks, and as for Meg, she's been posted. She's going to retrain – not sure what the course is for. I can't imagine why they should move her, but that's the Air Force for you. And I've been posted too, only mine didn't come till yesterday.'

'Ye Gods, we really are being torn asunder, then. You and Meg going. It'll leave just me and Shanna again.'

'No it won't,' Christie said apologetically, pulling the kettle over the flame. 'Shanna's gone on leave, but when she comes back she'll only be here for a couple of days. Then she's off to RAF Weeton to retrain as a driver.'

'A train driver? What on earth do the WAAF want with train drivers? My God, I can't leave you lot for two minutes without you do something daft!'

237

'Sue, I'm sorry . . . what a homecoming! And I said train as a driver, nothing to do with railways at all! Ah, the kettle was already hot, I'll just make you some tea . . . anyone else want a cup?'

The hut was half full of girls writing letters, mending, doing jigsaws – a recent craze – and knitting. Two or three girls raised their hands and Audrey and a friend came over and started to make-up Sue's bed. She grinned her thanks at them, then began to take off her damp outer garments. She hung cap and greatcoat on the wall-pegs, then slid her tie over her head, unbuttoned her jacket and kicked her shoes off. Then she sat down on the end of Christie's bed and took the proffered cup of tea gratefully.

'Thanks, Chris, I really need this; now tell me all your news again, very slowly. The cold's numbed my brain . . . you can't *all* be moving on?'

'We are. I'm retraining as an RT operator, Shanna's driving, and Meg's gone on this course – probably RADAR. And after you complete the course you get posted to a different station, you can't come back to the one you've left.'

'That's grim, really horrible. If there's one thing I hate it's losing me friends. Is Shanna very cut up?'

'Well yes, she was. Said she'd leave. But she went and talked to the Wing Officer and came out . . . oh, calmer, sort of. Said she'd decided to make the best of it, looked almost cheerful when she went off on leave.'

'Where did she go? Any idea?'

Christie thought back; to Shanna's bright face, to

her murmurs about a cottage somewhere ... she'd wondered what Shanna was up to this time, but hadn't bothered to pursue it. After all, the kid was happy, that was the most important thing.

'No, not really. She did say something about a cottage in the country, but you know Shanna.'

'I thought I did,' Sue said. She finished off her tea and stood the mug down. 'I've never thought of her as a cottage person, mind you. I suppose there's some bloke?'

'If so, she's keeping him very quiet,' Christie said. 'Or perhaps it's a fellow from the village, or another station. Anyway, you'll be able to ask her yourself in a couple of days.'

'True. She *was* all right, wasn't she, Chris? You know what I mean.'

'She was fine; rosy and happy,' Christie said definitely. 'She decided to take her leave all of a rush, went and told her boss, chucked stuff into her kit-bag and vamoosed. Don't worry about her, Sue. Shanna's learned a lot in the past year, she told me so herself.'

'Oh, well. Thanks, girls, that bed looks so tempting, but I suppose I'd better trot along to the ablutions first, though it's brass monkey weather out there.'

'I'll come too,' Christie said, hastily cobbling the last hole in her stocking and biting off the thread. 'I want to get to bed before the stove burns out.'

Shanna lay on her back in the big brass bedstead, with the blankets pulled up to her chin. She was mother-naked, just bathed, sweet-smelling as a baby. On the end of the bed Jacko sat, watching the door unblinkingly.

Presently, the door opened and Col came in, already in his pyjamas and with his sooty hair rumpled and damp from his bath. He smiled lovingly at Shanna as he slid into bed beside her.

'I do love a bath . . . I always sleep better for a bath.'

Shanna snuggled up to him.

'I do, as well,' she murmured. 'Cuddle me, Col.'

Col began to cuddle her; she was watching him and saw his nostrils flare a little, his eyelids droop over those bright, dark eyes.

'Where are your sensible WAAF pyjamas, Shanna? What are you tryin' to do to me, gel?'

'I'm trying to seduce you, I think,' Shanna said. 'After all, you did tell Mrs Roberts that we were man and wife.'

'You said it was all right,' Col pointed out righteously. His hand slid, warm and wonderfully confident, down across her breasts and over the smooth roundness of her stomach. 'I did ask you, and you said you'd answer to Mrs Blacker any time.'

'Oh, I'm not complaining, I just thought we might as well use this bed the way it was meant to be used, you having paid for it, or Mrs Roberts might think we weren't married after all, and then we'd be in trouble.'

Col laughed, then he sat up, took the candle off the bedside table and blew it out. The faint waxy smell lingered as he lay down again and pulled the covers up over himself.

'Good night, ladies, good night, ladies,' a hoarse voice remarked from the foot of the bed. 'Shut up, Jacko, shut up, shut up!'

'Take your own advice, me old pal,' Col said. 'Shut up or put up.'

The bird squawked and settled. Col turned to Shanna.

'Now what were we saying? Oh Shanna, oh Shanna . . . oh, your skin is so soft and sweet, I could eat you up!'

He began to kiss her and Shanna, shuddering with anticipation, knew, at last, the sheer delight of love-making, the pleasure which it brings when the man with whom you make love is the lover of your choice.

'Whoa, whoa, take it easy on the corners,' Jacko shrieked presently, as the bed began to creak and move. 'Slow down, man, slow down!'

Shanna opened an eye and saw, beyond Col's shoulder, the bird swaying as though on a wind-tossed branch, its wings half-spread to help it balance. Then Col's movements became more rapid, her own response more frantic, and she forgot Jacko, the old brass bedstead, their landlady in the room next door. She was caught up in the passion consuming them and knew, with complete certainty, that Col felt just the same.

Presently, appetites sated, they lay quiet, sweat cooling, heartbeats slowing. Col turned to her and kissed her gently on the mouth.

'I love you, Shanna,' he whispered.

Shanna's eyes filled with tears. No one had ever said that to her before, not a mother, not a lover.

'I love you too, Col,' she whispered back.

Lincolnshire seemed to go on for ever; flat fields and meadows, huge rivers, great sunlit vistas stretching endlessly on either side of the train as it chugged along, carrying Shanna to Lincoln and her first proper posting as an MT heavy lorry driver.

Shanna knew she had been lucky to go on the course without too many black marks on her charge sheet, considering that she'd overstayed her leave by four days to be with Col. He hadn't known, of course – he would have made her go back, would have worried that she might get into deep trouble. So their week had been a completely happy one for both of them, even though they were dreading having to say goodbye.

It came, of course. Tears – on both sides – desperate clingings on the station platform. Col was going to Southampton to join the ship which would take him to his new posting, Shanna was catching the train back to her old station, though she wouldn't be there long.

Perhaps they'll punish me by making me give up the course, she thought hopefully, as she and Col clung, she inside the train leaning out, Col on the platform leaning in. Losing Col was like losing an arm or a leg – worse – so being sent away from Sue as well seemed almost unbearable. I don't care if they demote me, make me work as a floor scrubber, she thought desperately. It wouldn't matter, if only I could stay with Sue.

But she knew it wouldn't happen, knew she'd lose both Sue and Col; which was why, after all her resolve, the tears began to run down her cheeks as the train gave a preliminary shriek and began to get up steam.

'I'll miss you so much, Col my love,' she sobbed, her tears soaking into the shoulder of his greatcoat, for it was bitterly cold still. 'You'll write often, won't you? Every day?'

'Every day,' Col promised, his voice choked with emotion. 'I've never loved no-one before, Shanna, but I'll love you for ever, I swear it. I'll be back for you just as soon as we dock in old England again.'

'Don't go, don't go!' Shanna wept, then took a huge, shuddering breath, withdrew from his embrace and dried her eyes on the backs of her hands. He had to go, she shouldn't make it worse for him. 'Och, I'm so silly ... I'll wait for ye, dearest Col. But it'll be a long, lonely waiting.'

And then, at the last moment, when the train was actually moving, he had put a finger through the bamboo struts of Jacko's cage, given the bird's head one last rub, then thrust the bird, cage and all, into the carriage with her. Jacko fluttered, swore, then settled.

'Take care of each other,' Col shouted, waving. 'Love each other! I'll be back for the pair of you!'

Shanna had waved until the station platform, and the tiny figure on it, disappeared round a bend. Then

she sat down and stared rather doubtfully at the bird.
She was fond of Jacko, he was funny and affectionate,
quick-witted and occasionally vulgar, but he was also
quite a responsibility – and Col loved him so! Next to
me, Jacko's his most precious thing, Shanna found
herself thinking. To give me Jacko – well, he really
does love me, and he trusts me, too.

Jacko looked round the carriage. It was full – and
several passengers were regarding Jacko with doubt,
not to say dislike. Shanna cleared her throat.

'My feller's been posted abroad,' she said. 'Guess
he thought the heat might be a bit too much for his
bird.' She inserted two fingers through the bars the
way Col had taught her and began to rub the soft
feathers on his neck. Jacko sank his head into his
shoulders and closed his chalky eye with pleasure.
'He's a good bird, is Jacko – he talks really grand and
he's clever, you can teach him anything.'

She was right, which was a good thing, because he
had to be left in her hut in Sue's doubtful charge whilst
she was marched before the Wing Officer accused of
being AWOL.

'You were daft,' Christie said disapprovingly, when
Shanna arrived back with the parrot. 'No man's worth
it. And as for the bird . . .'

Shanna couldn't explain about Col, how special he
was, how precious to her, so she had to suffer her
friends' complete lack of understanding on the
subject. Indeed, she never mentioned his name, let
the girls go on believing that he was just another of her
pick-ups, a feller good for one thing and one thing

only, who'd be forgotten in twenty-four hours.

And being absent without leave was a serious offence, it could have gone badly for her as a breach of discipline; but the senior staff knew they were getting shot of her, sending her off on the course, so they'd docked her four days' pay and given her two days' punishment drill. Sgt Shaw made her run round the perimeter track with a kit-bag full of bricks on her back, a sort of gloating lesson for Shanna's behaviour behind the hut so long ago. But Shanna had got the better of her by a truly convincing faint – she'd skinned both knees in the fall – so her last day on the station had been spent in sick bay, anxiously watched by the staff, while her friends came and visited her and muttered about seeing that old Shaw got what she deserved. Indeed, before nightfall the Section Officer came to see her and said she thought Sgt Shaw had been over-zealous and promised that she would speak personally to the other woman.

And then it had been off in the train to RAF Weeton, near Blackpool, with Sue and Christie waving tearfully from the platform – Meg had already left of course – and Jacko squawking ruderies at everyone from the luggage rack. He had been on good form that day, making everyone laugh, hiding behind Shanna's kit-bag and blowing raspberries every time someone new came into the carriage and sat down. He was a good way of breaking the ice, actually. First Shanna apologised for him, then she explained that her boyfriend had trained him, and after that Jacko made friends for himself. Some people disliked him of course, but he recognised their dislike instantly and simply kept away from them.

Her fellow trainees at Weeton had loved him, from the lowliest recruit to the Scottish Sgt MacEvoy, their instructor.

'Jacko can tighten nuts better than the best spanner,' someone had declared as Jacko imitated the sound of the nuts being tightened to perfection. His Scottish accent improved apace too, what with Shanna and Sgt MacEvoy to copy. He would flap up to perch on an engine cowling and would sit there, quiet and apparently content, now and again muttering under his breath, then copy a recent remark so perfectly that the most intense amongst the budding MT trainees would collapse with laughter. He could be a nuisance in billet since nothing pleased him more than to poke his long beak into one's make-up or try to peck out a lipstick; but the girls chased him off, shouted at Shanna to control him, and then he would say something which made them laugh ... or someone would call out, 'Poor Jacko, poor old feller,' and he'd hang his head and limp very convincingly for a few paces, to gales of laughter and much applause.

When they were alone, Shanna would repeat all Col's favourite sayings and Jacko would promptly drop into the voice he knew best. Shanna listened contentedly as Col's voice told her he loved her, wished her Happy Christmas and advised her to get her bleedin' beak out of his sock-drawer.

I wonder what he'll think of RAF Waldrington, Shanna thought rather apprehensively now, as the train hurried on through the spring sunshine; and I wonder what RAF Waldrington will think of him – and of me. Not all members of the RAF approved of women drivers, particularly drivers of the heavy stuff ... but that was their problem. I can do the work, Shanna reminded herself. Provided I pull my weight they won't have cause to complain.

And when the train drew in and she climbed down onto the platform with Jacko's cage in one hand and her kit-bag in the other, she had a pleasant surprise. Another figure climbed down off the train at the same time, a small, square figure with dark, frizzy hair and, when she saw Shanna, a very wide smile.

'Meg Aldford! What on earth are you doing here?' Shanna demanded, rushing over to the other girl. 'I canna believe my eyes. It's so good to see you! Are you coming to RAF Waldrington, too?'

But Meg, though she hugged Shanna, shook her head.

'No, worst luck; it would be fun to be on the same station. I'm at RAF Sellars, not far from Waldrington. I've finished my initial training, but I'm going to be a u/t flight mechanic actually on station, which should be an experience. It's lovely to see you, Shanna, because we can meet when we're off duty. We all centre on Lincoln, they told me the transports go to and from the city each day. Look, we'll meet ... they arranged for me to leave for the course so fast that I scarcely had time to think. Christie's in Oxfordshire somewhere, she's training as an RT operator ... we write. What about Sue?'

'Still in Hampshire, but she's driving the blood waggon now. I do mean to write to them, but Weeton didn't give you much spare time, then I did some driving at a station in Blackpool itself before my proper posting came through. How strange that we've both been doing work connected with engines . . . Oh look, there's my transport . . . can you ring me at Waldrington? I'd love to meet up again.'

Meg promised to do so, then glanced at Jacko, swinging on his perch and muttering to himself.

'Where on earth did you get that parrot? It's not yours, is it?'

'Oh, someone gave him me. Colin – that's the feller who trained Jacko – was posted abroad. See you soon, Meg.'

'See you soon,' Meg echoed. Shanna made for her own transport with the name of the RAF station stencilled in white on the side, then glanced around her at the city which she would soon know so well.

It looks all right, she decided. There was the cathedral itself, a landmark for miles around on its hill above the city, and a huge building, a castle or something, nearby. Looking about as the transport began to fill up she could see shops, a river, quaintly winding streets and above it all, the pale blue arch of the sky.

'Aircraftwoman first class – Douglas, S?'

An RAF corporal with a list in one hand and a stub of pencil in the other glanced questioningly in her direction. Shanna nodded and he put a tick against her name, then looked round impatiently.

'Notice someone else on your train ... another WAAF ... girl called Martineau?'

'Tha's me, sir,' a voice behind Shanna said. It belonged to a small, wispy-looking girl, with fair curls and red-rimmed eyes; she'd been crying, Shanna thought. 'Sorry, sir, I went to the wrong lorry.'

'Well, get aboard. And don't call me sir, I'm a corporal,' the corporal said admonishingly. 'Come on you two, shift your arses. I've got work to do, you know, apart from babying you lot.'

'Don't mind him,' Shanna said soothingly, just as Sue would have said it. 'I'll give you a leg up and we can sit and talk until we go. I'm Shanna Douglas, by the way, MT driver. Is this your first posting?'

'Yes,' the girl said. 'I'm Angela Martineau and I don't know what I'm going to do there. Probably office work, since that's what I know best.'

'Then you'll probably be a cook,' someone called out. 'That's what the Air Force do best ... mucks us all abaht!'

Shanna joined in the laughter; so did Jacko.

'Ooh, what a big bird! What's his name?'

'He's Jacko,' Shanna said. 'We're all going to Waldrington, then?'

There was a chorus of agreement. Shanna looked round, smiling; five girls and three men smiled back at her.

'Anyone know anything about the place?'

'It's a good station,' a tall, skinny leading aircraft-man volunteered. 'I've just come off leave, I've been at Waldo six months. There's a good NAAFI, decent types in command, not too much enemy action since it isn't en route for anywhere else really, and Lincoln's a beautiful city.'

'Then if we stick together we'll settle in fast,' Shanna observed. 'It's always nice to recognise a face or two when you go into the cookhouse or the mess, so us WAAFs should all report to the guardroom together.'

'There's a Waafery,' the LAC announced. 'And you girls have brick huts ... better than the Nissens. The WAAFs seem a pretty contented lot, it's a big station so there are all sorts. They fly mostly bombers at Waldo.'

'Waldo?'

'Oh, no one bothers with Waldrington, Waldo's easier. There's a beautiful village all built on a hill, a couple of first-rate pubs ...'

'On a *hill*?' one of the other men said incredulously. 'I thought Lincolnshire was flat – well, it looked it, coming along in the train.'

'Yes, but the airfield's built on what they call the Cliff Edge. You'll see for yourselves once we arrive.'

'We have arrived,' a small, lively brunette announced, peering out of the back of the lorry. 'That was the gates ... I can see a hangar ... and there's a plane, a huge one.'

'They won't do much flying while the snow stays on the ground,' the skinny LAC said. 'So it'll be a quiet start for us in MT, thank God.'

Shanna smiled at him.

'Thank God,' she echoed.

Seeing Shanna had brought it all back, Meg thought as she climbed into her own transport and settled down on the metal bench. Not just the happy times Shanna and she had shared with Sue and Christie, but her closely guarded secret. She had glanced at the posting on that fateful morning, and then pretended surprise, never confessing to anyone, not even Christie, that she had applied for a posting, asked to re-muster as a flight mechanic. Her astonishment when she'd been accepted for the training had had to be kept secret – she hadn't even told them what she would be doing, had muttered something about a trade, hoping they would assume it to be radar or wireless, both trades to which plotters transferred quite frequently.

She had felt a certain amount of guilt over being the one deliberately to break up their foursome; that was why she had kept it all so dark. Of the four of them, she was probably the only one to want to leave Hampshire, to move on. Not that she had ever put it into words. Partly it was because of Patrick, she could acknowledge that now. She had felt ... oh, such a failure, such a total wash-out after he had given her the brush-off. All the other girls in ops seemed to have some sort of a relationship with a fellow, or a boyfriend at home, but she had mucked up, and done it publicly, what was more. She had been so proud of her lovely Patrick! And when he'd died she felt her last chance of proving that she could hold a man was gone for ever; and alongside that, stupidly, was a feeling of devastating loss. How can you lose what you've never had, she asked herself, knowing with the practical part of her mind that it was impossible, yet persistently feeling it nevertheless.

In the end she'd come to the conclusion that it was the finality of the affair which upset her most, as though Patrick had walked out of a room in mid-conversation whilst she, Meg, had still got something terribly important to say. She knew this was silly, but it was how she felt.

Lenny probably had even more to do with her desire to move than Patrick's rejection, though. Lenny had told her he'd be glad to have her in his ground-crew and it had played on her mind more than a little. She did have an aptitude for things mechanical, she knew she did. She should be using that aptitude where it could do most good, not allowing the Air Force to waste what talent she had.

Then there were the rumours flying round the station that, with the Battle of Britain over and our aircraft more on the attack, large numbers of plotters were not as necessary as they had been. We'll be posted, the whisper ran round the ops rooms in the south of England; the Air Force needs people in the north now, where the big bombers fly from.

So she'd pre-empted the demand by going to see her squadron officer and explaining that she knew quite a bit about engine maintenance and would like to re-muster and go on a course for flight engineers. There had been some initial amusement, then an aptitude test which Meg knew she had passed with flying colours. Then the posting had come, telling her to report to the engineering school – and once more she had behaved badly, letting everyone believe that she, like Shanna, had been stunned by the news that she was being posted. She acknowledged, now, that she had always been secretive, inclined to keep her own counsel, and it had done her no good; quite the opposite in fact.

Still. The enormous complexities caused by lying to friends had taught her a lesson. Since then she had been totally honest to everyone with whom she came in contact, telling them firmly that her father was a farm labourer, her mother a shopkeeper and her home was the flat above the shop. She also said she didn't have a boyfriend, though she wrote often to Lenny: light, amusing letters about the trials and tribulations of being the only girl on the flight engineering course, about how the men teased her, made sure she got her fingers well and truly dirty – and then copied her diagrams and asked her to explain things when they were in the classroom, writing up their notes.

She loved it though, both the work and the company. She found that if she treated men as she had treated Lenny when they had both been young they soon stopped being slightly threatening and became simply friends. She went to the pub with them, worked alongside them, listened to their woes, showed them how to darn socks and cook over the wood-burning stove in their hut.

And she wrote regularly to Christie, too. She doubted that they would ever meet again the way things were so she didn't mention her home life or circumstances, but she wrote about everything else with a frankness which, at one time, would have been foreign to her nature.

The WAAF is changing me, she thought sometimes. At other times she decided it was knowing Patrick which had changed her, or the war itself. She knew Lenny hadn't changed her, they went back too far; but once or twice it did seem to her that perhaps the way she thought about Lenny had changed her, softened her in a way.

And now, Shanna had re-entered her life. They weren't on the same station, but they were very near – probably not more than ten miles apart and both centring on the same city, both using the same pubs, restaurants, cinemas.

She had never been as close to Shanna as she had to Christie, but she found her heart lighter because there would be two of them. Being in a male-dominated trade had meant that she socialised with her workmates rather than with other WAAFs. It might be the same at Sellars, it probably would be the same; but she would have another girl to laugh with, talk about girlish things to, someone who already knew her, who didn't have to learn Meg's ways because she knew them already.

Shanna would have to be told the truth about Meg's home and parents, of course, though Meg did not believe that the other girl would care one way or the other. That was the nice thing about someone whose moral values were ... well, unusual. Shanna would just shrug and say so what? and the subject would be dropped.

The transport was filling up now; not that there were many WAAFs, only two so far, but lots of RAF. Mainly ground-crew, Meg saw, but a couple of air-crew as well. She smiled at everyone cheerfully but did not try to instigate a conversation until the man sitting beside her, a leading aircraftman, offered her a cigarette.

'So, you're u/t flight mechanic,' he said when both cigarettes were drawing. 'I didn't know there were any WAAFs doing that sort of work.'

'There aren't many I don't think; but I worked on engines in civvy street,' Meg said. 'I was a plotter down south for a year, then when postings began to come through I put in for engineering of some sort.'

'And they took you? You must be okay, then.' The young man luxuriously inhaled smoke, then blew it out through his nostrils. Meg saw by his arm badge that he was a flight mechanic, too. 'Is this your first posting since the re-muster, then?'

'Yes. The course was wizard, but I'm looking forward to doing the work for real. We trained on Hampdens, Oxfords, Spitfires ... you name it.'

The man nodded, narrowing his eyes against the smoke drifting up from his cigarette.

'We've got mostly Hampdens and Beauforts at Sellars. By the way, I'm Ken Barker.' He thrust out a hand, one eyebrow rising.

'Oh ... Meg Aldford,' Meg said quickly. 'Nice to meet you, Ken.'

'You'll go straight to the Waafery, no doubt, to get yourself signed in. But how about joining me in the NAAFI this evening? I can introduce you to people, put you right on things.'

Meg looked at him carefully; he was about twenty-four or twenty-five with short dark hair, a broad, peaceful sort of face, and a friendly, forthcoming attitude. He looked reliable, she decided.

'Thanks, I'd like that; what time?'

He had been looking down at his half-smoked cigarette, clearly letting her have a good look at him; now he raised his eyes and grinned.

'So I'm respectable, am I? Shall we say eight o'clock?'

'It's a date,' Meg agreed.

A tiny spark of excitement ignited at the words. A date! Only a friendship date, of course, but a beginning. She loved getting letters from Lenny and writing back, but she never let herself think of Lenny as anything but good friend. She had believed Patrick wanted to be more than a friend and look where believing that had got her, so she wouldn't make the same mistake with Lenny. She would value his friendship, but not take it amiss if he suddenly produced a girlfriend from somewhere. But Ken was different; he had approached her, he'd had no need to suggest that they meet ... any girl would consider that Ken was trying to get closer to her.

She had barely decided this, barely rejoiced in the

fact that a man had asked her for a date without so much as a flirtatious glance from her, when the transport lurched and began to move. Whilst she and Ken had been talking it had filled up and now men and women were squeezed onto the metal benches, the air was thick with cigarette smoke and voices bounced eerily off the metal and canvas walls.

'We aren't far out, thank goodness, which means you'll see quite a bit of Lincoln. I can show you round, if you like. I was born there.'

'Thanks,' Meg shouted again. 'I'd like that, too.'

And she knew it was true. Despite all that had happened with Patrick and Lenny, she still hadn't quite given up on the male race. She would very much like a boyfriend, someone to share service life with as she had shared civvy life with Lenny the last time they were home.

'Don't thank me; I'm proud of my home, it'll be good to take you around, show you all the nicest parts of the city. Where are you from?'

'I'm from Nantwich, in Cheshire,' Meg said, leaning forward to make herself heard. 'It's only a small town ... but I love it. My mum runs a newsagent's shop, we live over the top of it.'

Ken nodded.

'Snap! My mother lives over a cycle shop! But you'll see for yourself soon enough.'

They smiled at one another. We're going to get along, Meg thought happily. I'll tell Lenny all about him in my next letter!

9

Christie was in the control tower, bringing the returning aircraft down safely after a mission. She had done her RT training on the spot, being taught the job whilst actually doing it, her teacher an impatient cockney sparrow of a man whose one desire was to be released from RT work so that he could re-muster as ground-crew.

He had been good to Christie though, once he realised how quick she was, and she got on well with the other operators, preferring the eight-hour watches, which meant you sometimes had a whole day and night off, to the five-hour watches she had worked as a plotter.

It was hard to be too far away to see Andy except when one of them got a forty-eight, but she soon realised it was better not to be listening for his aircraft all the time, dreading the moment when she would hear his identification passed on in the emotionless tones of an observer who had seen his plane plunge to earth.

What was more, watches were shared on a regular basis, so Christie's watch-mate, who shared a bedroom with her in the house the RAF had commandeered in the village, was even more a part of her life than Meg had been. Mary O'Hara was as Irish as her name, a broad-browed, placid girl with a milk-and-roses complexion and very long, shiny hair the colour of cream fudge which she wound into a tight bun on the back of her head for work and allowed to fly loose when she was off duty.

'Why did you join up?' Christie had asked her when they first started working together, and Mary told her that she had been married to a London-Irishman who worked in an aircraft factory. They were living in Southampton when she discovered he was being unfaithful to her.

'He was in the Home Guard an' I was fire-watchin', so the bombs started comin' down and didn't I pop into an air-raid shelter, to warn them inside not to come out yet awhile? And what should I see down there but Harry, on the job? Goin' at it hammer and tongs in a bleedin' air-raid shelter,' she added, widening her big, greeny-blue eyes at Christie. 'Imagine it, Chris, on a bleedin' camp bed in an air-raid shelter, with his gun propped up against the wall for any paratrooper to nick! Oh, I was so humiliated! I grabbed up that rifle – I never thought to fire a couple o' rounds up his active little jacksey, but I hit'm with the rifle butt, and I did a deal o' shriekin'. Then I went to the Father to ask'm about a separation and he told me many women had more to suffer in wartime than a feller with needs over an' above those fulfilled by marriage, and I wasn't to consider leavin' me man for one small lapse from grace . . . so there went me faith in the Cat'olic Church.'

'What did you say?' Christie asked, considerably fascinated by this vigorously told story. 'I bet you told him a thing or two.'

'Well, didn't I! One small lapse from grace indeed, when there was Harry bouncin' around till the camp bed groaned, an' that shameless whore holdin' him be the ears an' caterwaulin' like a vixen on heat an' never givin' a thought to who might pass by, let alone to his poor wife.'

'Perhaps she didn't know he was married, though,' Christie said. 'I don't imagine he'd tell her, do you?'

'Sure an' why should he need to tell her anythin', when she was me bridesmaid at me weddin'?' Mary said huffily. 'A total stranger would ha' been bad, but me bridesmaid – I ask you!'

'We were stationed quite near Southampton; the raids were terrifying,' Christie said, remembering the appalling noise, the smoking ruins next day. 'It was brave of you to fire-watch, Mary.'

'Ah well, if it had me name on it I'd ha' bought it wherever,' Mary said philosophically. 'Harry t'inks we'll get back together when the war's over, but he'd better t'ink again. There's no way I'd let a feller like that into me bed I'm tellin' you straight. But haven't you heard enough about Mary O'Hara, now? Tell me about Christie Bellis.'

Christie had felt quite ashamed of her own dull story – joining up to get away from the farm, meeting

Andy, never looking at another man. She said as much and Mary retorted feelingly that she wouldn't have minded a bit of dullness herself, if it meant she'd still got a husband she could respect and a religion she could believe in.

But right now, the two of them were working away, head-sets on, one hand on the transmit-receive lever, mouth at the right level to speak into the upright mike, the other hand logging each message as it was sent and received. It was daylight, the planes were all trainers, and Christie felt closer to them knowing that Andy was training now – for a month or two, anyway. He'd completed his first tour and had been sent to instruct on Spitfires, work he enjoyed. Yet she knew that he wanted to return to active service, would return when he was permitted to do so.

And in the meantime, there were letters. They both wrote; and Christie, struggling with the technical side of her job, slogged away at electronic theory and Ohm's law to say nothing of magnetism, simple circuits, aerials and their care. She and Mary went two or three times a week to the transmitting station for instruction, and though they often moaned to each other that it would never sink in, Christie at least was determined to show everyone that she was capable by getting her 'sparks' badge which would denote that she had passed her exams and was a fully-fledged RT operator.

Even now, in front of the mike, her pencil flying across the page whenever a message had to be logged, she was thinking about the letter she would write to Andy later, the phone call she would make when she had the opportunity.

'It's going to be a nice day,' Mary said presently, when they had brought the last trainer in to land and were handing over to their replacements, Wendy and Doris. 'The sort of day when you can see summer's on its way. Why don't we take a picnic out into the country? We could use our bicycles.'

The bicycles were not, strictly speaking, the property of any one WAAF; a dozen of the girls had pooled their money to buy two old bone-shakers and these were kept in the gardener's tool-shed at the back of the once-beautiful old manor house which had been requisitioned by the RAF. Anyone off-duty could use the bikes, though they had not come out of the shed often during the long cold winter.

'I wouldn't mind a bike ride,' Christie said, looking out at the blue sky above the control tower. 'We might find some bluebells.'

'Or a couple of nice young fellers to pick 'em for us,' Mary said, only half-jokingly. She had pointed out more than once that just because Christie was head over heels in love with some feller, that didn't mean that she, Mary, must behave like a nun. Christie said she wasn't Mary's keeper and Mary might have as many boyfriends as she liked and welcome, but Mary told her that this was not quite the point.

'Sure and what would folk t'ink of me, if I chased after the lads on me own, and me still officially a married woman?' she said. 'Now if 'twas the two of us . . .'

'Well, I'd just settle for a picnic and some bluebells,' Christie said now as they clattered down the stairs and out into the fresh May morning. 'Did you catch the news, earlier? There have been awful raids on the Midlands and we've bombed Cologne again. I dread hearing the news, now. It always seems bad. Shall we go to the cookhouse, or shall we skip breakfast and go straight to the letter-board?'

They might live out but letters were still sent to the mess.

'Oh, I'll get no peace unless you've been to the board and checked that lover-boy has written his usual ten pages,' Mary said resignedly. 'You must get more post than any other WAAF on this station, Chris. There's me, lucky if I get one a month, but you get a couple most days.'

'I write a lot,' Christie pointed out as they crossed the grass, still wet with early dew, and headed for the mess. 'Not just to Andy, either. To my relatives, friends . . .'

'Those girls you were with when you were plotting? I feel I'd know them if I met them in the street,' Mary observed, pushing the mess door open. 'Meg, Shanna and Sue . . . like *Little Women*, I always think.'

Christie chuckled and took her post carefully off the letter-board.

'If you met them you'd know they aren't a bit like that. But we were good friends – why, even Shanna, who's no letter writer, drops me a line occasionally.'

'And Meg writes once a week at least,' Mary observed, obviously recognising the writing on one of the envelopes. ''Tis unusual though, me dear – in the services you meet and pass on but you four seem almost like family.'

'We were together for a year,' Christie reminded her. 'Come on, I do feel like some brekker; I'll read these over a bowl of porridge.'

'Why not?' Mary, who liked her food, pushed the door of the mess open wide and the two of them retraced their steps, then swerved across the concrete apron and into the cookhouse. The air was warm and steamy, WAAFs, air-crews and ground-crews sat around the tables eating with dedication. 'Ah, they've got cornflakes again.'

'A rare treat,' Christie said sarcastically as they fetched their portions. 'Especially with dried milk!'

'Eat up and don't grumble,' Mary commanded her. 'My dear old mother, back in County Kerry, would faint if she saw the food her eldest and best was forced to eat. Still, it does keep body and soul together.' She finished her cornflakes and got up. 'Want some scrambled egg? And if we ask cooky nicely we might even get some bread and cheese for that picnic.'

The corporal in charge of the cookhouse obliged; not only bread and cheese was given them, but a handful of raisins, a hard, green cooking apple and a rock cake each.

'I know t'cakes are made wi' dried egg an' dried

milk,' the fat little corporal said, popping them into a brown paper bag and twisting the top to keep it closed. 'But they taste good for all that. You won't find better cakes than them, ah tell you.'

'It's good of you, Corp,' Christie said gratefully. 'We do appreciate it, don't we Mary?'

The corporal sniffed.

'Oh well, we do us best. Where are you goin'?'

'To find a bluebell wood,' Mary said gaily. 'Know any hereabouts, Corp?'

'Not off-'and. Have a good time, then.'

The girls left the cookhouse and made for the gates. Despite having been at the station for several months, Christie had not quite got used to going off-camp to her billet. It still seemed strange to her not to head for the Nissen huts hidden in the trees, but with eight-hour shifts and set hours they were less likely to be needed in a hurry so it was as easy – and a lot nicer – to live a bit further from their work.

The manor house was half a mile away, along winding country lanes bordered by high, unkempt hedges and set amidst trees, small copses, streams, hillocks and hollows. Christie, hailing as she did from a fairly flat county like Norfolk, was enchanted by the rich variety of scenery through which they passed whilst Mary, used to her own country's lush and ethereal loveliness, felt an immediate kinship with the beauty which surrounded them. And on a clear, sunny day in early May, with the birds shouting their heads off and the hum of questing bees in the air, nowhere could have been lovelier than this quiet corner of Oxfordshire, seemingly so divorced from the troubles and dangers of war.

'Would you believe there was a war on, and a busy airfield not a mile away?' Mary sighed, linking her arm through Christie's as they strolled on, almost mesmerised by the soft sweetness of the air and the sunshine warming them through their stiff-collared shirts, for they were in shirt-sleeves and carried their jackets. ''Tis impossible to reconcile battles an' death wit' a summery day like this.'

'For today, let's forget the war,' Christie murmured. 'Only . . . can we nip into the village before we cycle off? I really must try to ring Andy.'

'Why? Isn't it enough that you phoned him not t'ree days ago? Can you not be content to know he'll be in touch if he's got leave comin' up? 'Tis not as if he was on active service, Christie.'

'No–oo. But . . . oh please Mary, I'd be so much happier . . . aircraft are dangerous things, he might . . . just a quick word.'

'He'll be workin' . . . it's a fine day, he'll be airborne.'

Christie shook her head.

'No; they had a night-flying exercise last night. He flew until four a.m., then he'll sleep until ten . . . If we go home and have a bath, walk down to the village, he'll be around the mess somewhere.'

'And if he's not?'

'I'll leave a message, ask him to ring me back between seven and eight this evening. We aren't on until midnight.'

They turned into the manor drive, walking between ancient stone pillars with a coat of arms carved on them and an heraldic beast perched on the top. Centuries-old oak trees lined the drive, cutting out most of the bright sunlight, their leaves dappling what remained into a thousand patterns of shifting light and shadow. Christie walked on, enjoying the day yet still with her thoughts fixed on Andy; she missed the simple act of seeing him, just the fact of her eyes lingering on his tough, rather craggy face, his good white teeth, his unremarkable hair. She loved him but didn't quite know why; yet she drowned in that love, felt it lapping, like warm honey, across her mind whenever she thought of him, let the image of him form behind closed eyelids.

'Love's a funny thing, wouldn't you say, Mary?'

They had emerged from the sunlight and shadows of the drive onto the rough, once-gravelled sweep before the front door. The manor house was built of Cotswold stone, its tiles were patched with yellow lichen. There were shutters but they weren't efficient enough for the blackout and now they hung, neglected, several with hinges missing, spoiling the look of the house rather than enhancing it.

'Love? It's just nature's way of entrappin' the young and hopeful,' Mary said. "Get reproducin", says nature, an' fills you full o' feelin's that you don't really understand. But you know enough to want each other an' each one pretties the wantin' up by callin' it fallin' in love. It cloaks your animal urges in fine satin, that's what love does.'

268

'You're a cynic,' Christie said, crossing to the front door. 'Don't you believe in love at all, Mary? What is it makes me prefer to ring Andy and hear his voice . . . just his voice, mind you . . . when I could be off into this beautiful countryside, picking bluebells with my best friend?'

' 'Tis your animal urges,' Mary said, grinning, as the two of them entered the hall. It was a very grand hall, marble-floored, with a graceful staircase sweeping, shallow stepped, up to the first floor. There were four long windows, all filled with stained-glass, and the sun coming through the right-hand one puddled the floor with colours – ruby-red, amethyst, azure, gold. They both stopped short, staring.

'Isn't that lovely?' Christie said. 'It's like a rainbow, only a small, captive one. Who would have thought a mere window could have reflected such colours?'

'Aye; just like love,' Mary said. 'It makes the marble look like silks an' satins, but if you try to pick them colours up wouldn't they just slip t'rough your fingers? And leave only the marble there, all cold an' white.'

'Oh, you! I'd love a bath, but I suppose a wash will have to do. Light the Primus, there's a dear. I'll get some water.'

There was a big, rambling kitchen with two low stone sinks and a great, blackened range. There were ovens, two of them, in the wall on either side of the range, hooks in the ceiling from which no doubt generations of hares and pheasants had hung, towering dressers, bare and pock-marked now, which had once glinted with china and glass. There were pantries and still-rooms, a laundry with a vast copper in one corner and drying racks winched up to the ceiling. There was the housekeeper's room, with her big roll-topped desk – locked – and a faded carpet on the floor. Her bookshelves were empty, her spindle-legged chairs too frail to support the weight of healthy WAAFs, but the whatnot with an empty vase of spills to light the fire and a small occasional table waited still. The housekeeper had kept a little dog, and though the creature itself had long gone to dust its basket, even its faded blankets, were still by the side of the desk, a mute reminder of times past.

But the girls who now lived in the requisitioned manor house steered clear of the kitchen regions. They thought them uncanny, some even said haunted. So they got water from the small cloakroom by the side door except when it had frozen solid the previous February, and then they had trekked right round the house and out to the well in the cobbled yard, unwilling, they said, to go through the kitchen unnecessarily. Christie was one of the few WAAFs to nip into the kitchen whenever she wanted to take a short cut through to the yard and the gardens. Indeed, she often prowled round the back regions of the house, exploring, poking into cupboards; entranced by traces, no matter how slight, of the people who had once lived here and the lives they had lived; fearing neither ghosts – in whom she did not believe – nor the lingering sadness of a house once loved and now to all intents and purposes abandoned.

The WAAFs kept their Primus stoves (they had two) in one of the fine, high-ceilinged reception rooms, all white paint and Regency striped wallpaper, and there they cooked themselves snacks – soup, cups of tea, stewed apples or, on special occasions, pancakes.

They kept the fire laid in there too. They had a rota in winter so that someone would light the fire whenever there were personnel either on the premises or about to come back to the manor. In the evenings, girls in every stage of undress would congregate there, hot drinks and hastily concocted snacks to hand, and they would pile the fire with illicit logs gleaned from the woodland where once the squire had stalked the red deer and his keeper had reared his pheasant chicks, and have sing-songs in the firelight and try to forget, for a little, that there was a war on.

But now, in bright sunlight, the house seemed different; you could almost imagine the squire returning after riding to his plump wife, his pretty daughters, striding across the reception room, shouting for the butler to bring the port. Even Christie acknowledged that the kitchens seemed to have a lingering sadness about them where once there had been bustle and laughter, but the front of the house, in sunshine at any rate, seemed welcoming, as though the squire was glad to see a couple of pretty girls lighting up Primus stoves under his finest chandelier, and carting a bucket of water across the marble-floored hall, slopping it over at each step.

271

When the first kettle boiled Christie took it upstairs. The bathroom was very grand indeed, the bath and lavatory both lavishly decorated with blue poppies, even on the pear-shaped knob on the end of the lavatory chain. She looked wistfully at the bath, with the enormous geyser over it; it worked, and worked well, too. But because of fuel shortages and other restrictions the girls were put on their honour only to have one bath a week, and to keep the water-level down to the required four inches. Christie's bath-night was Sunday, so she would just have to be content with a wash.

Still, washing in the vast hand-basin was rather nice. Christie stripped to her skin, soaped herself thoroughly, then rinsed off, rubbed herself dry, and dressed again. She thought about a clean shirt as well as underwear, but decided it would be silly. After all, a sweaty bike ride followed by a picnic in a wood was scarcely the way to treat a clean shirt, with a starched collar which had cost her tuppence at the local laundry!

She and Mary shared a rather nice, if small, bedroom on the first floor. They had had a choice between sharing four in a large room or two in a small, and had chosen the latter. Christie, getting clean underwear out of her drawer, reflected, not for the first time, that this little room, with its delightful view of a corner of the cobbled yard, and a glimpse of the orchard, had probably belonged either to a lady's maid or to a child, too old for the nursery but not yet old enough for a main bedroom.

Having washed, she stood in the window, gazing out whilst buttoning her shirt and putting on her tie. Beyond the orchard and a little to her right she could see the red roof of the coachman's house. It, too, had been requisitioned and seven aircrew boxed and coxed it there, sleeping during the day and going off to work as dusk fell. It wasn't a large house, in fact it was tiny, so someone had told Christie that four of them slept upstairs and three in the large living-kitchen, which must have made for certain difficulties when someone wanted to write letters or talk.

Christie and Mary had been meaning to wander over to the coachman's house and tell the fellows that if they wanted to use any of the facilities at the manor, they had only to ask. The house had only been taken over for billeting recently, and Christie had explored it one fine spring evening and knew that it was neither well-furnished nor particularly homelike. She had said to Mary that the fellows could have given a hand with the perpetual search for wood, could have helped to chop it into usable logs too, and in return they could have taken a proper bath now and again. The coachman's house didn't have a bathroom nor an indoor lavatory, so probably a real bath in the enormous tub upstairs would be a rare treat for the air-crew of C for Charlie. And it might be fun for them, now the summer evenings would soon be here, to join in the occasional games of French cricket or tennis which took place on the overgrown lawn, amidst howls of laughter, much slanging and the occasional bit of horseplay.

If the men accepted the invitation though, they would all have to be careful. Fraternisation between WAAF and RAF was not encouraged, particularly in one's billet. But it must be pretty damned uncomfortable, with seven large men crammed into that tiny house, and having discussed it amongst themselves, most of the girls at the manor house had meant to do something about it, though so far, no one had.

'Christie! Are you coming or aren't you?'

Mary's voice rose eerily up the stair-well. Christie sighed, picked up her jacket and headed for the hallway.

'On my way,' she shouted. 'Has the kettle boiled?'

It had. They drank tea, washed up their cups and the pot in the downstairs cloakroom, then went out of the side door and round to the potting shed. The bicycles were both there; one had a flattish tyre but Christie pumped it up and then they set off into the blue morning.

'You know when you shouted up to me, Mary? I was just . . .'

'I shouted because you're so slow! Sure and don't you take a month of Sundays to do the slightest t'ing?' Mary said at once in an aggrieved voice. 'If you'd come down when you should've . . .'

'I'm not grumbling, you fool, I just meant that when you shouted I was looking across at the coachman's house and thinking we really should do something about the crew of C for Charlie. An official invitation to dinner at the manor . . . that 'ud be a laugh.'

'We'll pop in this very evenin', after we get back from our picnic,' Mary said, ringing her bicycle bell vigorously as they swerved out of the drive and on to the dust of the metalled road. 'We'll ask them to partake of tea and cucumber sandwiches on our tennis lawn.'

Presently they reached the village with the telephone box on the corner outside the village shop. They dismounted and Christie went into the box whilst Mary took herself off to the shop on the off-chance that they might have something – anything – for sale that needed neither coupons nor points.

Christie, meanwhile, asked for the number which she would know for the rest of her life, which she would repeat in her sleep, which might just as well have been engraved on her heart. She heard the ringing tone commence, and at once her nails began to dig into her palms, her heart started to leap unevenly in her breast. So silly . . . he was instructing now, he wasn't being shot at, he wasn't having to dodge the flak or the enemy, he was simply showing other young men how one flew an aircraft, so why should she feel this terrible apprehension?

'Hello, RAF Westerham, officers' mess.'

It was Andy, she knew his voice as well as she knew his number. As soon as his beloved tones sounded in her ear her worries dissipated, her heart slowed and steadied.

'Andy, darling . . . it's me. Is everything all right? How's it going?'

'Darling Chris, it's so good to hear your voice! Listen, is there any chance of you getting a forty-eight? I thought we could meet half-way, if I came, say, to Newbury?'

'Oh Andy, that would be . . . but when? I'm due a spot of leave, I'm sure I could wangle something.'

Andy's voice lightened.

'This weekend? I'm off eighteen hundred hours Friday until eighteen hundred hours Sunday. Oh darling, if only you could make it too!'

'I'm pretty sure I can; as I said, I do have leave due and our FCO is awfully understanding. Besides, I stood in for Patty when she wanted a forty-eight ten days ago . . . look, where shall we meet? And what's the drill?'

'A quiet little hotel . . . a guest-house, if there is such a thing in Newbury. Darling, so long as it's you and I together . . . but I mustn't be selfish, what would *you* like to do?'

'The same as you; anything which means we can be together. What time can you get to Newbury, though? Oh God, let me think, let me think . . . my shifts . . . yes, I can leave here soon after lunch, if I can wangle it . . . Mary will help, bless her.'

'First one there books in, then?'

'It'll be me; I'm not very rich right now, but . . .'

'They don't expect you to pay for a room until you've used it, scatterbrain! Um . . . Mr and Mrs Todd?'

Christie laughed.

'Naturally. Look, if I can't get away I'll ring you

tomorrow at this time, and leave a message if you're working, but if you don't hear you'll know I'll be in Newbury to meet you on Friday.'

'Great . . . and what have you been doing with yourself lately, sweetheart?'

Christie opened her mouth to reply just as the sing-song voice of the operator cut in.

'Caller, your time is up. The line is busy, please disconnect.'

'Oh . . . sorry! See you Friday, darling!'

'Friday . . . by the church, at eight!'

They were cut off. Christie put the receiver down and stepped out of the box. Mary, sitting astride her bicycle, was placidly dipping her fingers into a small paper bag and licking them. She smiled at Christie and held out the bag.

'Lemonade powder; it was all they had. Want some?'

Her fingers were bright yellow and there were traces of it round her mouth. Christie shook her head sadly at her friend, though she, too, dipped into the bag.

'What a baby you are, Mary O'Hara! Dipping sherbert like a kid of six. It's lovely, though if you eat too much it makes your throat ache to say nothing of dyeing your fingers bright yellow. I wonder who makes it up into lemonade?'

'Me gran does,' Mary said, finishing the last sweet remnants and screwing the bag up into a ball, then flinging it accurately into the bin outside the post office door. 'Lovely, it is too. Clear and cold as fresh spring-water, only spring-water tasting of lemons and sunshine. But tell your best friend – did you get to speak to Andy?'

'Water tasting of lemons and sunshine; very poetic,' Christie said, scooting her bicycle along to gain some speed, then mounting it as they turned on to the village street. 'Yes, I spoke to Andy. He's got a forty-eight and he suggested we might meet for the weekend. He said Newbury.'

'One room or two?' Mary asked. 'I knew you'd spoken to himself, mind. Only asked out of good manners, I did. Your little face was shinin' like the sun itself when you come out o' that box so it was.'

'Don't your good manners stretch to minding your own business about how many rooms we take?' Christie asked, feeling her cheeks warm and bending to the pedals with more enthusiasm than was strictly necessary. She drew ahead of Mary and had to turn her head to complete her remark. 'Do you know Newbury at all, Mary? We're meeting outside the church.'

'Not a whit, but you can't miss a church,' Mary said cheerfully. 'I wonder could we mix lemonade powder somehow widout a cup or a glass? We'll be rare thirsty by lunch-time.'

'We'll find a pub somewhere and buy some real lemonade,' Christie said. 'Oh damn, now my chain's come off.'

They stopped for a moment to adjust the chain, then cycled on. Mary began to sing in her sweet, surprisingly powerful contralto voice.

'Summertime, and the livin' is easy . . .'

The bicycle tyres hissed along on the sun-softened tarmac, the breeze brought all the scents of May to their nostrils. Christie thought about Andy, and remembered again his mouth on hers, his tender, exploring hands. Her mind whirled with the strength of her desire. Two whole days : . . a forty-eight spent alone with Andy! No need to hurry anything, they would have two whole nights in which to lie together, to make love.

Tremulously at first, then with more conviction, her voice joined Mary's in her chosen song.

'Your mommy's rich, and your daddy's good-lookin',

So hush little baby, do—n't you cry–y.'

The two girls sailed on along the empty country roads, now singing, now reciting half-remembered poetry, now pedalling breathlessly uphill or free-wheeling gloriously down. They were very happy.

They found the bluebell wood largely by the smell which wafted across a meadow towards them. Sweet and evocative, neither had the slightest doubt that they had found their bluebells at last and sure enough, after they had hidden their bicycles in the ditch and walked carefully round a meadow full of standing hay they pushed their way through a straggling hedge and there, they saw through the trees the blur, bluer than water or sky, which was the flowers they sought.

'Isn't it odd how you want them, even knowing you mustn't pick them?' Christie said, falling on her knees and putting her head down to drink the heady perfume. 'It's the colour, and the smell ... have you ever smelt anything so *blue*, Mary? ... and the cool look of them.'

'Twouldn't hurt to pick a few,' Mary murmured. 'For the big room.'

'No. They'd be dead by the time we got home. But we'll take some of those pink campions and some of the wood anemones, too. They don't smell but they look pretty in a vase, with some ferny bits of leaf.'

They ate their picnic beside the bluebells, drank from a stream, then cycled back as the sun was sinking. Christie's thoughts were all turned on a hot wash and supper plus an early night – she was going to conserve her strength for the weekend – but Mary stopped just before the manor drive.

'Hang on; look who's coming along the road, looking a bit battered. It's C for Charlie ... only they're still in flying kit ... a bit late in the day, isn't it? Why don't we offer them some of our flowers and ask them if they'll come to tea next Sunday?'

'Good idea; but I'm away on Sunday, it's my weekend, don't forget. Unless the FCO says no, and I can't imagine he will.'

'Oh yeah, I forgot. The following weekend, then.'

'Why not?' The men were walking wearily and now that they were closer, Christie saw that two of them wore bandages around their heads and another had his arm in a sling. 'But they're hurt ... Is this quite the moment?'

'Why, they've been shot up,' Mary said, with a gasp

280

in her voice. 'Surely to God they could have arranged for some transport? Oh, the poor fellers!'

As the men drew level Christie saw that they were having to help one man along; he was limping, his face contorted with pain. Impulsively she jumped off her bike and barred the men's path with the machine.

'Here, can he climb on to the saddle? I can push him on the bike the rest of the way.'

One of the men, presumably the pilot, grinned shyly. He looked no more than nineteen, Christie thought.

'Thanks ... we'll push it. Come on, Hobby, the lady's lending us her bike. Get him aboard, chaps.'

They hoisted the wounded one on to the saddle without any trouble and the pilot, his bandage drooping across his brow, took the handlebars whilst one of the others caught hold of the saddle.

'There you are, we'll have you home in no time. Then it's a nice cup of tea – if we've got any tea – and the best bed!'

'Did you eat at the station?' Christie said as the men shuffled along the road, obviously too tired to take much interest in the proceedings. The pilot shook his head.

'No, 'fraid not. We pranged the kite getting down, but she was riddled with bullets. Some Jerry took a right scunner against us, though mine's only a flesh wound,' he tapped the bandage on his head. 'But poor old Hobby's got a cut foot ... very painful.'

'And they've patched you up and sent you back to your billet?'

Mary's voice was incredulous, full of anger, but the pilot just nodded.

'That's right. Too late to lay on transport, they said. So we'll live to fight another day, eh, chaps?' They had reached the cottage and he helped the tall boy off the bike with great gentleness. 'Thanks for the loan, girls. It was kind.'

Christie would have turned away, dismissed, but Mary was made of sterner stuff. She propped her bike against the linen post, then went ahead of them and opened the door.

'You get him to bed; we'll boil a kettle, make some tea,' she said firmly. 'If you've got none we'll fetch some from our billet. I bet you've no milk, have you?'

'We've not got much of anything,' the second man with a head bandage said heavily. Christie could see from his brevet that he was a gunner. 'We're usually too tired to muck about trying to cook. But we're not flying tonight, thank God, so at least we'll get a good sleep.'

'Go to bed, all of you,' Mary said. 'We'll get some sort of a meal and that cup of tea. If you don't mind, of course,' she added, with so little meaning in her voice that there were several involuntary smiles. Mary's strong mothering instinct had been aroused, Christie saw, and she would mother these young men whether they would or no.

But it appeared that they would. They trooped into the cottage kitchen – Christie was appalled at the bareness of it, the signs of neglect – and through into the small room behind it where two bunks, neatly made up, were pushed against the walls. There was a fireplace, a mantelpiece with a jam-jar half-full of water on it, a tatty rug on the floor, two wooden chairs, one of which had only three legs, and various kit-bags and hold-alls doing the work of wardrobes and chests of drawers.

'It's a bit bare,' the pilot said, looking around him as though seeing it for the first time. 'We take it in turns to sleep down here so it isn't anyone's room, exactly. It's a bit warmer than the bedrooms in winter, but noisy when people are washing in the kitchen.'

'Whose turn is it tonight?' Mary said briskly. 'The rest of you, get up them stairs! Chris, go and get some grub from our place . . . don't forget milk and tea.'

'It's most awfully good of you,' the pilot said. 'You shouldn't bother . . . it's all right, we'll survive. But I must admit we'd be grateful for the tea; we've not had a drop to drink since last night and . . .'

'What the devil were they t'inkin' of, up at the station?' Mary said angrily as Christie slipped out through the kitchen and made for the brick wall which separated the manor from the cottage. 'Is water on tap in this place or do I fetch a bucket?'

But Christie, running down the cottage garden and climbing over the wall, heard no more. Just let's hope no one sees me, she thought, but without much real fear of such an unlikely event. Their senior WAAF officers might be dragons – well, they were – but they were quite careful which of the airwomen lived off-station and they appeared to trust those girls who were billeted at the manor. With reason, thought

Christie, as she pushed open the kitchen door and went to cross the gloom of the kitchen. We are, by and large, too busy to start turning the place into a brothel!

She was half-way across the kitchen when she had the most uncanny feeling; she felt she was being watched. She stopped short, looking carefully around her. Nothing. No one. The sunlight, diffused by years of dirt and dust on the windows, came faintly in, falling on the dirty quarry tiles, the low, brownstone sink, the great stove with its flanking ovens.

But nothing else. Dust-motes, gilded into visibility by the sun's rays, floated lazily in the air. A fly buzzed against an empty, glass-fronted cupboard. Somewhere else in the house a floorboard creaked as a WAAF walked across her bedroom floor.

Christie smiled at herself and shrugged her shoulders. Good thing she wasn't superstitious, but just for a moment she understood why the girls steered clear of the kitchen.

She had been standing just inside the back door but now she moved, crossing the room purposefully. She opened the big, heavy old door – it swung easily under her hand – and went into the passageway which led to the hall. As she passed the various pantries, still-rooms, larders, she glanced into each. No one. And the feeling of being watched had gone.

Fool, Christie chided herself. If it was haunted, which it isn't, this house would be haunted by love, not fear. Quiet spirits, friendly ghosts, who had lived out their lives in peace and tranquility, that was the story of this house no matter what the girls might say.

She reached the marbled hall and crossed it; the door to their living-room was open but she pushed it wider. Apple sat cross-legged on the big chintz sofa, sewing a shirt button back on. Apple was fatter than she had been in the peace; she blamed the RAF cooks but couldn't be persuaded to eat less. She looked up and grinned at Christie, her pink cheeks bulging attractively, a dimple appearing in one of them.

'Christie, it's you . . . where've you been? I put the kettle on half an hour ago, when Leonie and I came off duty, but she's still upstairs. There's a dance at the sergeants' mess tonight, we thought we might go. What about you and Mary?'

'Dunno. Apple, have we got enough tea to give two or three teaspoonfuls away? You know the crew who share the coachman's cottage? Well, as Mary and I came back from our bike ride . . .'

The story was soon told and Apple was all concern at once. She fetched out her secret supply of biscuits – homemade shortbread, sent by an aunt – and a bag of dried milk. Christie raided her own store – some of Mum's rich fruit cake, made not with fruit but with cleverly chopped up carrots and walnuts from the tree outside Christie's bedroom window – and then thundered upstairs to see if anyone else would contribute.

There were only five girls in, but when they heard her story they were immediately concerned.

'Wounded, and sent to walk a mile to get back to a billet with no decent food in it, not even tea? That is wicked,' Annabel Burt said, round-eyed at the horror of it. 'I've got a box of Horlicks tablets and a little jar of Marmite . . . Leonie's Scottish aunt sends her oatcakes, they're really nice with Marmite . . .'

Within ten minutes Christie was making her way through the kitchen once more, a laden bag in her hand. But half-way across the kitchen, for no real reason, she turned suddenly . . . and curtseyed, only half-mockingly. There was no one there of course, no one at all. But she thought she heard a little sigh, as though she had satisfied something – or someone – by her action. And then she was out of the door and running down the garden, climbing over the wall, hurrying back to the cottage.

Mary had lit the Primus stove and boiled the kettle. She had got plates out, and cups. She had arranged the rest of their picnic – there wasn't much – on the plates and the fat bunches of wild flowers which they had picked were now in two jam-jars, looking pretty as pictures.

'Did ye get the tea?' she demanded as soon as she saw Christie. 'And the milk?'

'Yes, though it's only dried, I'm afraid. But the girls were great . . . look here!' she tipped the bag out on to the wooden draining-board. 'The oatcakes are so good, though crumbly. Shall I Marmite half and jam the other half? Norma gave me a jar of her mother's raspberry jam.'

They made the men a meal out of the scraps they had collected, with a pot of strong tea. No one had any sugar, but the ubiquitous saccharine tablets came in useful here. When it was ready it was delivered to each bed; two of the seven airmen were already asleep but Mary woke them because they were sleeping with their mouths open, she said, and would wake in sore need of the very hot tea which they would miss should she allow them to slumber on.

They learned their names. The pilot was John Kimberlye, known as the skipper, or Skip. The wireless operator was Sparky; no further introduction was necessary, though he did whisper to Mary that his real name, his civvy street name, was James McDonald. The rear gunner was Tony, the mid-gunner Fred, the navigator Kyle, the bomb aimer Muffo, the flight engineer Bruno.

Presently, sitting on the edge of Skip's bed, watching him demolish a toasted sandwich with Marmite, cheese and thin slices of apple inside, Christie discovered that this very young man was actually twenty-one, a bit older than she, and was pathetically grateful for the WAAFs' friendship and interest.

'I'm not a bad pilot, but I'm a lousy housekeeper,' he admitted, taking a long drink from his mug of tea and wiping his mouth blissfully with the back of his hand. 'We're supposed to eat in the cookhouse, of course, but there's times when we come back from a mission so flipping tired that we can't think straight. We go to bed, then we're so hungry that we wake up and you can't sleep through hunger pangs, believe me. Sparky is sensible but he's a lousy cook. Muffo's got some idea of tidying round, but none of us can get our collars decently ironed – we take them down to the laundry in town if we have time, but we often don't have time.'

'Bundle your washing up and bung it over the wall; there's twenty-six WAAFs there who'd be glad to lend a hand,' Christie assured him. 'And any little mending jobs, or a bit of cooking . . . just come to the wall and holler.'

His weary, old-young face smiled hopefully up at her, the bloodshot eyes very trusting.

'Would you? Would you really? I can't tell you how chuffed we'd be. We've often watched you lot. Last Sunday, when you were playing French cricket with that frying-pan and a wash-leather tied up into a ball . . . well, if we hadn't been scared of getting everyone into trouble we'd have been fielding before you knew it!'

'Well, next Sunday, come right over. I'll be on a forty-eight but Mary was saying earlier that she and the other girls would give you Sunday tea, especially if you'd give us a hand, now and then, with things like wood-chopping and collecting.'

He grinned at her, suddenly looking much less tired, much less grey.

'Could we?' he said. 'We'd help like a shot if we could come over the wall now and then without getting anyone into trouble. Don't you have officers living at the manor, then?'

'Nope, just other ranks.' Christie stood up. 'Finish your tea and then go to sleep,' she ordered him. 'And we'll see you later in the week.'

* * *

Later still, back at the manor, they held an emergency meeting in the living-room. Christie and Mary explained how they had come to visit the crew of C for Charlie and the other girls were immediately interested and determined to help 'their' crew. Offers to wash, iron, mend, cook, came thick and fast. The WAAFs knew what it was like to be tired and lonely and guessed at the much greater depth of weariness which must be felt by the crew of a bomber, trying to sleep after narrowly escaping death themselves and seeing others brought down by enemy action.

'Tomorrow, you go to the FCO and ask him for your forty-eight,' Mary planned busily as the two of them got ready for bed. 'We'll look after C for Charlie for you ... particularly Muffo, the bomb aimer. Wasn't he the nicest feller? Handsome, too ... and just that wee bit older than the others – makes them a bit more interestin', the odd year or two.'

'Muffo; oh yes, the Welsh one. So you fancied him, did you?'

'He fancied me,' Mary corrected her. 'And why not? I like a big man.'

'Oh, he wasn't that overweight,' Christie said wickedly. 'Just the odd stone round his middle.'

'Overweight? Sure and didn't he tell you he'd boxed for the Air Force before the war? He's twenty-eight, not married, lived in a mining town in North Wales in the peace ... all the rest of his family went down the pits, see, but he didn't fancy it so he went into the Air Force when he was eighteen – that must have been in thirty-one– and he's been there ever since.' She gave Christie a wink. 'Guess who's taking Mary O'Hara to the pictures on Saturday!'

'My God, he's a fast worker! When did he ask you? Whilst you were ladling tea into him?'

'Who said he'd asked me? Anyway, he hasn't. But he will. He will.'

10

'Shanna, can you not keep that bleedin' bird quiet? I know the mornings are light and I know the Tannoy blurts off at six-thirty, but I'd really like to sleep through until then and not have Jacko tweaking me nose and insisting that I at least open an eye to swear at him.'

Shanna, sitting on the end of her bed rolling up her hair, grinned at Mandy Crewe, irritably plaiting her mass of bright brown hair into a long tail which she then looped up and fastened on top of her head with a couple of jealously guarded kirby-grips. Meanwhile Jacko strutted impatiently up and down the floor, now and then uttering, in the very tones of Corporal Rawlings, a threat to 'Put the bloody lot of you in bloody irons if you ain't on the bloody p'rade grahnd in ten secinds flat!'

'I'm really sorry, Mandy, but if I don't remember to double lock it he can get out of his cage, now. And it means he likes you, honest. He hasn't been opening your eyelids again, has he?'

Despite her annoyance, Mandy giggled.

'Yes he has, he did it this morning. I know you say

he's very gentle, but it's awful to find your eyelid raised against your will whilst Jacko peers inside as though he were hunting for worms.'

'Be thankful he isn't,' Angela said from the doorway. 'It really worries me when he's sitting on Shanna's shoulder and starts peering into her ear, as though he knows there's a friend down there but isn't sure whether it would be acceptable to call! If he ever did that to me I'd die, I'd simply die.'

'He's never hurt anyone in his life,' Shanna said stoutly. 'Stop bletherin', the pair of you, and get a move on. Brekker's in five minutes. You never know, it might be cornflakes and a fried egg . . . maybe a bit o' bacon or a sawdust sausage.'

'You give me hope,' Mandy said sarcastically. She finished her hair and reached for her cap, perching it at a provocative angle on her head. 'Is it today that you've got your reunion, Shanna?'

'Yes, later. Meg and me are going to have a rare old day out. She wanted me to meet her at the Stonebow, wherever that is, but I couldn't understand where she meant so we've settled on the cathedral. She said under the Lincoln Imp, but I'm not going into the place, I'd only get lost or make a fool of myself and besides, they might not approve of Jacko, so we're meeting by the west door. That's the main one, she says.'

'True enough,' Mandy said. She rolled up her shirt-sleeves and hung her jacket over one shoulder. Jacko promptly gave a squawk of excitement and tried to perch on it, only to be unkindly shoved off by Mandy.

'Get *off*, you dirty old parrot, go and ruin someone else's tunic, you've already woken me up an hour early! Are you comin', Angie?'

'I'll wait for Shan,' Angela said. She had clung to Shanna as the first person to be kind to her when she had arrived in this strange new world and now, Shanna thought, they remained friends, if only out of habit. But in fact she liked the younger girl, admired the way she had cast off her shyness and inhibitions and joined in the rough and ready life of the station. 'Will you be long, Shanna?'

'I'm ready,' Shanna said, getting to her feet. She checked her appearance as she approached the doorway in the long metal mirror hung beside it precisely for that purpose. Once she would have looked only at her face and hair but now, driving every day, she knew better than that. She had to have a smart appearance, every button polished, not a hair out of place. Col will scarcely know me when he comes home, she thought, with some satisfaction. But it's a good change, a change for the better; he'll be proud of me.

As she reached the door Jacko gave one of his more bloodcurdling cries and homed in on her shoulder. She could feel him tensing himself to avoid being shoved off but this morning, since she wasn't working, she could afford to be generous. Besides, he came with her when possible, even into the bus when she was ferrying crews from the buildings out to the airstrips and back again, though usually in his cage.

But she went alone if she was given a car and an officer to drive, nor was Jacko welcome in the cookhouse. That didn't mean he didn't go in there, because he did – he was about to join them for breakfast now – but if Corporal Bradshaw was on duty the bird would be harshly ordered to get out and Shanna, seeing the spiteful glint in the man's eye, would hastily take her pet back to her billet.

Corporal Bradshaw hated birds; he hated the feel of feathers, he hated beaks and shiny, round eyes. He detested scaly feet, squawks, and the strength of wings. Most of all though, he hated being laughed at, and Shanna could see that he thought Jacko's hoarse comments were directed particularly at him. Which, she was bound to admit, they were, some of the time. Corporal Bradshaw had a squeaky little voice, all the more peculiar when you considered his size, which was large, and his language, which was often foul. To hear him swearing and blinding at the food, the stoves and the WAAFs under his command was an experience no one was likely to forget and Jacko, instantly recognising something so eminently easy to imitate, began to copy him within seconds of the corporal opening his mouth. From the first time that Jacko squeaked, 'I'll 'ave your effin' guts for garters!', a mutual antipathy was born.

But right now the sun was shining, Shanna had a day off, and Corporal Bradshaw's second-in-command was serving breakfasts. The girls queued for cornflakes, strong tea and scrambled egg on toast and Jacko sat in his cage under the table and contented himself with a few sotto voce remarks whilst gobbling any scraps which came his way – and quite a number did.

As soon as breakfast was over Shanna went out to start up the transport. She wasn't the only person with a day off and most of them intended to go into Lincoln, so the officer commanding had decreed that she might as well drive the liberty truck into the city and park it, then drive it home at the appointed time. Jacko, sensing an outing, danced on his perch, but he didn't shout or swear at anyone; he was clearly anxious not to be left behind, Shanna saw with amusement. He did seem to understand that exuberant, not to say ebullient, behaviour led to his being abandoned in the billet for the rest of the day, and to act accordingly.

The truck started easily, with only a couple of turns of the handle. Shanna climbed aboard, adjusted the seat – whoever had driven it last had had very long legs – and then let the engine idle. She wasn't due to leave for another fifteen minutes but as soon as everyone realised the engine was running they would begin to congregate. With a bit of luck she might get away ten minutes early once every seat was full.

Whilst they waited, Jacko preened his flight feathers. Shanna always liked it when he did this because he often accompanied his actions with the only song of which he was capable, a sort of trilling purr. You could both see and hear his pleasure in the work on hand when he did this, since he usually half-shut his eyes and worked along each wing with his strong, curved beak, and what was more with his wing extended to its fullest extent you could see the greeny-blue sheen of his feathers to their best advantage, and appreciate that he really was a handsome bird.

Presently, the truck began to sway as passengers climbed aboard and long before official leaving time someone came round to the driver's window and announced that they were full.

'Might as well get moving, driver,' he said. 'Give us all a bit more leg-loose.'

So Shanna drove out through the gates and took the long, lonely road along the Cliff Edge, as it was called, heading for the golden city which could be so clearly seen through the bright summer sunshine.

She had been into Lincoln a couple of times and knew where to park the truck. She got down and turned to her passengers.

'Back at ten, please,' she said. 'I shan't be late leaving.'

Everyone said cheerfully that they would do their best and then they dispersed, most to make for the shops whilst Shanna decided she would go straight up to the cathedral and wait there for Meg. She had no idea where the other stations parked their vehicles, and did not intend to waste any of this glorious day finding out. She would be quite happy to wait outside the cathedral, dreaming in the sunshine. She just hoped that Jacko would behave.

And behave he did, as she walked steadily up High Street, crossing the river by the bridge and looking with interest at the black and white half-timbered buildings on her left and with even more interest at the river on her right where two stately swans floated, causing Jacko to give an almost human gasp as he caught sight of them.

Presently she noticed an arch across the busy road ahead and saw from a road sign that this was Stonebow; no wonder Meg had told her a trifle impatiently that she could not miss it! Still, she was cathedral-bound now, there was no point in hanging about down here.

There were a good few RAF and WAAF about in the streets, though she didn't see anyone she knew. Not that it bothered her – she was going to meet Meg, they were going to have a day out together! Besides, she had news to impart and being only human, Shanna loved imparting news.

High Street began to peter out as they climbed higher though; another street took its place, the road sign said simply 'Steep Hill', and it was certainly accurate. For a flat county Lincoln was quite a surprise, Shanna thought, trudging grimly up the cobbled street whilst Jacko, with a gleeful mutter, made yo ho ho noises as she heaved herself along with the help of the cast-iron rail which ran from top to bottom of Steep Hill.

At the top, the road widened out and Shanna saw the cathedral in its full beauty, rearing above the city. But she had scarcely admired it before she saw a familiar little figure staring up at it a short distance away – Meg! She must have arrived early ... better catch her before she plunged inside. Shanna was suddenly sure that Jacko and a cathedral would not mix; she had a nightmarish vision of hearing him unleashing some of his worst language, or seeing him suddenly deciding to dive-bomb some particularly religious and devout person, who would unerringly divine the connection between the red-haired WAAF and her irreverent charge.

'Meg!' she shouted, therefore. 'Meggie ... I'm here, hang on a mo!'

Meg, who had stretched out a hand towards the door, turned. Even with the distance between them, Shanna could see the smile which split Meg's crumpled, pekinese face. She's really pleased to see me, she thought. Isn't Meg nice? Because I'm terrible pleased to see her!

'But I really would like to see the cathedral – he'll be all right, won't he? I mean he's in his cage ... oh, I get you, language! Well, suppose we shove the cage down under the arch, wouldn't he be all right there?'

Initial greetings over, Meg had announced her intention of exploring the cathedral and Shanna, knowing Jacko's propensity for mischief, had voiced her doubts about the possibility of the bird behaving himself.

'He's a valuable bird, I daren't,' Shanna said, shaking her head.

'What if he was loose? You could hold his beak shut and tie a ribbon or something round his leg so he couldn't get away.'

There was something about Jacko's strong, scaly legs which didn't go with ribbons, somehow – and something about his curved and clicking beak which seemed to say that even if Shanna tried it a ribbon wouldn't last long, not once he wanted to get rid of it, it wouldn't!

'Give it a go with a shoelace, I've just bought a new pair,' Meg suggested. 'He'll probably be good as gold.'

'Or he might make a dreadful fuss,' Shanna said, watching Jacko, who was pretending to ignore them and pecking enthusiastically away at a crack in a paving-stone. 'He'd probably scream blue murder – and swear.'

'Oh. Well, I suppose swearing or screaming isn't the done thing in a cathedral. Look, let's just try the shoelace, see how he reacts.' She produced the brand-new shoelaces, then unlaced one of her shoes, threaded in the new one and handed Shanna the other. 'Go on, uncage him.'

Shanna opened the cage and Jacko sidled briskly out on to her wrist, head tilted the better to observe the shoelace . . . and then plainly leaped to the wrong conclusion. Uttering a purring trill of satisfaction he grabbed the shoelace and proceeded to try to swallow it. It was only quick-thinking on Shanna's part which stopped him having a pretty traumatic experience, since the shoelace could scarcely have aided his digestion. She held tightly to her end of the lace and jerked and Jacko relinquished his prize, cocking his head in a puzzled fashion, as though questioning her right to withdraw the proffered worm in such a brisk and unmannerly way.

After they had stopped laughing Meg agreed that tethering Jacko probably wouldn't work and suggested that they go into the cathedral, with the bird in his cage, hoping that he would keep quiet for once.

'Tell you what, we'll put him on the arch; he'll probably be happy enough scrambling about out here, but he won't come down for a stranger,' Shanna said at last. 'I'll take the cage in with me.'

They slipped into the cathedral's cool, dim interior, leaving Jacko attacking the paving-stone cracks. If he objected to their absence the walls were too thick to allow any sound through them so the girls were able to explore in comparative peace, though Shanna was nervous every time someone else came in through the heavy oak door.

'Aren't the colours lovely?' Shanna said, gazing up at the great leaded windows. 'Oh, isn't that round one beautiful?'

'That's the rose window,' Meg said. 'Yes, it's glorious. And the roof's pretty impressive ... but I want to find the Lincoln Imp, and the fellow with the geese.'

Left to herself, Shanna would have skimmed round, impressed by the size and colours of the leaded windows but otherwise taking in very little. But Meg was a cathedral-fancier. Because she enjoyed both the architectural beauty and the atmosphere of places of worship, she told Shanna, she never failed to pop into any cathedral in her immediate neighbourhood. Knowing where to look and what to look for, she was able to show her friend things which, left to herself, Shanna would never have discovered. Together, they scanned inscriptions and examined side-chapels, choir-stalls, tombstones and figures carved in stone and wood.

And Shanna enjoyed it. The Lincoln Imp, peering down at her from a pillar in the Angel Choir, reminded her of many a rude young aircraftman leering after WAAFs, and the austere features of St Hugh put her in mind of a visiting group captain at a recent parade.

But Meg was as intrigued as she when they came across one particular gravestone, wrought of black marble, behind the high altar in the Angel Choir.

'What does this mean?' Shanna said. 'Look, Meg.'

Meg read the words on the tombstone slowly.

Michael Honywood, dean of Lincoln cathedral, died 1681 . . . He was a grandchild of Mary, wife of Robert Honywood, and was one of the 367 persons that Mary did see before she dyed, lawfully descended from her – that is 16 of her own body, 114 grandchildren, 228 of the third generation and 9 of the fourth generation.

'Does that mean what I think it means?' Shanna asked, seeing Meg doing some quick addition on her fingers. 'It isnae possible, is it? I mean surely even if you did have sixteen children, you couldn't have a hundred and fourteen grandchildren . . . could you? And to see them all before she died . . . If her grandson died in 1681, then she must have been born around 1600 I suppose, and people didn't live awfully long in those days, did they? And anyway, fancy seeing your own great-great-grandchildren!'

'It adds up,' Meg said, then giggled. 'Well, 228, 114, 16 and 9 do make 367, at any rate. What an incredible old lady Mary Honywood must have been! I suppose if you're one of a big family perhaps you inherit more than the shape of your nose and the colour of your eyes – you inherit fecundity, as well.'

'What's that? It sounds rude,' Shanna said suspiciously.

Meg giggled again.

'It isn't, it just means fertile, able to have lots of babies. What's sixteen times sixteen, anyway?'

'Umm! . . . over 200 at any rate. So of course it's possible, though unlikely I'd have thought. But they don't put lies on tombstones, I bet. In those days they'd have thought it was asking for hell-fire.'

'You're right there. I wonder if there are Honywoods in Lincoln still? You'd have thought, with a start like that, there were bound to be.'

'Ah, but you're forgetting girls. She might have had sixteen girls . . . no, that can't be right or there never would have been a Michael Honywood. Good Lord, Jacko! We'd best get back to him before he does something really bad.'

But Jacko, when they got out into the sunlight once more, was entertaining a group of schoolboys by doing acrobatics on the arch which led from the paved courtyard out to the top of Steep Hill.

He spotted Shanna at once and shrieked at her, then came hurtling through the air to thump down onto her shoulder.

'Happy Christmas, Happy Birthday, good boy, nice feller, who's been at my cake then, get your bloody beak out of me bloody eye,' he gabbled as he landed. 'Clear orf, you old buzzard, clear orf, clear orf!'

'He's pleased to see us,' Shanna said, returning him to his cage as Jacko began affectionately nibbling at her ear and purring like a small sewing machine. 'He's always gabby when he's pleased. What about a cuppa, Meg? There's a place half-way down Steep Hill.'

'Yes, sure,' Meg agreed. 'Then we can talk; we didn't get much talking done in the cathedral, somehow.'

'There was too much to see,' Shanna observed. 'Come on then, I'm gasping for some tea.'

Shanna had been looking forward to a mutual gossip and catching-up of news with Meg, but now, facing each other across a small, lace-clothed table, she found it difficult to begin. It wasn't as if Meg were a stranger, but somehow so much had happened since they'd last been together that it was hard to act naturally.

Col was the most important thing – person – to have happened to her, but because she'd met him in Hampshire it seemed almost unnatural that Meg knew nothing of him. And Shanna, who had never been above a bit of discreet boasting, found that she didn't want to start trying to tell Meg about Col. She knew she couldn't do him justice, for a start, and Meg would probably think he was nothing special and Shanna could not bear that. So they sat there, the two of them, whilst the waitress brought them a fat brown teapot, two white china cups, a small jug of milk and a plate of highly coloured little cakes.

'Meg . . .' Shanna began at last, when the tea was poured and she had taken her first long drink. 'That woman, Mary . . . whatsername, Honywood; would you like to have kids one day? A lot of 'em, like she did?'

'I dunno,' Meg said looking doubtful. She chose a pink cake with hundreds and thousands scattered over the icing, then put it down on her plate and stared thoughtfully into space. 'I think about being married, of course – I'd like that – but not about kids. Even babies seem to belong to a different story, somehow. Perhaps it's because you've got to meet the right man before you can take babies seriously.'

'I'd like to have babies,' Shanna said dreamily. The thought had crossed her mind before and somehow, standing in the cool dimness of the cathedral and reading about the extraordinary Mary Honywood, bearing children seemed a good thing to do. Imagine looking along a pew packed with your own kiddies, she thought now. Me and Col, hand in hand, looking at our own kids, loving them, loving each other . . . it seemed idyllic, a future too remote and wonderful to have even entered her head before this moment. But when you love someone, she decided, helping herself to a pale green cake, it seems much more natural and desirable to think about having that person's child. Before, she had mainly worried that she might fall for a baby because some over-eager feller hadn't bothered to wear a rubber johnny. Now she remembered, with gentle pleasure, the times she and Col had made love. We could easily have made a baby, she thought dreamily, and it would have been the right thing, I'm sure of it. I wonder why we didn't? The first time, there was no talk of precautions . . . no one had planned anything the first time. Perhaps I'm just not fertile enough to be a Mary Honywood, then, with her sixteen fine lads and lasses . . . but I'm sure I'll have babies, one day.

Meg, however, not being privy to Shanna's daydreams, shattered the moment.

'You? Have kids?' Meg snorted into her teacup. 'I've never thought of you as the motherly kind, Shan!'

'It's meeting the right feller,' Shanna said. She stared down at her cake, waiting for Meg to ask the questions which would lead her on to describing Col and their feeling for each other. 'You said yourself you've got to meet the right feller before you can take babies seriously.'

'Did I say that? Well, who've you met then, Shanna?'

'A fellow called Colin.'

'Oh aye? How many times have you been out with him?'

There was just sufficient gentle derision in Meg's

voice for Shanna's slowly unfolding confidence to shut with an almost audible snap. She shrugged and began to pour herself a second cup of tea.

'Not all that many. He's gone abroad now. What about you, Meg?'

Meg must have sensed the slammed door because she put her hand across the table and took Shanna's. Shanna looked up at her and Meg's dark brown eyes were kind, all the mockery gone.

'Shanna? I'm sorry, that was a silly thing to say. Tell me about Colin, then. Where did you meet? Where is he stationed?'

Shanna tried, but it was too late. She no longer wanted to talk about Col It was as though their relationship was a soap bubble, rainbow-hued but fragile, which could be shattered by a wrong word. She dared not risk holding up what she and Col shared to Meg's bright, critical gaze in case that wrong word was said.

'Oh . . . it doesn't matter. What I really wanted to say to you, Meg, was that I'd heard from Sue. Her Sammy started school and ran off; they had the police and all sorts looking for him. But just as Sue was about to ask for special leave Sammy walked into her Auntie Florrie's place bold as brass with a puppy he'd found. The wee lad had been hawking it round the neighbourhood trying to find its home without success, so of course they're going to keep it. And guess what else she says? She's going to try to come up and see us, just for a day, perhaps. She's driving for a Groupie who gets sent all over the place and thinks

there's a good chance of coming north. He's understanding, she says, so if she asks for a few hours off, a
day even ... but you must read her letter, I've
brought it.'

'Really? It would be lovely to see her again, I've
often wished she and Christie could be posted up
here. But Sue's so happy down in Hampshire. Driving
the blood-waggon and ferrying the air-crews seems to
be everything a Sue could desire!'

'Aye, she seems pretty content. I don't suppose
she'll be applying for a posting, not even to get back
together with the rest of us.' Shanna heaved a deep
sigh. 'Wouldn't it be good, Meg, if she came up here?
I'd love Chris to be nearer, too, but she needs Andy.
He and she can meet when they get leave, she said so.'

'True. It's odd when you think about it, the feeling
between Chris and Andy. They'd never have met but
for the war and one of those horrible accidents which
happen in wartime, but they just seemed to fit, as
though fate intended them to get together all along.
Now the rest of us have been out with one or two and
never clicked like that.'

Shanna's mouth opened and closed. Then she
forced herself to speak.

'I understand how it is with Christie,' she said.
'When something happens to you, something real and
special, it's like suddenly being able to drive after
years of footing it – yes, I understand.'

The hint had been broad enough and now she
waited for the questions, for Meg to gradually winkle
the truth out of her; but instead Meg smiled shyly, her

round cheeks suddenly pink, her round eyes narrowing as her smile broadened.

'I don't like to talk out of turn . . . but I think, I just
think, I may have clicked too!'

'Oh Meg . . . who? What's his name? Where did you
meet him?'

Shanna was being good, but she felt a tiny bit
resentful, nevertheless. Why couldn't Meg ask her
these questions, make her confide? But Meg was
talking.

'He's lived just up the road from me for years – he's
the reason I changed my trade and I do love being u/t
flight mechanic – his name is Lenny Bowdler, he's a
rear gunner in a Wellington, and we had a good leave
together at Christmas and then a forty-eight in a
village just outside Market Harborough, of all places,
because we couldn't get home in the time but we
thought it would be nice to meet up. I've got a good
friend at the station, Ken, his name is, and somehow
being friendly with him made me see how – how
special Lenny is to me. And then the forty-eight was
such magic, Shanna, it was so wonderful to be
together . . .'

'Together? D'you mean . . . ?'

'No I don't,' Meg said firmly, but the roses bloomed
in her cheeks and she gave Shanna her most wrinkly,
Pekinese-type smile. 'We haven't reached that stage
yet . . . but we did a lot of cuddling, and spent all day
together, and most of the evening, too. The rest of the
time was spent travelling to and from, needless to
say.'

'You should have slept with him,' Shanna said with all her usual bluntness. 'If you're serious, it's something you can do for them. I know you aren't like – like I have been, but honest, Meggie, if I fell for someone who was air-crew I'd no' hold back, just in case.'

Meg's smile faded and an anxious look spread over her face.

'Yes,' she said quietly, almost to herself. 'All those years when we mucked about and laughed and sat in each other's houses having tea . . . what a waste it was, when time's so short, like now. I really think I'd like to . . . to do what you say. But it's up to the fellow, surely? I mean, don't they suggest it? Say something like "can I come to your room?" If he had . . . but he didn't.'

'Perhaps he feels it's a bit soon, then,' Shanna said, feeling awkward. Men, she supposed vaguely, were all different; the type of man who thought it too soon didn't come her way often . . . But now that she thought about it, hadn't Col said he wanted to take it easy? 'Particularly since he's known you as a friend for ages; it might be difficult, he might be afraid you'd not feel the same to him if he suggested it and you turned him down.'

Meg shrugged but Shanna thought she looked happier.

'That's probably it. I hope we meet again soon though, because perhaps I didn't exactly encourage him. Is it all right for the girl to suggest it then, Shanna? I thought it was the fellow, always.'

She sounded anxious again. Shanna frowned thoughtfully, feeling important. No one had ever seriously asked her advice over sexual mores before; she rather liked it.

'I think it's all right if you're serious and know that he's serious, too. Remember someone's got to take precautions – but I daresay you know that, there's enough talk in billet... Hey, Jacko, that's my shoelace, stop tugging it.' She slid a piece of cake under the table and felt the bird's beak take it gently from her fingers. 'It's different for everyone, the right moment I mean, only ... if you really love him ...'

She left the sentence unfinished. After all, who was she to preach about sleeping with someone you love when she herself had slept with anyone who offered for so long? She was sorry now, wished she'd been choosier, even wished she'd saved herself for Col, but what was done was done. And all those other fellers didn't stop me recognising the real thing when it happened to me, she told herself, resolutely cheerful. Nothing can spoil what Col and I have got, nothing. She gave the rest of her cake to Jacko, drained her teacup, and stood up.

'Better get moving, or we won't have a chance to look around before the film starts,' she said, lifting the cage out from under the table. 'I'm ever so glad you've got your Lenny, Meg. D'you think you'll marry him one day, like Chris will marry Andy?'

'It would be nice,' Meg said wistfully, as they halved the bill, paid and left. 'But we've not talked about marriage, nor about the future, not really. We just write about our next leave and what we'll do then.'

'When this war's over we'll all be expert letter-writers, anyway,' Shanna said as they stepped out into the still-sunny late afternoon. 'There's a river here, isn't there? Shall we go and walk beside it for a bit? I hate going into a cinema half-way through a film, I'd rather wait until the interval.'

Meg agreed and they walked down the hill and round to Brayford Pool with its swans, the boats moored to the quayside and the old warehouses clustered around.

Shanna was enchanted. She took deep breaths of the mellow evening air, and strolled along beside Meg, now and again glancing up at the cathedral, golden on its hill above them.

'It's a beautiful city, isn't it?' Meg said. 'There's so much about it that's special, different. If only the others were here ... if only Lenny could be posted this way!'

'Where is he?'

'He's in Suffolk, actually, but he says they may go abroad soon, to somewhere in the Middle East. If it was safer for him I wouldn't mind so much.'

'Has he nearly finished his first tour?' Shanna asked. She knew all about tours, now that she spent her time ferrying the air-crews to and from their kites. Everyone talked about the number of ops they had to complete before the end of a tour because that meant a decent bit of leave, perhaps some desk-work or a stint of instructing if you were a pilot. But Meg was shaking her head.

'He's half-way through his second,' she said rather bitterly. 'I don't think he was given much choice, they need air-crew so badly. Still, when he's done this one...'

'Oh, Meg, I do wish... Look, let's sit down for a moment and you can read Sue's letter. It isn't a particularly long one, her letters never are, but she sounds very happy and jolly, somehow. Look, there's a seat over there, let's sit down for a moment.'

They sat down. Shanna produced the crumpled, much-read letter and Meg took it and read it, then laid it down on her lap.

'She doesn't say all that much if you don't count Sammy and the puppy,' she remarked after a moment. 'But I think you're right; she's very happy about something and wants to share it with us. Wouldn't it be odd, Shan, if Sue's met someone she can really care for, just like Christie and I have? Oh, I do hope she pulls it off and manages to get her Groupie to bring her up here for a day or so!'

Sue sat on her bed polishing her buttons with Silvo to bring them to glittering perfection. Tomorrow she was taking Group Captain Alan Watson up to London again, not a particularly long drive but an important one, and she wanted to look her best.

Not that she should want any such thing, of course. Not after last time. Was it really only three weeks ago that she and Alan Watson had set off to attend aircraft trials on a sunny Tuesday in July? What an experience that had been, enough, one would have thought, to put her off driving officers about for life. So if that were so, why did she sit here polishing away so industriously, and why did she feel such a lift of the heart whenever she remembered that astonishing, frightening day?

The Tuesday in question had started off as most of her days did; with instructions to go along to the house in the village where the group captain was billeted to pick him up and take him to a remote station 'somewhere in the south of England' where tests were being carried out on a fighter-bomber in which the Air Force chiefs had considerable interest.

Sue liked Alan Watson and he liked her. A tall, fair-haired giant of a man in his late thirties, he was married with a wife and small daughter. He was a career Air Force officer who had been training pilots in the years directly preceding the war and had made Sue laugh with descriptions of his early flying exploits when he had not so much got into his aircraft as put it on, so snug were the cockpits and so large he himself.

But their relationship was strictly a business one. Sue drove him when he wanted a driver and drove the ambulance, or blood-waggon, when he did not need her.

This had been going on for months, ever since the other girls had been posted, in fact, and Sue was happy with the arrangement, could not imagine wanting it to be different. She and Alan could judge their journeys to a nicety now, always arriving on time, neither late nor early, working as a team when crossing difficult country, stopping off at pubs for a drink and a sandwich or taking one of the ubiquitous packed lunches which the cookhouse supplied, sitting on the running-board of the car to eat in hot sunshine or sheltering inside when it rained or blew.

So that Tuesday had started off just as usual. It was sunny and reasonably warm, their route was planned and familiar to them, the talk as they drove through the beautiful summer countryside was relaxed. Alan liked to talk about his daughter, Anna, though he was less communicative about his wife, Cynthia. Sue had met her several times; a tall woman with a narrow, aristocratic face, long, thin hands and feet and a great deal of white-gold hair which she wore in a low bun on the nape of her neck. Her clothing was put on anyhow, hairpins kept escaping from her bun of hair and she was shy, stammering if directly addressed. Sue called her, though not in front of Alan, the White Queen, after the slightly mad, nervy chess-piece in *Alice through the Looking Glass*. Alan called her Cynthia darling, and was very patient with her.

Sue, after some discreet probing, had been told by people who knew Alan that it was an odd sort of marriage; Alan had married his Cynthia – who was an heiress in her own right – when he had been twenty-eight and she thirty-six. Some said it was a love-match, others that it was a means to an end for both parties. Only Sue saw it for what it really was – Alan's strong, capable hand held out to a weak, unhappy

314

woman as a lifeline which she had thankfully grasped.

Alan, who never talked directly about Cynthia, let quite a lot drop when he was telling Sue all about Anna. How gentle Anna was, how clever, how beautifully she dealt with her mother when he was absent and not able to help. In order to explain how marvellous Anna was, Alan also had to explain to Sue that Cynthia had been the only child of aged parents who had neither expected nor wanted her to marry. When they died Cynthia had gone to pieces, bereft of their support as well as their dependence, and had only gradually learned to lean on Alan. Now, with the war taking him away from her so much, she leaned on Anna instead. And Anna, who was only ten, managed to give Cynthia the security she needed whilst never revealing to outsiders the extent of role-reversal in this particular mother-daughter relationship.

'It's an education to see Anna planning a journey or a meal or even a shopping trip, whilst managing to make it look as though Cynthia is taking all the decisions,' Alan said with a chuckle. 'It's a bit like you and me, Sue – I sit in the back seat like a lord, and you do all the driving, take all the decisions and get us everywhere on time. They think I'm responsible, of course, and I can scarcely disillusion them.'

But that Tuesday, driving along in the warm sunshine, with the prospect of a couple of hours or more spent at a strange RAF station where she would be fussed over as the driver of that delightful man,

Group Captain Alan Watson, Sue wasn't really thinking of anything in particular; the road was familiar to her, she knew just where she wanted to turn off, they planned to arrive before lunch which meant she didn't have to keep her eyes peeled for a suitable pub – in short, her mind could wander where it willed as she drove along.

Alan, she noticed through the mirror, was reading reports, so she didn't interrupt with light conversation. They drove in comfortable silence, therefore, only broken when Alan sighed, shuffled his papers back into his briefcase, and leaned forward in his seat.

'Next right, isn't it? I'll page you when I'm ready to leave. Get yourself some lunch, there's a good girl.'

'They'll feed me in the cookhouse, I should imagine,' Sue said, swinging the car in through the gate and pulling up to show their credentials to the waiting guard. 'Where will you be, sir? The control tower?'

Tests of exciting new planes could be watched from various vantage points. Now, through the rear-view mirror, Sue saw Alan nod.

'Probably. I doubt I'll be offered a spin, no matter how well the kite performs, but I expect I'll be allowed to take a peep inside once she's touched down.' Sue drew the car to a halt alongside the officers' mess. 'Thanks, Sue; see you later.'

With her cargo safely delivered, Sue parked in the prescribed area and was carried off to the cookhouse by a garrulous Scot who had been told to take care of her, a task he clearly enjoyed. He advised her on the choice of menu and then chatted amusingly whilst she

316

ate. When the last of a delicious apple crumble had been disposed of she went with Will, the Scot, to watch from afar as the new 'plane went through its paces.

'Your boss seems a pleasant fellow,' Will observed as they scanned the skies for the approaching aircraft. 'I was standin' near him at the last trials; he spoke to me several times. Not one of those toffee-nosed southerners at all at all.'

'No, he's very hail-fellow-well-met,' Sue said, nodding. 'He isn't one to stand on his dignity, not the Groupie. Ah, can I hear something?'

The tall young Scot was beginning to say he could hear nothing when the whine of a high-powered engine obviously came to his ears. He nodded, grinning down at Sue.

'Aye, that'll be it. You've sharp hearing, lassie!'

After that they watched in silence as the pilot banked, swooped, dived, and generally handled his aircraft with all the expertise expected of him. Several times spontaneous applause came from the small groups gathered around the airfield and when at last the display was over and the plane came in to land, Sue and her companion exchanged wide smiles.

'My boss will like it,' Sue said positively. 'Who's the pilot, Will? He really does know how to handle that kite!'

But Will could only shrug.

'No idea; he's a test-pilot from away somewhere, I believe. He's only landing here so that the high-ups can take a look in the cockpit, chat to him about any problems and ask any questions they've got in mind. Then he'll fly back to his own station. So it won't be long, lassie, before you're off again, more's the pity.'

'That was very charming of you,' Sue said approvingly. 'Any chance of a cup of tea, Will, before the boss and I make tracks?'

'Oh aye, there's always a brew brewing in the mess. Come along then . . . I'll see if someone can rustle you up a cake, as well.'

And presently, when the tea had been drunk and a slice of excellent cake devoured, Sue heard her name called over the Tannoy and with many thanks to Will for his hospitality, made her way back to the car.

'Well, Sue? Did you enjoy yourself? I saw you with that young sergeant, standing down at the edge of the runway. Pleasant fellow – I spoke to him a couple of times when I was here last.'

Wasn't that typical of Alan, Sue thought affectionately, to remember one sergeant amongst so many, just because they had exchanged a few words? But that was her boss all over; quietly, unassumingly thoughtful of everyone who crossed his path.

'Yes, he was an excellent host; I had a good time, thanks, sir,' Sue said demurely, keeping her thoughts to herself as she swung the car out of the gates and raised a hand to the guard, who winked at her as she passed. 'I thought the plane looked grand too, though I'm no expert. But Will – that's the sergeant – seemed to think it was a pretty good show.'

'It's Alan, when we're off-duty, not sir, and I'm off-duty the moment I step into the car,' Alan said reprovingly. 'Yes, the kite's all right and the pilot's brilliant – almost as good as me, in fact! Now where shall we stop for a meal? I know a nice little pub . . .'

'We could be home in three hours if we went straight through,' Sue pointed out. 'Wouldn't that be best? You'll want to put in a report.'

Alan sighed.

'Yes, I suppose . . . no, dammit, we'll stop! After all, we're in good time and neither of us should be on duty for so long without a break. You can't call lunch in the officers' mess a break, and I don't suppose the cookhouse was much better. We'll have a snack; I'll tell you when.'

They stopped at the pub, had a very good shepherd's pie followed by stewed apple and custard, and then sat back in their seats, replete.

'The custard was made with dried milk and the apples were sweetened with saccharine, but it was still delicious,' Sue observed. 'Isn't it strange how one person can make a lovely meal from ingredients which someone else just moans about? My mam makes a brilliant stew out o' nothing, but me Auntie Florrie's stews are tasteless no matter what she puts in 'em.'

'No stranger than how one person can play cricket when another can only sew a fine seam,' Alan said. 'You're not a logical creature, Susan Collins – but few women are. Now I suppose we must move ourselves or we'll be later than we ought to be.'

Outside, the fine evening was drifting towards dusk. Faintly, in the deep blue firmament above, stars pricked out and in the west the sky was gilded with

319

flame and gold. It was a glorious evening . . . Sue was just thankful that she was not driving straight into the sunset, however, but had it on her right hand.

She was saying as much to Alan as they made their way along a country lane, a short-cut through to the major road which would lead them straight back to the station, when they saw the aircraft, black against the sky, its nose-cone catching the light of the sun and turning it, for a moment, into a star in its own right, painful to look upon.

'Oh look, that plane's awfully low,' Sue remarked, as the plane came fast towards them. 'I do hope he isn't in trouble, though it looks as if . . .'

'Get into the hedge! Quick, Sue. Stop the car, get as close to the hedge as you can, it's a Jerry!'

Sue, instantly obedient, swerved off the centre of the road and into the only sort of shelter which existed right here – a tangle of hazel trees, overhanging the grassy verge – just as the plane dived towards them, its engine note rising to a manic scream. Sue felt Alan's hands seize her by the shoulders and push, then she found herself flat on her back across the front seats whilst her head was banged against the side door. Not daring to move, she was still trying to understand what was happening when Alan vaulted over the seat-backs and landed hard and rather uncomfortably on top of her.

She felt the breath whoosh out of her lungs, heard the staccato snarl of bullets ripping across the fabric of the car's engine and the shattering of glass, smelt the stink of petrol, and then she saw two things: the belly of the plane, looking only feet away from her, as it zoomed over the car and a tiny tongue of flame, blue and gold, creeping along the car's bonnet towards them.

'Out!' Alan shouted. Squashed and flustered, Sue only knew that Alan's weight was suddenly lifted off her, the door against which her head uncomfortably rested was swung open, and once more she was grabbed by the shoulders and apparently flung through the air, to land bonelessly and quite painlessly in the soft grass of the verge.

She was not, however, allowed to lie there long.

'Come on ... it'll explode,' Alan shouted. 'Up, Sue!'

Sue scrambled to her feet just as the car did indeed explode, with a whoosh of scalding hot wind which sent the pair of them several feet through the air again, to land in a confusion of limbs in a gateway.

This time it did not take Alan's urgent hands on her to convince Sue of the rightness of flight; this time she was ahead of him, running as fast as she could away from the raging inferno which, just moments before, had been the staff car of which she had been so proud.

But they made it. From a hundred yards down the road they turned to survey what was left of the car. Not much, by now.

'Whew!' Sue said. 'What next? Wharrer thing to happen, eh? I dunno whether I'm on me head or me heels!'

She turned to Alan, just in time to see him crumple, kneel for a moment on the grass, and then sink, slowly and rather majestically, on to his side.

In an instant Sue was on her knees too, trying to shake him back to consciousness, for his eyes were closed, his face deathly pale.

'Alan! Alan, wake up . . . Come on, you're all right, we're both all right, it was just the shock . . .'

She stopped speaking. Her hand on his right shoulder had encountered a sticky wetness . . . She rolled him further over and saw that his tunic had been slashed from one shoulder to the other . . . and that blood was stickily oozing out . . . as she moved him the ooze became a stream, then what looked, to her terrified eyes, more like a river.

Sue stared round her, at the increasing dusk, at the lonely little secondary road, at the dying bonfire which had once been the car. She stood up, her heart hammering, and ran to the gateway; beyond it, some way off, she thought she could just make out the dim shape of a house. It was unlit, of course, but she was pretty sure it was a dwelling of some sort. She would have to run there, get help, come back . . .

But first she must stop the bleeding. In her early days as a WAAF she and Shanna had attended first-aid classes on the station, both of them regrettably more interested in the young airmen who volunteered to be 'bodies' than in the bandaging and splinting which they were being taught. But now it all came back to her. When dealing with open wounds keep the edges of the wound as close as possible and apply pressure to stop the bleeding. Apply pressure, that was her first move . . . what could she find to make a

322

pad with, though? And with what should she bandage that pad tight against the wound? She must stop the bleeding, and fast!

Without allowing herself any more time for thought she rolled Alan on to his back and unbuttoned tunic and shirt. Then, urgently, she ripped his tunic off, rolled him on to his stomach and folded his shirt upwards, the better to reveal the wound. It looked as though someone had ploughed with an iron finger right across his back, leaving a bloody ditch . . . She shuddered, but automatically began her work.

She used her blackouts to make a pad which she pressed down on the wound. Whilst she was fitting it Alan came round and said he was all right, what the devil was she doing up there; but she told him to shut up and lie still, and then, because it was the obvious thing to do, she used her stockings as a makeshift bandage. Only when the pad was firmly held in place dared she pause to examine her work.

The bleeding had slowed, if not stopped. She had tied the stockings cruelly tight . . . that and the pad should have done the trick. She found she was weak and irritable from reaction and she still had to move him, to the farm she thought she could glimpse through the trees of a nearby wood. Her patient, lying on his stomach with his head pillowed on his arms, seemed quiet now, and actually had his eyes closed, though she was pretty sure he wasn't asleep.

'Alan, if you walk will it open the wound? Can you walk, come to that? There's a house over there . . .'

'I'm perfectly all right, just a bit weak and bloody,'

Alan said. He tried to sit up, swayed and stopped moving for a moment, then looked up at her and grinned cheerfully. He had a grass-stain along one cheek where she had hauled him from front to back and dirt in his fair hair and he was still rather pale, but Sue realised, with considerable relief, that he no longer looked as though he intended to die. 'Sue, don't look so worried, my dear, we're both alive, which is little short of a miracle when you remember the way that bloody Jerry dived at us, shooting like something out of a Tom Mix 'B' movie! If you could just give me a hand...'

She heaved and he managed to get upright; swaying, but upright.

'Where's the farmhouse?' Alan said breathlessly, leaning on her shoulder. 'Oh yes, we'll make it there without any trouble.'

Together, regrettably giggling like a pair of drunken idiots, the two of them lurched across a field, through a wood, and up to the buildings they had seen from the road. Only the buildings proved to be a couple of almost derelict barns, and by now daylight was no more than a memory. At a timid suggestion from Sue that she should leave him and try to find a village, Alan shook his head vehemently.

'No, not in the dark, my child. We'll be all right here until morning... Is there some straw or something?'

'Sit down whilst I explore,' Sue said firmly. How she regretted her gas-mask case with her torch in it, as well as all the other things the car had contained. 'Is this straw? Well, it's fairly soft. Oh! No not here, Alan, I wouldn't be surprised if we've found the midden.'

There was also a wall though, so she leaned him against it with more instructions – don't move, don't fidget, just wait – and made off, gingerly, into the dark.

Presently she found him again, and was able to give him good news.

'There's a loft full of beautiful soft hay. The ladder isn't too bad, it's only half-a-dozen steps. Do you think you could manage that?'

Through the dark, she saw the glint of his teeth as he grinned.

'Manage it with both hands tied behind me,' he boasted. 'Lead on, Miss Life-saver!'

'You make me sound like that mint with the hole in the middle,' Sue grumbled, leading him across the dusty barn floor. 'Here . . . you go ahead of me, then if you fall you'll fall on something soft.'

'No, ladies first,' Alan said. His voice was slurred and even as she shook her head and pushed him ahead, Sue remembered her knickerless, stockingless state and bit back a giggle. Good thing it was dark . . . not that it mattered, since she would mount the stairs last, but it came to something when you found yourself climbing up into a hay-loft with your boss but without your knickers. Whoever would believe me innocent after this, she thought, steadying Alan with a firm hand in the small of his back.

But despite the wound he did not stumble and

without further incident they reached the haven of the hay-loft. Sue made a round, secure nest, displacing a couple of hens who flew off with startled squawks, and settled Alan in it. Rather to her surprise he raised no demur but lay down with a sigh, half on his stomach so that his bandaged back was not against anything.

'Comfy? I wish I could get you a drink, you must need something, you lost quite a bit of blood,' Sue commented, finding a bale of hay and dragging it over so that she might lean against it. 'However, if you won't let me go off to get help you'll scarcely approve of my wandering around searching for water.'

'True. And to make quite certain . . . Come here, driver!'

Sue leaned forward and Alan caught her hand.

'Sit down by me, there's a good girl. That way I can make quite sure that you don't wander off.'

She sat down by him and presently, when he sighed and turned over, she lay down too, but let her hand remain in his. And when his breathing steadied and deepened, when he turned restlessly towards her, it seemed the most natural thing in the world to smooth the hair from his forehead, to tell him he was safe now, and to lie close so that, should he wake, she was immediately at hand.

As she lay there, listening to his breathing, it occurred to her that he had called her a life-saver when the boot was very much on the other foot. He had saved her life twice, if not three times. He had seen that the plane was about to attack and had ordered her to pull into the side, he had pushed her flat and thrown himself on top of her so that it was his strong shoulders which had taken the bullet instead of her own breasts and face, and he had dragged her out of the car when the first flames had flickered along the car's bonnet. She sat up on her elbow, peering at him in what faint light entered the hay-loft.

'Alan? You really saved my life, and not with a silly bit of bandaging, either. Alan? Are you asleep?'

He seemed to mutter something, then groaned and sighed. She thought he had spoken and bent closer to him.

'What? What did you say?'

His arms came up and enfolded her, pulling her down. Gentle arms, but strong. She knew then that he needed her closeness, regardless of who had saved whose life. It didn't matter, not really. What mattered was that they were both alive, and that right now, they should cling to each other in the dark and be thankful for their escape from death.

'Turn your back to me,' Sue murmured into Alan's ear. 'Then I'll lie round you, spoon-fashion, and that way your bandage won't slip.'

Obedient even in his sleep, Alan rolled over and Sue curled round him. Very soon, they both slept, regardless of the tickly hay, wounds and various other small discomforts.

Next morning Sue woke to find her nose resting against a broad, blue-shirted chest. She frowned, half sat up and glanced around her, at the soft piles of hay, the underside of the tiles with light shining around the edges, and lastly, at Alan, still sleeping. Recollection was cold as a bucket of water – the Jerry plane firing and destroying her beloved car, Alan being wounded, the two of them finding their way here.

Alan had not yet woken but as she moved a little away from him he mumbled something and grabbed her. Sue extracted herself from his arms with some difficulty, for it appeared that in sleep he had all the qualities of an octopus, but she managed to get away without waking him and stood up to shake off the hay seeds and decide what to do next.

Alan looked quite well this morning she thought, though a trifle flushed. He might have a temperature, or it might simply be the result of two people sleeping closely entwined in a quantity of rather grubby hay; but whichever it was, now was her chance of fetching help before her companion woke and insisted on being included in any such expedition.

She went down the ladder slowly and carefully, and across the barn floor. Seeing it in daylight, she realised they had had a very lucky escape from death by impalation the night before, since there were agricultural implements scattered all over the place, including a number of pitchforks. But fate had favoured them, so now she sidled through the half-open door and blinked at the morning.

The sun wasn't yet up but the sky was blue and in the east a brightness heralded the sunrise. A seagull, high enough in the sky to be gilded by the unseen sun, swooped overhead and birds sang, whilst on the country road along which she and Alan had lurched last night a herd of cows moved, lowing placidly, obviously going in to be milked.

And where a herd of cows went, Sue suspected that people went too. She wasn't a country girl, had never even thought of flung-down pitchforks in a barn, but as a driver she had been forced to wait often enough for cows to cross the road to know that they seldom, if ever, went anywhere unaccompanied. And if she was right, then help was at hand, ready and waiting for her to use it.

She ran across the yard, skirted the midden, and plunged into the belt of trees which, last night, she had thought an extensive wood. When she reached the road the cowherds, a youth with a round, red face and a skinny eleven-year-old, were standing stock-still, staring at the remains of Sue's beloved car. In fact so intent were they on the wreck that they jumped like a couple of shot rabbits when Sue spoke to them.

'Oh excuse me, could you possibly give me a hand? My officer's been shot . . . never mind the car, it is only a car, a Jerry plane shot at us . . . so we spent the night in that barn over there. He's still sleeping, but I don't think he ought to walk. Could you help?'

Once they got over their surprise they were helpfulness itself. The red-faced youth said his aunt's farm was nearest and pointed to a small, square house nestling in a hollow on the far side of the road. With all the lights out and situated as it was, it must have been invisible in the semi-dusk of the previous evening, Sue realised.

'Bertie, get aunt to gi' you a jug o' tea for the gent

329

and lady,' the youth said, addressing the small boy.
'They're in Blake's old barn, so bring un there. Oh,
an' best bring Cousin Kenneth too, in case the gent
needs liftin'. And be quick as you like.'

He was quick. Sue and the red-faced one herded
the cows past the burnt-out car and into their
destination, which was a cowshed further up the road,
and were only half-way back to the barn when Bertie
caught them up. He had a jug of tea and two tin mugs
and announced breathlessly, that 'Cousin Kenneth
and Uncle Simon will be over 'ere in a brace of shakes,
wi' a couple o' blankets, in case the gent needed
carryin'.'

Alan woke as they creaked up the stairs and was
grateful for the tea, but said he didn't need carrying,
thanks, and in fact was feeling fine, if filthy, this
morning. Sue fancied he leered at her as he said the
last words, but decided it was just her over-active
imagination. For now, he was very much the wounded
hero and should be treated as such.

Kenneth and Uncle Simon proved to be father and
son, two silent, square-faced men who took one look
at Alan and did not unfold their blankets; carrying
him would have been a task to make most strong men
quail, Sue supposed, seeing her boss's bulk with new
eyes. However, Uncle Simon said he would go into
the village and get transport for them, and Kenneth
said he'd ring the RAF station, so that was two
problems solved.

'If you needs a doctor . . .' Simon began, but Alan
pooh-poohed the suggestion and even Sue was

beginning to see that a doctor was probably not necessary.

They reached the farm slowly, but without anyone assisting Alan in any way whatsoever. Sue offered a shoulder but this was declined.

'It's a flesh-wound, that's all,' Alan declared. 'A bit sore, but that isn't going to affect the way I walk.'

When they reached the house the farmer's wife, a practical person who told them that before she married she had been a nurse, undid Sue's makeshift bandages – without commenting on the materials used, to Sue's relief – and said it was a neat job and had saved the gentleman from losing a good deal of blood. She then bathed the wound, patted it dry, bandaged it more conventionally and offered breakfast.

'Potato cakes, fried eggs and a nice bit of bacon from our own pig,' she said, casting ingredients into a big black frying-pan and jiggling it expertly over the heat. 'By the time the men get back you'll be outside o' this little lot.'

They were, too. The menfolk arrived with a message to say that the RAF station was sending a car and driver in half an hour just as Alan was leaning back carefully in his chair with a satisfied sigh.

'Mrs Tomthorpe, that was a marvellous meal and you're a perfect cook,' he said gratefully. 'I dare not ask you where you got the coffee from, either, but it was ambrosia. I ought to feel guilty, but you're such a good hostess that even guilt is denied me!'

Mrs Tomthorpe chuckled.

'All 'ome-growed an' 'ome-reared,' she said. 'Can't go far wrong wi' stuff like that. What about one more cup o' coffee for the road?'

The journey back to the airfield was a silent one. Alan snoozed and Sue was too conscious of the WAAF driver listening to want to say much. In fact there was only one question which she longed to ask, and she supposed that she never would; when she had woken in the small hours, to find herself being clutched and kissed, she had assumed that Alan was asleep and had mistaken her for his wife.

But if so, why had he said it? Why had he muttered, deep in his throat as he released her, 'Ah God, I love you, Sue!'

11

'Have you nearly finished that darning, Mary me old prune? Because there's a transport going into town later and I thought I might go along with it. Fancy a trip?'

Christie and Mary were sitting on the back lawn, darning. Christie, inexpertly cobbling up the seam of her only decent silk stockings, bit the cotton off and leaned over to examine Mary's work. Mary, who really could darn, made a work of art out of the plebian task so that Muffo's beautiful civilian socks, a gift from his mum last Christmas, would be nicer when they were finished than when they had been brand-new.

'Holy mother of God, Chris, why on earth d'you want to go into town on a day like this? The trouble with you, me darlin', is that you're restless. You ought to be takin' advantage of the sun, so you should. September's half over, we won't get many more days like this, I'm thinkin'.'

'It's just that it's Skip's birthday tomorrow. I thought I'd see if I could get him something . . . just something small, you know. I've got five bob I can spare, at a pinch.'

Ever since the girls had accosted the battered crew of C for Charlie months before, the friendship between the WAAFs and the air-crew had grown stronger and steadier. Mary, true to her promise, was 'going steady' with Muffo, or so she claimed. To the others it seemed a friendly, easy relationship, more like brother and sister than lovers; but it suited Mary as the sun of summer had suited her, gilding her fawn-coloured hair with sun-brightness, turning her pale skin to a warm shade of gold. And now, basking in the paler sun of autumn, she had an air of dreamy contentment which Christie envied. Mary didn't worry, or if she did it didn't show, whereas Christie knew herself to be a bundle of nerves.

Christie supposed that they were all anxious for the well-being of the crew of C for Charlie, because they had become good friends, but she herself worried about Andy constantly, because he was back on active service. What was worse, they'd posted him to RAF Shipton, up in Lincolnshire, flying fighters still but too far away for the sharing of a sneaky forty-eight. Phone calls were briefer, the lines cracklier, his dear voice fainter ... she missed him so badly, so constantly, only that her friendship with Skip saved her from despair.

Skip had a girlfriend in the WRNS, stationed up in Scotland. They weren't engaged or anything like that; but he had told Christie once that she reminded him of Sarah and somehow just that one small remark had made him her responsibility so that despite her lack of expertise, it was she who darned his socks, starched his collars and cooked pancakes for him when she could lay her hands on an egg and a bit of fresh milk.

Because she so longed for Andy, though, she was considering asking for a posting, yet was scared that if she did so she might simply lose Mary and Skip and end up in Scotland or Cornwall, somewhere further from Andy than ever. And she did not think she could bear that. If only one was able to ask for a specific station – but the Air Force moved you at their whim, not yours. All you could do was your best ... and send up prayers for the man you loved and save up your leave so that you could spend time together every six months or so.

And in the meantime ...

'I'm too lazy to spit and polish meself up for a trip to town,' Mary grumbled, finishing the sock and laying it neatly on top of its fellow. 'Sure and you're as likely to find a little somethin' for Skip in the village as in town. You know what the shops are like ... bare, mostly.'

'Yes, you're probably right. Are you going to walk into the village with me, then? Oh come on, Mary, be a sport, you know I hate going off by myself.'

Mary sighed and picked up the neatly darned socks.

'All right, I'll come with you. On one condition.'

'What's that?'

'That you go down the garden and climb over the wall and put these socks somewhere in the coachman's house where they can't be missed. Sure and you'll be there and back before the cow can cough.'

335

Christie, who had seen Mary's wall-climbing efforts, grinned and held out her hand for the socks.

'No sooner said than done. Go and brush your hair or whatever you want to do; I shan't be a tick.'

Accordingly, whilst Mary went towards the manor – skirting the back regions automatically and entering by the side door – Christie legged it for the coachman's house. The wall was perfectly climbable, but you could snag your stockings or catch your skirt easily on the mellow old bricks, so she went over it carefully. She was bare-legged, but would have to don her stockings again before they visited the village shop. Old Mrs Bailey, the shopkeeper, would have looked askance at a WAAF without stockings.

Christie reached the coachman's house and knocked perfunctorily before pushing open the door. The boys never bothered to lock up; what was the point? As they said, there was nothing worth stealing inside unless a thief happened by with an appetite for dirty washing or Air Force issue bedding.

Christie stepped over the threshhold and looked around her; without the crew of C for Charlie the big kitchen looked empty, though cheerful and expectant, as though knowing full well that it would be pleasantly reoccupied soon. Indeed there were enough signs of their presence to tell Christie that they had only recently left and would be back before too long; a dirty collar, a packet of fruit gums, a letter, half-written, a bottle of Kwink and a pen nearby. Like all young men they usually left everything to the last minute; Christie could well imagine the panic when they realised they must leave or be late for their flight briefing. They were flying tonight, she knew, and were on stand-by at the station, so it would be a good few hours before Muffo would want his socks. Still, she would leave them somewhere obvious ... she looked around, then laid them carefully on the dresser. There were dishes waiting to be washed but she didn't have time right now. Mary and I will come back after we've done our shopping, she promised the dirty dishes, and deal with you then. The boys would eat in the cookhouse before leaving for whatever raid had been planned for them; they wouldn't be needing clean dishes until after debriefing tomorrow morning.

With one last glance around, Christie left, closing the door carefully behind her. She reached the wall again and swung over it, taking care, but caught her skirt and had to pause to unhook it from the rustic brick. Then she loped up through the orchard, across the patch of lawn over which the girls, turn and turn about, pushed the rusty old mower a couple of times a week, and in through the kitchen door.

It was dark in there after the bright sunshine of the garden. Christie slowed for a moment so that her eyes could get used to the gloom, then began to pick her way round the central table, making for the door which led into the long corridor. It was cool in here after the garden, and if she half closed her eyes and let her imagination have a free rein she could see a maid clattering dishes at the sink, cook rolling out pastry at the big table, the butler majestically polishing goblets over by the tall glass-fronted cabinets and a skinny, tow-headed boy plucking pheasants on the long counter under the window, carefully saving the feathers in a big canvas bag, whistling as he worked.

If she didn't look around her they were all there, but as soon as she looked they disappeared because they were only a mixture of shadows and wishful thinking ... but it's nice to have an extended family of yesterday's folk, Christie told herself.

Now, she gave one last valedictory glance around the room, empty save for shadows and sun-motes, and left the kitchen to hurry along the corridor, pushing open the green-baize doors – tattered but intact – and crossing the marble hall at a trot. Upstairs, she could hear Mary singing 'The Rose of Tralee' at the top of her voice, which meant that she was happy, and also that she was almost ready. Christie took the stairs two at a time and burst into the bathroom where Mary was cleaning her teeth and somehow managing to sing snatches of song in between vigorous brushings.

'Ah, here you are!' Mary made a hideous gargling noise and spat a mouthful of foam into the basin. 'Everyt'ing all right over there?'

'Yes, but they didn't have time to wash up their brekker plates so I thought we'd do them after we've done our shopping. I've left the socks on the dresser and I thought, since it's Skip's birthday tomorrow, I'd leave his card and whatever I manage to buy him on the dresser too. Then he'll get it as soon as they get back.'

'Good idea,' Mary agreed. 'Come on, girl, let's

get a move on. They're showing a fillum at the village hall this evenin' that I'd like to see, for once. You comin'? We can afford a late night, seeing as we're not on again until midnight tomorrow. Ah, Holy Mother, I do most dearly hate the twelve to eight.'

'Yes, it's the shift I'm always scared of falling asleep on,' Christie said, untying her ribbon and shaking her hair free, then attacking it with someone's hair-brush until it stood out like a bright, chestnut-brown dandelion clock around her head. 'Of course I'll come to the flicks with you; what's on? Not a war film, I hope.'

'No, it's a nice, ordinary romance, starring Myrna Loy. I've got some sweet coupons left. I'll see if I can get some boiled sweets while you're gettin' Skip's present.'

'I'm just going to our room to put some stockings on,' Christie remarked. 'You know what old Ma Bailey's like, she'd probably refuse to serve me if my legs are bare.'

'And you might meet Killer Attila,' Mary said, grinning. 'The most efficient Section Officer in the WAAF, and she's got it in for our little Chris! Oh yes, she sees right through your spit and polish to the little slut underneath; wasn't that what she said?'

'Yes, she said it, but she's jealous as hell because she's got her eye on Skip, and thinks I hang around with him too much,' Christie protested. 'Not that he'd go for Attila even if I wasn't here . . . well, who would? She's got a cruel face.'

'Mm hmm. Remember the wicked Queen in *Snow*

White? Attila reminds me of her – same cutaway nostrils and slanting cheekbones.'

'I do so agree, but Mary, I wish you'd stop calling her Killer Attila; her real name's bad enough – fancy calling a child Sandra Kendra – but I'm bound to forget and use it in her hearing and I'll be up on a charge for insubordination or something before you can say knife.'

'Or Killer Attila,' Mary agreed brightly. 'Don't you see, Chris, that's the beauty of it? We can discuss her in her hearing and then deny, flatly, that it's her we're talking about.'

'Yes, I suppose you've got a point. Are you ready? Then let's go and fetch my stockings.'

A rather flowery birthday card was purchased at the village shop, but Mrs Bailey, though eager to help, could provide nothing suitable for a young man of twenty-two who needed almost everything. Mary had some sweet coupons left but even with those Mrs Bailey looked doubtful. Her supplies hadn't arrived, though they should be coming in a day or so. But seeing that Mary did have coupons she rooted through her dusty cupboards and produced some rather weary-looking Pontefract cakes. Christie, meanwhile, had been desultorily going through a drawer full of odds and ends and was just about to turn away when she reached what at first she had thought was the bottom of the drawer. Closer inspection, however, revealed that it was a largish box, the writing indecipherable, the picture so faded that she could not make it out.

'Mrs Bailey – what's this?'

'Blessed if I know,' Mrs Bailey said, taking the oblong box out of the drawer and regarding it doubtfully. 'It's nothin' much, it's too light ... ah, I know – that's a kite that is. When my son was small he used to enjoy flying a kite ... I wonder if 'tes still all in one piece?'

She opened the box, not without difficulty, to reveal a magnificent triangular kite with a long tail, its colours – red, yellow, blue and orange – as fresh and bright as on the day it was made.

'Oh, Mrs Bailey, it's perfect – he spends all his working life flying a kite, now he can play with one when he has time off! How much is it? May I buy it, please?'

'Well, I wonder how much I should charge, like?' Mrs Bailey mused. 'You could say 'twas beyond price ... But for one of they flyin' chaps – shall we say three bob?'

'It's worth more than that,' Christie said honestly. 'But if you're sure ...'

There was no spare paper to wrap it up but the box was so faded that no one could possibly make out what it was supposed to contain. Christie tied it securely with a precious length of the ribbon she used to tie up her hair and then she and Mary carried it across to the coachman's house, where Christie borrowed the letter-writer's pen to inscribe the birthday card and to write, *Happy flying, Skip, from your friend Christie* on the lid of the once-blue box.

'And now to wash the dishes,' Mary said. 'Then we'll have to scamper back to the station. We'll grab a meal in the cookhouse before we go off to the flicks.'

'Who is this Skip, anyway? I'm really envious of that kite, sugar-bun; we get some high old winds up here, a kite like that could really travel.'

The line was almost clear, Andy's voice only slightly distorted by the distance between them.

'Skip's just the lad who's billeted at the end of our garden,' Christie explained, not for the first time. 'He's not the youngest of his little lot, but it's a near thing. He's ever so fatherly to them, though. He's nice, Andy, you'd like him.'

'I doubt it very much; I'm not inclined to like my rivals, you know!' He was teasing, yet was there a darker note in his voice? It would be fatally easy to imagine that she had fallen out of love with him, given the distance between them. Christie hastened to reassure him.

'Darling Andy, you're the only one I care about, you know that. Oh, if only we were nearer! If only we could touch!'

'Sweetheart, don't worry, don't sound so anguished, I'm not jealous, honestly, I was only pretending, mucking about. What have you been doing with yourself this evening? Had any fun?'

'We went to the flicks in the village hall. The film broke down three times and Mary cried so hard she made her face all puffy. She adored the film, though, we both did. What about you?'

'Played high cockalorum round the mess and Freddy Newnes fell off the sideboard and broke his ankle. Lucky blighter, he's off flying for twelve weeks! No, I shouldn't have said that . . . he's champing at the bit I can tell you, and so are his pals. He's a good pilot, Freddy. Now just you go back to your manor house and have a good night's sleep. I'll be in touch. Is Mary with you, by the way?'

'No, she was worn out so she went straight back to the billet. Andy, when are you flying again?'

His reply was immediate – too quick, too facile.

'Not for a few days, so don't go worrying! You're on the midnight shift tomorrow, then. Station watch or Darky watch?'

'Station, Mary's on Darky. Andy, when . . .'

The familiar interruption, the voice gabbling out the words regardless of meaning, indifferent to their anguish.

'Caller, your time is up; the lines are busy, please disconnect.'

'Christie . . . love you.'

'Oh darling, I love you too! Take care of yourself, don't take risks, don't forget . . .'

Click and burr; the connection was broken. Christie replaced her receiver, sighed and looked around her. For a moment she could scarcely focus on the familiar scene, the faces of the WAAFs waiting their turn at the telephone. Then she glanced at the clock; it was almost eleven but the waits for a line got longer and she simply had to speak to Andy, to reassure herself that he was all right. Mary had gone back to their billet and would have been snoring for the past hour so she would have a quiet walk back. Not that she minded; she loved a walk on a night like this one, cool but balmy, with the autumn moon swinging in the sky and a million stars looking down.

She left the warmth and buzz of the mess and made for the gates; it was a clear night, the moon huge in the sky overhead. As she walked a little breeze teased tiny movements from the branches of the old oak trees, brought the country sounds to her ears, sounds as familiar as her mother's voice. Water tinkling in the ditch, a sleepy bird chirping as it was disturbed, the squeak and scuttle of a tiny mouse, the silent flight of a big barn owl, swooping along the hedge, intent on prey, never noticing the girl who watched appreciatively as his great white wings carried him past.

She reached the end of the drive, turned up it. The house was blacked-out, of course, but she could hear, as she neared it, the soft murmur of voices from the big room. The girls would be there, darning stockings, writing letters, chatting. Someone would have the kettle on, someone else would be spooning mean spoonfuls of cocoa into mugs, a biscuit tin would be produced, Silvo would be passed around as girls buffed their brass buttons into whiter brightness.

And here am I in this magical moonlit evening, with the softest of breezes touching my cheek and darkness and star-shine my only companions, Christie told herself. And in there, not two feet from me now, is warmth, brightness, good talk . . . hot tea!

She climbed the half-dozen stone steps, mossy with time, and pushed open the front door. The hall, unlit, picked up the moonlight, but under the living-room door a ray of lamplight gleamed gold.

Christie glanced quickly behind her, at the soft darkness, the thinning foliage on the branches of the stately old trees which lined the drive. Then she slid inside and closed the front door on all that natural beauty. What I want is tea, then sleep, so I'm fresh for tomorrow, she told herself, a hand already on the door-knob. She entered the room and smiled hopefully round at the girls.

'Evening, one and all! Any chance of a cuppa before I get my head down?'

Next day they woke to a high wind, clouds snatching across the sky, and guessed that WAAFs would be walking across to the cookhouse clutching their skirts whilst the men's forage caps took off despite their owners' jamming them hard down on their Brylcreemed hair.

'A lovely day off,' Mary said blissfully as they lay in their room contemplating the tossing window curtains and the fast-moving cloudlets overhead. 'What'll we do, Chris? We ought to get our heads down around four o'clock, then we'll be fresher for the midnight to eight a.m. watch.'

'Let's go out on the bikes; I like the woods on a windy day,' Christie suggested. 'Once winter sets in we shan't be able to ride much.'

'Sure, I'd like that,' Mary agreed and presently, washed, dressed and with hot tea inside them, they walked leisurely down the garden towards the potting shed. The bikes, however, were not there.

'Someone's pipped us at the post,' Mary said regretfully. 'Well, we could walk ... hey, it's Skip's birthday! Should we go over?'

'Not until after lunch, they'll be sleeping,' Christie pointed out. 'You know how it is, they'll just crash out until mid-afternoon, then begin to come round. We'll go over in time for tea and sandwiches – we'll take the tea and sandwiches.'

And we'll walk to the woods,' Mary said with unexpected firmness. 'It'll do us both good.

She was right. It was a four-mile round trip but fighting the wind on the way there and being propelled by it on the way back was exhilarating rather than anything; they sang as they walked, and shouted out scraps of verse and pointed out to each other the dance of the yellowing leaves as they were torn from the trees and the beauty of the flickering sunlight and shadow through the wind-tossed branches.

They re-entered the manor in mid-afternoon, tired but still full of the beauties of the countryside.

'We ought to get some rest ... but let's go round to Skip first, see how he liked his present,' Christie said. 'Grab my biscuits – they're in the yellow tin – and I'll take a loaf and some tomatoes.'

'Can we walk round?' Mary said pathetically. 'Me legs ache from all that walkin' but I doubt I'll ever get over the wall.'

'You walk round, I'll climb over,' Christie said. 'You go now, I'll rush upstairs and fetch that packet of tea my aunt sent. Gosh, aren't we good to go when we're both so tired?'

''Tis always nice to see the boys, they're a cheerful bunch. Now if you arrive first be sure to knock,' Mary urged. 'They were flying last night, don't forget, they may still be asleep.'

'I always knock,' Christie said. 'The tomatoes are a bit soft . . . never mind, in sandwiches, who notices?'

Christie watched Mary walk tiredly to the front door and then she turned and ran up the stairs. She had grown thinner than ever despite the Air Force food and knew she was several inches taller than she had been when she signed on so long ago, but she was both fit and healthy; whereas Mary, who certainly ate no more than Christie, puffed and panted after a short run or a long walk.

We all make different uses of food, she was thinking as she retrieved the packet of tea, shoved it into her gas-mask case and thundered down the stairs again. Everything I eat goes into length and energy, everything poor Mary eats tends to settle contentedly round her hips!

She went through the house and out into the garden, threaded her way between the trees, automatically reaching up for an apple as she passed the big Blenheim orange pippin tree, then remembering that she had her work cut out to carry the tea, the loaf and the tomatoes. The wind had brought down the first windfalls, she noticed. They would have to have an apple-picking party and put their crop up in the hay-loft to keep all winter through, or perhaps they could preserve them in some way. Bottle them? People did, she supposed vaguely, with pleasant memories of apple pies at Christmas.

She reached the wall, climbed carefully over, and crossed the cobbled yard. Mary wouldn't have arrived yet. Her friend had done a great deal of walking already today and would be taking it slowly.

Christie put the packet of tea into her tunic pocket, slung her gas-mask case more securely over her shoulder, and knocked. Quietly, just in case they really were asleep. Then she knocked again and, like Goldilocks, she cautiously opened the door a crack.

She poked her head inside the cottage and immediately knew that it was empty. She frowned, then pushed the door wide and went inside. Had they been and gone? She was a bit late – that could well be the answer. It was Skip's birthday after all, they might have decided to take themselves off into town to see a flick and have a birthday tea.

Still, she was inside now. She would just check the bedrooms.

She ran up the stairs, knowing the rooms were empty, feeling already a deep sense of disappointment. Damn, and she had been looking forward to seeing the air-crew, making them sandwiches and tea, sharing round the biscuits. Most of all, perhaps, she wanted to see Skip with his present, wanted to watch him out there, with the wind in his hair – and it couldn't have been a better day for kite-flying – as he got the kite airborne. In her mind's eye she could see already his thin face, eyes bright with excitement, as he bucked the kite against the wind and taught it how to fly. A childish pastime perhaps, but the sort of pastime which would do Skip and his crew more good than a dozen packets of cigarettes or several pounds of toffees. It wasn't easy to relax, to divorce your mind totally from the war, but Christie was convinced that kite-flying would do it.

Then it occurred to her where they were, and she hurried down the stairs and across the kitchen. Of course! They would be up on Raddlewell Hill, the whole lot of them, flying the kite! If she went up there . . .

Something stopped her in her tracks, some second sense, or perhaps her eyes had already seen without her brain absorbing. She turned, slowly, towards the dresser.

The kite, still in its box, her piece of ribbon intact, lay on the sideboard. Beside it, the birthday card.

She knew, in a moment, what had happened and stood there, a hand unconsciously laid across her heart, whilst she slowly turned ice-cold. The room knew, too. Now that she looked at it properly she could see that it knew itself deserted; the dust was already settling on their beds, their odds and ends of possessions. The half-written letter seemed to cry out to be finished, stamped, despatched, but Christie knew it would never go, now. The birthday card, the present, the pile of logs by the fire . . . they looked like a stage-set, a cleverly contrived message to those with eyes to see. For a moment she could almost believe that Muffo, Skip, Sparky and the others were hovering here, wanting to get through to her, trying to get through, telling her that it was over, that she might as well leave; there would be no celebration now.

She was out of the cottage and half-way to the wall when Mary came puffing round the corner. She smiled at Christie and mopped her brow dramatically.

'Oh no – have they gone out? And didn't I run me best this last quarter-mile? Christie! What's the matter?'

'They . . . they've not been back. Not at all.'

The smile slipped. Mary's rosy face suddenly drained of colour and looked pinched, old, with a yellowish shade round her mouth. Christie remembered Mary's friendship with Muffo, the way they had all teased her about him. God, how could she have been so stupid, so selfish! If the loss of C for Charlie and her crew had been a cruel blow to her, how much worse for Mary, who didn't just like Muffo the way she, Christie, liked Skip. She loved him.

'They probably landed at another airfield,' Christie said quickly. 'It was probably an emergency . . . it could have been anything . . . a wounded man, no time to get back here, no fuel . . . Mary, it doesn't have to mean . . .'

Mary walked past her, going towards the cottage. She went inside. Shut the door.

Christie waited. She had been a fool, jumping to conclusions the way she had. What she had just said must be true; they must have done an emergency landing, it was happening all the time, just because they weren't back yet didn't mean they had pranged the kite. When she and Mary went back to the station they'd go straight to the control tower, try to find out what had happened to the crew of C for Charlie. Someone would tell them when they saw Mary's stricken face.

She waited, in the blustery wind and sun. Time passed. The door of the cottage remained closed.

Suddenly, it opened. Mary came out. She was quiet, composed. She didn't look as though she had been crying, but her eyes had a fixed, shiny look. Together they walked the long way round, ignoring the manor, heading without a word spoken, for the station.

They found out what had happened quite quickly. The bomber C for Charlie had been hit by flak; there had been an explosion, observers had only seen one parachute descend and they didn't think it had made it to the ground.

'It was Skip's birthday; he was going to be twenty-two,' Christie said helplessly, with tears running down her cheeks as she and Mary returned, with lagging steps, to their billet. 'His birthday, for God's sake – why in the name of Christ do they make them fly on their birthdays?'

There was no answer to it, or not one that made sense.

'It wasn't Muffo's birthday,' Mary said flatly. 'But he died just the same. Oh, Chris, I'm sick of it – sick to death! Tonight we'll do the midnight to eight o'clock, we'll sleep until three, we'll walk down to the cookhouse . . . in a few days we'll think about them a little less, in a few weeks there will have been so many others . . . we shan't remember the colour of their eyes or the way their hair grew. God, I'm sick of it!'

It could have been Andy, Christie thought. It could have been Andy and I wouldn't even know! I love him, he's a part of me, if he dies then I'll die too, I won't go on like this, accepting the unacceptable, seeing them snuffed out, taken off the board before they've had a chance to do half the things which are theirs by right. I can't take it any more, I'm going to get out, go home, let them get on with it!

She and Mary went to their room and got into their beds. Despite secret convictions that they would never sleep they slept at once, and deeply. Worn out emotionally and physically, they simply sank into sleep. They were on watch at midnight so the alarm was set, but neither girl thought about the shift to come. They didn't think at all, they just slept, taking the only way out that was open to them.

Christie dreamed. In her dream she was sitting on the wall between the manor and the coachman's house in bright sunshine. Skip sat on the wall next to her. He was doing something to the tail of his kite, adding more coloured bows. Presently he finished his task and looked across at her. He grinned and reached out to ruffle her hair. She could feel his fingers on her scalp, she could feel the wind on her cheek, she knew it was a good day to fly a kite. She grinned back at him.

'Thanks for the kite, Chris; you're brilliant, it's just what we wanted, the lads and I. We flew it earlier; it went like . . . like a Spitfire, way up into the sky, it tangled with the clouds and when we brought it down a cloud came, too.'

'I'm glad you like it.'

She found she was suddenly shy with him, which was natural since he was dead and she had not before talked to a dead man. But he seemed to have no such feelings.

'I do like it. Flying this sort of kite is even better than flying my other kite – safer and all. We all think so . . . we all like being dead much better than we liked being alive. But now that we're on our way, you and Andy can have the kite.'

She frowned over at him and noticed, for the first time, that she could see through him, that he was ever so slightly transparent. She blinked and put out a hand to take his. At first her fingers closed over warm flesh, then his hand in hers grew cold and the smile on his face faded; she could see the haunted eyes, the tremble of his lips.

'I didn't want to die; there's so much I've not done. I never told Sarah I loved her, never kissed you, Christie, never even thanked you for the kite. Why didn't I see the flak this time? Why didn't we dodge it? Muffo's lonely, he wants Mary. And I'm so cold, Chris, so damned cold!'

He was fading fast now. She gave a heartbroken cry and tried to take him in her arms; it was like trying to hold mist. She jumped off the wall and called his name but he didn't hear her; he and the others, all pale-faced, hollow-eyed and transparent, were drifting upwards, like smoke, towards the sky which had grown dark and threatening.

Christie screamed . . . and woke. She was bathed in sweat and her heart was hammering away in her breast. What an absolutely horrible dream; she looked over at the alarm clock and it was only half past ten, no need to get up for another hour. She turned over, meaning to try to get back to sleep, and found herself on her feet. If she went back to sleep she might have another nightmare, she couldn't bear that. It would be more sensible to go down to the living-room and see whether tea was on the go, or at least have a chat to someone. Mary was snoring gently and didn't seem to be dreaming; best leave her, she would need all the sleep, and forgetfulness, she could get. It would be time enough to wake her when they had to get down to the station for the midnight watch.

Christie dressed slowly in the moonlight and then left the room and padded down the stairs. She was about to go into the living-room, actually had her hand on the door-knob, when she had a great desire to look at the coachman's cottage; as though she might find the whole thing had been a horrible dream and the crew of C for Charlie were sleeping in their beds, or playing poker round the kitchen table, or even trooping up through the orchard to reassure her that they were safe.

She went quickly across the kitchen. It was empty, moonlit. She went out of the back door, across the yard, over the grass, though the orchard. She leaned on the wall and looked across at the coachman's house and knew, with a sort of dreadful, sad finality, that her hopes were in vain. The crew of C for Charlie had gone and would never return. It was no use buoying herself up with false hope, no use filling Mary's mind with that same hope. They must accept that they'd lost their friends and get on with life.

She returned slowly through the garden and slipped into the kitchen. And there, for some reason, grief hit her. She sat down at the kitchen table, buried her face in her hands and wept as if she could never stop. Tears rained down, tears for all of them, for Skip who hadn't quite made it to his twenty-second birthday, for Muffo who might have married Mary, for Sparks and all the others who had laughed and joked and done their damnedest to remain sane and to keep their fears and worries to themselves.

She was at the choky, gasping stage when she felt suddenly sure she was not alone. She didn't look up, because she knew that there was no one else in the room . . . but there was a warmth, a strong feeling of sympathy and understanding, which had not been there earlier. Someone, at some time, had sat at this kitchen table as she was sitting, had wept as she was weeping; and that person, soul, spirit – ghost, if you must – was doing its best to comfort her, telling her that she must grieve and then put her grief to one side so that she could remember her friends with pleasure and warmth because that was the only good thing she could do for them, now.

And presently she stood up, wiped her eyes with the heels of her hands, and set off up the stairs to wake Mary. She felt composed, almost capable of facing up to the sense of loss she was bound to feel. It's probably been happening as long as there has been a world, she told herself, climbing the stairs. In a house like this, which is probably three or four hundred years old, girls have wept for men killed in battle over and over; and have gone on to lead useful lives. And instead of thinking it might have been Andy I should be thanking God that it wasn't. Not this time.

She slid into the bedroom just as the alarm began its frail tinkling. Mary sat up groggily as Christie pulled the blackout blind down and fumbled for the matches and the lamp.

'Chris? Is it time to get up?'

She sounded about five years old, Christie thought affectionately. She lit the lamp and trimmed it until the flame burned steadily.

'Yes, it's time. We're on watch in thirty minutes. It's quite cold outside, so I'll get our greatcoats.'

On the way along the dark country road, arms linked, Mary said, 'Christie, you know Muffo and I . . . well, you know we liked each other?'

'Yes, love,' Christie said gently. 'I know.'

'It . . . it wouldn't have come to anything, not really. I guess we both knew it. He had a girl back in Wales . . . a land-girl. I reckon he'd have gone back to her in the end.'

'And you've got your husband,' Christie said. 'It does complicate matters, I suppose.'

Mary nodded.

'Aye. There's times when I remember our honeymoon, and things which happened when we were courtin' . . . they were good times.'

'That's right. They're what you should remember. Because all that other business ... it wouldn't have happened but for the war, would it?'

Mary sighed and shrugged. 'I dunno, maybe you're right. But ... I'll never forget Muffo, Christie.'

'I hope I never forget any of them,' Christie said. 'We'd better walk a bit faster, Mary, or we'll be late for the change-over.'

Mary glanced at her watch in the moonlight and gave a squeak.

'Holy Mother, we'd best run, Chris!'

It was a hard winter. Christie and Mary left the manor with the snow-flakes whirling round their heads and limiting their vision to a few yards. Christie's hands were like ice even in her warm woollen mittens and her nose felt as if it might fall off at any moment, but she was so worried for their fliers that the cold seemed of little importance. When they had taken off, four hours earlier, it had been icy cold but clear; poor blighters, little had they known what they would have to face on their return – the met. bods had got it wrong again.

She and Mary hurried into the control tower, hung their snow-wet greatcoats up on the hooks outside the door, and went into the warmth of their small room. The two girls on the four to midnight watch turned and smiled at them; Anita was knitting herself a scarf, Freda was embroidering a tablecloth for her trousseau. The tablecloth was a mass of sweet peas and butterflies and was large enough to cover a table for eight, or so she told anyone who would listen.

Right now, however, Anita was bundling up her knitting and jamming it into her gas-mask case and Freda was carefully folding the tablecloth round the silks she had brought with her tonight. There was clearly nothing doing – the FCO was changing shift too. FCO Charlesworth taking over from FCO Ribbins, talking in low voices, Ribbins pointing to the board with the call-signs of the aircraft flying tonight chalked on it, to the head-sets, to his ledgers.

Christie was on station watch tonight, Mary on Darky watch. They slid into the chairs still warm from their predecessors' neat rears and picked up the head-sets. As soon as Christie put hers on the sounds were there; the metallic, maddening sound of German jamming. Horrible in its persistence, the jamming continued whilst under or over it the voices of pilots talked to each other, commented on conditions, engine notes, sometimes on personalities, getting nearer, then further, then fading into silence . . . except that there was no silence, only the jamming, the static and the morse code bleeping away. Probably the most important, and difficult, part of the job of an RT operator was to ignore these sounds, to hear only the voices which were addressing her: the pilots and radio operators, their call-signs on their lips, asking for help, landing instructions, guidance from the ground. Learning to ignore all the outside sounds was hard at first, but became possible, especially since, after a time, the jamming and the static became a part of silence, albeit a noisy and sometimes irritating part.

Sitting comfortably in her chair with the snow

tapping on the window before her, Christie checked her equipment; pencils, pad, the mike, the set. The big window through which, on a day-watch, she watched the approach or departure of the planes was blacked out with a very efficient blind. The blind had lines running across; it didn't do to stare too hard at the lines or try to imagine what was happening beyond them or you lost concentration and didn't listen as closely as you should. Listening, straining your ears for that all-important call-sign from out of the welter of jamming was what it was all about. So Christie sighed, leaned forward in her seat, a pencil ready in her hand, and waited, as she would continue to wait until the first planes began to return.

Beside her, Mary slid into her own seat. She was on Darky watch, the emergency safety watch which dealt with lost pilots who needed an emergency landing-place. Months before, in that warm September, Christie had hoped that the crew of C for Charlie might have gone into the nearest station on a Darky call. They had not; but it was the most important watch there was, Christie thought, and also the most boring because so often – thankfully – there were no Darky calls. When the planes began to return to their station then Christie would be working all-out until they were down . . . but should there be a Darky call, Mary could find herself giving vital, life-saving information to men who had never landed at this particular airfield before, had no knowledge of the sort of country they were in but were simply in desperate need of help.

Now, the two girls exchanged small smiles as Mary

settled down. Christie saw out of the corner of her eye Mary doing the checks she herself had just completed, saw Mary select one of the pencils, rub a finger across the point, pull a face and turn to the FCO who sat behind them, his books spread out in front of him.

'Lend us a penknife, sir, me pencil's gone and blunted on me.'

The Flying Control Officer handed over his penknife; he yawned as he did so and said it had been a quiet night so far but would be pretty lively when the kites began to come back in these rotten conditions. Rumour had it that there were razor blades on sale in Boots the Chemist in town, he added; had the girls heard if it was true? And why were razor blades always in short supply during wartime? He remembered his father saying it had been just the same in the First World War.

'They're steel, I suppose,' Christie said, wondering whether it would be a good time to produce her knitting. Some officers hated seeing other ranks knitting or reading on duty, but FCO Charlesworth was a nice bloke; he knew very well that the girls could knit and listen and he also knew how cold and boring the midnight to eight a.m. watch could be.

'Steel! Yes, of course, that must be it. Oh well, I'll have a quick zizz in the morning and then go into town after lunch, see if I can pick up some blades. It's pretty quiet right now, I'll put the kettle on, I think.'

'All right if we knit, sor?'

Mary scarcely waited for the FCO's nod before whipping out the square she was knitting. She was going to make a blanket from the squares when she had enough and got a good deal of pleasure from unpicking any woollen garment she could acquire and knitting it up again for her famous blanket. Already it was half-completed and she vowed that it would be cosier than a real blanket when it was finished.

Christie was making Andy a pair of socks in Air Force blue. The men always complained of cold hands and feet in winter but she did not feel capable of the intricacies necessary to produce gloves, hence the socks. Thank God toes are too close together to want separate little compartments, she thought, painfully knitting with four pointed needles and seeing the sock growing a little nearer its completion with every row. What on earth would I do if people wore socks with fat little fingers?

'Tea up.'

Flight Control Officer Charlesworth put a steaming mug carefully down in front of each girl, then returned to his own place.

Christie sipped her tea, then did another row of knitting. In her ears the jamming buzzed and tinkled and clattered. Steadfastly, she listened through it, for the voices out of the night, calling to her.

The long night passed. The planes began coming back in the dark – in January daylight comes late. Christie was working all out, as she stacked up the planes for landing. Behind her, the FCO rubbed out the aircraft identifications as they landed safely. Beside her, Mary listened intently for Darky calls, and knitted, and occasionally got up and made tea.

Pilots called out to each other, asked her to get a move on, bring them in before they ran out of juice or fainted from hunger. It had been a raid over Germany and seemed to have gone well.

Eight o'clock came without them noticing, and when Doreen touched Christie's shoulder in an interval when there were no planes waiting, Christie jumped, was startled. Keyed up to do her job, as soon as relief was at hand she immediately realised she was tired, stiff and cold. She slid out of her seat and Doreen sat down; the head-set changed hands and Christie stepped back, out of the way, whilst Doreen began to do her checks.

'Let's get some brekker,' Mary said as the two of them descended the stairs and pushed open the door. 'Holy Mother, look at that!'

Snow lay everywhere, deep and crisp and even; the sky was still dark, though it was grey in the east, and the wind brought a chill with it.

'They won't fly in this,' Christie said with satisfaction. 'Andy's lot haven't been airborne for several days, they've got bad snow up in Lincolnshire. Perhaps, who knows, they might let us have a spot of leave!'

12

In the early days of January '42 the weather closed down and there was very little flying, but Col and the rest of his crew were back in Blighty at last and Col was to go before a promotions board. Consequently, Shanna was in seventh heaven.

He had rung her as soon as he landed, bubbling with excitement.

'Dunno where I'll be posted,' he said. 'Nor whether I'll get my promotion of course, but it 'ud be great if I came up north. Anyway, it won't be long before we're 'avin' a cuddle. Gawd, I can't wait!'

Shanna couldn't, either. Every day she examined the letter-board with deep interest and desperate hope, every evening she hung about, hoping for a phone call. Her friends teased her, her passengers in whatever form of transport she drove commented on her pink cheeks and sparkling eyes, and even Jacko was infected by her excitement, squawking indignantly when she left him in his cage to go to work, welcoming her return with raucous comments and his sewing-machine purr.

Exactly a week after the phone call Shanna

wandered into the mess on the off-chance that there would be something for her, and met Angela about to leave with a brown envelope in her hand.

'Hi, Shanna; there's a letter for you,' Angela said. 'We're going sledging when we come off shift this afternoon. Coming?'

'I don't know,' Shanna said. She recognised Col's writing immediately and longed to open it, but instead she shoved the letter into her pocket, crumpling it considerably. Once, she would have torn it open on the spot, but she was learning self-discipline. To open it here and now would mean answering well-intentioned questions, sharing the contents. If she waited, she could read it in peace and quiet, and enjoy it all the more. 'Thanks for picking up my mail, Angie. What are you doing after work?'

'Exchange clothing parade,' Angela said. 'I'm in great need of another shirt, mine seems to have shrunk. How about you?'

'Might as well. I've some stockings which are more ladder than anything else, not even the nastiest officer could expect me to wear them. And there's a hole in the elbow of my working denims; I caught the material when I was trying to crank up that pig of a lorry the other day.'

'And we're going sledging this afternoon,' Angela said again as the two of them fell into step to make their way to their respective jobs. 'You aren't likely to be busy – going to come along?'

Shanna nodded, but her thoughts were elsewhere. Col must have had his posting – suppose he was coming up north! Her hand stole into her pocket and she fingered the envelope thoughtfully. It was a fat letter . . . lots of detail, lots of love-talk. Wonderful. A treat in store.

Shanna and Angela parted outside the offices and Shanna went to the MT pool to do the daily inspection of the vehicle she would have driven should circumstances warrant it. The NCO in charge then ordered everyone to clean the hangar and get their vehicles spotless, so Shanna worked away with everyone else, not thinking of the letter more than ten times a minute, and finished her work in good time. She joined Angela, Mandy and the others in the cookhouse, but bolted her food and then got up.

'I'm going to give Jacko some seed,' she announced. 'I shan't be long. Where are you meeting for sledging?'

'By the main gate. Don't be late, or we'll go without you!'

Half-way across to her billet Shanna was hailed by their Wing Officer's second-in-command. The Wing Officer was a pleasant woman in her mid-thirties but the Squadron Officer was a very different kettle of fish. She was autocratic and vindictive and not popular with her WAAFs. Shanna stopped in her tracks and saluted smartly, assuming that she was about to receive a lecture for not doing so at once, but instead the SO came over to her, holding out a letter.

'Douglas, there's a letter for you. Seems to have got muddled up with my official mail.'

Shanna, thanking her politely, looked at the long

brown envelope with dislike. More instructions from on high, or reprimands, or something similar. When had a letter such as this meant good news? But she saluted smartly and made for her billet. What did the official letter matter? Nothing could take away her pleasure in Col's epistle!

She reached her billet, hung her coat and cap on the hook, and took Jacko's seed from the bag under her bed. Jacko, who had been snoozing in his cage, began to dance expectantly up and down, shouting about Christmas, bloody birds' beaks and his latest passion, snatches of rude limerick. Shanna got him out of the cage and scattered the seed so that he would get some exercise searching out every last grain, then sat down on her bed and drew out her letter. She opened it and began to read.

It was a happy letter, full of his pleasure in being back in Blighty, anticipation over seeing her, hope for a posting somewhere near her so that they could spend more time together. She read it through twice, began to read it again, then remembered the second letter. With a strong sense of doing her duty she drew it out of her pocket, slit open the envelope, pulled out the page within and began to read.

When Shanna had read the second letter through twice she stood up and the letter, which she had placed on her knees, fluttered unregarded to the floor. Her greatcoat, still with damp patches on the shoulders, was on the hook behind her bed. She took it down and pulled it on. Then she put on her cap, wrapped her scarf round her face, fished her gloves out of her pockets and put them on, too. Then she made for the door.

Outside, it was cold but clear. The snow was deep and the wind had dropped. A small, cold part of her mind noted that it was good sledging weather, but she did not turn towards the group of girls heading for the gates and freedom; instead she began to walk out across the airfield to where, only a couple of days before, she had joined in a snow-clearing party, shovelling and brushing at the snow as the plough cleared most of it from the concrete until they were all glowing, muscles aching, and the runways were clear.

She walked right round the airfield without seeing anyone or indeed wanting to see anyone. When she reached the gates the sledging parties had left; no one took the slightest notice of her as she walked out of the camp and turned left, away from the village.

She walked briskly, but presently she noticed that her legs felt very heavy, as though she were wearing, not her issue lace-ups, but lead boots. Not that it mattered whether she walked slowly or fast; she wasn't going anywhere.

She walked on, meeting no one. She passed through a village, not the one they usually visited, and glanced without seeing them at thatched cottages, a church, a tiny general store. Presently she found herself in truly open country, with the wind getting up and whipping the surface off the snow whilst the bare-branched trees protested as they were bent and shaken by the force of the gale.

To walk against the wind it became necessary for Shanna to bend forward, to fight against it. As she went it grew darker. It snowed in little flurries. Shanna had abandoned the road now and was walking over what seemed like moorland. Not that it mattered; a walk taken for no purpose at least freed you from the obligation of going anywhere.

Presently the wind dropped and the moon rose. High in the dark sky, ringed with mist, it shone emotionlessly down on the snowy landscape, on the small, greatcoated figure who was walking much more slowly now, head bent, hands thrust deep into pockets.

Soon it shone down on an empty landscape. A dutch barn bulked against the stars, a thin hedge meandered along beside what had once been a country lane and was now little more than a dimpled snowfield. A great white barn owl swerved, hovered hopefully for a moment . . . flew on.

To the owl the moon in the sky above was a hunter's moon, a friend. To the mouse over which it hovered the moon was an enemy whose brilliant light could lead to its death. To the searchers hunting for Shanna it was a relief, a help in their task. They called out to one another, commenting on the improvement in visibility, shouting her name, finding footprints which looked hopeful, now discovering signs that someone had passed this way.

But they did not find Shanna.

Angela and Mandy had sledged without Shanna,

since she hadn't turned up to join them. They came back to the station just as darkness was falling, flushed, tired, happy.

'I'm going to tell Shanna she missed the most fun of the entire war,' Angela stated as they trekked wearily across to the cookhouse to return their borrowed metal trays. She had shared her tray with a sergeant pilot called Tony who had kissed and cuddled her when they had ended up in a snowdrift; the stars in her eyes were bright enough to make a torch unnecessary. 'Still, the snow doesn't look like thawing just yet – perhaps she'll come tomorrow.'

'I wonder what she was doing whilst we were rushing down the slopes,' Amanda mused. 'Let it be a lesson to you though, Angie – girls with regular boyfriends miss all the fun. She was probably writing to that Colin of hers.'

'Probably. Did you know he was back in England? He's somewhere down south, going before a promotions board in a week or ten days. She was over the moon when she got his phone call.'

'Lovely for her. I wonder where she's gone, though? We could try the mess, only I must get out of these wet clothes first.'

'Yes, I'm soaked,' Angela agreed. Even the best of sergeant pilots upended trays occasionally. They entered the cookhouse, which was by no means full since it was an hour before the next meal. 'Thanks for the trays, Corp, we had a wizard time.'

The cookhouse corporal, frying potatoes in spitting fat, nodded grumpily, and the girls put their trays on the long counter and left, turning towards their billet.

They opened the door and slipped inside, following the usual routine; you stood between the blackout curtain and the door, closed the door behind you, then pushed the curtain aside and entered the hut.

There were several people in the hut, changing their clothes for an evening out or just sitting on their beds writing letters. But the most cursory glance was enough to show Angela that Shanna was not amongst them though Jacko, hunched and offended, was sidling up and down between the beds, now and then stooping to peer beneath the frames as though he were the proverbial old maid searching for a man.

'No, she's not here, but she's probably in the mess . . . or was there a transport into town earlier?' Angela asked Mandy as the two of them began to struggle out of their wet clothing. 'I wonder why she didn't take Jacko? But he can be a nuisance, and he does hate the cold.'

She removed her skirt, then sat down on the bed in her blackouts and began to peel her stockings off, dropping them soggily onto the floor. Mandy, doing the same on the bed next to her, said, 'Have you got dry stockings without ladders, though? I washed a pair yesterday, they're probably still hanging in the ablutions.'

'Here, have these.' Angela rooted in the locker which separated her bed from Shanna's, then paused, stockings in hand. 'There's a letter half under Shanna's bed.'

'So what? She gets quite a lot of mail one way and another.'

'Ye-es, but it shouldn't be on the floor, I'll just . . .'

'It's rude to read other people's letters,' Mandy said reproachfully as Angela, having retrieved the sheet of paper, stood as if turned to stone, her eyes fixed on the handwriting. 'If Shanna catches you . . .'

'Hush, Mandy,' Angela said. 'Oh my God . . . listen.'

> *Dear Miss Douglas,*
> *It is with great regret that I write to inform you that LAC Blacker, whilst servicing an aircraft in a snowstorm, was today knocked down and killed when he slipped on the icy wing and fell into the path of an approaching ambulance.*

Angela stopped reading and stared across at her friend.

'That's Shanna's Colin, it must be. She's as good as an orphan, she doesn't have relatives and things. Why, I was just telling you that Col was back in England . . . oh Mandy, what shall we do?'

'Does the letter say anything else?' Mandy asked. 'I mean LAC Blacker could be a long-lost cousin or something . . . doesn't it mention . . .'

'Hang on a minute, I'm just reading the rest. It's mostly details which don't . . . ah, this is the last paragraph. Listen.

> *Colin was a delightful chap as well as a first-class*

371

mechanic; he often spoke of you and the future he planned with you. We are all deeply sorry for what has happened; you have our sincere sympathy.

Yours sincerely,
Charles Cavanagh (Flt Lt)

'That's it, then,' Mandy said heavily. 'You're right, it is Shanna's feller. What'll we do, Angie?'

'Find her,' Angela said briskly. She and Mandy had conducted their conversation in hushed tones, now she turned to face the rest of the room and raised her voice. 'Girls, has anyone seen Shanna?'

Heads were shaken doubtfully.

'The place was empty when I came in an hour ago,' someone volunteered. 'Jacko was quite polite – I'd saved him some peas, mind.'

'She had a letter from her feller,' Mandy said suddenly, remembering. 'At least, I thought it was from Colin. We asked her to come sledging but she wanted to feed Jacko first and I guessed she wanted to read the letter, too. We should've searched for her when she didn't come ... but how were we to know?'

'We'd better get over to the officers' mess and tell them she's not around,' Angela said. 'Such terrible news ... where will she have gone?'

'Somewhere quiet, where she can be alone,' Delia Brown said. She was a small girl with night-black hair and big, grey-blue eyes. She had married a rear gunner three months ago, and he had been killed seven weeks later. If anyone knew how Shanna would

372

feel it would be Delia. 'She won't want anyone, not at first. Leave her to come to terms with it.'

'But the weather,' Angela explained. 'If she's out in this . . .'

She stopped speaking. Outside, the wind howled eerily round the huts, snow tapped now and then on the metal walls.

'It's a pig of a night to be out,' Wendy Prothero remarked. 'Perhaps someone should be told. I'll take a look round whilst you go over to the officers' mess. Anyone coming?'

They all went in the end, a great gaggle of anxious girls. They alerted the authorities and searched the airfield from end to end. But they saw neither hide nor hair of Shanna.

'It was a real cock-up,' Angela was saying earnestly into the telephone. 'Her fellow's Squadron Leader wrote to our Wing Officer and enclosed a letter to Shanna. The WO was supposed to have a word with Shanna first, so that she knew what to expect when she opened the letter and had some support. But her second-in-command opened the letter, didn't bother to read it, just called Shanna over and gave her the letter to read.'

'And Shanna's gone? Just walked out? What about the bird?' Meg's voice was thin with fright. 'She wouldn't leave him, surely?'

'She did. He hates the cold and I don't suppose she meant to go for as long as she did . . . she went mid-afternoon yesterday, it wasn't until this morning I thought of you, wondered whether she'd made her way over to Sellars.'

'She hasn't. I wonder ... did she have any money on her, do you know? She was closer to Sue Collins than anyone else, she missed Sue horribly when she was first posted. I've got Sue's number, I could ring her. And there's Christie ... she might think of something. Only if Shanna's got no money I don't see how she could get far.'

'I don't know what to think,' Angela said, her voice perilously close to a wail. 'She's been out all night, Meg, in the most terrible cold. I keep thinking she's probably lying stiff and – and dead in some ditch.'

'She's got more sense than that,' Meg said, but Angela could tell Meg wasn't too sure, not too sure at all. 'Have you tried sending Jacko in search of her?'

Angela snorted.

'Him! Useless blighter! He went straight to the cookhouse and started menacing people for food. He's not like a dog, he's only got a little bird-brain so I suppose we shouldn't expect anything different, but we did think he might try to go to her. Anyway we're going out again this morning – everyone who isn't actually on duty that is, and most of us aren't working because of the close-down the weather's caused.'

'I'm off-duty apart from checking a repair,' Meg said. 'I'll get a few of the girls together ... we'll take a look round.'

Putting the phone down, Meg thanked the officer who

had called her in, explained what it was all about, and then went slowly out of the office block and back to the big shed where she was engine testing. She picked up the spanner she had been using when the phone call came, then put it down again, staring vacantly into space, trying to think. She had known, vaguely, that Shanna had a boyfriend, but hadn't thought much about it. Shanna had always had boyfriends, she took that for granted. Not being on the same station she hadn't realised that the boyfriend was a serious one, a boy Shanna liked enough to correspond with, to talk about sharing her future with.

She remembered that first meeting, when Shanna had started to talk about a fellow and she, Meg, had not been very sympathetic, had actually interrupted Shanna's timid explanation with the story of her own leave, her feelings for Lenny. Now, she could have kicked herself because when Shanna wanted help she would most definitely not turn to Meg.

What would she do, then, where would she turn? To Sue, of course, because Sue had never let her down. So I should ring Sue, Meg told herself, that is the obvious thing to do. But if Shanna turned up in Hampshire, Sue would ring in, explain. So Shanna hadn't turned up there, not yet at any rate. Suppose she'd wandered off, blinded by grief, and simply got lost? If so she'd be dead now – no one could sit down under a hedge in weather like this and survive.

Better ring Sue. And Christie, because she might easily think of something.

Meg put her spanner down and went over to Corporal Jackson who was drinking a cup of tea and laying down the law about hydraulics.

''Scuse me, Corp – that phone call was about a WAAF from RAF Waldrington, a friend of mine. Her feller's been killed and she's gone missing. Mind if I go and make a couple of calls? I've had a thought.'

'Missing? When?'

'Last night,' Meg said unwillingly. She did not want to begin long explanations. 'Can I go now, Corp?'

'Yes, off you go, Airwoman. Got enough pennies?'

'Lor', no . . . Can anyone lend me . . .?' Meg said hopefully. Everyone in hearing began to rummage through pockets and respirator cases. Meg took their contributions with promises of repayment, smiled round at them and set off. 'Shan't be long, Corp.'

She hurried across to the mess. She picked up the phone and asked the operator for the number of her first operational station. She tumbled the pennies into the slot and found she was holding her breath. Expelling it slowly, she found she was praying beneath her breath; *let Sue be there, don't let her be out on a job*!

Meg was fond of Shanna, fonder than she'd realised. We're special, we four, she found herself thinking. If only I'd been more understanding, more sympathetic. If only I'd realised . . .

Let her be with Sue, let her be safe.

Someone answered the phone, went in search of Sue.

Meg waited.

It had been November when the mutual attraction which had flared between Sue and Alan Watson again reared its head. The two of them, without exchanging a word on the subject, had done their best to pretend to themselves – and each other – that the night they had spent in the barn had meant nothing to either of them. Indeed, Sue sometimes wondered if it had meant anything to Alan. He was a married man, he had a child he adored, and a reputation which did not include the seduction of an M/T driver who was young enough, at a pinch, to be his daughter. Perhaps his abrupt reversion to a rather cooler attitude towards her was not merely a mirroring of her own feelings but a natural act for a man who felt embarrassed over his behaviour on that one solitary occasion.

Besides, Sue was all too aware that, should either one of them show again the feelings which had very nearly risen to the surface that night, a near-to-impossible situation might arise. So they both behaved with slightly stilted friendliness which might have continued for the rest of their working lives together had it not been for Sergeant Johnny Smith.

Johnny Smith was a sergeant pilot, flying a Beaufort with great skill, much admired for his handling of the tricky, not always reliable aircraft. He partnered Sue at a dance in the sergeants' mess and after that, often chatted to her when she was driving the blood-waggon, or having a meal in the cookhouse, or just on the transport, going into town.

Johnny was a Canadian, who had joined up in '39 and found many English ways odd, not to say eccentric. He loved Sue's Liverpool accent – she thought she'd shed it, and was quite surprised to find it was still there – and teased her to teach him Liverpool slang, falling on some of her sayings with great glee.

'Say it again, Suzie-Woo,' he would beg. 'Tara, whack! Gee, you slay me!'

Almost without noticing it, Sue began to go around with Johnny. He was a tall, gangly young man with an engaging grin, a crew cut, and very white, even teeth. He would never have claimed to be good-looking, but Sue found him good fun, a friend in need, and began to take it for granted that if they were both free then whatever they did they would do together.

Johnny chose to get amorous at a dance to raise money for the war effort, when there was quite a lot of mingling of ranks, and Sue enjoyed feeling that she mattered to this nice young man. She never kidded herself that Johnny was serious, she was sure he had girlfriends back home; but she saw no need to repulse him when, after the dance, he walked her home to her billet and kissed her very thoroughly just outside the door.

Next day, when she went and picked Alan up to take him up to a meeting at Adastral House, he behaved strangely, taking his place in the car with only a mumble, ignoring her remarks about the weather, the possibility of snow. Now and then she felt his eyes on her and turned her head – he was sitting in the passenger seat – only to find him gazing

378

front, a frown on his brow, his lips set.

Finally, it all came out. He had seen her kissing that Canadian, he had heard the man call her by that ridiculous name – Suzie-Woo indeed! – and had thought it all a bit silly, a bit tasteless. Sue, stung, had answered him pretty sharply and they'd had a row so bad that he'd ordered her to stop the car, growling the command out through gritted teeth.

Furiously, Sue indicated that she was turning left and swerved into a gateway. She turned to tell him just what she thought of him – a dog in the manger was the politest thing she said – and was in very satisfactory mid-flow when he leaned across the car and took her in his arms.

Sue struggled and fought and ordered him to let her go, was actually swearing at him when his mouth descended on hers.

After that there was silence in the car for two long, gloriously happy minutes until Alan drew back a little, still holding her to his breast.

'Darling ... my God, I've wanted to do this for months! Oh Sue, I've loved you from the first moment you saluted outside my billet and said you were my new driver! Don't remind me about Cynthia because I've thought of her non-stop ... oh Sue, you little wretch, *how* I love you!'

'You shouldn't, you aren't free to love me,' Sue said in a small, uncertain voice. She reached up and stroked his cheek. 'I can love you – I can't stop myself – but I can't do anything about it. And you mustn't love me at all. You must love ...'

'I didn't want to fall for you, it just happened,' Alan said. He sounded both guilty and complacent and a smile twitched at his lips. 'This is rather a public spot, my darling, but . . .'

He drew her close again, kissing her in a way which made Sue's heart pound and other strange things happen so that she moaned and moved her body closer, wanting him so much that suddenly their situation, his wife, scarcely seemed to matter.

A man wobbling past on a bicycle brought them both to their senses.

'Oh Alan, people are . . . I'd better move.'

She drove him to Adastral House, waited for him, drove him out of London just as they heard the hum of aircraft in the night sky.

'Raid,' Alan said quickly. 'Stop at the next pub.'

Sue knew what would happen if she stopped, knew she ought to insist on driving on. Instead, she drew into a small car park, got out, went inside with him. She heard him booking two rooms, knew that one bed would never be slept in, accepted that what was going to happen was the natural conclusion to all that had gone before.

That night she lay in his arms and wept because she had never lain with a man before and had meant to save herself for marriage. They were both naked, lacking any kind of nightwear; she had never seen a naked man before save for younger brothers and was astonished by his erection. She had danced with scores of young men, kissed them, cuddled with them, and had never realised what was going on beneath their blue serge trousers. Talk in the Waafery had not prepared her for this – she could scarcely take her round, astonished eyes off him.

She said as much to Alan and he laughed and kissed her, his tongue exploring her mouth, something which astonished her anew. She had heard of French kissing, knew what it was, but had never allowed any man such an extraordinary intimacy. She told him that, too, as soon as their mouths parted, holding his straying hands tightly whilst she talked, and he laughed again, and kissed her lightly on the nose, then pulled his hands free and began gently stroking her small, peaking breasts.

He cupped one breast with his warm palm and said he could feel her heart-beat, that it was beating too fast; then lay down beside her so that they were pressed together down the length of their bodies and just cuddled her, moving his hands almost absently from her slight shoulder blades down across her back until she whimpered and moved restlessly, eager for ... what? She had no clear idea, she just knew, vaguely, that whatever was to come was somehow necessary to her.

Presently, they made love, and Alan's gentleness – and undoubtedly his experience – made it unforgettable for Sue. Any pain, any fear, was quickly swamped by desire and very soon, by fulfilment. And Sue, who had always been niggardly with her body, was suddenly generous, suddenly abandoned.

So this was what it was all about, she marvelled, as Alan slept, his head in the hollow of her shoulder. So this was what poets wrote about and singers sang about! She hadn't imagined it a bit like that – it was all a lot more *physical*, rather like the PT they all tried so hard to avoid. Not *quite* like it of course, but much harder work than she had imagined, needing energy and enthusiasm as well as the urgency of desire.

Likening it to PT made Sue imagine her PTI, a leathery WAAF with a blaring voice, doing it, and that made her smile. No, perhaps it wasn't really like PT after all. It was more like ... well, it was like nothing else, it was in a class of its own. No wonder Shanna had behaved the way she had, no wonder Christie went off for sly weekends; because when someone does *that* to you, you know yourself valued ... or at least, that was how she had felt, in Alan's loving, intimate embrace.

I wonder if it's as nice the second time? Sue thought, stirring restlessly in Alan's arms. I wonder if it's possible to do it first thing in the morning, as well as last thing at night?

And when morning came, she found it was perfectly possible.

It had been several weeks after that first night together that Alan's conscience began troubling him. It might have come to a head sooner, probably would have done but a 'flu epidemic had swept the Waafery and Sue, usually the most healthy of girls, caught the bug and was in sick bay for three miserable weeks. Alan visited her but the visits were, perforce, formal, and no sooner was she up and about than Alan also succumbed and the visits, as Sue put it, were on the other foot.

As a senior officer he had a room to himself, so she smoothed his brow and yearned over him without a ward full of sneering onlookers; but as soon as he was able to be moved he got a friend to drive him home and that meant that he and Sue didn't meet until he was back on the strength once more. Christmas came and went and the snow came down and it was well into January before Sue found herself driving him back to London and hoping that they might get 'held up' again on the way home, for the look in his eyes told her that absence had, if anything, made the heart grow fonder and the body more eager for the consummation of their love.

But she had reckoned without Alan's conscience, it appeared.

'I really ought to tell Cyn; I shouldn't go through life acting a lie,' he said heavily, once they were driving along the main road into London. 'She was very sweet when I was ill, though one didn't want to catch 'flu herself – for Anna's sake, of course. Only I can't tell her, she'd never stand it. Sue, I love you with all my heart, but I've got to go back to Cyn and spend the rest of my life with her . . . thinking of you, longing for you. She'll know something's wrong but she'll just make the best of it, as I'll have to. I've behaved like a complete cad and now I'm getting what I deserve. I'll spend the rest of my life wanting you and dreaming about you and having to pretend. Oh Sue, my darling, how can I bear it?'

'What about me?' Sue said stoutly. 'I love you, Alan, and I ought to be able to enjoy that, but I can't because you belong to someone else. My life will be ruined through no fault of my own . . . unless you feel you can ask for a divorce? Though I don't know what me mam would say if I told her I was goin' with a divorced man.'

'I can't bring myself to hurt her so; Cynthia's very dependent, my love. She has no self-esteem, no independence of spirit. She clings . . . God, how she clings! You're tough, terribly pretty – you have a good life. But Cyn would just crumble to nothing if I left her. I know it.'

'Right. Then we mustn't be alone together again,' Sue said miserably but with decision. 'That first time was also the last.'

'We're alone together now,' Alan said gloomily. 'Driving along the Great West Road, about to spend the day apart. Going back to our lonely beds . . . But Sue, sweetheart, it needn't be like that. Is it so very wrong to take what we can? Love whilst we can? I've been honest with you, I've told you that I can't divorce Cynthia or tell her about us. Does that mean it's all over? Can't we salvage something for ourselves?'

'When the war ends, or I get posted, or you move on, the less there is between us the easier parting will be,' Sue said, trying to be practical. 'It'll be hard enough now, don't make it harder.'

'You're wrong, life's too short to deny love, if we kill it then we'll be lesser people because of it. Yet in a

384

way I know you're right . . . If only I'd met you a dozen years ago! If only I'd waited!'

Despite the tears trembling on her lashes, Sue giggled.

'A dozen years ago I was eight,' she pointed out.

Alan smiled mournfully.

'What a literal girl you are, and how delicious you look when you laugh! So you'll really go through with it? Apply for a posting, or ask to drive someone else? Because if we're in the same car, sooner or later I'll forget myself and so will you, and we'll make love again.'

Leave him? Go somewhere else, where she wouldn't see him every day? Even thinking about it hurt so much that Sue gasped, put a hand to her heart as though to comfort an actual, physical pain. She couldn't imagine not even having the comfort of his nearness. But it was sensible, the right thing to do, she acknowledged that drearily to herself.

'I hadn't thought of that, but . . . yes, I suppose it's sensible.'

They had reached their destination. Sue slowed at the gates, showed her pass, drove round the back and pulled up. She and Alan got out.

'Thanks, driver,' Alan said formally. 'I'll see you back here at fifteen hundred hours.' He bent down as though to adjust his trouser creases and lowered his voice. 'Sweetheart, I know a wonderfully discreet little place out by the river, near Bath. We could be together there, we could truly enjoy one another. Would it be so wrong for two people in love?'

Sue stepped back, her body shouting its need of him even whilst her mind struggled with the precepts of right and wrong which she had been taught as a child. They saluted and Sue could see the gleam in Alan's eyes as he turned away, knew the same gleam was reflected in hers. What on earth was she to do? She loved him, she wanted him... He would go home to Cynthia and his daughter, nothing she could do or say could stop that, but was it so wrong to lie with the man you love? Why shouldn't she have some pleasure from life as well as the endless round of duty, of serving one's country, of doing her job?

But if she gave in, agreed to love him, then she would be his mistress. That was just another word for his whore, her mam would say. But Mum was old-fashioned, she simply didn't understand.

''Scuse me, Aircraftwoman, can you move that motor up agin the wall? There's a dozen more to come, yet.'

Startled out of her reverie, Sue got back into the car, moved it against the wall, then climbed out and contemplated the day.

Pale sunshine, piles of filthy snow and slush in the gutters, the subdued hum of traffic in the West End. And three hours to kill.

I'll look at the shops and have a good think, Sue told herself, heading resolutely for the outside world. If only the girls were here ... Christie would know what I should do. But even as the thought crossed her mind she knew it was no use; this was a decision only she could take, because it would make or mar the rest of her life. It would not have been fair to put the burden of such a decision on any shoulders other than her own.

Sue mooched around the West End for a while, but the shops bored her and it suddenly occurred to her that it would be awfully nice to have a chat to Shanna. And why not? The weather was bad country-wide, the chances were that Shanna would be in the motor-pool, playing cards with the other drivers. She might even be off . . . no harm in checking.

To think was to act. Sue went to the telephone kiosks in the foyer of the nearest shop, arranged her pennies along the top of the box and asked for the familiar number.

As soon as she said who she wanted she was aware of a certain tension on the other end of the line, though the brisk young woman in the office gave nothing away.

'Driver Douglas isn't . . . hold the line, please.'

Whilst she waited, Sue wondered why it comforted her, in moments of stress, to speak to Shanna. Because she knew that she liked people to need her. She was a carer, she enjoyed taking care of people and it occurred to her now, as she waited patiently for someone to come to the phone, that it was this which made her enjoy being a driver. She took care of her officer, of her wounded when she drove the blood-waggon, of her air-crews when she took them out to the dispersal points. So perhaps it was natural when she was distressed that she looked, not for support exactly, but for someone she could mother and support in her turn.

Someone picked the receiver jerkily off the desk, someone who was breathing heavily, as though she had been running.

'Hello, Sue? It's Shanna's friend Angela. Could you ring Meg Aldford? She's been trying to get in touch,' the girl said. 'She's at RAF Sellars, just down the road. She's coming round here presently, but if you ring right away you'll probably just catch her.'

Sue would have liked to ask about Shanna, but sensed the urgency in Angela's tone and realised something was up. She rang Sellars and Meg, who must have been almost sitting on the phone, snatched it up.

'Hello? Is that ... oh, Sue, thank God! What made you get in touch with me? I tried you, but ...'

'I suddenly felt I wanted to speak to Shanna; Angela whatsername answered the phone and said you'd been trying to raise me ... Meg where's Shanna?'

'Oh Sue, I can't believe it! I tried to get you but they said you were driving an officer to London and wouldn't be back until very late ... Shanna's gone missing. Her fellow was killed and she just walked out, straight into a blizzard. That was yesterday and she's not been seen since though they've had search parties out. Can you possibly come? I don't know what it's like down in London but here there's thick snow, the conditions are awful, I don't know if

Shanna can possibly be . . . it isn't the sort of weather to be out in the open but so far there's not been a sign . . . can you come?'

'Of course. I'm in London, I'll catch a train. I'll be with you as soon as I can. Have you phoned Christie?'

'Yes, but she's on an eight-hour shift and they won't interrupt her, not even on a life and death matter, they said. She'll ring me back, though. But if you just come, won't you get into a row?'

Sue shrugged. 'Dunno. Probably. It doesn't matter, does it? Shanna matters. I'll be as quick as I can.'

As she made her way to the nearest underground Sue wondered what Alan would think . . . then stopped wondering and stepped out. Alan would have to cope for himself; she was needed elsewhere. Only one thing mattered now; Shanna, lost in a blizzard, knowing her lover was dead.

I'm coming, Shanna love, Sue thought. I'm on my way and you'll be right as rain once I arrive.

Christie and Mary came off watch and made for the mess. A WAAF came to meet them; Audrey, cheerful, red-faced.

'Phone message, Chris. Meg something-or-other rang; she said Sheila's gone missing in a blizzard, can you phone Waldrington?'

'Sheila? I can't remember a Sheila. And Meg's at Sellars, not . . . oh my God, Waldrington . . . you mean Shanna, not Sheila! Yes, I'll ring right away . . . Mary, go on without me, I'll catch you up.'

She got through after ten minutes; bad weather always seemed to affect telephone lines. Meg was called to the phone and came quickly. Her voice sounded thin and strained.

'Christie, it's Shanna. Her feller was killed and she walked out . . .'

Christie listened to the story, cold despair creeping into her mind. Poor Shanna, as if she hadn't had enough to put up with. Once, in a reminiscent mood, Shanna had told Christie how she came to be turned out of the flat in which she lived when she was fourteen, not by her own parents, but by people to whom she was not even distantly related.

'My mam left my da, he took up wi' another woman. When he left her, I stayed. Then the other woman took up wi' another feller. When they parted . . .'

Four or five down the line came a step-father who beat her up. Six or eight further on, a step-mother who hated her and wouldn't feed her when the rest of the kids had a meal, then chucked her out because the new step-father fancied Shanna and was unwise enough to show it.

Wandering the streets, hiccupping, crying, she had been noticed by a lorry driver who stopped his vehicle and picked her up, took her round with him delivering tatties, then took her home, into his bed.

What he did to her had hurt, because she was only a kid, and under-developed – but he must have loved her, mustn't he? He kept her for several weeks before dumping her. She'd always liked lorry drivers after that, had sought them out. Stood by the road . . . they fed her, let her sit up in the cab with them, sometimes bedded down with her in the cab, sometimes just used her and put her down, to wait for the next man.

Christie remembered Shanna's reaction to the WAAF.

'It's wonderful, isn't it? I'd no' thought anyone would ever give me clean clothes, food, and pay me to do a wee bit work. I dinnae understand why some of 'em grumble. To me it's wonderful.'

Poor Shanna, she had been satisfied with so little, had wanted affection and three meals a day, that was about all. And now she was lost, perhaps already dead . . .

No! I won't even think it. Christie turned her thoughts resolutely back to Meg's sad little tale as it drew to a close.

'. . . they've organised search parties, they've scoured the countryside, but there's no sign of her. I rang Sue . . . she's coming up here though God knows what anyone can do. Oh Chris, can you think of anything?'

'She'll be safe; Shanna's a survivor,' Christie said. 'She'll always fall on her feet, mark my words.'

When she said it she meant it, thought she probably wasn't too wide of the mark. After all, Shanna had had so many fellers . . . Could she possibly feel about one of them the way she, Christie, felt about Andy? But . . . but just suppose she did? Suppose that for Shanna, this feller was the equivalent of Andy? Was it possible that Shanna, who had had so little, could lose so much, and even want to survive?

'I shouldn't have said that, it was tempting fate. I'll come up,' Christie said huskily. 'Life's bloody unfair . . . I'll catch the first train.'

13

By the time Christie and Sue arrived in Lincoln, the weather had done its worst and was beginning to ease off. They had met at one of the many changes they had been forced to make – railway journeys had to take into account so many things these days that you sometimes had to travel twice the distance just to avoid stations which had been bombed or lines which, for one reason or another, were temporarily unsafe – so in the waiting-room of a small station, blue-lit, dismal, Christie and Sue fell into each other's arms, and shed tears, and hugged convulsively.

'Chris, it's so *cold*! I can't bear it that she's likely freezin' to death under some hedge,' Sue said, pale from worry and red-eyed from tears shed. 'She never had much, our Shanna. Why did it have to happen to her feller?'

'I don't dare ask myself that,' Christie said soberly. 'Andy's on operational flying again. It's – it's tempting fate to question what happens, you just have to face it. Oh Sue, I pray Shanna comes through it, I pray she's holed up somewhere, safe.'

'Meg's been a brick,' Sue said after a moment. 'Of

all of us, she was the one who didn't really understand Shanna but when they found themselves up
here, just the two of them, Meg stuck by our Shanna,
went around with her, treated her nice. Meg's your
best friend, I know, but I always felt she couldn't
really see why Shanna went after fellers the way
she did. She was innocent, somehow. Like – like I
was.'

'Sue, you always seemed to me to know just where
you were going and why. The rest of us were fumbling
in the dark, but you'd got it all sussed. You struck me
as innocent-knowing, if you see what I mean.
Shanna's trouble is never having seen a happy
marriage at first hand and not having any sort of
family life. You're always talking about the kids and
your parents, you know how wonderful a good
marriage can be, and you want it just like that
for yourself. So I always thought you'd pick and
choose pretty carefully, and never let your heart
rule your head ... in the nicest possible way, of
course.'

'Oh, let's light that bloody gas-fire and blue a few
bob in the meter,' Sue said, suddenly brisk, as though
Christie's opinion of her had given her back her self-
confidence. 'They said a short delay before the next
train arrives but I bet it's ages. The meter takes
sixpenny pieces; I've got some.'

Sue rooted round and produced her box of matches
– she didn't smoke but most of her passengers did –
and lit the fire, fed it with a sixpence each, then settled
back on the hard wooden seat once more. They were

alone in the blinkered waiting-room with the darkness of the platform outside seeming to press against the blackout blinds and the chill of the windy, deserted platform creeping under the door despite the gas-fire flickering and popping away in the small, dusty grate.

'So; you were saying that I wouldn't let me heart rule me head, and you were right,' Sue said. 'I liked havin' fun, but I didn't want no permanent relationship, nothin' I couldn't walk away from. I've always seen meself, you see, as marryin' someone just up the road or round the corner, someone just like me, really, so's I could live cheek by jowl with our mam and the rest. I wanted to wait till the war's over so I could take me time, make me choice of fellers livin' round Vauxy. I must've been mad,' she added reflectively. 'Now, right this minute, I'd give ... oh, a lot ... for a permanent relationship. But you know what? I'd chuck the feller I thought I loved into the nearest river rather than have Shanna hurt.'

'I couldn't go as far as that, because Andy's my life,' Christie said simply. 'But – I do want her to be all right. She doesn't deserve to lose everything. In fact when I think about it, it's stupid to say Andy's my life because I've got Mummy, Daddy, two of the best brothers in the world, a super sister-in-law-to-be, lots of friends ...'

'That's right. Me family means a lot to me; I find it dead difficult to imagine how our Shanna manages without one. I mean she doesn't even know who her parents are, in a sense. If she met 'em, she'd walk right by 'em. Think about that, chuck.'

'I do; I am,' Christie said. 'You know, Sue, a while back I promised a friend that I'd talk about marriage to Andy. But I never did. It's such a big step and somehow I'd always imagined a white wedding, from home, with lots of friends, relatives... To have a service wedding and then just go back to work seemed wrong but maybe I should have asked Andy how he felt. We can't go home for our leaves often because it means being apart... I daresay you've guessed Andy and I are lovers? ... and that's unbearable with ... with no certainty, any more. But I can't hurt my parents by creeping into Andy's bed under their roof. Oh Sue, isn't war the most dreadful, cruel thing?'

'It is,' Sue said soberly. 'Did I tell you I was in London with my boss when I got this feeling that Shanna needed me? And rang through? Well, my boss is going to be driving himself home, and I'll find meself on a charge when I do go back. And I don't give a monkey's.'

'Oh, I got permish,' Christie said, using the schoolgirlism without a second thought because she was talking to Sue, and Sue was as good as family. It was odd, she reflected, how the dependence, the closeness, that the four of them had taken for granted had come back as soon as they met again. 'I think they knew I'd go anyway, though. But I'd got a week's leave due ... our officer was awfully nice about it, got me a travel warrant and everything.'

'Meg asked permission, too,' Sue said ruefully. 'Oh well, it's just me and Shanna that's AWOL then. At least we're in it together.'

'Your boss will understand,' Christie said comfortingly. 'If you ring first thing in the morning . . . Didn't you leave a note or anything?'

'I'm norra fool, you know; I rang Adastral House from the station and left a message,' Sue said indignantly. 'But whether he gets it is anyone's guess – you know what these bureaucrats are like.'

'Oh, he'll get it. Besides, when you don't turn up at the car he's bound to go back into the place to see if there's a message. That will remind someone, surely. Shall we get a bit closer to the fire? We might as well be warm whilst the money lasts.'

Despite their best efforts, it was seven in the morning before the two girls arrived at Lincoln station and headed for the nearest taxi.

'Waldrington please,' Sue said firmly when the taxi driver asked where they wanted to go. 'And make it snappy.'

'Give 'em a uniform and they think they're bleedin' Queen Elizabeth,' the taxi driver grumbled, but he winked at Christie in the mirror and drove as fast as safety permitted over the hard-packed snow on the flat, straight road out to Waldrington.

'Here we are; it looks just like every RAF airfield in the world, only flatter and barer,' Christie said as they climbed wearily out of the taxi, paid the man and turned towards the guard on the gate. 'Got your ID?'

Not that they needed it; the man on the gate looked at their identity cards, remarked that 'They 'aven't fahnd the poor lickle blighter yet,' and waved them

397

through, obviously having been primed to expect them. He directed them to the hut where Meg had been given a bed and then, red-eyed and chilly, continued to guard the gates.

They went straight to the hut. Reveille here was at six-thirty but there were plenty of WAAFs still preparing for the day ahead. Meg came over to them, her smile broad but her eyes red-rimmed. Two other girls, a slim blonde and a stocky brunette, accompanied her.

'I *knew* you'd make it, though I really couldn't imagine how! Oh Chris, it's marvellous to see you . . . you too, Sue. I've borrowed Shanna's bed, but there will be room for you somewhere, I'm sure. By the way this is Angela, Shanna's buddy, and Mandy, another friend.' Meg swung round and pointed at a large green parrot, pecking desultorily at a stale half-round of bread. 'And that's Jacko, Shanna's bird, looking fed up.'

'He's been shut in here for two solid days, no wonder he's cross,' Angela said. She held out a hand. 'Hi . . . you'll be Sue and you'll be Christie. Shanna talked about you . . .' her voice wobbled and failed her and she stared down at the floor for a moment. '. . . talked about you a lot,' she finished. 'I'm sure if she knew you were here she'd come home.'

'Come and have some breakfast,' Meg suggested. 'Got your irons? You poor things, you look worn out. Have you been travelling all night?'

'Either travelling or sitting on cold stations waiting for connections,' Christie said. 'We were awfully

398

lucky to meet up early on; I don't know what I'd have done if I'd been all by myself. Some of those stations were creepy, weren't they, Sue?'

'Pretty horrible,' Sue admitted. 'I wouldn't say no to some brekker, though. And I've really gorrer make a phone call later.'

'Right. Breakfast first though,' Meg said decisively. 'What's it like outside?'

'Not bad; cold, but the sky's clear,' Sue said. 'It don't look like snow, that's one blessing.'

'Good; they said they'd bring the dogs out again if it wasn't snowing,' Meg said. 'Apparently the scent isn't any good when it's snowing and blowing.' She turned to Angela and Mandy. 'Better get our coats.'

Presently, coated and capped, the five of them were about to set off when Angela said rather doubtfully that perhaps they ought to take Jacko.

'He's usually awfully bossy and noisy in the mornings,' she said. 'But I don't suppose the poor fellow knows whether he's coming or going, not being allowed out, and not having Shanna. I'll take the responsibility if anyone says anything.'

She called the bird and he stretched his neck and looked hopefully at them, cocking his head, his eyes boot-button bright.

'Happy Christmas?' he said hopefully. 'Get your bloody beak out of me bloody eye, I'll crucify that bugger if 'e imitates me again!'

'That's the cookhouse corporal,' Angela said when the girls laughed. 'Jacko likes unusual voices, and Corporal Bradshaw sounds just like that – sort of high and squeaky. Well, come on then, old bird.'

Jacko, thus invited, flapped over to Angela's shoulder and the five of them – six if you counted Jacko – set off across the crisp snow towards the cookhouse.

After their long, chilly journey, followed by the brisk walk across the snow, it seemed extra warm in the cookhouse. Christie, glancing round her, thought that all cookhouses were much the same – this one, though larger and lighter than the one in Oxfordshire was otherwise pretty well indistinguishable from it.

At this time of the morning all cookhouses probably smell the same, too, Christie thought, sniffing. She could smell frying sausages, scrambled eggs and stewed tea, with overtones, unfortunately, of sweat – the big, old-fashioned coke-burning stoves were at their hottest when a meal was in full production – and now burning toast was added to the other breakfast odours. A red-faced WAAF flapped a tea-towel at the flames under the grill, then rushed to the sink with several curled, blackened slices.

Ahead of them, WAAFs and airmen queued patiently, holding out their plates for sticky porridge or a stiff, artificial-looking sausage and a scoop of dried egg. Angela and Mandy went ahead and began to explain to the nearest cook about Christie and Meg, about Shanna ...

The corporal in charge, a large man with what looked like a permanent scowl and a heavy-lipped, sulky mouth, came towards them just as Angela began to ask if the newcomers might be given some breakfast. He broke in at once.

'What's all this? You want somethin', you asks the boss, not the bleedin' staff. The boss – that's me, get it? Whaddyer want, eh?'

The voice, high and squeaky, sounded familiar. Christie frowned. Now where had she heard that voice before?

'Oh, Corporal Bradshaw, these are friends of Aircraftwoman Douglas, the WAAF who's gone missing. They've come to help find her and they want to have some brekker, if that's all right.'

Christie noticed Jacko leaning forward, head cocked, and light dawned. The bird was brilliant; it was this man he had been imitating earlier!

'Oh, I *see*.' Corporal Bradshaw's voice sounded heavy with sarcasm now. '*That* gel. Well, I dunno why they're botherin', she's a gonner, she is . . . dead in a ditch be now, take my word for it. Along wi' that green bastard of hers, an' good riddance to the pair of 'em, I say.'

He could not have seen Jacko, who was sitting on Angela's right shoulder, probably hidden from him by the girl's head. Jacko, however, leaned round Angela and peered at the corporal.

'Good riddance to the pair of 'em, I say,' Jacko said, in exact imitation of the man's squeaky, malevolent tones. 'You can't 'ave sausage an' egg, you greedy little bugger!'

Christie laughed; she couldn't help it, it was such a brilliant imitation. Indeed, when the corporal vaulted

401

over the counter she flinched back, thinking he was coming for her, but she was not his intended victim. He gave Angela a push and snatched the bird in the same movement.

'Gotcha!' he shouted. 'I'll teach you a lesson you won't forgit, you bastard, I'll teach you to laugh at your betters. I'll tear you in two!'

For a moment, surprise and horror rooted everyone to the spot, and in that moment Corporal Bradshaw, little eyes gleaming madly, began to pull on the bird's neck. No one noticed the door of the cookhouse as it swung open, no one paid the slightest attention to the small, red-haired figure who swayed in the doorway. All eyes were fixed on the corporal and his victim.

'Stop that!'

'Let go of 'im, Corp, that ain't funny . . .'

'What the devil do you–'

Men were on their feet, women began to scream, the girls pushed forward whilst Corporal Bradshaw tugged at the bird as though he were pulling a Christmas cracker and laughed madly as Jacko gave one harsh, despairing squawk.

'There you are, you bugger,' he shouted breathlessly above the hubbub. 'That little bitch has gone and now you're goin' to join her . . . and you won't never cheek me again, not unless you can do it wiv a neck a foot long and no bloody head!'

One moment Corporal Bradshaw was standing triumphant with the bird between his hands and feathers floating in the air, the next he was swamped by what seemed like a sea of girls. Sue punched him in the stomach, Meg bit his hand, Christie caught hold of his greasy hair and pulled with all her strength. But Shanna outdid them all; she flew across the intervening space, punched the corporal in the mouth and went for his eyes with stiff fingers, all the while shrieking abuse at the top of her voice. She had not spent the formative years of her life in the Gorbals without learning how to street-fight!

'You've kilt him! You wicked, torturin' murderer, you've kilt my bird and now I'm goin' to kill you!'

Corporal Bradshaw reeled beneath the onslaught and went down, flat on his back. Shanna knelt on his chest, one fist smashing weakly into his face whilst with the other she sought, apparently, to gouge his eyes out.

'It's Shanna! Shanna, you're alive! Oh God, we thought ... oh Shanna, you're all right!' Sue was almost sobbing with relief at the sight of her friend diligently whacking the corporal's head. 'Don't kill him, chuck, tell us where you've been these past two days.'

'I'll bluidy crucify 'im, do ye no' ken he's kilt my bird?'

Christie pulled Shanna off the corporal; the other girl felt light as a child, there could be no real strength left in her, yet the man beneath her had a bloody nose, a tooth decorated the front of his shirt and already one eye was puffy and split, the other darkening ominously. Christie was glad to see that the corporal had taken a good deal of punishment.

'Take it easy, Shanna,' Christie said soothingly. 'Let's take a look at Jacko, shall we?'

The bird, unregarded in the scrimmage, lay some way off. He was on his back, his grey claws pathetically curled. The once-bright eyes were hidden by wrinkled grey lids and his beak gaped. He looked very dead to Christie. Shanna shook her off and fell on her knees by Jacko. She picked him up and he lay still in her hands, his head flopping sideways.

'It was only a bit o' fun,' Corporal Bradshaw was saying thickly as he struggled to his knees. 'Christ, my face! I'll 'ave you on a charge, I'll report you ... causin' a disturbance in the cook'ouse ...'

'No one caused a disturbance except you,' Christie said at once. 'You had the bird in your hand and whilst you were handing him to his rightful owner, you fell. And unless you want to fall again, even harder, I'd not talk about reporting people.'

Corporal Bradshaw looked round. Stony faces looked back. Christie unobtrusively dropped the handful of greasy hair she held – ugh – on to the floor, then rubbed her hands down her skirt. Nasty creature, he must have used cooking lard on his hair the way it clung to her fingers, she couldn't wait to have a good wash.

'Oh, yes? You're all goin' to stand by that, are you? Nah, there must be someone here who saw what happened and ain't skeered to tell.'

Silence. Shanna's voice broke the hush. She had

not even glanced round at the corporal but addressed the suddenly small bundle of feathers between her hands.

'Dinnae die, my wee mon, dinnae die and leave me! You're all I've got, Jacko, now that my Col's gone. It's just you and me, feller, against the whole world. Oh, say you willnae leave me!'

Sue moved forward and put her arm round Shanna's skinny, heaving shoulders.

'We'll get help for him,' she said. 'We'll take him to the MO, he'll know what to do. We'll save Jacko, love, never you fret.'

Shanna sagged against her. She had shown no surprise at finding her friends suddenly on her station, now she turned as naturally to Sue as though they had never been parted.

'I cannae bear to lose Jacko too,' she said heavily. 'I cannae bear it.'

But she let Sue lead her out of the cookhouse and Christie, following on their heels with Meg beside her, found herself close to tears. Then she sniffed, lifted her chin and took Meg's arm.

'She's wrong, isn't she, Meg? It's not just her and the bird against the whole world; she's forgotten. She's got us. We're a family, as good as, and we won't forget it.'

'You're right,' Meg said. Christie saw that her friend's eyes, too, were shiny with unshed tears. 'She'll always have us.'

The Air Force is usually believed to be a pretty

heartless sort of institution, but on this occasion at least, it certainly came up trumps. Shanna was bundled into sick-bay by the MO and Jacko, in a blanket-lined box, was allowed to remain by her bedside.

Despite everyone's fears, including the MO's, the parrot had not turned up his toes.

'He's a tough old bird,' the doctor told the girls once Shanna had been tucked up in bed, fed with hot bread and milk and given a very small glass of whisky to help her to sleep. 'I'll take him into Lincoln tomorrow to see a vet, but he's breathing. He's got a good chance.'

'How long can we stay?' Sue asked him bluntly, as soon as he had reported on the parrot. 'I'd like to make sure Shanna doesn't do this again and I know the others feel the same.'

'You can stay as long as it takes,' the MO assured them. 'Don't worry about it – we're as keen to have Shanna fit again as you are.'

'I'll have to ring my Wingco,' Sue said rather heavily. She made the call as soon as she could and returned to the other girls, smiling.

'It's all right, I can stay too,' she said. 'I haven't taken all my leave so they're letting me stay until she's all right again.'

It was two days before Shanna left sick-bay and returned to the fold, with Jacko convalescing beside her.

'He's no' so bad,' she admitted when asked about the bird's health. 'But he willnae speak to me. The vet says he probably willnae talk again – some trauma in his throat I think he said.'

'Does it matter?' Meg asked gently. 'So long as he's alive and well.'

Shanna smiled.

'It doesnae matter at all,' she admitted. 'Weel, no' much, any road.' She paused, looking from face to face as her friends gathered round her. 'Sue says you'll stay here a wee while.'

'That's right. We thought, having come so far, we might as well have a bit of a holiday,' Christie said. 'The MO says it will be at least a week before you can go back to work so you can show us round. I'd love to take a look at Lincoln, it's such a surprising town, perched high on that hill in the middle of all this flat countryside.'

Shanna's pale face flushed slightly and she began to smile.

'Och, that would be great! I've no' been everywhere in Lincoln mysel', I'd like to see more, too. You must see the cathedral, the Stone Bow, the river . . . we can go to a flick, there's lots of cinemas . . . the shops are pretty guid, eh, Meggie? I can't wait!'

'It'll be like old times,' Christie said contentedly. 'I've a good friend in Oxfordshire – Mary – but us four are different. We're more like sisters.'

'Better than sisters,' Sue said. She had three sisters and had frequently suffered from the complex love-hate relationship which sisters so often share. 'I dunno that it's definable, what we've got, but I know it's the best thing this war's given me.'

'If only Jacko can get his full health back,' Meg said that night, as she and Christie settled down in their borrowed beds in the guest wing of the mess. Sue was sleeping in a bed squeezed in beside Shanna's. 'Because at the end of the week, when I go back to Sellars and you and Sue leave, Shanna will be terribly lonely if she's without her bird.'

Christie, with an old stocking tied round her head to keep her hair tidy, began painstakingly spreading cold cream across her cheekbones.

'No, you're wrong, she won't be lonely even if Jacko doesn't make it. She's got Angela and Mandy, and what's more, she knows a great many people are genuinely fond of her, she isn't the outcast she always thought herself. Look how people rallied round in the cookhouse that awful morning. Look at all the little presents she's been given since, from people who hardly knew her name before. They're all on her side and she knows it. Good has come of this whole episode, unlikely though it seems.'

Meg was plaiting her hair into two thick, springy pigtails. She nodded thoughtfully and secured the last pigtail with a red rubber band.

'Yes, I see what you mean and you're right. It's too soon to say Shanna will be truly happy one day, but I think it's quite likely. Hasn't she *changed* though, Chris? She's very different from the old Shanna.'

'We've all changed,' Christie said soberly. 'And this business has changed me more than almost anything else. I've talked about marrying Andy, thought about it, worried over it, but I've never actually done anything about it. Now I shall. We're in love, neither of us will ever change, so there's no reason why we shouldn't marry. Then if he ... if the worst happens, I'll have something to cling to, something really marvellous to remember. He'll be mine to mourn, mine to miss, in a way he can't be unless we marry.'

'I can't think why you didn't marry before,' Meg said frankly. 'Anyone could see you were made for each other.'

'That's what I think, but I'll never try to make Andy my whole life, because that's the mistake so many people make when they marry. He'll be the most important person in my life but I'll never forget my friends. So many girls do just that – they marry and turn inwards, and then if the – the worst happens, they've nothing to fall back on. I won't ever let that happen and I hope that us four friends will be together for always, even though marriage must change things. Because, when it comes to the crunch, it's your friends who see you through.'

'Yes, I can see that,' Meg nodded. 'I'm really fond of Lenny, but in war, it's mad to put your happiness into one man's hands and let the rest of the world go hang. Friends who won't turn their backs on you are worth more than diamonds.'

'That's right. So I'm going to beg Andy to let us get married even if it does make me more vulnerable. I went along with his arguments before, because Mummy and Daddy said just the same sort of things... You know, if something happens it will break your heart, you're too young to be widowed, why not wait until you can have a real married life, but now I can see that nothing matters except that Andy and I are together. But I won't chuck over my training and leave the WAAF because that's where my friends and my interests are. I joined up to help win the war and I'm going to carry on, no matter what. Marrying Andy won't make a jot of difference to that.'

'Good for you,' Meg said. 'You'll ask us to the wedding, of course.'

'Of course. But whether you'll be able to come is a different matter, what with taking this bit of our leave and everything. Still, I'll have to talk to Andy first.'

Shanna got into bed and watched the billet orderly switch off the lamp and check the blackout curtains. She didn't open the windows, though; despite the thaw it was still terribly cold.

Lying there, with Sue's humped silhouette before her eyes, she remembered the night she had turned back, made for the airfield once more. She had spent the previous night in a barn, had gnawed on a turnip to ease her hunger-pangs, but was miles away from Waldrington, simply walking on because there was no shelter and to go to sleep here would have meant death, though death seemed almost good to her now. What was the point of going on without Col? Losing him was the worst thing in a long line of bad things which had happened to her, her mind couldn't take any more so why not just end it, lie down in the snow and sleep and let death take her? Yet she kept on walking, kept herself awake.

And then the strangest thing had happened. She believed that Col had actually got through to her from whatever sphere he inhabited, had spoken to her.

Under the stars sparkling in the black night sky, as she continued to drag herself through the thick snow, his voice had sounded in her head, his tones as clear and matter-of-fact as though he stood close beside her, smiling down at her as he had once done.

'Don't you go doin' nothing' desperate, gel,' he said. 'We didn't know each other all that long, an' I can tell you you'll know someone else better, an' you'll love 'im better an' all, one of these days. But don't forget me, eh, sweet'eart? Cos I loved you an' you loved me, an' that's a good thing to 'ang onto, when the chips is down.'

She had stopped short, in the dark little lane with the snowdrifts piled up on her left and the blackness of the hedge showing through the whiteness on her right. For a moment she felt delight, warmth, a sense of homecoming so strong that she smiled and spoke aloud.

'Col ... I'll never forget you, I swear it! An' I'll always love you, never look at another bloke. Stay wi' me; don't go!'

There was a chuckle in his voice and something, somewhere, wiped away the cold tear trickling down her cheek.

'I'll never quite leave you, not if you think abaht me. But you've got a long life to live ... you've gotta get on wi' living, sweet'eart. Don't make me your excuse for chickenin' out.'

'I willnae, I promise,' Shanna said fervently. 'Oh Gawd, Col, I thought I couldnae live wi'out you . . . but I'll try.'

'That's my girl. And look after old Jacko for me, eh? Best get back to the station, 'e could be in all sorts o' trouble, you know what a blighter 'e can be.'

She had turned at once, seeming to know by instinct that she was now heading for the airfield. Somewhere, fainter now, she could just catch Col's words.

'That's my girl,' the voice said, so far away now that Shanna had to strain to catch the words. 'Give my love to life, sweet'eart! You've gotta live for us both, now.'

Shanna stood quite still for a moment, all her senses straining after the voice, but she knew it was no good; as she began to walk the warmth gradually receded and the ordinary sounds came back – the drips from the hedge, the rustles of wild creatures, the squeak of her feet on the soft snow. She knew that she was alone once more. But she had a purpose now, a mission. Steadily, she trudged back along the lanes, heading for the station, and Jacko. Returning to life.

Sue woke in the early hours, knowing in the way you do that she wasn't in her own bed or her own hut but not able to remember just where she was. She turned over and saw Shanna's small, pale face, relaxed in sleep.

Of course! She was at Waldrington and Shanna had been found. Shanna had had a bad time, but what happened to her happened to a lot of girls now. Their men were killed, leaving their lives empty for a time.

She'll get over it, Sue thought, glancing at the window and seeing that it was still pitch-dark outside. They all had to get over it, the girls who'd lost their men. I've lost Alan, and I've already got over it.

Even as the thought formed in her head, however, she had sufficient generosity of spirit to deny it. She hadn't lost Alan, she'd never really had him, and what was more for the first time she knew it, acknowledged it. Oh, he'd slept with her, talked of love ... but it hadn't been real talk, it had been war-talk, designed to let Alan have his cake and eat it. The fact that she'd gone along with it for a short time merely meant that she was less grown-up and sophisticated than she believed. Her pain had not even been a pale imitation of the pain she had seen etched into Shanna's face, it had been more like the vague sense of grievance felt by a small child who sees the nicest cake on the table taken by someone else. Now, having seen what real love had done to Shanna, she could acknowledge that she simply didn't know the emotion, had never really felt it. She liked Alan, found him physically attractive, but there it ended. She would love, one day, she acknowledged it now, but her lover would be someone she had not yet met. Not Alan Watson. When the chips were down she would have sacrificed him for Shanna any day of the week.

Sue snuggled deeper down the bed. Might as well get what sleep she could before reveille sounded and the billet orderly pulled the blackout curtains across once more. She would have to tell Alan, if he needed telling, that she intended to apply for a posting the moment she reached her own station again. There were plenty of other pretty WAAFs in the m/t section who would enjoy ferrying a good-looking officer about the country. And sleeping with him. Now that she'd come to terms with it she realised it was unlikely that she was his first adulterous partner, nor would she be his last. But that was no concern of hers; Alan must be the keeper of his own conscience. She, Sue, would be far too busy living her own life.

'It was marvellous to be together again. We talked non-stop and Shanna was extraordinarily brave. She seems to have recovered completely and she's certainly found her feet at Waldrington. Meg's close, only ten miles or so away and they can meet in Lincoln when they are neither of them actually working, but we've already arranged another get-together.'

It was a quiet night and Mary and Christie were on the midnight to eight a.m. shift, Christie on Darky watch, Mary waiting for the returning planes, the numbers chalked up on the board, her knitting in her lap.

'Another? With this one only just finished? Where will you find the time?' Mary marvelled. 'You have to see Andy whenever you can . . . incidentally, are you going to talk to him about marriage?'

'Yup. I've got to persuade him it's what I want, I've just got to. I'll need time though, so it'll have to wait till my next forty-eight. But we – the girls and I – have arranged to take four days leave next November. We'll meet up somewhere and we'll do it at least twice every year until the war ends.'

'What does Andy think?' Mary asked lazily. She picked up her knitting, measured it along the desk, then began to knit. 'I thought you were marrying him so you could spend every spare second together.'

'Yes, that's so, but he understands about my friends, how important we are to each other. We damn' nearly lost Shanna, you know, and that would have hurt us all. So we won't risk it happening again, we're going to have much more contact in future. Letters, phone-calls when we can manage it, and the meetings.'

A faint crackling came from Christie's ear-phones as she finished speaking and she flapped a hand at Mary, shushing her.

'It's a Darky call; someone's lost out there.' Christie began her call-sign, contacted the pilot, gave him directions, listened intently for the note of his engine so that they could briefly put on the landing lights and see him down safe. 'Hello Darky, hello Darky, I can hear your engine so you aren't far from us now; are you receiving me?'

Small and lost from the vast blackness of the sky a thin, strained voice answered her.

'Hello Nemo, Hello Nemo, receiving you strength niner; where are your bloody lights?'

14

'T'row that bag over here, gorl, and let's see what an expert can do wit' it. My word but you're no packer, Christie! Don't just jam stuff in, persuade it, talk to it, find out each tiny corner and then fill it up!'

'Thanks, Mary, if you're sure you don't mind. Over to you!'

Christie tossed the half-filled canvas bag over to Mary, who up-ended it over the bed, tutted, and began to sort through the contents.

'Look at this lot . . . there's no method, Chris, no method at all. Now if you roll your undies up inside your shoes . . .'

The two girls were in their bedroom at the manor, packing for Christie's forthcoming move whilst outside the window the September sunshine fell mistily through the trees in the orchard, already mellow with fruit.

It had been quite difficult to convince Andy that they should marry because of his tender conscience, which said he had nothing to offer Christie except worry and waiting, but she had made him see sense in the end. And then her parents had said they didn't know Andrew, they'd only met him once . . . she was not yet twenty, why not wait just that bit longer?

In the end though, they had waited partly so that they could get married from High Tree farm and partly until Christie's requested posting to RAF Edenham had been granted. Andy said he had no intention of getting married and then kissing his wife goodbye for six months. Christie's Wing Officer had been very understanding and kind, had done her best to get the posting put through; but the mills of the Air Force, like the mills of God, grind slowly, and it had taken from mid-May until early September for them to confirm that Christie would be sent to Edenham as an RT operator, the u/t part of her job description now being null and void as she had passed the necessary exams and wore her sparks badge with some pride.

Then it was all rush, of course. Andy's application for married quarters had been refused; but he had been granted a living-out allowance instead, which he said jubilantly was as good or better since it would enable them to get right away from the airfield for a bit.

And planning even a small wedding in wartime wasn't easy. Cousin Phyllis, who had married in the summer of '39 with much pomp, lent her ivory satin wedding dress with the ruched train. Cousin Phyllis was small and Christie tall, so the train disappeared to be turned into a deep additional frill round the hem. The head-dress which Phyllis had worn proved to be battered beyond repair – old Phyl must have taken it on honeymoon with her, Dan Bellis said irreverently – so Christie said she'd wear a circlet of rosebuds in her hair, from the bush outside the stable.

'Like Jesus?' Frank commented, and Christie decided that perhaps roses weren't such a good idea; the rose bush by the stable was notorious for its thorns.

'I'll make you a wreath of artificial flowers if you'll let me have the rest of that train,' Jane the embroidress said. 'I won't need even half the material for the flowers so I'll use the rest to cover a cushion for myself.'

Christie, feverishly writing letters to tell everyone when the wedding would be, was grateful to Jane, especially as the circlet of tiny, ivory satin blossoms were every bit as pretty as the original – exceedingly expensive – head-dress.

Bridesmaids were out of the question, of course, but Christie had hoped the girls would be able to come. So far, Sue was definitely out, Meg was definitely coming and Shanna was a possible, provided she could get enough leave. Mary, on the other hand was, as she put it, 'stickin' by me pal'. Since she had no relatives in Britain and most of her friends were in the WAAF, this wasn't the sacrifice one might have assumed, but Christie was delighted anyway and knew that Mary would have done her best to come no matter how difficult it was. They were good friends and would miss each other when the move was accomplished.

'Is that the lot?'

Christie turned from dreamily shoving her uniform into her kit-bag and saw that the canvas hold-all was packed and bulging and that both bed and floor were now empty of her possessions.

'Mary, you're a blinking genius,' she said, genuinely impressed. 'That's wonderful – how much time have we got?'

Their train left at ten the following morning, so they were taking their gear down to the station and leaving it with the friendly station-master. Then they meant to get themselves a meal and after that return to the manor for Christie's last night.

'It's gettin' on for half four. If we want to catch that transport . . .'

'Oh lor'! Right, I'll get a move on.'

'He seems a nice enough lad, I'm not denying that, but she's our baby, far too young to know her own mind,' Becky Bellis told her sister-in-law, Zena Elliott, as the two of them did their best to perform the miracle of the loaves and fishes in order to feed all the wedding guests.

'Chris is twenty,' Zena said mildly. She had always been aware that Becky adored her boys and regarded her only girl far more critically, but she knew it was often the way with mothers and daughters. 'She's known Andy for the best part of two years. That's no small thing these days when kids tumble into bed at the drop of a hat, or so they say.'

'Only a certain type. No child of mine would do such a thing, but anyway, I'm talking about marriage, which is longer lasting than ... They've simply not thought past the physical side, I'm sure. I asked her what he intends to do with himself when the war's over and she just looked at me, and when I pressed her, she said, very slowly, "I expect he'll just live, Mum", and there were tears in her eyes ... I felt so foolish, I wished I'd not asked.'

'He's a fighter pilot, isn't he? Poor little Christie! Perhaps, Becky, we shouldn't deny them the only thing they can have, which is a bit of closeness. After all, if the worst happens ...'

'She'll be widowed before she reaches her majority,' Becky concluded. 'No, it's not that which worries me, though I've had to pretend it is. What worries me is that they may look at each other once the war's over, and realise that they don't have a darned thing in common. It'll be too late, then, for regrets.'

Zena, slicing onions, snorted through her tears.

'That's arrant nonsense, love, and well you'd know it if you were thinking straight! What did you and Dan have in common, may I ask? You were a nurse, he was a farmer. And what about me and Reggie? We met at a dance, fell in love, married ... it was pretty chancy, really.'

'You met at a dance in a private house,' Becky corrected . 'Now if he'd been a waiter or the trumpet player then I'd agree, it would have been chancy. But he was a fellow guest, Zena, which means more or less hand-picked! As for Dan and me, we both came from county families who knew each other, and I wouldn't want more than that for any of my children. I've had to put up with Frank's young woman – she'll probably make him a good little wife – but I'm really not in favour of all this *togetherness* for young people. Why, for years Queenie Woolton and I thought that her Derek would be the perfect match for Christie, we talked about it from the time Chris was born, I believe. They got on most awfully well always, Derek taught her to handle a rod, kept his eye on her when they went pony-clubbing ... and then along comes the war and she never gives him another thought.'

'Derek Woolton is a smug, self-satisfied... Besides, last time I saw him – I was shopping, on the market – he was with the most dreadful little floozy. He tipped his cap at me and gave me a horrid leer – he's in the navy, isn't he?'

'Ye-es, but if Christie had only given him the slightest encouragement he wouldn't need to cultivate little floozies, would he? I'm sure Queenie probably blames me, and I dare not even mention his name to Chris or she'll say something crushing.'

'Queenie's having an affair with a spivvy-looking RAF johnny whose moustache is so big he could take off if only it would rotate,' Zena pointed out, wiping a hand across her streaming eyes. 'These bloody onions ... good thing I don't use mascara! So I don't see Queenie criticising anyone else's behaviour, not right now at any rate.'

'*Is* she? Having an affair, I mean. Gosh, poor old Bart – I wonder if he knows? Mind you, Queenie was always a lively girl. I remember Dan once saying that she'd made a pass at him, only I thought she was just being . . . oh, you know, friendly.'

Zena snorted again.

'Don't be so ingenuous, Becky. Women like Queenie only have one attitude to men and that's horizontal. Be thankful Dan didn't follow up that pass. And be even more thankful that Chris didn't get entangled with Queenie's very nasty young son.'

'Oh,' Becky said. She sounded thoughtful. 'You're only two years older than me, Zena, but you're a lot worldlier, somehow. I suppose it's because I married a farmer and you married an international business-man, if that's what you call Reggie. Do you like Andy, then?'

'I only met him once, for about half an hour, but . . . yes, I liked him very much. He's been reared in a hard school, but it's brought out the best in him.'

'He went to an ordinary grammar school; he got a scholarship,' Becky protested. 'Or didn't you mean it that literally?'

Zena laughed.

'Becky, you're incredible sometimes! I neither know nor care where he went to school and nor should you, because things like that aren't going to matter after the war any more than they matter during it. What I meant was that he'd not had things easy. According to Chris his mother died when he was eleven and his father turned round and married a girl of twenty-two who didn't want a thumping great step-son about the place. Andy will take care of Christie better than most young men because he's been taking care of himself ever since he went into long trousers.

See? But tell me, what does Dan think of Andy?'

'Oh, Dan likes him, but then he would, wouldn't he? He idolizes Christie, always has, so anyone she likes, Dan likes. Which isn't much help when I'm trying to prevent her from ruining her life.'

Becky sounded plaintive. Zena leaned across the table and gave the other woman's hand a squeeze.

'Marrying Andy is the most sensible thing she's ever done, and this is your worldly sister-in-law speaking. So don't upset yourself, and above all, don't alienate your daughter by showing her you don't trust her choice. Christie's a good girl, easily my favourite niece, and she's sensitive as hell; I wouldn't want her hurt.'

'Sensitive! I love her dearly, but she goes for what she wants like ... like a hot knife through butter. David's the sensitive one.' Becky rolled out a great sheet of pastry, then began to spoon a filling on to it. 'I sometimes think Christie is the most selfish person I know. She doesn't even consider me or her father, she just thinks about what suits her best.'

'She's not like that,' Zena said, her voice quiet in an attempt to disguise her thinly veiled anger. This was total, blind prejudice! 'Right now, your little girl is in love; very deeply in love. And the object of that love, may I remind you, is in danger of death every time he flies. Every time, Becky! If that were Dan up there, wouldn't that make you feel that he was the only thing that mattered? Wouldn't that make you seem, to the cold, outsider's eye, totally selfish?'

Becky started to fold her pastry over the filling,

then stopped and sighed. She stared down at her hands for a moment, then looked across the table at Zena, her expression rueful.

'You're right. I suppose love is a selfish emotion.'

'And I was right about you having an outsider's eye too, love, because you can't know how Christie feels. She's seeing things from a different angle because she works with planes and pilots, she talks them down, reassures them . . . hears them die. So you see, dear Becky, her fears for Andy are bigger and more real than any fear you may have for Frank or David.'

There was silence for a moment whilst Becky continued to work on her pastry, then Zena saw the tears trickling down the younger woman's cheeks. She put out a hand at once, instinctively wanting to comfort, but Becky shook her head.

'Don't say you're sorry for telling me the truth, Zena. You've made me look at myself and at my reasons for not wanting this marriage and you're right, I'm the selfish one. I've been foolish, too. Andy is right for her and even if he wasn't, he's her choice. And now for God's sake pass me those onions for these pasties . . . I nearly forgot what they were for!'

'That's my Becky,' Zena said, scooping up the raw onions, diced into tiny pieces. 'Right now you may only be trying to like Andy from a sense of family duty, but you'll end up loving him. You mark my words.'

The church was large but even so it was full. Friends, family . . . and all nicely spread out, too, because there were so few on the bridegroom's side.

Meg sat next to Mary because Shanna, like Sue, had been unable to get leave. She watched Andy's broad back, his shoulder almost touching that of Christie's brother, Frank, who was acting as best man. If things had been different, it would have been Patrick standing by Andy, Patrick feeling in his pocket for the ring . . . but only the faintest pang of sadness went through Meg at the thought. Time had wrought its healing just the way everyone said it would. She seldom thought of Patrick now, it was Lenny who was most often in her thoughts.

There was a stir from the church porch. Like everyone else, Meg turned her head slightly to see Christie coming up the aisle on her father's arm. She looked stunningly beautiful, her chestnut-coloured hair gleaming through the veil, her wide-open, dark blue eyes fairly blazing with nerves and excitement.

Her father had light brown hair and the same tranquil expression which Christie's face had once worn, though now it was a little sad, a little anxious. They reached Andy and Mr Bellis slid into the pew beside Christie's mother, a pretty, fashionable woman in a marvellously tailored dark blue suit and matching hat with a blouse so crisp and white that it might have been bought yesterday, only Meg knew for a fact that it was Mrs Bellis's wedding outfit from Cousin Phyllis's marriage in '39.

As soon as he glimpsed Christie, Meg saw Andy's hand shoot out and catch hold of her fingers. Chris looked sideways just as he did and they smiled into each other's eyes – Meg, with tears threatening, thought she had never seen such raw emotion on two faces and found herself praying for them – let it last, dear God, don't let anything terrible happen. They're two good people, they need each other, don't go letting the bloody war hurt them any worse than they've been hurt already!

Meg knew that the rector had known Christie all her life and now he smiled at them both, his gentle, child-like face full of loving-kindness. He didn't need to read the words of the marriage service because he knew them by heart so he said them directly to the couple before him, his voice low but clear. Christie and Andy made their responses in the same way, glancing at each other, at the rector, towards the altar. No one fidgeted or rustled and the hymns – all old, well-known ones – were sung with more meaning than usual because this was a service wedding, even though the bride had forsaken her blues for once in favour of ivory satin and fine, creamy lace. Meg, watching, could almost imagine danger as a palpable thing, waiting to pounce. She renewed her prayers, gripping her hands so tightly that her nails dug into her palms. Keep them safe, God, love like this is rare, don't spoil it!

'The blessing of God the Father, God the Son and God the Holy Ghost be upon you and remain with you, always . . .'

The sonorous words rang out, Meg surreptitiously wiped her eyes – and saw Mary doing the same – and as the organ began to play the wedding march the bride and groom emerged from the vestry and, with various members of the family, paced slowly down the aisle and out of the church. The organist broke into a lighter air and the congregation began to pick up gloves, arrange hats, straighten tunics and caps and make for the churchyard once more.

'Sure an' wasn't that the prettiest weddin' you ever did see?' Mary sighed as they assembled outside the porch. Mary, Meg knew, had come down with Christie the previous day whereas she herself had not arrived until the evening. But once at the house, she and Mary had shared an attic bedroom where they had talked half the night and become rather good friends. 'I was married once, as I told you, but these Bellises really pushed the boat out, didn't they? All those gorgeous flowers an' that!'

Whilst Christie, Andy and relatives were photographed by a tall, thin man with a pointed bald head ringed with silvery hair, the two WAAFs relaxed and had a good look at the rest of the wedding party.

'It was a lovely wedding, the nicest I've ever been to, and isn't Christie's mother pretty? Her hair's ever so like Chris's ... did you see Andy's step-mama, though?'

'Is she the blonde in the white tulle hat? There's a discontented face if ever I saw one. And not a job does she do, lazy cow ... she ought to be ashamed, an' her scarce a day over t'irty.'

'Women like her always find a way round things they don't want to do,' Meg said. 'Andy hasn't lived with them since his father married her, though.'

'Sure and isn't that just what I was sayin'? But when's the weddin' party leavin'? There's a good spread, Christie says, her mum and her aunts all clubbed together ... I ate a good breakfast but I'm hungry all over again now so I am.'

Meg chuckled.

'Who isn't? Oh, they're starting to move away ... we won't go back. Frank brought the tractor and trailer down last night but he won't drive it back in his best blues, so one of the farm-hands is going to take it. Come on, if we hurry we can bag a decent share of the seat.'

'Happy, Mrs Todd?'

The train was crowded. Christie and Andy were so squeezed together by the pressure of other passengers that they were wedged in their places, tighter than two peas in a pod. Nevertheless Andy put his head very close to Christie's to whisper the words.

'Yes thanks, Mr Todd, quite amazingly happy. I did think it would have been nice to have a proper honeymoon, but the one we did have was marvellous, wasn't it?'

'Marvellous,' Andy confirmed. 'Just like married life will be. What are you going to give me for supper tonight, wife?'

'Oh ... I thought we'd have jam sandwiches,' Christie said airily. 'After all, we'll both be eating in the cookhouse for most meals, and getting off-ration grub takes some doing, these days. But I'll find you something nice for tomorrow night, I promise.'

'I thought your mum might have sent something delicious back with us,' Andy said hopefully. 'What's in the brown paper carrier bag?'

'You peeped! Actually it's a cold egg and bacon flan. They're gorgeous hotted up, with potatoes baked in their jackets.' Christie lowered her voice still more. 'And there's a marmalade roll wrapped in grease-proof paper, only we ought to keep it quiet, there are lots of hungry passengers in this carriage. We don't want to be lynched for a marmalade roll, just at the start of it all, do we?'

'Not really. Actually I wouldn't mind a nibble right now.'

'What of? Me or the marmalade roll?'

'I'll leave you to guess,' Andy said. 'It's our station next, though. We'll get a taxi back to Mrs Denman's place.' He heaved a sigh and gave Christie another squeeze. 'I wish it were a nicer room, but it was all I could get.'

'I'll love it,' Christie said stoutly. 'It'll have you in it, which is all that matters.'

'Wonderful Chris! We're going to be so happy!'

It was late, and dark, by the time the Todds got back to their new home – one room with use of bathroom in Mrs Denman's narrow cottage, abutting straight on to the main village street. Mrs Denman answered their knock herself, shielding a candle with one hand.

'Yes? Oh, it's you, Mr Todd. Come in . . . you're later than you said.'

'It was the train,' Andy said patiently. 'Trains are

always late in wartime, Mrs Denman. This is my wife
. . . Christie, Mrs Denman, our landlady.'

Christie held out a hand and Mrs Denman shook it,
her fingers knobbly and stiff in Christie's grasp. She
was a highly coloured, irritable-looking woman in her
forties, with hair cut in an Eton crop and small, hard
eyes which seemed to Christie to barely hide her
regret at agreeing to share her home with a couple of
strangers.

'How d'you do, Mrs Denman? It's nice to meet
you,' Christie said trying not to glance round her too
obviously. 'I'm sorry if we've kept you up.'

'I'm an early riser so I'm never late to bed,' Mrs
Denman snapped. 'You'll be wanting a key, no
doubt.'

'Oh, yes, but . . .'

'Off early tomorrow, are you? You do work, I take
it? Your 'usband said you'd both be out, like as not,
all day.'

Andy stepped forward.

'We neither of us start work tomorrow,' he said
pleasantly. 'So anything you want to say to us you can
say then. But right now we've had a tiring journey and
would like to go to our room, clean up, and then get
ourselves a meal and go to bed.'

'You can't use the kitchen after seven at night,' Mrs
Denman said decidedly. 'It's after ten now, Mr Todd,
I really can't see my way clear to changing my
rules . . .'

'It doesn't matter,' Christie said, giving Andy a
desperate look. He'd not mentioned that their

landlady was Hitler's sister! 'We'll make do with a hot drink for tonight, Mrs Denman.' She simply didn't feel strong enough for a row, she told herself as she began to mount the stairs. 'Come on, Andy, let's get some rest.'

Andy, muttering, followed her up the stairs. At the top, on the small, square landing, he passed her and threw open a door.

'Here we are. I'm pretty sure there's a little stove-thing, perhaps we could heat up a tin or something . . .'

His voice died away. They didn't have any tins to heat up, Christie was well aware of it. For a moment they stared at each other, then Christie slung her kit-bag on to the bed – a saggy double – and went smartly out of the room once more. Mrs Denman was on the landing, hovering.

'Where's the bathroom, Mrs Denman?' Christie said brightly. 'I need to use it,'

'It's beyond the kitchen, Mrs Todd,' the older woman said. 'It's the door straight in front of you as you come in, end of the 'all. But you won't want to go down there after dark, there's a chamber pot under your bed. If you can empty it before you go off in the morning . . .'

'No, I'm afraid I can't. I'll just go down to the bathroom . . .'

Mrs Denman, a large but slow-moving woman, got half-way back across the hall, but not before Christie was well down the stairs. 'Oh, Mrs Todd . . .' the landlady said, her tone already censorious, but was cheerfully interrupted by her tenant.

'When you said we might use the bathroom you didn't specify daylight hours only,' Christie said. 'And I'll just pop the meal I've brought into the oven as I go through, then we can have something hot. Don't worry, I won't leave lights on or waste fuel or anything, but I won't have my husband going to bed hungry.'

Mrs Denman began another sentence, but Christie did not wait to hear her finish it. People might boss her about, bully her, ignore her rights, but no one was going to allow Andy to go hungry whilst she was around. Deaf to her landlady's angrily rising voice, Christie made her way determinedly down the hall and into the kitchen.

Married life, Christie thought as she turned out of the gates, was wonderful, the best thing that had ever happened to her. Of course the war made it cruelly difficult, because once things got back to normal she would worry over Andy as she had worried about him before, possibly more, but for now she was enjoying life.

They had been married for a fortnight and during that time the main runway at RAF Edenham had been out of commission, which meant that very few flights had taken off, and when they did it was likelier to be for training purposes rather than the real thing. Later, when things were back to normal and the kites were taking off on missions to Germany and beyond, the strain would start again. When she was on Darky watch and Andy was expected back she would have to force herself to keep her mind on her own work and not to allow herself to listen to her partner's words as she counted them in. But even taking that into account, even guessing at the suspense and pain to come, she would not have changed places with anyone else in the whole world. She was with Andy whenever possible and with every day that passed she fell more deeply in love.

Fortunately, life in the Edenham control tower was no different from life in any other tower. The work was the same, she was fully in control of it, and her partner, Stevie Collard, was a pretty, lively girl who was engaged to a wireless op. Together the two of them worked their shifts, shared meals, grumbles, jokes, and hid as best they might their worries over the men in their lives. But they both knew the helplessness of constant worry, and their mutual sympathy and understanding helped to fill the gap which losing Mary as well as Meg, Shanna and Sue, had left in Christie's new existence.

But when work was over for the day, Stevie went off to her billet whilst Christie, lucky Christie, trundled across the airfield, out through the gates, along the country lanes and into the village street and The Lilacs.

Despite its pretty name, The Lilacs was not a happy house. Mrs Denman was just as nasty on closer acquaintance as she had seemed that first night, but Christie and Andy didn't care. They avoided her. Christie ignored the vast number of rules which Mrs

Denman produced every time her lodgers did anything, from walking on her carpets to sneezing in her
air. The rules governing what Mrs D referred to as
'Use of facilities' were endless; and since the landlady
seemed, to the Todds, to make up new rules
whenever she wanted to prove she was in the right
there really wasn't much point in trying to please her.
Easier and better to go quietly about one's business,
agreeing to everything she said whilst never taking the
slightest notice.

Shift work being what it was, Christie wasn't always
available to cook Andy a hot meal, but then he could
eat in the cookhouse, as she could herself. But when
they were both free then cook she would, no matter
how loudly Mrs Denman asserted that it was against
the rules . . . not her turn . . . too early or too late.

Besides, Christie had quickly worked out a ruse
which had Mrs Denman muttering impotently into
her tea. Whenever the older woman bounced into the
kitchen with a cry of: 'Not cookin' *again*, Mrs Todd,
when I've said a 'undred times not . . .' she would
simply look up, smile, and say smoothly, 'It's a swop
cook-up, Mrs D. I didn't take my turn at the oven two
days ago, and we had a cookhouse brekker yesterday,
so I'm owed.'

Of course Mrs Denman always tried to prove her
wrong, but Christie could go back days and days and
tie the landlady up in a knot of statistics, imaginary
rights and phantom occasions. Indeed, her proudest
moment had come when she had been making
macaroni cheese, to be served with hot jacket

potatoes. She and Mrs Denman argued all through the preparations, through Christie serving up, splitting the potatoes, spooning out the crunchy-topped macaroni, enlivened with Christie's bacon ration, carefully snipped into tiny pieces and scattered over the dish. Mrs Denman was just remarking, as Christie carried her tray across the room, that she was very sure . . . when Christie played her trump card.

'Do you know, I believe you're right, Mrs D,' she said sweetly. 'It isn't my turn . . . but since the dinner's cooked, I can't do much about it, can I? I am so sorry!'

She and her tray swept triumphantly out whilst Mrs Denman's jaw dropped so low, Christie told Andy later, that she was in danger of bruising her chin on the tiles.

Remembering that triumph as she walked along in the evening hush, Christie smiled to herself. Despite Mrs Denman they were managing well enough. Andy kept saying that when they had more time they would find new quarters, but goodness knows how they would manage that. The village heaved with evacuees, people bombed out of the big cities, relatives who had fled the confusion or been turned out of seaside properties. And if they went further afield it would mean a long, hard cycle ride which wouldn't be too welcome once the winter truly arrived. There was a nip in the air tonight, Christie noticed, feeling the chill on her cheeks. They had been married two whole weeks and already the leaves were thinning on the trees, the grass was losing its summer brightness.

I hope we have bad weather when winter comes,

Christie thought, trudging along. They can't fly when the weather's really bad ... not that Andy's flown much since we married, but sooner or later he'll be away again and then ... oh well. At least I'll be on the spot, it can't be as bad as worrying from a distance, never really knowing what's going on.

She reached the village street and stopped for a moment to admire the display in the window of the village shop. There were some extremely dusty toilet rolls, three feather dusters made by the farmer's wife up the road when she'd killed her cockerels earlier in the week, and a large pile of onions. Good, she could do with some onions ... Mrs Denman objected to her cooking anything like onions or kippers on the grounds that they stank the house out, so perhaps she could cook them this evening. It was Mrs D's night for the Women's Institute and she would go out early and come home late, so if Christie fried up the left-over potatoes from yesterday with the onions and a couple of tomatoes, that would make an acceptably tasty supper. It was a pity that almost all meat was rationed, but they were luckier than most. The Air Force fed its people pretty well, all she had to do was to make tasty snacks most of the time, and Andy was so easily pleased. He just liked to see her pottering about the kitchen – she usually slipped out of her uniform and put on an ancient green overall which she had once worn in her chemistry class – or sitting opposite him at the dingy, pock-marked table in their room, encouraging him to tell about his day. He would grin at her and touch her cheek then tuck into whatever food she had

437

provided with a will, talking with his mouth full, occasionally reaching across the table to take her hand or chuck her under the chin; any excuse for physical contact.

She went into the shop and bought three large onions. Mrs Ablard, who kept the shop, asked her if she wanted a bit of fatty bacon, just a heel, like, off the piece. She knew how hard Christie found it to feed Andy and would help out whenever she could. Christie, accepting with heartfelt gratitude, realised that had the fatty bacon not been available, she would have been hard put to it to fry the cold potatoes, let alone the onions. Lard was rationed, too, as were butter and margarine.

'There y'are, luv. Anything else? Not that I've got much ... how I'm supposed to keep the shop goin'...'

Familiar plaints, echoed all over the country, Christie knew. But she murmured sympathetically and set off for the short walk to The Lilacs.

The dying sun slid out of sight just as she reached the front door, and half-way up the stairs she heard Mrs Denman coming from the direction of the kitchen. Good, so she was off out, as usual on a Thursday.

'Ah, Mrs Todd, I'll thank you to remember...'

Christie, feigning deafness, ran up the last few stairs and went into their room. She sat down on the bed and felt peace and joy envelop her in their warmth. The room smelt subtly but deliciously of Andy, the pillow was still dinted where his head had lain last night, his old felt slippers were where he had stepped out of them, heels together, toes apart, Chaplinesque, ridiculous, deeply loved.

Downstairs, the front door slammed. Crossly. Feet in sturdy, old-fashioned shoes clumped down the short path. Christie lay back on the bed and smiled up at the crazed cracks on the ceiling, recognising with affection the old man with the pointed nose, the goose, the horse with three legs and the cloud formation.

Home! Soon, Andy would come. Soon, very soon, they would be together, free to touch, to cling, to kiss. She really should start chopping the bacon, slicing the onions, preparing their meal. But Christie, awash with happiness, continued to smile at the ceiling.

Andy sang softly beneath his breath as he walked out through the gates. The main runway would be ready for use in another couple of days and he and the rest of his squadron would have to forego their unexpected break in routine. Today was Thursday; probably by Sunday he'd be back on active duty. He felt a frisson of feeling, part fear, part excitement, chase up and down his spine. He had so loved flying, the tremendous exhilaration of manoeuvring his kite through that most elusive of elements, using every ounce of skill at his disposal; seeing the earth below, no bigger or more important than a cleverly constructed relief map, whilst his kite darted in and out of a snow-field of cloud, now in brilliant sunshine, now in dark cloud-shadow.

Not any more, though. Now he was too tense, his nerves tight as violin strings, his reactions so sharp that at times he even frightened himself. Now the pleasure came in a safe landing, the feel of the ground beneath his feet, the wind on his cheek.

Yet there was the excitement still, the thrill. He was very conscious of the heightened awareness which danger brought, so that he could *feel* the Hun on his tail even when he couldn't see him, would jink his kite to one side, gain height, lose it, all with only that awareness to guide him.

It had stood him in good stead so far, though. Only . . . he'd not had so much to lose before. He'd not had Christie. He loved her so much! The pleasure he got from just seeing her in the same room, moving quietly around, quick and deft at cooker, sink or table, could not be over-estimated. And she was looking so wonderfully pretty, too – a bonus that marriage should have restored the roses to her cheeks, the lightness to her step and the smile to her deep blue eyes, but it obviously had.

She looks like she did when we first met, Andy told himself, turning into the gate of The Lilacs and remembering to latch it carefully behind him. She had begun to look pale and jaded, permanently tired; but a fortnight of loving marriage had given her back her youth . . . and why should it not? She was only twenty, after all!

He went quietly into the house and stood for a moment in the narrow hall-way, listening. Sure enough, he could hear her moving about quietly in the kitchen . . . it wasn't that dreadful old woman, Mrs D, she could no more move quietly than fly to the moon. But was she lurking somewhere, waiting to pounce? Andy didn't mind for himself, but he deeply resented the fact that she tried to make Christie's life more difficult. I'll have to have a word with the old bat, Andy told himself resignedly, tiptoeing towards the closed kitchen door. Christie will be working again properly, all-out, once the runways are all in commission. The strain of a twelve-hour shift when you're really busy is bad enough without a carping old woman deliberately making things difficult at home.

Still. It was a home, of sorts, and once they closed the bedroom door . . . Andy smiled to himself and opened the door slowly and carefully. He loved to catch a glimpse of her before she knew he was there, and now he saw her, in profile, bending over the cooker. She had got Mrs Denman's big black frying-pan off the shelf and was cooking something, concentrating so hard that she did not even look up as the door slowly opened. For a moment he feasted his eyes on her – the soft, burnished hair swinging forward, half hiding her face; the slim figure in the stained green overall, one hand gripping the knife anxiously, white-knuckled as she poked tentatively at the contents of the pan.

'Hello, sweetheart; something smells good!'

Christie jumped, dropped the knife and swung round, the faint flush in her cheeks deepening to rose.

'Andy, you pig, you scared me half to death – I

thought you were the old bat! This is her pan and you know how she feels about onions.'

'Onions! I'd almost forgotten how they smell, believe it or not.' He crossed the room in a couple of strides and stood behind her, putting his arms round her, kissing the tender nape of her neck, then pulling her hard against him. 'Oh, Chris . . . is the old bat out? Have you ever made love on a kitchen floor whilst cooking onions?'

'You know just where and how I've made love if anyone does,' Christie said. She turned in his embrace and kissed his chin, then sighed and turned back to the onions. 'Go and lay the table, you bad person, stop molesting the cook or I'll burn something. Oh Andy, isn't it nice here on the old bat's WI night?'

'Has she been pestering you again, darling? I really must do something about getting us a move. There's a rumour that Freda Simpson's joining the WRNS and if she does her mother might let her room. It wouldn't hurt to ask.'

'Who's Freda Simpson? Where does she live?' Christie turned a potato over and sighed. 'Wouldn't it be lovely not to have to listen to that awful monotone voice, always grumbling? Not that I mind, of course,' she added hastily.

'You know the Simpsons; he's that square little man with no hair who always wears a cap so his face is red and his forehead's white. The sidesman in church with the wobbly voice, you know. And she's the one who cleans the church, the one with bird's-nest hair and a laugh like a parrot. They live in the end cottage next to the church. I don't know which one Freda is, but she's one of the girls who stand outside the chip-shop in the evenings, you can take a bet on it.'

'Yes, I know who you mean. They seem nice, but would they really be any better than the old bat?' Christie asked doubtfully. 'We don't want to jump out of the frying-pan into the fire . . . quick, get the plates out, darling, they're hotting in the oven. Everything's cooked to a turn so let's be really naughty and eat down here since she's out of the way. Then our kit won't smell of fried onions.'

'Okay,' Andy said, snatching the plates out of the oven with the aid of one of Mrs Denman's tea-towels. Had their landlady been present it would have been more than their lives were worth to use any of her linen; she would far sooner see third-degree burns than know unhallowed hands had touched her tea-towel.

'I wonder if I dare use her salt? Oh, no need, I've got some in my cupboard.' Andy watched as Christie delved into the one meagre cupboard she was allowed and produced a small packet of salt. She thumped it down triumphantly on the wooden table-top. 'There! Dig in, I stewed some apples for a pudding but they're upstairs, I'll have to fetch 'em.'

When the meal was finished they washed up, boiling up a whole kettle of water for the purpose on the kitchen stove, which would have caused Mrs Denman to have an apoplexy had she known, and returned to their own room. It was dark, but they had not drawn the curtains and through their window they could see the arch of the dark sky, the stars and a great golden moon.

'We'll go for a walk, then pop into the pub for a quick one, then go to bed,' Andy said contentedly, watching as Christie struggled out of the overall. 'Unless there's something you'd rather do?'

'No, that's fine. And darling, if Mr Simpson's in the pub, do you think we might just ask about his Freda? Only next week, when you're on duty and flying again, I can't say I much fancy cosy evenings with the old bat.'

'I'll have a word, or go round,' Andy promised. She was out of her overall now, standing there in her underwear, reaching for her skirt. He put his hands on her shoulders and kissed the tip of her nose, then drew her close. 'Mind you, I'm not absolutely sold on a walk; I could easily be persuaded to give it a miss tonight and go straight to bed.'

Christie giggled, then pushed him away.

'Nonsense, we'll sleep better for a bit of exercise, we can just walk round the village and . . .'

'There are other forms of exercise which can be just as pleasantly tiring and far more fun. Why don't you put that silly skirt down and take off all those . . . I say, they aren't your issue undies!'

'No, I only wear the issue ones to work, now. Come on, Andy, let me get dressed – think how cross you'd be if someone else got to the Simpsons first.'

Andy sighed but let her go.

'All right, but if Mr Simpson isn't in the pub we'll come straight back here. Agreed?'

Christie buttoned her blue shirt and reached for her tie. She smiled up at him, her eyes blazing with love. 'All right. Agreed.'

He was not aware, at first, of what had woken him. He lay on his back, looking up at the ceiling, at the old man with the pointed nose, the goose, the horse with three legs. Before they slept they always pulled back the curtains though now, with the leaves gone off the trees and their marriage a month old, winter threatened and Andy foresaw that it would not be long before they needed all the extra blankets that Christie's mother had pressed on them.

He listened, expecting to hear a village dog bark, or perhaps the sound of an aero engine heralding the return of the kites which had gone out earlier. Instead, he felt Christie move beside him, turned . . . and froze.

She was sitting bolt upright, her hands to the sides of her head in a gesture which he knew well but could not at once recall. And even as he went to touch her, she began to talk.

'Hello Darky, hello Darky, can you hear me? Can you hear me? Receiving you, but only just . . . receiving you strength two . . .' She turned her head slightly and said, in a low voice, 'Someone else will pick him up, surely? His engine's on fire, he's got to get down . . .' She put her hands to her ears again and spoke urgently. 'Hello Darky, Nemo calling, Nemo calling . . .'

Andy realised that she was asleep and dreaming . . .

that she was still working, in fact. And in a state of desperate anxiety. The hands holding the imaginary head-set close to her ears were shaking, her face was sheet-white, her eyes dark-rimmed. He hesitated, afraid suddenly to touch her, to attempt to wake her. Wasn't there something about not waking sleep-walkers ... but she wasn't sleep-walking, she was sleep-working ... and she was in such distress, he would have to wake her.

'Chris darling, wake up my sweet, you're having a horrid nightmare, wake up!'

He put a hand on her shoulder but she shrugged him off.

'Don't ... I can barely hear him, he'll crash, he *must* be near enough to someone to ... Hello Darky, Hello Darky, Nemo calling, Nemo calling. I am receiving you, strength two, are you receiving me?'

'Sweetheart, you're dreaming, you must wake up! Darling Christie ...'

She woke. Hands were gripping her shoulders, someone was trying to push her down on to her back. She struggled, trying to explain, to push her attacker away.

'No, please ... it's a Darky call, he's in desperate trouble ... please let me help him, please don't let him go too far away, please don't let him die!'

She heard her own voice, high and terribly young, and then she was in bed, with Andy's arms round her and there was no head-set, no desperate boy's voice in her ears, no jamming to listen over or under. Just the old man with the pointed nose, the goose, the horse with three legs.

And Andy. She relaxed on to her back and he was looming over her, his face clear in the moonlight which flooded through the window. His eyes looked very black and something shone on his cheek, spilled over from those dark, dark eyes.

'Andy? Whazzermatter? It's the middle of the night, are you all right?'

He put his arms round her and buried his face in her neck. She felt the wetness on his cheeks, his whole body was trembling. At once all her protective instincts were aroused. She sat up, cradling him, crooning love-words.

'Darling, sweetheart, have you had a nightmare? You're all right, Chris has got you, I won't let anyone hurt you!'

'Sweetheart, it wasn't me having the nightmare, it was you. Oh, my pet, it's bloody killing you, that job! I've seen you age years in the past two weeks, ever since the station went fully operational again. You were taking a Darky call, in the middle of the bloody night, when you've only just come off a twelve-hour shift. That means you're working twenty-four hours out of the twenty-four ... no one could stand it and I can't let you go on. I want you out of it, safe!'

He clutched her convulsively. She could feel his tears running down the skin of her bare breasts. His pain hurt her more than her own could possibly have done and now she remembered the Darky call, her distress, the feeling that if she didn't listen, if she

447

failed, somehow, to hear those small, lost voices in the night, she would have killed the boy as surely as if she'd plunged a knife in his heart. How could she be so foolish, wasn't it enough to have the pain in reality, on her shifts, without imagining it at night, too? But it was her cross, not his; he should not have to bear it for her!

'Did I dream? Well, I guess we all dream. It's ... it's rather a responsible job, you see, and ...'

'I – want – you – out!'

Christie sighed and sat fully up in bed. She pushed the covers back and padded over to the window, drew the blackout blind down, pulled the curtains across, then fumbled her way back to bed and lit the candle. In its slight light she looked with love and sorrow into the dark face so near her own.

'No can do, Andy. I'm in for the duration, you know that. Look, it's all right, they've told me on other stations that sometimes at night I – I go on working when I've had a – a difficult shift. Others are the same. The Air Force might take me off r/t work I suppose, they do that sometimes, when it makes someone ill, but it's what I know, what I'm best at. I'd feel I was letting everyone down ... oh darling Andy, I'm sorry I worried you, but I'll be all right, honest I will.'

He shook his head, clutching her to him so hard that it hurt.

'You don't *know* – you looked so well and peaceful that first fortnight, I thought marriage suited you, was doing you good. But as soon as the ops started again you got thinner somehow, paler. Darling, you look so weary and ill and I want you rosy and glowing and happy! There's nothing I can do about the worry I give you, we both thought of that before we married, but there is something I can do about your work and I intend to do it.'

'Don't try to get me moved, I couldn't bear it, I couldn't . . .'

'No. That would be worse. I want you out, but we must be together. Come here, my love.'

He was gentle suddenly, the tears drying on his cheeks. He took her in his arms and began the familiar moves that would end, she knew, in love-making.

'Oh Andy, it's the middle of the night, you're on call tomorrow night, don't you think . . . oh Andy, that is so nice, do it again!'

Presently, she leaned over to open her bed-side drawer. She had attended lectures which had been given by an MO to personnel contemplating matrimony and as a result had a birth-control device, a diaphragm and some cream which had to be inserted before they made love. It was rather a messy business but she understood the necessity. It had cost a great deal of money to train her fully; she would not want to spoil the war effort by . . .

Andy leaned across her and shut the drawer. He stopped her protest with his mouth, his hands urgent on her, bringing her to a peak of desire beyond which she would think of nothing but him.

'No, sweetheart,' he said gently against her lips. 'It's the only sure way.'

She struggled, but not very hard or very long. And presently, he made love to her with a trembling intensity and a tenderness which surpassed all their previous experiences. Christie forgot her job, her dreams, her responsibilities, and knew ecstasy, and fulfilment, and the joy of giving pleasure without stint.

When they relaxed on to the pillows once more, Andy put a hand on the smoothness of her stomach.

'It's the only way,' he murmured. 'The only way.'

15

It had been a wet winter rather than a wild one, and when March came in, Christie and Andy moved out of The Lilacs and into a farm labourer's cottage a mile outside the village. Freda Simpson had joined the WRNS but her parents decided not to let her room; indeed, it was only as a result of constantly asking the Simpsons whether they had changed their minds that Andy and Christie heard tell of somewhere else which might – just might – be available for rent. Christie, who had recently had the embarrassment of being requested by Mrs Denman to explain strange creakings and rustlings coming from her room at night, would have lived in a pigsty to escape from her landlady and said at once they would like to take a look.

''Tis a tumbledown place,' Mrs Simpson said doubtfully. 'Us moved outer there when this 'un came 'vailable. Still, no 'arm in looking.'

Ivy Cottage was certainly not much to look at. Birds nested not only under the eaves but also in the roof-space, dead leaves were piled up in corners and the small rooms smelled of damp and worse. Cracked and broken windows, walls with great patches of plaster missing and an earth floor downstairs completed the picture; but Andy and Christie, desperate to get away from Mrs Denman, were prepared to have a go if the farmer would agree.

The farmer, hearing of their plight – and also of their lodging allowance – promised to make it presentable. New building materials would have been impossible to obtain but he used glass from an old greenhouse for the windows, patched the roof with slates which had once graced his lean-to scullery, and got an odd-job man to replaster the walls and repair the pump.

When it was finished Christie and several WAAF friends scrubbed the place through thoroughly, cleaned the windows with great care and even forked over the tiny front garden. Then Christie broke the news of the impending changes to Mrs Denman.

Christie had expected it to be greeted with muted cheers, perhaps even loud cheers, but instead she got almost biblical wailing and lamentation.

'You've been like a daughter to me,' Mrs Denman snuffled. 'And I'm that fond of Mr Todd ... dearie me, I'll be rare lonely ... never 'ad no childern of me own ... well, truth to tell me title's only for decency's sake, a woman alone ... it wouldn't do to let on you wasn't wed ... but there you are, if you're determined to go there ain't nowt I can do to stop you, I daresay?'

''Fraid not,' Christie said, trying not to sound too cheerful. She thought that if Mrs Denman's treatment of them was what she would have meted out to a daughter then it was a fortunate thing indeed that her title was honorary. 'But we aren't far from the village, so no doubt you'll see us from time to time.'

'She's got used to the money coming in each week,' Andy said with cruel practicality when Christie told him their landlady's reaction to the news. 'She'll get someone else soon enough – Sandy Crewe's getting married in a couple of weeks, I never did like him – he and his wife can move in with pleasure.'

So he and Christie hired a horse and cart and took their few possessions out to Ivy Cottage. Mrs Denham had assumed they were lodging with someone else and had scarcely been able to believe that they preferred a tiny, run-down cottage with no running water, no electricity and precious few other amenities to her bijoux residence; but she put a good face on it and waved them off, probably because half Andy's squadron had piled into the cart to give a hand with the move.

'I want a house-warming party, just a little one,' Christie said that evening, when they had lit the lamp and drawn the curtains and were cosily ensconced on the rug in front of the log fire, lacking any easy chairs at present.

Their new home was rather empty, but in the small, low-ceilinged bedroom they had a bed with a huge feather mattress, two packing-cases masquerading as a chest of drawers and a washstand complete with a basin and ewer in bright blue china. In the second bedroom lurked an ancient tin hip-bath which they planned to carry downstairs on a Saturday night to have their baths; and downstairs they owned two upright kitchen chairs to draw up to the wobbly kitchen table, and a primus stove. There was also a brick copper with a fire space beneath it, the rug, a spare lamp, two tin buckets for water, a huge enamel jug and a couple of saucepans which Christie had bagged from home.

Outside, a long thin garden with the lavatory at the end of the path completed their domain. Christie rather liked the lavatory with its double seat and the heart-shaped hole cut in the top of the door so that you could read the newspaper before using it for a more mundane purpose; but she thought Andy might well be right when he said she wouldn't be so sanguine on a rainy night or when it snowed.

'A party?' Andy said now, shifting uncomfortably on the rug. 'My btm says this rug isn't thick enough, it needs something softer, may I sit on your lap? How can we have a party with no chairs, no food and not much of anything else? But if it's what you want . . .'

Christie chuckled and knelt up, looking consider-ingly round the room. Andy was right, the hearth-rug was too thin to make a good seat, but there was always a way . . . she ran upstairs and fetched the pillows off their bed. She emerged from the boxed-in ladder which was Ivy Cottage's answer to the staircase and chucked the pillows at Andy's head.

'There! Make a nest.'

'For Mr and Mrs Dormouse; certainly I will.'

Two minutes later, lounging on pillows, Andy re-opened the discussion.

'But why a party, sweetheart? Who could we ask, apart from the blokes and girls we meet every day? And most of them helped us to move in, so they've seen the place, had a cup of tea, even.'

He sounded so complacent that Christie giggled.

'A cup of tea isn't exactly a party, but I know what you mean. Perhaps I shouldn't have called it a party, because I really only want to ask Shanna, Sue and Meg. Shanna and Sue missed the wedding, but they're my three best friends; I'd love to have them see our very own home. Why, they could stay with us! There's the little room, we could shove the tin bath in the yard and they could bring bed-rolls and kip down on the floor. Why not, Andy? It would be such fun.'

'No reason why not. In fact, it's a good idea.' Andy made a long arm and pulled Christie closer, snuggling her against his chest. 'Look, I haven't said anything before but in a couple of weeks I'm due to go off on a three-day course, and you can't come with me. Why don't you ask the girls if they've got some leave, and try to arrange for them to visit you whilst I'm away? Then you won't be here alone. That's the only thing that worries me, the thought of you stuck out here by yourself.'

'Oh, but I won't get in such a state now we've got our own home,' Christie said. 'I was worrying so much over Mrs D listening to our every movement that I was afraid to turn over in bed. And anyway, I've got the doctor's tablets.'

Andy had hoped that Christie would get pregnant quickly once she stopped using her Dutch cap, but it hadn't happened. Instead, she got nervier and nervier until she scarcely slept without dreaming that she was on duty. Andy stuck it for a week, then marched her off to the MO.

She doesn't sleep and when she does she dreams she's still got her head-set on,' he told the doctor. 'So she gets no rest at all and she's constantly at full-stretch, nerves, mind, everything.'

The doctor prescribed a mild sleeping-pill and suggested re-mustering in another job, but Christie could not bear to be sent away from Andy for weeks whilst she retrained, and obstinately refused to put in an application. However, she stopped dreaming, though her sleep was shallow and twitchy and she often woke with a headache.

'Bloody tablets,' she had stormed to Andy only a couple of days earlier. 'They're making me worse, please let me stop them, please!'

'Oh, love, but those awful nightmares . . .'

Christie remembered how her bad dreams had constantly woken him, constantly worried him, and pretended that she didn't mind the tablets really. But here, in the quiet countryside, surely her need for such things would just go away? She would be able to relax out here – surely? In their own little home, far from the horrors of Mrs Denman, she should be able to forget the job, her anxieties, and the constant click and tinkle of the jamming which filled her ears day and night, night and day.

So now, sitting on the floor propped up by pillows, they planned their very first social event.

'I'll write to all of them straight away,' Christie said busily. 'Well, not straight away; tomorrow, when I'm on the eight to sixteen hundred shift.'

'Yes, you get time on that shift,' Andy agreed. 'I'll probably be flying tomorrow night, but you can post the letters on your way through the village. You'll eat in the cookhouse, won't you? Then you can come straight back here and have an early night.'

'Oh darling, give me a lovely cuddle!'

Even the thought of his plane leaving the ground sent the familiar, hated shudder through her. But she couldn't let him see it, he worried enough over her already. She snuggled in his arms for a moment, then sat up.

'I got about an inch of cheese and half a loaf from the NAAFI this morning, strictly on the q.t. of course. We can have toasted cheese before we go to bed. And some cocoa. A feast!'

They laughed ruefully together.

'Well, Meggie, are you going? I'm really excited – I mean, I missed the wedding, but there's no' a chance of me missin' this! Their own wee house ... och, I cannae wait!'

Meg and Shanna were perched on the anti-tank defences half-way up the Strait, relishing the clear spring sunshine and waiting for Mandy and Meg's friend Fay, who had gone into one of the shops. Meg had a bunch of flowers in one hand, bought from a youngster further down the street who had probably stripped his mother's garden to make himself some pocket-money. There were two daffodils, a sprig of flowering currant, some yellow forsythia and a few violets, and now and then Meg bent her head and inhaled blissfully. Shanna could see that the small posy was giving her friend as much pleasure as a box of chocolates would have done, and at least flowers weren't rationed – not yet.

'I'm going,' Meg confirmed. 'So you'll abandon Peter for a couple of days, then? Have you heard from Sue, incidentally? Can she make it?'

'She wouldnae miss it. We both missed the wedding, but things are easing up a wee bit, don't you think? There's no' the same urgency. As for Pete, we're only good friends, you know.'

'Sure,' Meg said, looking unconvinced. 'Will you bring Jacko?'

'No, not this time. He can be such a nuisance, and Pete likes him; he enjoys having him, he says.'

'What about his mum, and his sister?'

Peter Canning was a local boy so he lived in Lincoln and not on station, in a small flat over a menswear shop on High Street. He was an M/T mechanic and because she had been unhappy and often lonely after Col's death, Shanna had spent quite a lot of time the previous summer watching him servicing the engines and helping when she could. At first she suspected that he just tolerated her, being too polite to tell her to get lost, but gradually she became useful. She fetched and carried for him, asked intelligent questions about his work and wasn't at all averse to getting dirty in the good cause of removing a head or repairing a clutch.

Peter was shy, but because she made no demands he got used to her presence and eventually seemed to enjoy her company. She had seen him glance around restlessly when she was out of his sight, and saw, too, that his eyes lit up when she came into view.

He wasn't conventionally handsome or particularly clever but he was a first-rate motor mechanic who enjoyed his work and, as the months passed, she learned more about him. He was a good son and a good brother, too. He didn't go out with girls; but that was mainly because he was saving up, and because in a way his job was also his hobby. He had a big old Harley Davidson motor-bike which he loved passionately and when he wasn't working on service vehicles he was stripping down his motor-bike.

By the time autumn came, Peter had grown so accustomed to Shanna that he began to miss her, he said, when he was off the station. Without a trace of the shyness which had made him so gruff and monosyllabic at first, he announced that he wanted to take her to the cinema, home to tea with his mother and sister, and out to the surrounding villages with the fascinating names – Greetwell, Cherry Willingham, Fiskerton and Stainton-by-Langworth – on the back of his beloved motor-bike.

He proved a delightful companion, interesting and dependable. He knew everything there was to know about his city and shared his knowledge with Shanna because she was interested and did not moither him, or so he said. Even after he grew confident in Shanna's company he was a man of few words, but

Shanna knew he thought things over carefully before he did speak. He told her that when peace broke out he wanted his own garage where he would repair cars and motor-bikes, sell petrol and do re-sprays and servicings. He was saving up already towards the happy day when the war ended and his new career could begin; and though he had not yet actually said it in so many words, Shanna knew that he wanted to marry her. But she thought he was going too fast; she, who had once lain down for any man who asked was now so different that she could not contemplate another lover. One day, perhaps ... but right now Pete was the person she most wanted to spend her time with, the perfect friend, and she did not want this relationship jeopardised by talk of marriage or even of a deeper intimacy.

'Well? I asked you what Mrs Canning and Pete's sister think of Jacko, dreamy!'

'Oh, sorry ... they like him. Marjorie would love a bird of her own, but she's not too well so she's happy to take care of him for me. She'll make a great fuss of him whilst I'm in Edenham – they all will.'

The shop door opened and Mandy and Fay came out. Shanna slid off the warm concrete block and dusted down her skirt and Meg followed suit.

'Got what you wanted?' Shanna asked the two girls, slinging her respirator case over her shoulder as they began to move off. 'Good ... then let's go down to that cafe on Silver Street and have waffles and coffee. All the Yanks go there.'

'And why should you be interested in Yanks?' Meg

said censoriously. 'You've got Pete, haven't you?'

'I'm no' interested in Yanks, to tell the truth,' Shanna admitted. 'Isn't it odd – that was a completely reflex remark, because that's what the girls on the station would say. But I've no' *got* Pete, as you call it. We're just good friends.'

'I've seen the look in his eyes when he's watching you, and it's a very *got* sort of look,' Mandy remarked. 'Everyone likes Pete though, Shan, so if you really do want him, I should grab before someone else does.'

'Not everyone has that sort of thing in mind whenever they take a wee ride on a feller's motor-bike,' Shanna said righteously. 'We're just friends, I'm tellin' you.'

'Bet you hold hands in the flicks,' Mandy muttered. 'Bet you kiss goodnight.'

'That's just being friendly,' Shanna said, then grinned as the other three made derisive noises. 'Aye, it is, just friendly. We don't do ... other things, I'm tellin' ye!'

'No. Well,' Meg said, linking her arm with Shanna's. 'Tell you what, Shanna, I think you probably like Pete more than you know, if you understand me. And liking comes awfully close to love, in my experience. Come on, best foot forward, I'm hungry!'

It was all downhill to Silver Street. The girls swung along, crossed Corporation Street at a run and swerved into Silver Street. There was a slight altercation at this point because Fay didn't like coffee and would have preferred to visit Minns on Guildhall Street, where she might have had a toasted scone and a nice pot of tea, but she was out-voted on this occasion.

'Toasted scones and pots of tea are lovely when it's icy cold or raining cats and dogs; waffles and coffee are best when it's sunny,' Meg declared. 'Besides, though they probably can't provide toasted scones I'm sure they'll do you a cup of tea. Come on, girls, I saved some bits from brekker this morning; if there's time after tea I want to go down to Brayford Pool and feed the swans.'

'Oh all right, I give in, and I think you're right about the tea,' Fay said. 'Let's bag a window table!'

Shanna, following the other three into the small cafe, wondered dreamily if Meg was right; was the strong liking she felt for Pete akin to love? Was she still secretly waiting for Col? But Pete, dear Pete, never tried to hurry her or do more than chastely kiss her cheek, hold her hand. Perhaps, if he did . . .

'Here we are, best table in the place! Come on, let's order before the hordes arrive.'

Shanna took her seat at the window table and thought about the lovely leave she and Meg and Sue would have, at Christie's little house. Wonderful to be together again . . . She would tell Sue about Pete, see what she thought. Meg liked him . . . well, how could anyone do otherwise? But marriage was a big commitment and she had made up her mind when Col died that she would never marry.

'Waffles and coffee for three, please, and tea for

one. What'll you have to eat, Fay? Waffles are delicious you know, you really ought to try one.'

Christie had brought her old bicycle from home so that she could get back to Ivy Cottage quicker than on foot, and now that spring had arrived, bringing with it lighter evenings and balmier air, she rather enjoyed the cycle ride.

Particularly, she thought, now pedalling along in the sunset's glow, when Andy, on his bike, rode beside her. They had been married for six months but nothing had palled; his every glance, every smile, every touch, was welcome and delightful to her, his company was the sweetest she had ever known, his absence the saddest.

But in two days' time the girls would arrive and though it also meant that Andy would depart for his three-day course, at least on the course he wouldn't be on active duty. British raids were pressing deeper into Germany now as the tide turned in the Allies' favour; but this only meant, so far as Christie was concerned, that Andy did not only attack enemy aircraft coming in over the coast to bomb British cities, he went with the bombers to Germany on the offensive rather than the defensive. Danger, scarlet and black, dogged him from the moment his kite took off until it landed safely, but she tried very hard – and usually unsuccessfully – not to think about that.

Andy was far more news-conscious than she. She had listened as the wireless announcer told of victory in the desert in the autumn of the previous year, cheered when the Russians turned the tide on the Nazis in February, wept with the rest of the nation when almost two hundred people were crushed to death in a panic on the underground in early March; but smaller items of war news passed her by.

Andy listened to most news programmes on the wireless and usually had snippets of information from other servicemen, too. He seldom talked about his own experiences or those of the rest of his squadron, but Christie realised that the larger picture was important to him; they all longed for the end now. Three years and almost seven months ... it was a long, long time.

But Andy believed, with Winston Churchill, that they were making real headway at last.

'We're pushing 'em,' he would say exultantly, when the news-reader announced that another U-boat had been destroyed or our defences had brought enemy raiders down. 'They've got the Yanks to reckon with as well as us now, a fresh fighting force. The Red Army are unbelievable, they say Hitler himself fairly gibbers when they're mentioned, and we've got Rommel on the run. At this rate the Jerries will be on their knees by the end of the year.'

He had been quiet the night they announced that the Germans had recaptured Kharkov, though. One of the most industrialised of Russian cities, this had to be bad news, and was all the harder coming after a string of Russian victories over their hated foe.

But although she appreciated that all these things were important, to Christie only one thing really mattered; if their kite's all right then they'll fly tonight, she reminded herself, pedalling hard uphill and then swooping triumphantly down. But I'm not on tomorrow until noon, so I can get him some breakfast and tuck him up before I have to go on ... oh, how I wish someone, somewhere, would decide to call the raid off!

They wouldn't, though. Weather conditions were just about perfect and you needed good weather for the long, boring flight right across France and into Germany. Would it be the Ruhr, or somewhere else? Andy sometimes hinted at a destination if he thought she might worry less ... oh God, if only that big raid on St Nazaire had been the end of it! Andy had been in the fighter escort and had come home glowing with achievement ... Yet it hadn't been enough, still the enemy's heavy bombers droned in over the coast, night after night, and attacked.

Still. Tonight would be his last raid, anyway; that was something to be profoundly thankful for. She was actually turning in at the gate of Ivy Cottage when she realised her last thought had been badly phrased. An arrow of sheer terror shot through her breast, stopping her breathing, sending palpitations surging through her. No! *Not* his last raid, just the last one before the course starts, she told the fates. No! Andy's my dear love, my heart's darling, he's got to come through all right, he promised, he promised!

She wheeled the bicycle round into the back yard, abandoned it there and went into the cottage. How homely it was when Andy would be back soon, how lonely when she was on her own. But they had two hens now, in a run at the end of the garden; she would feed them presently, she always enjoyed that. They had been the proud owners of a kitten, but it had been run over whilst they were at work and Andy hadn't wanted to get another. Christie had not seen the kitten's little corpse, as Andy had, but she did miss its friendly presence when Andy was working.

She put the kettle on the Primus stove, considered lighting the fire, decided not to bother. She would lay it so it could be lit in time for Andy's return in the morning, but she would wrap herself in a blanket this evening and go early to bed. Perhaps she might even sleep, because she did have good thoughts to mull over, and good thoughts helped.

The curse was late, she was eighteen days overdue. Andy desperately wanted her to have a child so that she could leave the WAAF, but Christie wasn't at all sure what she wanted, except that she wanted to please him. And she was beginning to realise that he was right about one thing. The job was getting to her. Lately, despite the doctor's little blue tablets and Andy's loving care, she had begun to feel as though something evil lurked just behind her, waiting to strike her down. She was living in a state of nervous tension in which a loud noise could cause her total, blind panic, or someone entering a room and speaking without warning could actually make her faint.

She managed to hide most of these manifestations from Andy because in his presence she relaxed much more, but colleagues had noticed and friends worried. Stevie, her opposite number, had spoken to the Wing Officer about her, and wing officers could do all sorts of things, they were powerful people. Suppose the WO said she must re-muster and they sent her away from Andy? I'd die, I know I would, Christie thought now, mixing potato peelings, cabbage and chicken meal with half a kettle of hot water into a tempting mash in one of the buckets. I couldn't go on without Andy; I wouldn't even want to go on. But suppose I am having a baby? Or suppose it's just that anxiety has screwed all my muscles up so tight that the curse can't come, even if it wants to? What should I do? Suppose I say nothing and the curse just goes on building up and building up, can it kill me? Should I see the MO? I could ask for a pregnancy test, I remember someone telling me you give them a sample of your wee and they inject a poor little lady frog with it – ugh – and if the frog lays eggs then you're pregnant. Horrible . . . cruel and unnatural . . . but at least I'd know for sure.

The bucket of mash was hot and smelt delicious. Christie carried it out to the hens in the last long rays of the sun. Andy called the hens Flanagan and Allen because he said they were a pair of comics, but Christie insisted that they should be called Elsie and Doris, after the Waters sisters. Despite a certain amount of confusion over names and sexes, the hens seemed none the worse. They answered to their names – that is, they charged the length of their run, large feet slapping on the hard earth, wings half raised

– and hurled themselves hopefully at the wire netting whenever Christie called them; and although some birds might have looked askance at a hen-house which was really a disused dog-kennel, Elsie and Doris – or Flanagan and Allen – laid a couple of eggs most days in the straw of their new abode and raised no objection to Christie stealing their produce on a regular basis.

'Grub up, chaps,' Christie called as she neared the run. 'Swop it for an egg, kind ladies?'

The kind ladies uttered croodling cries as the mash descended, and began to eat devotedly. If we had a cockerel they might get pregnant too, Christie thought, going quietly into the run and extracting an egg from the kennel. Only then they wouldn't let me take the eggs, and I do love to see Andy tucking into an egg . . . If I was a pregnant hen I'm sure I wouldn't want people interfering with my babies . . . but that must mean I can't be pregnant, because I don't feel anything, I mean not possessive, or fond, or starry-eyed or anything like that . . . Oh hell, thank goodness I didn't say anything to Andy about my dates being wrong, he'd have got all pleased and excited and now I'm absolutely *sure* I'm not pregnant, I'm just ill.

Ill? No, I feel quite okay, Christie decided. People do miss periods when they're very strung up, I seem to remember that MO telling us so. She took the egg and the empty bucket back to the house, first rinsing the bucket under the pump. Indoors, she perched the egg on the mantelpiece where Andy would see it as soon as he came in and refilled the kettle. A lonely night, then Andy, then a day-shift in the control tower, then seeing Andy off on his course, and next day, Sue, Shanna and Meg!

Christie went to bed early, having cleaned the cottage relentlessly first because she wanted the girls to have a good impression. She thought about taking a little blue tablet, then decided, as Andy wasn't with her, that she would jolly well skip it for once. She knew they made her feel worse, and if she had nightmares tonight, at least they would disturb no one but herself.

She woke in the dark, knowing that it was still the middle of the night, not knowing what had woken her. She propped herself on her elbow, heart hammering, and peered across the darkened room. Someone outside? The wind in the trees, perhaps, or a fox, barking at the moon? If she leaned over to one side she could just see the moon; perspiration trickled down between her breasts, making her jump and starting her heart, which had slowed, hammering fast once more. It was nothing, just a dream, probably . . . Lie down, girl, and go back to sleep, she scolded herself. Stop making a fuss about nothing, it's hours before you've got to get up.

She was lowering herself back on to the pillows when she saw the movement; quick and dark, something darted along beside the wall. She shot up, grabbed her torch, clicked it on and swung the beam.

Backed defensively against the wall, a large mouse glared beadily across the room at her, its whiskers casting spider-like shadows on the wall behind it. Christie, who had stopped breathing, let her breath out in a long sigh.

'You stupid creature ... go back wherever you came from and stop waking me up,' she commanded it. 'Some girls are scared of mice, but I'm not amongst them, so vamoose, scat! I'm going to get another kitten from the farm tomorrow, that'll keep you in your place.'

She lay down, listening as the mouse scuttled dementedly across the room and dived down a hole she had noticed days ago in the wainscotting.

She was almost asleep again when the most tremendous explosion woke her. It shook the bed and brought her out of bed, eyes black with terror, heart hammering once more, already running over to the window. What on earth was it? Something awfully big had gone up – had there been a raid on the airfield, or on the nearby town ? Was there an ammo dump nearby which had inadvertently been hit? She glanced at her watch; ten past three in the morning so it wasn't likely to be blasting from the local quarry or anything of that sort.

She reached the window, opened it and leaned out. A gentle breeze blew in and a bird moved, cheeping sleepily, but other than that the countryside lay peaceful in the moonlight. Nothing stirred, not even a mouse. No smoke drifted across the clear sky, no flames lit up the horizon. Whatever the noise had been, it had gone without trace so far as she could see.

Presently, she went back to bed but for the rest of

the night sleep eluded her. She counted sheep, wondered about babies, chose a kitten from the farm cat's half-wild brood. She saw the pale grey of dawn creep across the sky and was down in the kitchen making herself some tea and toast when the sun rose.

By seven o'clock she had fed the hens, sliced bread and spread it thinly with margarine, boiled the kettle again. Ten minutes later, she got on her bike and cycled off in the direction of the airfield. She had hoped he would get home before she left, but she'd heard the thrum of the returning planes only half an hour ago so they must have gone further afield. Andy was probably debriefing now, but she'd see if anyone knew what the noise in the night had been and have a word with him, tell him she'd left him an egg on the mantelpiece, before going to the control tower for her shift.

She reached the airfield, padlocked her bike and went over to the cookhouse. Stevie, Millicent and Avril waved to her; she went over, accepted a cup of tea and asked about the explosion. Heads were shaken, faces puzzled.

'God, you must have heard it – it nearly turned my bed over,' Christie exclaimed. 'It sounded like an ammo dump going off, honestly.'

'I sleep like a log,' Stevie said. 'Nothing disturbs me. Drink up that tea, Chris, I know Theresa and Joan counted them in, but they won't be too pleased if we're late relieving.'

They made their way to the control tower. Christie

found that she was walking like an automaton. She suddenly knew that it was pointless hanging about waiting for Andy to come out of his debriefing. She could tell herself that he would pop into the tower to have a word with her; well, so he would in the ordinary way. But today would be different. He would not be popping in to see her today.

She reached the tower and went straight to the board. Only one plane was overdue. She knew his call-sign off by heart, even the shape of the letters and numbers were familiar to her. She did not have to read the board; she just stood there and felt the cold black water creep slowly up her body, to her knees, hips, waist, shoulders . . . just before she slid under it, she knew, with complete certainty, what the explosion was which had woken her earlier. It had been Andy's plane, crashing to earth. With the thought she let go, spiralling without protest or effort into oblivion.

'His squadron leader, Muzzo, came and told me. They were over the Ruhr when he went down. He's missing, they say he's missing, but I suppose they mean . . .'

Christie's voice faltered to a halt.

The girls had arrived in a group at the cottage, to find Christie dry-eyed, blank-faced, sitting on the hearth-rug and staring at the fireplace where the fire was laid but not lit. She had barely looked up when they crowded in, but now she sighed and shook herself.

'I'm awfully sorry, how rude I'm being. I fainted when I saw ... anyway, they put me in sick-bay but I told them you were coming today so they let me out. I got back an age ago ...' She glanced at her wrist-watch, then frowned and shook it, holding it to her ear. 'No, it hasn't stopped ... well, perhaps I've only been here for half an hour ... it seems impossible, it feels ... I'll light the Primus and put the kettle on. We've got a well, but Andy says ... well, we'll need running water if ... can someone light the fire? There's matches on the mantelpiece – mind Andy's egg, it's for his ... Ah, God, I'm in a muddle.'

Meg put her arms round Christie, cuddling her, but Christie pulled away.

'No, don't,' she said sharply. 'It's all right, I'll be all right. I've just got to come to terms with it and I'm almost there. Can someone light the fire, please?'

'I'll do it,' Meg said. 'Is there any food in the place? We didn't bring anything because we thought we'd probably eat on the station.'

'I'll have a look for food,' Sue said. She smiled brightly at Christie. 'If there's a loaf and some milk we'll manage something ... or we could go down to the airfield one at a time, I suppose.'

'There's food,' Christie said flatly. 'Eggs, a loaf, some marg ... I don't know about real milk but there's some dried.'

Shanna sat herself down on the hearth-rug beside Christie and took her hands. When Christie would have pulled away she shook her head gently.

'Christie, love, have ye no' cried? Get some o' the grief out of your system that way, naturally, the way it should come out.'

Christie shook her head.

'No, I haven't cried. I feel too cold and empty. Besides, they're going to do a pregnancy test presently and perhaps I shouldn't cry.'

'Oh, Chris, are you having a baby?' Meg's voice lifted. 'That's marvellous ... Well, it'll give you a reason ...' her voice trailed away under the disapproving glare Shanna was giving her. 'I'm sorry, I hadn't thought ...'

'A baby is great; I'd have been proud to have Col's baby,' Shanna said. She shook Christie's hands reprovingly. 'A baby's a very special, personal thing and you'll have to keep yourself fit and well to look after it ... though of course you'll have to leave the WAAF.'

'Andy wanted me to,' Christie said. 'But I might not be having a baby, only the curse is almost three weeks late and Andy wanted a baby, so I thought perhaps I might be pregnant.'

'Were you trying for one?' Sue asked. She had lit the Primus and filled the kettle, now she was making up dried milk powder in a small yellow jug. 'I thought you'd decided not to ... I remember that letter you wrote about the MO's birth-control instruction to brides, it was so funny, it had me in stitches.'

Christie smiled. It was a bit wobbly, but it was a real smile.

'Yes, I remember that letter too. I meant to be good

474

and use that cap thing they gave me, only Andy decided we'd try for a baby, so we did. But I was in such a state, so muddled, you know, that I never even told him the curse was late. He'd have been so excited, and if it was just a false alarm . . . well, I never told him, anyway.'

'Never mind. Besides, you said his squadron leader said he was missing . . . Christie, it needn't mean – the worst, he really could be just missing. You mustn't give up hope too soon.'

Meg's quiet words had the desired effect. Christie smiled again, then rubbed her eyes with the heels of her hands.

'Thanks, Meggie. Only I've accepted it now, I dare not start hoping and have to suffer losing him again. Anyway, they've given me compassionate leave so when you lot have to go back to your stations I can go home to Mum and Dad for a bit. And if it really is a baby . . . well, I don't suppose I'll come back here.' She turned round on the hearth-rug and addressed Sue, who had emerged from the cupboard with various foodstuffs and was lining them up on the draining board. 'Is there enough to make a meal or shall we go down to the village for fish and chips?'

It was an extraordinary three days, Shanna reflected, lying wrapped up in her bed-roll on the spare room floor. It should have been a dreadful, difficult time, but instead it had been somehow peaceful, almost pleasant.

'Missing means just that, it does not mean killed,'

475

Meg had insisted. 'You've always met trouble half-way where Andy's concerned, but this time, be sensible. Think of the baby, and of yourself. Miracles do happen, men do bale out of aircraft.'

And incredibly, Christie listened. She even listened when, on one occasion, Sue said irritably that she'd not saved Christie's life to have her waste it crying over spilt milk. She had smiled rather sweetly as Sue began to apologise, her voice growing more and more Liverpudlian as she tried to explain why she had snapped.

What was more, Shanna, who had been through it, realised that ever since Christie had fallen in love with Andy she had been expecting the worst. Now that the worst had happened, a sort of peacefulness came over her. The terrible fear of harm coming to him had come true, she could dread it no more, so her nervous terrors left her. She was deeply unhappy, they all knew that; but she was tranquil with the tranquility of one who had, in a sense, accepted her loss. And she clung to her friends. She was determined that they should not waste their leave being sorry for her – what had happened was past mere sympathy – so they must enjoy themselves.

And we did enjoy ourselves. Shanna thought wonderingly now, seeing Sue's small, humped shape in her own bed-roll the other side of the room. Sue was really tired because they had lived life to the full for their three days, visiting the nearest town, taking picnics to the woods, digging Christie's garden, mucking out the hens, doing unusual and interesting things. They had volunteered to help Christie choose a kitten and advised her to take up the farmer's offer of a collie bitch when the pups were old enough to leave their mother.

'Andy didn't like leaving me here alone,' Christie said steadily, when they had chosen the kitten and were talking about the possibility of a pup. 'I know he'd rather I had the animals. Hens are all very well but you can't call them companionable, can you? Besides, there are mice in the house and rats in the garden. The kitten will be a cat one day and you don't get mice and rats where you have cats.'

It was a nice little kitten. Ginger, with white paws. There was something at once innocent yet bold in its round amber eyes and little pink nose and its playfulness had captured their hearts. Right now it was sleeping with Christie, curled up on her pillow, all purr and fur. She'll need that kitten, Shanna thought wisely, snuggling down in her blankets; look what a comfort Jacko was to me.

Was. She was startled to find herself using the past tense. She still loved Jacko despite the fact that he no longer uttered a word; but she had just realised that she didn't need him in quite the way she once had. Her strength had grown, and her independence, too. Now she could cope with losing Col, being left. Perhaps she could even cope with loving Pete one day, if it was love she felt for him.

But Pete and their relationship was for the future, for tomorrow morning, when the four of them would go their separate ways once more. It's over a year since Col was killed and it's time I thought seriously about what I'll do when the war is over, Shanna told herself. I loved Col very much but he's gone and Pete's here, waiting. Not pushing, not trying to get into bed with me, but waiting. Mandy was right, I can't expect him to wait for ever; he's a lovely bloke, someone else will appreciate him if I can't.

Being together again, the four of them, had helped her to see things clearly, she reflected now. Meg, who had a few days more leave due, would be going back to Nantwich; she, too, had talked about her boyfriend, Lenny, and whether she would spend her leave with him, the way he wanted.

'Together ... you know,' she had said shyly to Shanna and Sue; and they had told her to go ahead if she was fond of Lenny, the unspoken words hovering in the air between them that rear gunners didn't usually make old bones.

But right now, Christie was the one who mattered. She was going to see the doctor tomorrow, to get the result of her pregnancy test; Shanna couldn't decide whether Christie wanted the baby or didn't want it, she couldn't even decide whether she thought a baby would help her friend, but she admired the way the younger girl was coping. Christie was calm, with a deep sadness which only time, Shanna knew, would erase, but she was also collected, as though she knew where she was heading and what she would do when she got there.

Which is more than the rest of us do, Shanna thought now, wishing she could go to sleep and knowing that sleep was going to elude her for the next hour or so. There's me still wanting Col and being stupid over Pete, there's Meg wanting Lenny but thinking he only wants her because it's wartime and he's afraid. Even Sue can't quite forget making a fool of herself over a married man so she won't let anyone else get near her. But Chris knows she had the very best, and she's content with her memories, for now. Later, she'll be like us, perhaps . . . She'll agonise over someone else, over whether she should take the risk, a second time, of losing a lover . . .

The thought brought her up short, astonished by her own subconscious perception. That was it! That was what made her hold back from Pete, what made Meg dilly-dally about spending a leave in bed with her Lenny, why Sue hadn't been out with a feller since her groupie told her he wouldn't divorce his wife; they were all afraid of suffering once more the agonising pain of loss. She had known it with Col, Meg with that Patrick fellow she'd dated for a bit, Sue with her groupie. We're all too scared of losing to take part in the game, Shanna thought with deep self-contempt. Why, if you win you have what Chris had, if you lose you get nothing . . . I'll tell Pete yes when I get back home to Lincoln.

And on the thought she turned over, burrowed into her pillow, and was asleep in seconds.

'I can't get over wharra good leave it was,' Sue sighed as the three of them, laden with all their luggage once more, walked along the quiet roadway, heading for the bus which would take them to the nearest railway station. 'I feel almost guilty that we could enjoy it, knowing how Chris must have been feelin' all the while.'

It was a glorious morning, and very early still. The sun shone with that pale, lemony brilliance which only April brings, and the mist on the low-lying water meadows was slow to lift, swirling gently round the pied cattle which grazed contentedly amongst the reeds and clumps of golden king-cups. It hung thickest and whitest over the river itself, but even there the warmth was drawing it up, making it gradually translucent as the sun climbed the sky.

The girls walked slowly, each one of them affected, to one extent or another, by the beauty around them. Shanna, still comfortable from the conclusions she had drawn the previous night, glanced around her with great contentment as she walked.

'Is it no' beautiful, girls? Look at the primroses on that bank – I'll remember this walk all the days of my life. As for Christie, she's strong – brave, too. She's going to have a dreadful time over the next few weeks, but she'll come through it.'

'I don't envy her,' Meg said quietly. 'People who don't know will ask after Andy, her parents will try to comfort her . . .'

'You should envy her, Meggie, because I do,' Shanna said emphatically. 'She had a marvellous marriage even though it didnae last long, and maybe she'll have a wee baby to remind her of Andy. That's no' such a bad thing.'

'She had a marvellous marriage all right,' Sue agreed. 'They had some laughs, didn't they? Why, even that awful old woman she told us about – Mrs Denham wasn't it – they laughed and joked about her, Christie said so. Perhaps it's a bit like a real good 'oliday – you're sad when it's over but you've gorra lorra good mem'ries.'

'Ye-es, but won't remembering hurt?' Meg asked doubtfully. 'I'd have thought it would have done.'

'I don't think it does; it comforts,' Shanna said from the depths of her own experience. 'It hurts when you cannae see his face clear in your mind's eye any more, when you cannae hear his voice, but by then you understand it's got to happen; life moves on and you must move with it.'

'You're very philosophical all of a sudden.' Meg slowed as they reached a gateway and turned to lean on the mossy wooden bars for a moment. 'Now there's beauty for you . . . What's that thing . . . "sheep may safely graze." The man who wrote it must have walked past here just like we're doing, and seen that.'

The meadow she indicated was fringed with willows; sheep cropped the grass, their fleeces steaming as the sun touched them, their wool diamonded with drops from the rising mist. Lambs frolicked and called, their voices shrill soprano to their mothers' basso profundo. The girls leaned over the gate, silent for a moment, each of them taking something from the beauty and peacefulness of the scene before them.

'I suppose that's what we're fighting a war for,' Meg said slowly, when no one else spoke. 'That's what men like Andy die for. Oh, come on, we'd better get a move on; I shall start howling in a moment.'

They walked on.

They reached the bus stop and piled their luggage up on the side, then sat on their kit-bags, chatting inconsequentially, knowing that the moment of parting was near.

'Christie's going to get the results of that pregnancy test this morning, isn't she?' Sue said. 'Will she write an' tell us, d'you reckon?'

'She said she'd come down to the station if she got the result in time,' Meg volunteered. 'After all, none of our trains go until after ten, it's just that we couldn't afford to miss the early bus. She'll come on the transport, though. You go first don't you, Sue? Then it's Shanna, then I leave last.'

'You and me could have caught the same train, Meggie, if you hadn't decided to take some more leave and go home,' Shanna grumbled. 'I hate train journeys, especially alone. What's the use of us both bein' stationed near Lincoln if we cannae take advantage and travel together?'

'Don't moan at her; at least you had company on the journey down,' Sue pointed out. 'I'm alone in both directions . . . aha, this looks like our bus!'

They piled aboard, amongst business people going to work, girls travelling in to the munitions factory, schoolchildren heading for local grammar schools.

They squashed on to the back seat, their feet on their kit-bags, and listened to the talk around them and tried not to think about their imminent parting.

We're important to each other still, Shanna thought happily. We'll always be important to each other. I'm glad.

They reached the station much too early, had a cup of tea and a tired currant bun in the refreshment room, bought a paper and shared it between them, then walked out of the station and on to the dusty roadway outside.

No one put it into words, but each knew she was looking for Christie. No one knew what was best for their friend, a positive or negative result; they just knew they wanted her here, to say goodbye, to promise another meeting, to give, wordlessly, that support which each of them needed from time to time.

Meg spotted her first but Sue and Shanna weren't far behind. Christie was running, waving. She must have been dropped off by the transport round the corner and now she was bearing down on them, breathless, pink-cheeked; talking even as she ran, talking at the top of her voice, what was more, so that jerky, disjointed words came to their ears even as, with one accord, they dropped their belongings and tore up the road towards her.

'Digger was waiting for me, he's the groupie, he knew all about it, oh girls, I'm so bloody happy, so *bloody* happy!'

They reached her. They surrounded her, mystified

483

whilst she beamed at them and tried to talk, only her words came out too fast and disjointedly for them to make sense.

'Calm down, Chris, or we'll never get the message. I take it you are having a baby, then?'

At Meg's quiet words Christie stopped short and stared. Then she shook her head dazedly from side to side.

'A baby? Good Lord, I haven't the faintest idea, I forgot to go along to the MO, but it doesn't matter, not now. Girls, it's all right! Oh, I'm so happy, so – so *bloody* happy! Andy's a prisoner of war! He really was missing, the presumed dead part was *wrong*. My darling's coming home to me!'

They laughed and wept a little and clung, and then Christie went with them back to the station and saw them off on their respective trains. She was in a daze of happiness, she glowed with it to such an extent that everything around her seemed bathed in the same rosy light.

Andy was safe! He would cuddle the kitten, meet the puppy – love their child, if she was going to have a baby. And now, more than ever before, Christie realised what her friends meant to her, how dearly she loved these three girls who had stood by her, comforted her when she needed them most.

But you couldn't say things like that, not to your mates. Instead, she told them they must all meet again, mustn't leave it so long next time.

'We'll meet when peace is declared, Meg said. 'Just

us ... well, we might let Andy join the party, if he's very good.'

'No, just us,' Christie insisted. 'I might have to bring my kid, though, if I'm having one, that is. We'll meet on Victory Day, shall we, if that's what they decide to call it?'

'Yes, let's do that,' Sue said excitedly. 'Where'll we meet?'

'Trafalgar Square?'

'No ... Why not under the clock at Victoria?'

'That's bloody borin' ... why not the top of Blackpool Tower?'

It caught their imaginations; smiling, they agreed that they would meet again, when peace was declared, at the top of Blackpool Tower.

The first train arrived moments after they'd decided on Blackpool and they bundled Sue and her kit aboard.

'Tara then, flowers,' Sue shrieked as her train pulled away. 'Be good, an' if you can't be good, be careful. And don't forget, Blackpool Tower!'

'Goodbye, girls,' Shanna called when her train left, leaning out of the window at a perilous angle to wave to Meg and Christie. 'Dinnae forget – we'll meet on Victory Day!'

'Be good, Chris, and keep your pecker up,' Meg shouted, waving hard to the small remaining figure on the platform. 'Give Andy my love, and do write! I can't wait for Victory Day!'

Christie, alone, stood at the foot of the stairs she must presently climb to leave the station, and watched

Meg's train disappearing down the track in a cloud of steam. She was smiling though her eyes smarted with tears.

Andy was safe; it was the best thing, the most important thing. But close behind her love of Andy came her feelings for her three friends. They would meet again, she knew it. In a year, two . . . She had no way of knowing how much time might pass, but it was a date, nevertheless.

The war wasn't over, even though Churchill had said months ago now that it was the end of the beginning. London was still suffering air-raids of tremendous ferocity, other cities had been almost razed to the ground. The Nazis might be rocking back on their heels a bit but they would have more dirty tricks up their sleeves, she had little doubt of that.

But eventual victory was assured, everyone knew it in their hearts. Andy was out of it for now, but wars have a way of continuing to inflict hurt on those who wage them. Nothing was any safer today than it had been yesterday – but was it that which made the sunshine a little more gold, the sky overhead a little more blue?

'*The train now standing at platform five . . .*'

At home, loneliness waited. The years before Andy would be released stretched ahead of her, disappearing into the distance as the train had disappeared down the track.

But she was young and strong and she had her three good friends who would always stand by her. The future had seemed black, but now, way in the distance, there was a gleam of rose and gold.

Christie straightened her cap, checked that her buttons were all done up and her seams straight. Then she hitched her respirator strap higher on her shoulder and began to climb the stairs.